PATAGONIA JACKS

Geoff Brookes

AN INSPECTOR RUMSEY BUCKE NOVEL

Print ISBN 978-1-9161619-7-9

Published by
Llyfrau Cambria Books, Wales, United Kingdom.
*Cambria Books is a division of
Cambria Publishing.*
Discover our other books at: www.cambriabooks.co.uk

DEDICATION

To Liz, on the occasion of our Golden Wedding anniversary,

To our children, Laura, Catherine, Jennie and David,
To their spouses, Richard, Dave, Dan and Emma
                    and
To our grandchildren, Alex, Will, Bethan, Sam, Emily, Isabelle,
Jessica, Tilly and Olivia.

The Rumsey Bucke Collection

In Knives We Trust (2019)
Our Lady of Mumbles (2020)
The Swansea Camel (2021)
A Swansea Child (2021)
Patagonia Jacks (2022)

For more information, visit www.geoffbrookes.co.uk

Reviews of the Inspector Rumsey Bucke Series

In Knives We Trust

A twisting tale of violence, poverty and policing…a must-read for anyone interested in historical portrayals of our ugly, lovely town (Delyth Williams in Swansea What's On March 2019)

Great story, really gave you a feel of what it was like to live in that part of Wales at that time. (Amazon Review)

I was hooked. I thoroughly enjoyed reading it and loved that some of the characters were real people.(Reader comment)

It is packed with fascinating characters – a flaky headteacher, assassins, failing industrialists, prostitutes, criminals and corrupt policemen, all of them surviving as best they can in an unsympathetic world. (Welsh Country Magazine)

Our Lady of Mumbles

'Our Lady of Mumbles' is much better than simply a piece of history with a melodramatic plot; it's a clever, engaging and thrilling detective novel. Very highly recommended. (Lloyd Rees, Author)

A Swansea Child

I really enjoyed it, there were some very grim goings on but it had me gripped until the end (Melanie Heath, Reader)

Another cracking story with great historical detail. Highly recommended (Tristan John, Reader)

Patagonia Jacks

A story of new love, lost love and cannibalism. What a treat! {Jason O'Brien, Artist)

1832
To Record Murder

This stone was erected by general subscription over the Body of Eleanor Williams aged 29 years

A native of Carmarthenshire living in service in this hamlet of Llangyfelach

With marks of violence upon her person she was found dead in a well

By Llywngwenno Farmhouse

Although

The Savage Murderer may escape for a season the detection of Man yet

Doubtless God hath set his mark upon him either for time or eternity

And

The cry of blood will assuredly pursue him to a terrible and righteous judgement

Vengeance is mine. I will repay, says the Lord.

CONTENTS

Prologue

The man stood in the shadows as a weary August night wrapped itself around the exhausted garden at the rear of the house and its oppressive heat slithered through the single open window.

A short man, a dark man, a vengeful man. But careful, too. A man who waited. A patient man; someone who listened.

And he listened to the voices in that simple threadbare room, nodding occasionally. What he heard was everything he had hoped for throughout those long featureless days; the perfect expression of a plan nurtured during dark, cold hours in a solitary cell. If he had ever troubled himself to write the dialogue for this long-anticipated evening, he knew he could never have expressed it as successfully as those words which slipped thickly from the window, coloured with terror and tears.

'I have done bad things…I have been cursed…' There were other words now that he couldn't hear, that melted away. Then, 'I may be mad.'

The man nodded, slowly, with approval. Powell Street in Swansea, close to High Street Station, was not a happy place. He was responsible for that and he smiled. Had it ever been a happy place, he wondered? How could it be, when everything in it was based on a lie?

'But I still love you, honest I do.'

What a waste. Why would a young woman waste her only life with someone as clearly unworthy as Rhys Price? He lifted his head and looked carefully around the dirty window.

'I know,' he heard Price say, and he watched her gently smoothing his hair. He looked as if he was possessed by demons, which made the man in the garden smirk with pride at what he had achieved. He saw Price's raw eyes blaze suddenly. 'But I have been cursed!' Then, quietly. 'You have to understand. I am cursed.'

'Hush now,' he heard the woman say. 'You have not been cursed; you have only been unlucky. Yes, you have had bad times, my love, but all will be well for us, now that you are back. I know that's true, Rhys, please do not doubt it.'

Hers was a sweet voice, the man decided. Full of tenderness and love. It was more than a waste; it was a needless sacrifice. He smiled and stepped away from the flickering glow of the candle. He remained in the shadows, waiting, nodding. What will be, will be. What will be, will be deserved.

'There is a face at the window!' shouted Rhys. 'I saw him! He has come for me!'

'Hush, I say,' she said softly. 'There is no one there.' She dared not turn her head.

He sobbed again, more loudly this time. 'No one understands!' His voice dropped to a whisper. 'No one. Not even you, Molly.' Rhys looked anxiously around the room, as if there had been someone else there, who he now could not see. 'I am so sorry for the things I have done.'

Molly was terrified but she took his hand and squeezed it gently, trying to be brave. 'You are back now. And we are together. We will face whatever we have to face, together. This is your home. This is your family. A new start. A new life. Together we are strong, remember that.' She was not sure what else she could say.

'But what have I done to you all? We will never walk the road before us together. It is too late, now.' His head was bowed.

'It is never too late. We can be strong together, if only you will tell me-'

Rhys looked up and stared straight into her eyes. 'No one knows what is inside my head. No one ever should. The ship had sunk and he fell and we pulled him out of the water, you see. And then I did it again. I told them I had done it before but I should not have done it.'

This all made terrible sense to him, but Molly was floundering, trying to tease some meaning from his words, something she could hold on to, but horrified by the emotions in which these words were wrapped. 'You are troubled, that is all. It is rest that you need, Rhys, I know it. You have been through so much; it can't be a surprise if you are over-wrought.'

He shook his head. 'I never wanted to do any harm. I never wanted to hurt anyone. I just wanted to come home, to you and the children. But now I am haunted and my head will burst.' He screwed up his eyes and large tears fell. 'There is a bird that comes to peck out my eyes! It comes every night and sits at the end of our bed, waiting. And I know that one day soon he will come in the daytime and then there will be no escape.'

'Things are getting better, Rhys, I truly believe it. Whatever it was that you did, you don't have to do it again. You have a good job, now. You are a policeman. Everyone respects you. You won't have to travel anymore.'

'Those spirits want to destroy me. And they will, I know it. They live inside my head. They shout at me. They laugh at me. Then they whisper poison in my ears.' He pulled at his hair frantically, as if he could drag those spirits from his mind.

'Tomorrow, Rhys. Tomorrow. We will go and see a doctor. I will come with you. I am sure Inspector Bucke knows someone who will see you.'

'And what will he say, Molly? That I have an ague? Or will he talk about a visitation from God, will that be it? But I tell you something, it isn't God who has come to call. It is not God who has taken up his dwelling inside my head!' Rhys screamed, but no noise emerged. 'And now this!' he waved the letter around that had been pushed under the front door, as if it was poisoned. It fell from his hand and fluttered to the floor.

Molly was shaking in fear. She glanced for a moment at Griff, their baby son in his cot, but he remained, thankfully, undisturbed. How would Rhys react if he started to cry? Little Georgie was asleep upstairs, she hoped. She knew that Rhys had started to unsettle him; she saw how he now looked at his father warily.

Rhys suddenly stood up and started to pace their shabby room, round and round, stopping every few moments to write something on a piece of paper on the table. Molly bent down quickly and picked up the letter and pushed it into the pocket of her apron. She felt powerless and could only watch as the agony and the anguish creased and twisted his face. Rhys had been unhappy before, but never as bad as this, or for so long.

Rhys dropped his pencil, grasped the edge of the table with both hands and lowered his head. 'Leave me alone! Leave me alone!'

She went to him and laid her shaking hand on his shoulder. 'Come to bed, Rhys. Let me hold you. Let me ease your mind.' She took the paper he was writing on and put that in her apron, too.

'You must understand, Molly! I have done some terrible things. You do not know. You must not know, or they will come for you, too. But I have been cursed, and the demons have taken their place in my head to mock me. And they push hot needles into my mind. Again! I can't… I can't…'

By four o'clock the following morning, Molly had been stabbed to death in a frenzied attack and the different parts of Rhys' body had been pulled out from the beneath the milk train from Llanelly at High Street Station.

One

Sergeant Stanley Ball stood in the same place behind the counter of the police station on Tontine Street every day. He was always surprised that there were no indentations in the parquet flooring to match those sturdy boots of his that rarely went anywhere else. He was the permanent presence the constables needed, the fixed point in the chaotic world they were expected to police and they all relied upon him a great deal. There were days when they exasperated him, days when they angered him with their evasions and idleness, and days when there was nowhere else he would rather be, and no one else he would rather be with, other than Lillian, of course.

This daily morning meeting was the part of the day he liked best, when the constables and the Inspectors turned up in the foyer and exchanged greetings and gossip before their duties properly began. These were his people; this was his place and this was his time. There was a camaraderie that cheered him; the teasing, the minor insults, the news. It was the time when he could share in those peculiar policing stories that his fixed position as desk sergeant denied him. He enjoyed watching the constables, noting their different characters and their moods, which Ball always believed enabled him to more successfully deploy them around the town.

All of them had been a little subdued for a few weeks now. They hadn't known Dai Price for long – certainly not long enough to get to the bottom of why he was called Dai when his name was Rhys- but it was still a shock that someone they worked with had taken his own life. Under a train, too. He hadn't been a constable long enough to know just what an unpleasant thing that was to clean up. He surely wouldn't have done it if he had known, one of them had said, unsuccessfully trying to lighten that grim morning when they heard the news.

He had been an old friend of Iago Morris, and Ball knew he had taken it very badly. They had worked together years ago, sailing on the copper ships to South America, and it was Iago who had persuaded him to try life as a constable. Safer he had said, especially for a man with a young family. And then this new, hopeful, start in his life had ended in such a horrible fashion.

It hadn't helped Iago Morris much at all; Ball was sure that he felt responsible for this inexplicable death. If he hadn't suggested the job as a constable, perhaps Dai would not have murdered his wife or taken his own life. Everyone knew it was a hard job; perhaps Dai couldn't find a way of saying that it wasn't the job for him. There was no way of knowing now, but a dark cloud had settled over Morris, one that seemed in no hurry to disperse. He had always had a tendency to the morose and, though he was tall, there were days when he appeared much shorter, his body crouching in on itself in unhappiness. He was known as Bonfire, though preferably not in his hearing, for he had *Love* tattooed on one set of knuckles and the unfortunate *Heat* on the other. He did not enjoy being reminded of this. He was older than the other constables and sometimes his irritability with their youth was too-readily displayed. On those days he believed in punishment, not redemption. However, Ball recognised that he was a good officer. His colleagues would grudgingly admit that they felt safer when he was around and Rumsey Bucke valued him for his good sense. Stanley always felt that they all could gain more from his experience and that his recent irritability was a small price to pay. This morning Morris was sitting on the bench in quiet conversation with Lemuel Turner, the great hope of the Swansea constabulary.

Stanley knew that they hadn't had a constable like him for a long time. He was educated and intelligent, attributes which, in his own dealings with the great and the good on the privileged west side of Swansea, he knew did not always go together. Turner wrote things down in his little notebook to the extent that this eagerness to learn and remember made him a little unpopular with some of his colleagues. He was barely twenty-one and his good looks and bright blue eyes added to their irritation. In their envy, they called him 'The Blue-Eyed Boy', believing that he had become the favoured one through ingratiation. Ball found that irritating. Perhaps they should instead show the same conscientious interest and be as keen to learn as Turner. Ball preferred the nickname 'Page,' which he had invented and which Turner was sensible enough to take in good spirits most of the time.

It was however a nickname that confused Constable Evan Davies mightily. But then, thought Stanley, most things confused Evan. He was the shining light of his mother's life but not, sadly, of the police force. This morning he was leaning on the front of the counter; he was always leaning on the counter, encouraged by his mother to believe that the job of desk sergeant was his birthright. As he did most mornings, Ball reflected on the boy's peculiarly round and unexceptional face, one that was possessed, on occasion, by a remarkable vacancy. Stanley felt that this could be the only explanation why he seemed to spend most of his time either avoiding his duties or inventing remarkable and different ways to get things wrong, whilst believing he was the single most important stitch in the tapestry of their days. Deploying Evan Davies became Ball's most difficult daily challenge, once he had accepted that there were few tasks which he could ever successfully complete. Ball took what little comfort he could from observing James Flynn's difficulties in managing him, for it was Evan who proved that the Inspector's patience was not infinite.

James Flynn was the dependable man who, in most other circumstances, always brought a sense of calm with him. He was tall and imposing, clean-shaven and with thinning grey hair which he frequently smoothed into place with his large, encompassing hands. He was almost always unruffled and sensible for, as he liked to remind the constables, he had seen many things in his long career; only rarely had Ball seen him properly lose his temper. Sometimes he became exasperated when constables did not display what he defined as common sense, but Ball had considerable sympathy with that. He had also once been a desk sergeant and so if Flynn gave the impression, as he sometimes did, that he had seen it all and done it all too, then he was probably right.

This morning Flynn was in hushed conversation with Constable George Smith, probably offering some gentle advice that would inevitably be ignored. This would be advice which had frequently been offered; advice to Smith about keeping his hands to himself. He was short in temper and in stature, aggressive and someone Ball knew he had to watch closely. It wouldn't be long before someone on the Strand took a swing at him and that was when things would get complicated. Yesterday, Flynn had said that Smith was volatile, which was probably the right word, though he wasn't entirely sure what it implied. He was sure they were merely counting the days before Mrs Dolphin hit him with a poker; she had attacked constables before and previous custodial sentences had done little, it seemed, to inhibit her enthusiasm for this unwelcome hobby.

And then there in a corner, wrapped in his personal thin grey blanket of eternal misery, was Constable Byron Midwinter. He had seemed worse recently, his lips twisted by the sudden eruption of ulcers. For reasons that Ball didn't know, Midwinter was teased unmercifully whilst on his beat by the young boys of the town. Why him? What had he done? Or was it just the fact that, like chickens, the boys had established a pecking order and Midwinter was at the bottom of it, a position from which he could never hope to escape? Ball had not helped either by calling him 'Bleak,' after a poem Lillian had read to him from a magazine, but there were no two ways about it. He was such a bleak streak of unhappiness. Ball always wondered why he was so troubled. But all the constables had their stories, they all had their past that they carried with them. Price must have had something terrible inside him to make him murder his wife like that, with the little baby next to her and his other son trembling in terror beneath his bed, and then throw himself, in his nightshirt, under the milk train. An argument? A nightmare? No one would ever know.

So yes, they all had their stories, their secrets, and they were entitled to them. He had his own. The secret that no one knew, not even Lillian. A year ago – was it really as long ago as that? – Stanley Ball, solid dependable Stanley Ball – had murdered a journalist because of the trouble he was causing. He felt no guilt though, about which he was surprised, but relieved. He remembered the feelings he had experienced, of unexpected hatred for the man and the fear of being caught, but no, there had been no guilt at all. So he could worship quite happily in the chapel and teach in the Sunday school, because he never considered for a moment that he had done anything wrong. Because that man Baglow, that maggot, that scavenger, that dishonest twister of words, had targeted Rumsey Bucke through his vitriolic newspaper columns and for Stanley Ball that made him irredeemable, for the Inspector was the man he admired most in the world. He believed that Rumsey Bucke was a paragon, the perfect police officer made real. All those virtues that Stanley Ball believed in, had been made flesh in the person of Rumsey Bucke. But in some ways, he did not see Bucke as flesh and blood; rather he was an expression of the qualities, and the ideals he wished he possessed himself. He too wanted to be able to display the authority, the integrity, the intelligence that he saw as the essential qualities of a policeman.

By extension then, to criticise these attributes was nothing less than an assault upon Rumsey Bucke and an assault upon himself. Ball knew he could never match his daily heroes, but his greatest pride was that he worked with, and was respected by those who were, in his mind, so much more able than him.

At this moment, Bucke entered the police station with Constable Gill. Ball would never start this daily 'morning shout' until Bucke arrived, and he had known that he would be late because he had promised Mother Superior Hillereau at the Convent that he would call with the beat constable, Gill, after some boys threw stones through the windows of the kitchen.

Bucke looked around him as he advanced, in order to place his hat upon the counter, nodding his greetings, trying to assess the demeanour of the constables working this morning. This was going to be a busy time; perhaps, he speculated, the busiest period ever in the history of Swansea constabulary, for the Prince and the Princess of Wales were visiting Swansea and the whole of the

9

town, in fact as far as Bucke could see the whole of Wales, was in a frenzy of excitement. It wasn't something that he welcomed at all.

Had he been fully aware of the hero worship that Stanley Ball was silently offering him, he might have been even more uncomfortable, for he did not relish attention or praise. He had once been a serving soldier, once a widower and now a more rounded, more balanced person through his relationship with Constance White. He was brave, resourceful, sympathetic and humane. Ball was naturally proud to know him, though a professor of human behaviour might find it significant that Stanley consciously chose never to speculate about the true nature of Bucke's friendship with Constance, the abandoned wife, busily seeking a divorce.

Ball nodded in greeting. Like any disciple, he was a student of Bucke's moods and anything that troubled him must, by definition, trouble the constables. But all looked well this morning. His beard was neat and trimmed as always, his hair ordered, those brown eyes bright and sympathetic. Ball no longer noticed that missing piece of his ear that the Inspector had left behind in hand-to-hand conflict on the North West Frontier.

Iago Morris was loudly expressing his new irritation, this imminent Royal visit to open Swansea's east dock which he considered unnecessary and tedious; the way it had dominated public life in the town for months had fuelled his anger. It had become, inevitably, an enormous shadow on the constabulary's horizon and Morris was not the only one unhappy about it, either. But he was the most vociferous. This morning, once again, there was no escape from his familiar theme. 'Have you heard what The Roe has been shouting?' he began, referring to the newspaper vendor at the bottom of Wind Street. 'He had quite a crowd there yesterday, listening and laughing. "Factory owners to have seven course meal with Bertie. Price of bread to go up." He is not wrong.'

'Got a point,' said Midwinter with a sneer.

Ball disapproved of such seditious talk about authority.

10

'Dangerous man that. Spreading unrest. Need to watch him. Anyway, gentlemen. On to business.' The constables gathered closer to the counter to listen to the announcements. They always left the police station muttering that the whole thing was a waste of time, but they would all quietly understand that one day they could be told something that might save their life.

'First off. Bit trivial, I know. But someone pinned a bunch of flowers to the door of Cox's Farm. Forget Me Nots, I am told.'

'Do we care? I mean, so what?' asked Morris, exasperated.

'It will get old Ma Derrick off my back,' said Davies, nodding. 'Was on at me all day yesterday in the market about someone nicking her flowers. She didn't say what sort, though.'

'Just keep an eye open, is all I am asking. It is a strange thing to do, I'll give you that. But why? What is it supposed to mean? Something or nothing. So, if you hear anything I'd be obliged. Thank you.' Ball looked around the assembled policemen, believing that an appearance of attention was enough. 'Now then, listen up. Had a telegram, yesterday.'

'Managed to read it did you, Stan?' muttered Midwinter, but only Bucke standing behind him heard.

'Been delayed, see. Got sent to Cardigan for some reason, and them being woolly tails they didn't know what to do with it. Not a lot of call for brains down there. Anyway, Arthur Riverton was released from Dartmoor. Months ago, I reckon. Now that name might not mean much to you young 'uns, but it does to Inspector Bucke and me. Am I right, Inspector?' Bucke nodded. 'I was a constable just like you lot, and me and the Inspector tracked him down when he had escaped from Cox's Farm and went to ground in Gower. isn't that right?'

Bucke smiled. 'Absolutely, Stan.' It wasn't quite as he remembered it but that didn't matter. He made light of it. 'You see? Stan did such a good job he was promoted to Sergeant. Let that be a lesson to you all.'

'And Cox's Farm? Am I right in thinking that is what older people call Swansea gaol?' asked Turner, unsuccessfully supressing a grin. Bucke was pleased to see it – a sign that Turner was finding his feet amongst his colleagues. They smirked, apart from Midwinter, who remained stony-faced.

'Enough of your cheek young man or I shall change your beat to Regent's Court. You'll be lucky to come back with your breeches, and well you know it. Don't any of you approach Riverton. You lot don't know him but if you get a whisper about him being around, you tell me straight away. No one should approach Riverton on their own.'

'I haven't got a problem with him,' said Morris.

'Do you know him then, Iago?' asked Bucke, who watched him shrug in reply.

'I am just saying you don't go near him on your own,' continued Ball. 'And if he has turned over a new leaf and become a law-abiding citizen, which I most sincerely doubt, then there will be much rejoicing in chapels across Swansea. But until then, if you hear anything, you tell me, is that clear? Don't need heroes. Especially not dead ones.'

There was muttered assent.

'Other news? Well, Simeon Simons says that his cart has gone missing. Came in to tell me earlier.'

'Shouldn't be difficult to find. You can smell it for miles,' muttered Smith.

'Someone has to collect the night soil on Mount Pleasant,' replied Constable Gill. 'You don't want them leaving it in the streets again. And anyway, it isn't a job you would want to do, Smithy, is it?'

'Not saying it is. But it still stinks.'

'Thank you, gentlemen. Just keep an eye open.'

'Or a nostril,' added Smith.

Midwinter spoke out. 'Can one of you have a word with Joseph Padley? I have tried, but he won't listen to me. I hardly know him.'

'What has he done now?' sighed Ball.

'He reckons he is going to do his wife in on 1 April next year.

12

As if I care,' said Midwinter.

'Not again, said Ball. 'He has been banging on about murdering her for months now. And it is always going to happen on 1 April.'

'Fair enough,' said Midwinter. 'She might deserve it, but why tell anyone? I don't understand. He is bluffing, I reckon.'

'Unless, of course, it is nothing more than a double bluff,' said Turner, looking thoughtful, with his pencil resting on his lip. He wrote something down in his notebook.

'What are you on about, Page? asked Smith, who resented his perceived position as teacher's pet and always used the affectionate name Ball had given him as an insult. 'Double bluff? What is that supposed to mean?'

'Simple, really. He wants us to believe that it is a lie, when in fact it is true. He is going to murder her on the 1st April and we won't stop him because he knows we won't believe him.'

'Perhaps it is his birthday,' said Davies, for whom ignorance had never been a barrier to making a contribution.

'It is all a bit deep for me, that,' said Ball. 'But I shall put a note in the diary and we can bang him up at the end of March.'

'Simple. That should bugger up his plans,' said Smith. 'That's your problem, Page. You make things too complicated.'

Turner continued to write in his notebook. He added an emphatic full stop. 'Of course, he could be lying too. He tells us he is murdering her on the 1st of April and we don't believe him, but in fact he is lying and he is planning to murder her, but not until the 3rd of April. Clever.' He nodded.

'You are just playing games, Page,' said Smith.

'No. I am not. It is Padley who is playing games. We must always be alert, Constable Smith.'

'Let's just get on,' said Morris, who had been even more irritable than usual lately. 'If you want me to do my beat twice, like on a normal day, then I need to get started. Unless today we are just talking. Up to you, really. All I am saying is that we have enough on our plate with this bloody royal visit, without all this bloody gossip.'

'Oh, come on, Iago,' said the usually affable Constable Gill. 'Where is your patriotic spirit?'

'Patriotic spirit be buggered. A waste of time and money. All this palaver and he gets a dock named after him and the Princess gets a road. That really is a good day out. Worth coming for that, then.' Morris turned and trudged wearily out of the police station and the others, eventually, followed reluctantly.

Bucke went through to his office and looked out of the window for a moment. He had some passing sympathy with Morris, for this visit had come to dominate their duties and their plans. The visit of the Prince and Princess of Wales in just over two weeks' time would be, without doubt, the most important event in Swansea's year. A huge number of visitors was expected and the consequent commercial opportunities considerable indeed. Everywhere there was bunting for sale. So many different decorative items were filling shop windows. Telescopes and binoculars were particularly popular, it seemed. Seats at upstairs windows along the royal route, most notably on Walters Road, were already fetching a high price, in some cases the cost inflated by the offer of fully-catered arrangements. Welsh costumes were for hire in shops across the town 'for the nobility and the gentry.'

And yet, thought Bucke. And yet. Ordinary people would be kept at a distance from these visitors. Edward, Prince of Wales was their future king but he would spend his time with the better-off people of the town, whilst the poor were invited to wave and cheer. The women of Swansea market wore Welsh costume as a matter of course, a proud expression of their origins. And yet the royals turn up and the rich and the prosperous, those people who have a choice in most parts of their lives, choose to ape the garments of the poor. And not only that, as the advertisements said, 'Demand will be so great that early orders are solicited.' Iago Morris had a point.

*

Constance sat down at the kitchen table to write her reply. She

14

tucked the permanently errant strand of hair back behind her ear. If it didn't start to behave, she would cut it off.

Dear Flora, she wrote. *I was delighted to receive your letter and to hear how you are all settling into your new life in Aberystwyth. It is so long since you were here and there is so much news to share.*

She paused and thought about the last time they had met. Almost a year ago now. A terrible time for everyone, in the aftermath of the evil church of Our Lady of Mumbles and particularly for the Beynons. Emily, their eighteen-year-old daughter, abducted, raped and almost killed. Constance almost died too, but the assault upon Emily had been especially brutal. They had moved away to find peace, though it might take her a long time to heal. She would never forget what had happened. How could she?

It is always a great joy to write to you and even more so when the town stands upon the threshold of great events!

They had exchanged letters only occasionally over the past year and so this message had arrived unexpectedly. Now they were coming back to Swansea, though not David, a doctor pleading pressure of work, though perhaps, thought Constance, he could not face returning to the place where, in his distress, he had said too much and offended those who had cared for him most. They were coming apparently for two reasons. One was to be part of the celebration of the royal visit, the sense of excited anticipation spreading even as far as the distant west coast. The other reason was to attend a lecture by Frances Power Cobbe. She was a leader of the anti-vivisection movement and her speaking tour was bringing her to Swansea. According to Flora's letter, animals and their welfare were Emily's new and consuming passions and she had been corresponding with Miss Power Cobbe for some time. This was an opportunity to meet her at last.

I am quite excited at the thought of seeing you again. And I was delighted to hear that Emily will be accompanying you. Please, Flora. You will not be imposing at all. I am sensible of the many kindnesses which you granted me when I was most in need of friendship and I am anxious to be able to repay that debt, no matter how modestly.

She meant that too. The Beynons had been the first to recognise and accept that her relationship with Rumsey Bucke went beyond mere friendship, in spite of its potential for scandal. She could never forget that they accepted her and did not shun her because she was an abandoned wife.

I understand that the Mackworth Hotel has been refurbished for the occasion of the Royal visit and I am sure you will be both comfortable. I shall be happy to render any assistance within my power to ensure your all-too-brief visit is comfortable, for I have missed my conversations with both of you.

Constance had been Emily's confidante and friend, her greatest support when they were both trapped in that collapsing pit. That sort of experience created a bond that remained indissoluble.

It is my fervent wish that the clean air and a new life will have eased the terrible pain through which dear Emily had to live and has restored the heart and soul of the girl we both love.

Constance read the letter once again. 'That will do,' she thought. It was short and perhaps she ought to write more, but it said what she wanted it to say. She put it inside an envelope which she addressed carefully. 'Aberystwyth' was a difficult word to spell. She looked at the stove where a simple leek soup was bubbling to greet Ramsey when he called, far too briefly, for their daily supper. How did she feel about seeing the Beynons again? In truth, she wasn't sure. David had said some difficult things - unkind, untrue things - blaming Rumsey unfairly for Emily's abduction. What did Flora think about them? Did she agree with him? Constance had never found out. Had Flora spoken to him about it, told him he was wrong? She didn't know that either. After some awful days contemplating the loss of their daughter, then knowing first that she was alive, but then understanding what she had been through, David needed someone to shout at and Rumsey had been the easiest and nearest target. Rumsey had understood why it had happened and would bear no grudge. But he had been very hurt by his words and if they hurt Rumsey then, of course, they hurt her too. If Rumsey had been responsible, for even a small part of what happened, she would have told him so. But he hadn't, and really, he was the one who had ensured they were rescued. But

Emily had not been rescued intact, she thought with unusual delicacy, and perhaps that was the point.

Legally she was still Constance Bristow, though emotionally she had abandoned that name a long time ago. Her Bristow years were over, a desolate place where thankfully she had stayed only briefly. The only treasure she kept from those empty years was Agnes, her daughter, now a governess in South Africa who she missed terribly and with whom she exchanged long and gossipy letters most months. Agnes too, had consigned her father to the past. When William Bristow had left his wife, he had abandoned both of them. Constance had much to thank him for, she now realised, for when he fled to America, believing he was a suspect in a murder investigation, Bristow had inadvertently introduced her to Rumsey Bucke and it was meeting him that had changed her life entirely.

Constance had reverted to her maiden name as much as she could, but the change of name did not change how she looked. She was still short and slight; her large brown eyes and a slightly upturned nose had not altered. But now that she had been liberated, her face displayed an intelligence and a sympathy that made others wish to confide in her. She knew that she was an entirely different person now. In not-quite eighteen months, she had witnessed a failed assassination, had helped rescue people in the Calvary Pit, had almost died herself, had defended herself when assaulted, had rescued a woman from a murderer in the street, had met all manner of people – everything all so very different from her previous life of tedium, punctuated only by frequent episodes of domestic abuse. She had grown, and that was visible in her face.

So now she was Constance White, piano teacher, awaiting a ridiculously expensive appearance in the High Court in London, where she hoped to be granted a divorce and finally marry the man she loved. She had ferocious loyalty to Rumsey and had uncovered for him an unexpected passion so profound, that she regretted so many wasted years. She had found within herself courage and resolve, qualities which she didn't know were there. She knew that she had been waiting all her life for Rumsey, and that so many of her adult years had been wasted ones. But she always tried not to think in clichés. Perhaps she had met Rumsey at the right time, which of course was another cliché. But he represented all that she had ever wanted and a life without him, after eighteen months together, seemed unimaginable.

Two

Thankfully, it had been a quiet day – something they all needed. The lull before the storm of the royal visit, Bucke thought, and he was looking forward to a few short hours with Constance – with the added bonus, he believed, of leek soup. This was their time; the door was closed and social convention and the fear of moral outrage were locked outside. After all, they had both almost died in Calvary Pit and if their love had found its ultimate expression in the aftermath of almost losing each other, well, it should not be a surprise. So Bucke would go and visit Constance as often as he could and then there would follow the very worst part, that long walk home along the cold streets to his bare, brown room on Fisher Street, above the surgery of Mr Scott the dentist. He regarded the room as nothing more than the place where he slept, and often not very well, and sometimes as nothing more than a place of solitary confinement. In fact, he had started keeping clothes – what few he had – in Constance's rooms on St Helen's Road, away from the damp that worked its way inexorably up the wall of a room that faced St Mary's Church, with a window that appeared to block out the light but suck in the noise of the church bells whenever he could not sleep. He was frequently cold and lonely, the contrast between Constance's home and his own was sometimes almost too great for him to bear and he dreaded leaving her and waiting for the silent anonymity of those tedious moments when he hovered on the threshold of sleep.

The spectre of his departure hung over him at every moment of his time with Constance, even during their most intimate moments together, when the little devil of departure laughed at them, waving his pocket watch. Even those wonderful moments of shared silence were stained by time's inexorable decay. It always felt so unfair.

He tried to believe that ending his day in solitude enabled him to think more clearly about his work, but of course it was a lie. He thought more clearly, more incisively, when he was with

Constance, for she had become his oasis after the grim, featureless desert through which he had travelled when he was first bereaved; she was something he never thought he would find after he lost his wife and children.

People accepted their relationship, perhaps blinding themselves to any shameful possibilities, but at the moment they could not marry. He was a widower of course, but she was an abandoned wife and so there were aspects of ordinary life that remained beyond their grasp. Their days were often simultaneously wonderful and difficult for them both, and it amused them that they were each envied by others, who could never appreciate the dank cell of depression into which they were often separately imprisoned.

And so tonight it would soon be leek soup and there was nothing in the police station to detain him. The cells were empty, the streets were quiet, the constables reasonably contented…and then it happened; one of those moments which Bucke instantly recognised would set in motion events that would change lives forever. There was a visitor, one who always turned lives upside down.

He was coming to the end of a short report for the Watch Committee, supporting the request by the Chief Constable for urgent improvements in the quality of the constables' footwear, when the bell above the police station door sounded and he heard an unexpected voice, but one that he knew very well.

He looked into the lobby and saw a distinguished man, a military man, still trim and fit, well-dressed in an expensive three-piece suit, a golden watchchain hanging neatly across his waistcoat. He was clean, healthy, glowing – not a man who battled daily with Swansea's tainted air. A little taller than average, clean-shaven, neat hair, piercing eyes. This was Colonel Grey, affable, confident, a man in control, a man with an un-named role in the Home Office. A man, it seemed, with responsibility for the nation's security.

'Ah! Inspector Bucke. A good afternoon, indeed. Constable, a pot of your finest Assam, if you will.'

It was everyone's misfortune, especially his own, that Evan Davies was idling away the end of his shift at the counter, pretending to assess the entries in the ledger for today. He had no option but to comply. He nodded, then watched as Bucke and Grey went into the inspector's office and closed the door.

They talked companiably for a while, catching up and gossiping casually, both recognising that something serious was to come. The weather, the difficulties of train travel, the inaccessibility of Swansea. Grey had heard of the Abramovitch case, for he had his sources everywhere. He listened to Bucke's report carefully, nodded and said, 'Well done. Abramovitch was a person of interest to authorities in most of the countries of central Europe. We think he robbed and murdered his way across the south of England before he arrived with you, but to be frank, we will never be sure who he really was.'

Sergeant Ball opened the door and Davies came in with a tray, precariously arranged. 'Don't have any of that Assam stuff but we do have some tea so I took the liberty, like.' He put the tray on the table rather too noisily and then left. Nothing spilled; a job well done.

'His mother is very proud of him, Colonel.'

'I see,' said Grey, his tea. 'Welcome to Swansea, the town of low expectations. Still, Bucke, the tea looks perfectly acceptable. His mother taught him well.'

'If only his mother had been a constable. There are so many other things she could have taught him that would be much more useful to us.'

Grey shrugged. 'There are some things that even Her Majesty's Government cannot resolve, Inspector.'

'My greatest fear, Colonel.'

'Be strong, Bucke. Be strong. Though we have other pressing issues to discuss, short term difficulties I think, in comparison with the long-term nightmare of Constable Davies' appointment. So pleased that he is not my concern.' He scratched his chin briefly. 'You see, thought I would pop in, have a word. I wanted to see

21

you before we have a formal meeting with the Lord Mayor – Jones Jenkins? Jenkin Jones? - about this visit by the Prince and Princess of Wales that you must endure. I have come down this afternoon with Colonel Pollard of the Royal Division to finalise all the arrangements, particularly, as far as Bertie is concerned, the catering arrangements. He takes no hostages at the table, I can assure you. Pollard is in touch with all the practicalities and I want you to know that I trust Algernon completely. He comes across at times as a little pompous, bit of a stuffed shirt, you know the type. But I would want him next to me in a crisis.' He sipped again at his tea, and then placed the cup decisively on the saucer.

'Naturally, this is all off the record. Wouldn't want your Jones -Jenkins fellow having a seizure, now do we? I am here now for a few days and I shall have a bit of a poke around. But I have to tell you, this visit could be damned tricky for some of us, including you.

'It is a relief all round that Princess Alexandra is coming with him, so there will be no need to lock up the local show girls. She takes the edge off his tiresome behaviour. Quite obviously, the whole thing is a waste of time, but it keeps the common people contented. Such a huge amount of work and money just so that he can give a dock a name. But then Bertie is quite popular, they say. Goodness knows why. He is to be the next king of course, so I suppose one needs to make the effort but sometimes I wonder. But anyway, Pollard will have this meeting with the Chief Constable and the Lord Mayor and I have requested that you attend. And that is why I am here. There are things I need to mention, between the two of us.'

Bucke remembered the last time they had met, when the visit of Ferdinand de Lesseps had briefly put Swansea at the centre of political conflict and military planning. Then, he had felt like a piece in someone else's jigsaw, only finding out about the part he had played after the picture was complete. At least it appeared that this time, he had a chance of knowing what was going on. The Colonel trusted him, that was clear – and reassuring.

'You see, a royal visit brings out the worst in people, never think otherwise, and my sources are suggesting that there might be a problem with the Fenians, with the Irish Nationalist Brotherhood or whatever they call themselves at the moment. They appear to be gathering for a bit of mischief.' He shrugged. 'They can be brutal.'

'I see. We have a large and rather secretive Irish community here in Swansea, though our relationship with them is currently reasonably cordial.'

'Indeed, your Little Ireland. But then so does almost everywhere else. We have some people amongst them, as you might expect. Nothing certain at the moment. Just whispers. But they are gathering here in Swansea. Just before Bertie's visit? That is not a coincidence. Hoping to have a little more clarity in the next couple of days and, with good fortune, we should be able to nip it in the bud. Does the name Giblin mean anything to you?'

'James Giblin? Oh yes. Involved in most things. An important person in their community and, to be honest, we do manage to work together to smooth things over when we need to, but he always manages to keep his nose clean and that sometimes worries me.'

'Clever then. What about Duggan?'

'Not a name I recognise.'

'Not a surprise. Bit of a longshot, really. He does move around rather a lot. He knows we are looking for him. This is our difficulty, you see. Be on your guard.' He paused. 'You see, I would be grateful if you didn't get drawn into the petty arrangements for the visit. I need you with me. Bertie and the Princess need to leave here alive, whatever we might think. After that, to be frank, I care little. If the mayor survives then of course I shall celebrate, though quietly. And if Bertie survives but I don't? Well, Bucke, I will have done my duty. Everyone will say so. Then they will move on.'

He took a sip of his tea again, never removing his gaze from Bucke's face.

'Let me be frank with you. Least I can do. At the moment, apart from Giblin and Duggan, we have no names, no numbers, no idea of what their plans might be. But we are hopeful, ever hopeful. We'll muddle through, we usually do. All I can be sure about is that the forces of darkness are already gathering in Swansea in time for the visit by this mad Irish woman. Do you know her? The anti-vivisectionist woman, Power Cobbe? She has some exceedingly dangerous ideas. Can't quite see the connection, even if she is Irish, but we are watching her too.'

'Earlier, Colonel, you accused Swansea earlier of being inaccessible, and yet you seem to be putting us at the centre of unwelcome events.'

'True enough. And you are right, it does seem damned peculiar. It could all be rather more entertaining than perhaps you would like. But if we stay in contact, it should make it more manageable and deal with whatever nonsense they are planning.'

Bucke nodded, wondering which of his constables would be able to step up to this particular mark and realising that it was not a crowded field.

They walked together out of the station. 'Some of the Royal Brigade will turn up. They will be in full uniform. You know the sort. Colonel somebody, Major someone else, Admiral no one has ever heard of – they do like a do. They will have impressive swords, don't doubt it. Creates an impression. They will expect deference and a handsome supply of Glenrosa, the pure Highland malt, or some such. Don't exercise yourself about them. It is the ones you don't see who are the ones we need, not the fancy Dans. I will be here with my small team and so you need not concern yourself with us. With good fortune, my men will come and they will go and you will never notice them. Pollard will deal with the arrangements; your constables will deal with the crowds and we will deal with the security. But if you think you'll be presented to the Prince, or the rather more pleasant Princess, if that sort of nonsense is important to you, then think again. I've done it and to be frank, it is not worth losing sleep over. Strictly in the background please, and if you feel the need to lock up some of your more excitable villains as a preventative measure, then be my guest.'

Together they walked on to Tontine Street where a young boy in a tweed jacket and with a flat cap tucked into a pocket was shouting, loudly advertising his collection of flags, clutched together like a fan in his hand. Bucke stood in front of him, smiling.

'Thank you, Jack, but I think it is time to move on, don't you think? I should be grateful if you could control your enthusiasm for the royal visit and not make quite so much noise.' The boy grimaced but moved on towards the station. There would be a train coming in soon anyway, a train full of opportunities. The two men watched him walk away. 'A boy for an opportunity is Jack Dawes,' said Bucke. 'He has been selling small binoculars of dubious quality on the streets, which has been troubling the market traders no end, since he doesn't pay any rent but intercepts their customers at the entrance. That is probably why he has drifted up here too. He is good at what he does though. He can be very persuasive.'

Grey watched him carefully, seeing a small, dark, quick opportunist. 'Enterprising, then. Is the raven-haired boy really called Jack? Jack Dawes?'

'I don't know. It does seem unlikely, of course, but that is what we call him. There are many boys like him around the town, but he is perhaps the most intelligent, I think. I can see him as the sort of corporal the army runs on – always knows where things are, always finds something to eat, always has somewhere to sleep. Has answers. He is a survivor.'

Grey watched him carefully as he drifted off into the crowds. He raised his eyebrows.

*

He had a lot to think about as he walked briskly to Constance's room. He was eager to see her and he had much to talk about. Grey's suggestion that he should speak to no one about their meeting did not, as far as he understood it, encompass Constance. How could it? She was not a separate person in these matters,

25

merely an extension of himself, and as such it was inevitable that she would have to know.

Paul Roe's pitch tonight was on Oxford Street. One of the constables must have moved him on, but as far as The Roe was concerned, it made no difference. He had a message to deliver and newspapers to sell, though he realised that they were not always the same thing. Some of the things he said had an almost revolutionary tone, but he sold papers and that is what the proprietors wanted, no matter how much they might tut in public.

'Read all about it! Bertie to visit Swansea! The Poor are obliged to come out and cheer! Stop Press! Factories to close so workers can greet next king! Pay to be docked.'

Roe waved at him and inclined his head, encouraging Bucke to invest. He shook his head gently, raised his hand in acknowledgement and walked on.

It was amusing, of course; the man with newspapers over his arm offering an iconoclastic version of events. But that was all it was, thought Bucke. A different version, that is all. Yes, the workers in the factories were expected to come out to cheer. And yes, their pay would be stopped. And somehow, they were supposed to be happy about that? Presumably it was a question that never crossed the minds of the factory owners. Patriotism was designed to reinforce the status quo, to maintain social order. Bucke could see that, even though he had no such dangerous opinions of his own. But he knew that not everyone was possessed by obsequious loyalty. It wouldn't be a surprise if the visit revealed a number of tensions across the town. And when an event like this one attracted all sorts of outsiders to the town, for any number of reasons, it was inevitable, to his mind, that these people brought trouble with them, too.

There had already been a small and disorganised group who had gathered outside the Town Hall last week. It had been organised by members of the Operative Bricklayers Society, who objected loudly to the Royal visit on the grounds of unnecessary expense. Bucke had watched them as they listened to a speech from Gwyn Williams, their General Secretary, and noticed how their attention was increasingly drawn towards the streets that led, ironically perhaps, to the Queen's Hotel - and refreshment. It was not the most convincing speech Bucke had ever heard and he could understand their impatience. When Williams suddenly linked the visit to the government's excessive expenditure on the military, his audience began to drift away. A bricklayer's current set of pressing issues did not seem to include the need for a passionate denunciation of the army, *'which sapped the life of countries and taught its manhood destruction instead of productive habits.'* As an ex-service man, Bucke was rather pleased to see their response. But even before his meeting with Colonel Grey, he was aware that a high-profile visit by the royal family could provide an opportunity for those who had a grievance. The news about the Fenians did not surprise him, but it was a further complication the Swansea police did not need.

He looked across to a shop where the window display was disappearing as the oil lamps were being systematically extinguished and saw the hunched, brooding figure of Iago Morris turning slowly into Plymouth Street. He was carrying such a burden at the moment. The death of Price was a weight that he couldn't shake off. Bucke understood that. It came with the job – you found you could bear most things and then, often unexpectedly, something would happen and it would turn you inside out. For him it was usually anything to do with children. He could manage the rest, but it was the cruelties inflicted upon children that kept him awake at nights. Bucke resolved to find Morris on his own and try to talk to him, though that was not always very easy.

Three

Constable Turner had been entertained for a number of weeks now. It was, he recognised, his great good fortune that his daily beat took him down the steep incline of Powell Street for, half way along, he would always be intercepted by Mrs Lambrick, leaning against the door frame of her ramshackle house, waiting there, ready to advise him of her most recent dealings with the supernatural. As far as Constable Turner was concerned, it was hard to believe that beings from the unfathomable spirit world would find space within their busy diaries to regularly haunt Powell Street. But apparently, according to Mrs Lambrick, they did and with considerable enthusiasm, too.

At the very moment he arrived, neighbours would suddenly appear from nowhere to lend muscle to her argument. They stood sagely, with their arms crossed aggressively, if such a thing were possible, nodding their support. Turner would then endeavour to look thoughtful and serious, occasionally writing in his notebook at this shocking state of affairs. Something should be done. And it was clear that he was the someone who had been selected to do the something. And so today he had. He had brought his dog, Vasco.

In those quiet moments as he proceeded with his beat beyond Powell Street and on to Neath Road and all the terraced accommodation in the industrial streets of the Hafod, he always asked himself whatever could have possibly possessed Mrs Lambrick to move into this house, as opposed to one of the many available alternatives, a house in which a young woman had been so recently murdered. He repeated that sentence in his mind quite frequently, for he enjoyed his use of the word 'possessed,' which made him smile quietly to himself. Thus, he could understand why Mrs Lambrick would enjoy the soothing comfort of being able to repeat the same conversation almost every day, whilst new, and previously ignored evidence, attached itself to her story like barnacles.

'I am telling you,' she would say. 'That woman keeps coming back. In the nights. I see her. She knocks on windows. She keeps moving the kitchen table, which is very annoying, constable, and I'm not inclined to be putting up with it. And then there is that sobbing. Every night.'

'You sure it's not the wind?' he would reply knowingly, a private joke, always ignored, but that didn't matter. It was a reply without which his day would not have been complete, without which his young face would never have been creased by a smile. A simple pleasure, and he relished it.

'I am telling you now, constable,' Mrs Lambrick would continue, 'this house is possessed and I know it is her. It can't be my sister Hazel, because she died of pleurisy. They should never have buried her clothes in the garden, like they did. She keeps coming back for them. Someone,' she said looking at Turner significantly, 'should dig 'em up. We don't want 'em here. It was terrible what happened to her, but there's no call for us to be possessed, is there?' At this point she always folded her arms beneath her bosom and lifted it up, shaking her head. 'Lovely funeral, they say. Beautiful wreaths. From the police.' She nodded for emphasis.

'You see, Mrs Lambrick, I do have an idea...'

It was a sentence he never completed, for she ploughed on with her monologue relentlessly. Turner realised that it was highly unlikely that Mrs Lambrick would ever be prepared to show confidence in any of his ideas. 'That man comes, too. Dai Price. Keeps looking through the window of a night, trying to cop a look, I shouldn't wonder. And I will tell you something else,' invariably squashing Turner's attempt to reply, 'I was pegging my washing out on the line and the dirty bugger laid his dirty, murdering hands all over me. Clammy, they were. I turned to give him a slap and he disappeared into thin air, not a word of a lie. And there is more. He keeps taking my smalls off the line.'

Turner routinely speculated on the remarkable leap of faith required to regard those particular garments as small. 'Now, what I -'

His contribution was still not required, for it was at this point that Mrs Lambrick moved effortlessly to the conclusion of her complaint. 'So, I wants something done. I wants them clothes dug up and then I shall be able to go and wave at the prince and not fear that I am going to be interfered with.'

He would nod respectfully, for every woman, great or small, should be allowed their dreams. However, no matter how entertaining this ritual exchange had become, he knew, regrettably, that one day it must end. And that was why today he had brought the dog.

It was, he felt, by far the best way. Bringing the dog made it seem that he was taking her concerns seriously, and bringing a modern, scientific approach to her problem, something thoughtful, rational, reassuring. For how else were you to confront a ghost, or even two? Mrs Lambrick had never been entirely consistent about the number of supernatural beings haunting this small and dismal house, which only remained standing because each property in the terrace was supported by the ones on either side. One good sneeze would bring the whole lot down. But even in polite society, one ghost in a house was regarded as more than enough, so why should it be any different here?

He had learned a great deal during his first year in the force. He was acknowledged as a quick learner and the one who had taught him the most was undoubtedly Inspector Bucke. With such a skilled officer as Bucke to model himself upon, Turner had become adept at avoiding overt confrontation and gently easing those he dealt with into the place he wanted them, before they ever realised it was happening. Turner had realised that he could make his own life so much easier, and hers, if he removed the clothes from the garden. It would cost him nothing. She would relax then, she would no longer feel the need to see ghosts everywhere and Turner would be allowed to find bigger issues with which to fill his days, rather than her gin-soaked imaginings. So, he brought Vasco, so that the dog could find the buried clothes, so that he could dig them up and so that everyone would then be content.

Mrs Lambrick was mightily impressed. This was clearly

policework of the highest order and certainly no more than she deserved, when you considered how haunted she had been. When he asked for an onion, she knew that this was the right constable for her.

Turner produced from his pocket an old piece of flannel and, quite unnecessarily, rubbed the onion all over it to add detail to this scientific approach. Very proper, thought Mrs Lambrick. Very clever. The neighbours would be jealous.

Then Constable Turner led the excited dog down the passageway through to the garden, its tail bouncing furiously, ready to play the old game, his favourite game. He sniffed the flannel, ran around the muddy desolate space littered with broken bricks that appeared to erupt from the ground, for the sheer pleasure of doing so and then returned to a patch of ground, down by a grey broken wall, and then sat down and yelped.

'Duw! Duw! That is a marvel! That dog o' yours has gone right to the place where them clothes is buried.' This was possibly one of the most exciting moments of her life. She might appear in the newspaper; people would want to view her garden.

'You knew where the clothes were buried then, Mrs Lambrick?' Turner asked.

'Of course I did,' she said scornfully. 'You don't think I am dull, do you?'

Turner had learned that sometimes it was best to keep your own counsel. At least Vasco had found some enjoyment, even if it hadn't taken him long.

The ground was soft and easy, having been previously worked when the clothes had been buried, and the trowel Turner had brought with him was sufficient.

Mrs Lambrick offered a detailed commentary to her neighbours, who sat on the low wall and leaned over to watch. 'See the footprints? That's where that bloody ghost has been standing, churning up my garden,' she said.' Look at the size of them boots.'

Turner hadn't seen any prints at all, but turned, offered a smile and then removed a bundle of clothes from the ground and knocked off some of the wet earth that clung to them. Their burial, not unexpectedly, had served them badly, for they had been thin and worn and hardly serviceable when they had been used. Now, as the final, lost remnants of an innocent life, cruelly taken far too soon, they appeared forlorn, an inadequate representation of a caring young mother.

'Here we are, Mrs Lambrick. You will be troubled no longer. I am sure of it.'

'Sergeant Turner, you are a treasure. I told you, Mrs Hampson, didn't I?'

'Constable, Mrs Lambrick,' said Turner as he broke the thin string that held the parcel in place. 'I am a constable.'

'Same difference, my lovely. I shall tell your mam, next time I sees her in the market. Hasn't been for a while, mind. I notice these things.'

He made a mental note to tell his mother of this; one of the very few benefits of her recently acquired immobility. 'I will take these with me. I am sure they will throw them in the furnace for me down at the copper, if I ask them. You can rest now. The ghosts won't come looking for the clothes, not once they know they have been removed and then burnt.' He shook them out. There wasn't much in the bundle. Just a black skirt, a blouse that might have been brown and an apron with a large pouch along the front. It was sad, he thought; the insubstantial reminders of a life that had gone, ended in fear and agony. But, as he arranged the garments to carry away with him, he felt something in the apron, lost within the folds of the material. He pushed his hand inside the pouch that ran along the front and felt a piece of paper. This was unexpected and he thought it best so say nothing. It was probably unimportant, but he realised that it would not be wise to set more rumours racing up and down the street.

'Restless spirit, was Dai. Lots of trouble in his life. Never happy. Still, not an excuse for doing your wife in, is it?' said Mrs Hampson from the wall. 'And now what has he left behind him? Two orphans. Breaks your heart, it do.'

32

Turner smiled at her supportive words. He knew about Dai Price. Everyone did. His was a terrible story that had appeared without warning, horrifying the town with its elemental rage and ferocity. A domestic argument, they said, that had moved first to murder. and then on to suicide. That such a thing could have happened amongst them all was so bewildering for the residents of Powell Street. Such things happened elsewhere, not here.

Turner led Vasco, his tail still wagging with pleasure at a job well done, along the damp passage back to the street. He tipped his hat to his audience and then turned down the hill to the right and under the bridge beneath the main railway line before entering the Strand. He stopped and, with the dog sitting alert and happy at his feet, he examined the contents of the apron's pouch. He found first a single piece of paper folded tightly. Of course it was damp, but thankfully not wet, and very carefully Turner was able to open it. There was a message written in pencil, still legible, and he read it carefully. Then he scrabbled around in the deep pocket and found a second scrap of paper. This one appeared to have been written in ink, which had spread itself across the wet paper, dissolving much of the message. He looked at it for a while and then returned to the first one and read it again.

He lowered the paper and looked along the Strand. All was quiet at the moment, though that was rather irrelevant. He knew he had to return to the police station immediately. He re-folded the paper carefully along the existing creases and put it in his pocket. He patted the dog's head and was rewarded with a devotional look, though Turner didn't really notice, lost as he was in his thoughts. 'What a thing to find,' he said softly. 'Come on, Vasco. Let's go and find Inspector Bucke.'

*

'So, what do you think, Constable Turner?' Bucke looked at the paper again.

'It is a message from the grave, in effect. That is what I believe. It seems to be a confession, of some sort.'

'Yes. And so, the first thing we have to do is to ask ourselves two questions. Firstly, who wrote it? And then, is it genuine?'

'Both of those questions are hard to answer, Inspector. Sometimes it is too convenient to accept such things at face value, I imagine.'

'Yes, it is. So, Constable. What do believe we have here?'

'A piece of paper, handwritten in pencil and folded, which was found in the pocket of an apron that has probably been buried for six weeks or so. These are the facts, simple to establish.'

'Yes, those are all true. So now, what do you think?'

'I would say it is unlikely that someone dug up the parcel of garments once they had been buried in order to hide the paper. If they wanted to destroy it, burning it would have been a lot easier. So, without any proof, I would say that Mrs Price found the confession and pushed it into her pocket, perhaps to keep it from her husband at that time. Therefore, if you were to ask me, I'd say it was genuine.'

'Good work, Constable. We can't regard it as proper evidence, then?'

'No. I think it is background – but important background, if it helps to explain Price's actions.'

'Do you think that it does?'

'I think it might help us understand his state of mind. But it is hard to believe it is true. But it does show that the case cannot be closed.'

Bucke picked it up carefully and looked at it again. He read it aloud.

I hope that one day you can forgive me for all I have done I never wanted to bring shame on my family I cannot be a good father there is evil inside me I am going to hell they punish me I should not have eaten the boy

He put the paper down. 'My goodness.'

'What do you think it means, Inspector?'

'It might mean what it says, Constable. Or he was having visions. Best to keep an open mind. But if he wrote it, he appears to be telling Molly something she did not know. Something from

34

his past. But what a thing to say.'

'It doesn't sound like he was about to murder his wife. He wants her to forgive him in the future. He is not suggesting she hasn't got one.'

Bucke picked up the second scrap of paper. It was creased, damper and more fragile, written in ink, most of which had expanded into thin black stains. There was only a small, incomplete section that was still legible, and barely so. He looked at it with care, turning it round in his hand before handing it over to Turner. 'Your thoughts?'

'Obviously I read it. It is easier outside in the daylight. But it appears to have been a threatening letter. As you can see there is no ink where a signature might be. So perhaps it was anonymous.'

Bucke nodded. 'We don't know whether he saw it. We can't assume he did. Molly might have kept it from him and kept it in her apron.' He paused. 'And what can you read?'

'It is not very clear. But what I think it says is *Remember Aucaman*.'

'And what do you think it means?'

'I have no idea,' said Turner. 'I imagine it is a noun, but what it is I do not know. A place? I shall consult my copy of *Fullerton's Gazetteer of the World* this evening.'

*

He found Morris leaning against the pier, looking down into the black restless sea, as if the trouble in his eyes was being projected on to the water. He wanted to talk to him about Constable Price and the letter, but he had drifted away after the end of his shift, like a ship abandoned.

'Iago, I have been looking for you.'

'Oh aye? Well, you have found me.'

'Dark night,' said Bucke, looking up at the sky. 'No stars. The harbour office is talking about storms after the weekend, just in time for the royal visit, it seems. It will be a hard day, if they are right.'

Morris said nothing.

'You seem pre-occupied, Iago,' said Bucke, patiently.

He sighed again and then turned away from the water to look at the inspector. 'I'll be alright. There is a deal of death at the moment, that's all.' His eyes glistened, as if they were wet. Perhaps it was the wind from the sea.

'There has been a great deal of death over the last eighteen months, Iago. Don't know when it's going to end.' Bucke rubbed his cheek, wondering where this conversation might be heading. 'There are times when anyone of us can say that they cannot bear anymore. Anyone who denies that isn't being truthful to himself. We have to pick up the pieces of such a great deal of unhappiness and that's hard. There are many people in the town who don't realise this. That is why we have to support each other.'

'It was Price that got to me, Inspector. Poor Rhys. I never knew it had got so bad for him. He'd only just started. His boots were still new. I told him it would take a while to break them in. I told him he had to be patient.' Morris screwed up his face briefly. 'But to do that to Molly and...' His voice faded and then he appeared come to a decision. 'It was my idea he become a constable, Inspector. Did you know that? I said he should do it.'

'Yes, I had heard. You sailed together, didn't you?'

'Yes, that's how I knows him. He gave it up, just like I did, but he went and worked in the tinplate works in Morriston for a while. It didn't suit him, though. He got a bad chest and so he and Molly decided he should go back to sea. One last trip. To clear his chest. And then, when he come back, I met him one night in the Troubadour, by accident. He'd had a bad trip and so I said to him, why not become a constable? Won't be inside or anything. You'll be outside and that's got to be better and so that is why he did it. Become a constable. And how long did he last? Ten days? And then he did for Molly and then did for himself. And they had two little 'uns. Her sister's got them now.' Morris sighed. 'Why did he do it? What was wrong with him? Eight stab wounds she had. It

36

was the one in the neck that did for her, you know. Was it my fault? I ask myself that all the time.'

'You said he had a bad trip. Do you think that might have had anything to do with his state of mind, Iago? It is what the magistrate said, isn't it? A crime committed in an unsound state of mind. What made it like that, though? Was he ill in his chest? Was he anxious about that? Had something happened to him? Do you know?'

'He was unlucky, that's all. He was on the *Para*. To Newfoundland. Well that's a cold trip, always has been, and this time they got stuck in the ice. You might have read about it in the paper.' Bucke shook his head. 'I did, but then I follow all the shipping news; it is a habit. But the *Para* got stuck in the ice in Notre Dame Bay and the hull was crushed. It happened to me once. It is a terrible thing, stuck out at sea and listening to all those creaks and groans and cracks. The ship is all you have got and it feels like the ice is eating it. You can't see anything, no matter which way you look. Just ice. No clear water. No nothing. I was lucky, we got out of it. We dug the ice away for days. As fast as we dug it, the more that came. But we got out. Rhys was not so lucky. The hull of the *Para* was crushed and splintered and it sank. Straight to the bottom. So what do you do? You have to get off the ship, that's obvious. And then what do you do next? You have to get to land or you have to find water where you can drop your rowing boats. But it is hard. My god, it is hard. Dragging the boats across the ice. And what people don't realise is that it isn't flat. And there will be channels in it and you have to go round them or across them. A couple of the men fell through the ice into the sea, Rhys told me. What do you do then? They'll never get warm again. They will have tried to sleep underneath the upside-down boats. But all night they will always have been thinking that at any moment the ice is going to crack. And when that happens, do you want to be awake or asleep?'

There was a sudden gust of wind that chilled them as they stood there, with images forming in their imaginations. Bucke turned to look out to sea. 'And what about food, then? What would they have eaten?'

'They will have taken as much food from the ship as they could, but it is never enough. You don't know how long you are going to be out there. The *Para* was only eight miles out, they reckon, but in those conditions it might as well have been eighty.'

'Did you know that Price left a note, Iago?'

'I've heard, yes. About the eating.'

Bucke turned to look at Morris, but it was his turn to look out into the darkness and to imagine. 'And what do you think, Iago? In your experience.'

'It is possible. Of course it is. Out there on the ice. I have heard of it. A crewmate dies of the cold or he falls or something. So what are you going to do? You are going to keep yourself alive, aren't you? It is what your dead pal would have expected, anyway. We all know that it might happen. Not a secret.'

'Really?' Bucke wondered what he would have done. It was impossible to say unless you had been part of such a desperate situation.

'I mean, I have not done it. Never had to. But I have heard.'

'So you think it might be possible. It could have happened that, in these terrible circumstances Price and the others found themselves in, the survivors ate the body of a dead colleague. To stay alive.'

'Yes, inspector. I think it is possible.'

'And it is possible that something like that could have unbalanced his mind.' Bucke nodded to himself. He thought it was a possibility. Nothing more than that, but a possibility. He noticed that Morris was still looking out to sea, as if the whole terrible circumstances were vividly pictured there. 'Poor Price.'

'It didn't get any better. The survivors made it to land. Got places on the *SS Merima* and that got stuck too. Now that is unlucky. They got themselves free and then they were lost for a couple of days in dense fog. Not knowing what you might sail into, what might sail into you. Unsettle anyone that would. And Rhys was not the sort of boy to forget things, neither.' He turned suddenly from the sea and looked at Bucke. 'Do you know what? It wouldn't surprise me at all if the poor boy thought he was cursed. That is what I reckon, Inspector.'

'Interesting,' said Bucke. 'I can see that. Two bad voyages, some terrible experiences. I can see that it could have unbalanced anyone.'

'I didn't know he was so troubled. I just wish he had said something.' He shook his head. 'He never touched the baby, did he? The one that was in their bed that night. Killed Molly but never touched the baby.'

'These things can dwell with you, Iago. We both know that. As you say, having someone to talk to does help sometimes. All of us in the police station need to talk. Perhaps if Price had been with us a little bit longer, he would have. But thank you for your help, Iago. It has been really useful. We'll never know what was going on inside his head, but I think I have more of an idea about him after speaking like this. There is just one other thing. There was a scrap of paper too. Turner found it with the note in the pocket of an apron. *Remember Aucaman.* Any idea?'

Morris turned and looked away again. 'A place, I think. A seaport. Venezuela? Not sure. Don't think I have been there.'

'It puzzles me,' said Bucke. 'Why would anyone send that in a letter to Price, do you think? There may have been something else, but those are the only words we've got.'

Morris continued to stare at the sea. 'Something happened there? Who knows? Who can say? We'll probably never find out. Died with him, I shouldn't wonder.'

Four

They had not met for almost a year now and so much had happened that had changed all three of them, for extreme experiences that reshape lives, can never be shrugged off lightly. Flora and Emily had finally arrived at the Mackworth Hotel on Wind Street on their very first return visit. They were staying here for the week, bridging the gap between Power Cobbe's lecture and the Royal visit and this extended visit reflected Flora's desperate need for re-engagement with Swansea society, her thirst for news and gossip only otherwise matched by that of a parched man in a desert. Emily, apparently exhausted by the rigours of the journey across country, had taken to her bed and, once she was resting, Flora hurried to the lounge to see her old friend, Constance, without the troubled presence of her daughter. She entered the lounge, glancing around nervously, and Constance saw immediately that she was thinner, haggard almost, certainly unsettled and nervous.

Constance was different too, but in a much more positive way and Flora noticed those changes in her immediately. She was more confident and relaxed, a person who now had a status and a reputation in the town that she had never had before. Some was reflected from Rumsey Bucke, of course, for it was a woman's fate to be seen as a male adornment, and he was, without a doubt, Swansea's favourite policeman. But escaping death in a mine rescue, assaulting attackers in the street and developing an informed social conscience, after years spent oppressed in an abusive marriage, had brought a light to her eyes that could not be dimmed. She was known and acknowledged, respected and envied, a woman who thrived, a little, on a racy reputation as a wronged woman, but who was still welcomed into shops across Swansea in the hope that her patronage would add lustre to their profile.

All this made Flora not a little jealous. The Beynon's had left, sacrificing their comfortable and recognised status in the town, and exchanged it for the uncertainties of lives as newcomers in Aberystwyth, which brought more challenges to them than they ever expected. All those social threads that had linked them to others, that had secured their place in the town in which they had lived for so many years, had been severed. Flora would never have found it easy to build new ones, but in her state of constant anxiety, it was an impossible task in an unfamiliar place and she had been cut adrift. Flora's infrequent letters had mapped it out in painful detail.

She had no idea of how to deal with Emily, had no idea what she needed or how to react. In the first few months in Aberystwyth, she had kept Emily constantly by her side, often sleeping with her, terrified that if they were apart, even for an instant, Emily might disappear once again.

Emily's experiences when held captive by Milo Rogers' religious cult were rarely spoken about now by either of them, unless Emily wanted to upset her mother, but its presence was always there in the background, leering over their shoulders, troubling their days, stealing their ease.

And what did Constance see? That David Beynon had wanted a new start, in an attempt to close the door on the horror that had assaulted all of them in Swansea, but that the family had soon realised that they had taken the horror with them; they would never be able to leave it behind, wherever they went. It was part of them now and lodged deep in their bones, Constance thought. They desperately needed to rebuild not just their social lives, but also themselves, but that would never be easy. She watched how Flora tried to re-immerse herself immediately into what once had been her life, but which was hers no longer and in which she no longer featured, believing that it would reshape immediately around her as if nothing had changed. But it had and she was now nothing but a visitor.

Flora had not wanted to move to Aberystwyth, and for that reason alone, Constance knew their relocation would never succeed. Surrounded by people and places that she knew, she might have healed more successfully. But not now. Constance recognised that Flora was now a stranger in her new home and a stranger in her old. She could also sense the jealousy, too, for she was stuck in a horrific past whilst Constance was excited by a sparkling future. And so Flora was lost and bewildered; everything about her seemed so desperate and frenetic. Constance knew that living in such a maelstrom of emotions must be exhausting.

Flora for her part, felt that Constance had usurped her place in the hierarchy of Swansea and feared that she would never get it back. My God, Aberystwyth was a mistake, though she could not acknowledge that. Everything would have been so much better if they had stayed in Swansea. That was the problem. She had lost what she had once had, and had replaced it with nothing.

Emily, however, had found an interest. Her new enthusiasm was animal rights and the Anti-Vivisection League and her great hero was Frances Power-Cobbe. In this way, Emily had found something with which to fill her mind, to block out the hellish images, although it was an interest which, in Flora's mind, had become a disturbing obsession. What she had originally believed was a straw to be clutched at, offering a healing distraction, had become something much less welcome.

That Power Cobbe was a woman was undoubtedly helpful, and she had become the channel into which Emily directed all her attention, writing letters, distributing leaflets to the indifferent of Aberystwyth, now flirting with the concept of vegetarianism. This was how she intended to live her life. She could not change a world that was dangerous and hostile and soulless – but she could try to change herself and find the solace in animals that she could not find in the humans who had betrayed and abused her.

'That is why we are here, you see. I must have told you. I have written to you, haven't I? I always forget what I write to you the moment I take them to the Post Office. I wanted to see the visit of the Prince of Wales. What an opportunity that is. I am so excited and I would never forgive myself if I missed it. David is too busy with his patients, of course,' she said, rather too quickly, 'but Emily wanted to come because her great heroine, Frances Power Cobbe is speaking on Saturday at the Music Hall and she is desperate to see her. Have I told you this? She has been corresponding with her, you see. Everything is animals with Emily now. It is exhausting, but it seems that there is no room in her mind for anything else.' Flora sighed, looking around the lounge in search of threats and dangers.

'Whenever Frances writes to her, Emily reads every word again and again for days on end. She is more devoted than a puppy. This woman can neither be questioned nor doubted. Now Emily is talking about vegetarianism. We bought her a dog, Prince, to take for walks along the front, to get her out of the house. Emily hardly ever goes out, hardly knows anyone. She now says that unless she stops eating meat, she will forever be a hypocrite when she strokes Prince. So, if we don't stop eating meat, she will give him away. There will be arguments with her father, I know that. He is not going to embrace such ridiculous ideas, even for the sake of Emily.'

'And how is David?'

'Still angry, Constance. Angry at everyone and everything. And mostly at me.' Flora realised she had said too much and hurried on. 'I think, Constance, that Frances guides Emily away from her troubles, for which I am profoundly grateful. I merely wish that Frances, a powerful and formidable woman as she is, was a bit more conventional. She seems to be telling Emily, in so many words at least, that it is best of all to be different; I don't want Emily to be different. If I am honest, Constance, there is no one stranger in the entire world than Frances Power Cobbe. But Emily can't see it. She must not model herself on her, if she is to avoid becoming a laughing stock. There, I have said it.'

'Perhaps all that Emily wants is to be Emily? Who of us knows what that might be?'

'Well, Constance, I know, because I am her mother,' Flora replied abruptly. 'But you see, I wouldn't want you to misunderstand me, Constance, and of course I don't want to see cruelty to animals, but there are more important things to do when you have moved to a new town than handing out leaflets in the street to people who do not want them.'

'And how is Aberystwyth, Flora?'

'Windy and wet. Some days wet. Some days windy. Most days, both. One of the reasons why we lead a quieter life, I fear. There seems little chance of it improving.' She pulled at her earring anxiously and then decided that it was time to refocus the conversation. 'Tell me, Constance,' said Flora rather too brightly. 'How are you?' emphasising the last word, as if the success of her own life had given her the right to offer her wisdom to all others around her.

'I am very well thank you, Flora. I keep myself busy with my work and I have an opportunity sometimes to help Rumsey with his.'

Flora ignored this. 'And what is the news of your status? Of your legal struggles?'

'Well, Flora. We had hoped that the case would have been heard in the summer, but we now know that I shall have to attend the High Court in London in the spring of 1882, so it is frustrating. But it is only a few months away now.'

'How difficult that must be,' said Flora sympathetically. 'You must be so anxious to be called a wife once more.' Flora smiled faintly, clutching at an illusion of superiority.

Constance was by now, and despite herself, feeling irritated. 'The title has little meaning, in the end, but it will make life so much more convenient. The commitment, Flora, has already been made. Quite regularly, actually.'

Flora appeared lost for words, which for Constance was no bad thing, although part of her regretted shocking her like this. But really, was there any need for her to be so pompous? Flora's face coloured and she fiddled agitatedly with her handkerchief. 'Oh, I see.' She wasn't really sure what to say.

Poor Flora, thought Constance. The world was far more complicated than she wanted it to be. Her emotional state was much more insecure, than the pretence she had tried to project of the experienced. confident woman. Emily's abduction had ripped the stability from everyone in the family. 'Please don't be shocked,

Flora. Such things are quite common amongst the ordinary people of the town.'

'Really, Constance! That does not make such arrangements right, now does it? The lower classes have always been victims of their own base desires. Those of us in society should set a better example. I am deeply shocked, Constance, to be frank. Perhaps you are unwell, or you have for whatever reason, forgotten your obligations.' You should not submit yourself to his needs, Constance. You are not married to the man.'

'Hmm. Sometimes he has to submit himself to mine, Flora.'

'Really! There are times when you disgust me, Constance. Do you realise what you have just said?'

'Yes, Flora. I was listening.'

'To be frank, I am so disappointed. I never expected that Rumsey Bucke, of all people, would force himself upon you. You should have resisted, called a policeman...' Her words skittered away, as she realised the absurdity of what she had said.

This was much harder work than Constance had anticipated. She wondered about asking Flora about her own intimate life but decided against it. She chose her words with care. 'I have obligations only to Rumsey, to my daughter Agnes, to myself. To no one else. Not to you, not to society. You and I, Flora, live in the same society but our paths are very different. And we have to find our own way to happiness, because no one else will do that for us.'

'But without a husband, Constance, surely you can see your life is incomplete?'

'Don't be silly, Flora. I had one of those before and he made my life incomplete. Don't look so shocked, Flora. The world is changing and I owe your friend Frances Power-Cobbe a huge debt of gratitude. Without her enthusiasm for the Matrimonial Causes Act, I would have a life without hope. But with it...'

'Her again! I can't escape from the woman, if that is what she is.' Flora sighed. 'Yes, she is Emily's new devotion, but I am not sure that it can be a healthy one. I am worried that Frances will

45

introduce her to an unorthodox way of life.'

'I am sure that Emily will make the decisions that are the right ones for herself, Flora. I don't think she can ever change the kind of person she is.'

'But will she? She hates men now. All men. Sometimes she flashes her father such a look. I know that she had a horrific time, but if she continues in this way, what will become of her? Will she dress like a man and live with some sort of female sculptor?' She shook her head, her tongued loosened after finally finding someone to talk to. 'I do wonder whether, in your current state of folly, you are a suitable companion for my daughter, but her current enthusiasm troubles me so. Please can you have a word with her? Like you did before? Please, Constance.'

Constance smiled and nodded. She wondered how successful that might prove. There had always been walls around Emily. But now those walls must be topped with broken glass.

'It is so hard being a mother,' sighed Flora, ignoring the fact that Constance was one too. 'I shall see if she is ready to see you, Constance. She is in our room upstairs. Perhaps she would prefer to see you there.'

The reunion with Emily, of course, was a tearful one. They hugged and stared and hugged again. They talked. The story of Henry Fry was a scandalous one and she wanted all the details the newspapers hadn't mentioned. And she felt she had a right to know. After all, he had once been sweet on her, hadn't he? She had never encouraged him of course, but everyone knew and look what had happened now! Fighting in the street? Henry? And a man killed? And Henry did it? Was this woman really a music hall singer? And truly that much older than him? And when was he to be released from prison? Did anyone know? And the judge had extended his sentence because he had brought the legal profession into disrepute? What an awful thing to do to your mother! And poor Harriet! What a terrible thing to do to her! She didn't deserve it. She corresponded with the poor girl and she was still refusing to leave her bedroom. She had never liked boys much and now she knew why. 'Men? How can you trust them?' asked Emily,

46

whilst Flora smiled, twisting her handkerchief into a desperate and inelegant ribbon of distress.

Emily was still the dark-haired jewel that Constance had known but she now had a single, startling streak of white hair that ran across the top of her head and which she had no intention of hiding. Flora had written about it but this was the first time she had seen it. It was her badge, sometimes of shame, sometimes of defiance, it seemed. It certainly brought drama to her hair, as a dramatic swirl within the tight bun on the back of her head. It was an obvious legacy from those awful days of abuse and torture which had brutally stolen her childhood. Her face had once been open, with wide-eyed innocence and curiosity; now it seemed to Constance that Emily was permanently exhausted and unwilling to emerge from the shadows for any length of time.

Her eyes were still almost black, of course, but now they were darting around the room to avoid contact, for her trust and her faith in the decency of others had been destroyed. Constance saw she was always biting her lip, as if only discomfort could keep her alert and safe in a world that was eager to betray her.

As she watched them both, Constance found that everything about their relationship and emotions seemed fragile, their lives resting upon the thinnest ice, revealing creeping fractures. How could any of this be repaired? But for now, it was gossip; they were back in the world they missed, gossiping. It was important because it was not important, and even more important since it wasn't your pain, thought Constance. Your own pain was so much greater.

*

Rumsey Bucke was not really gossiping either, rather he was bringing the Chief Constable up to date about Arthur Riverton. Captain Colquhoun had never met him, but felt in the interests of the town's security he should find out as much as he could. 'Should I assume, Rumsey, 'asked the Chief Constable, 'that he must become our new enthusiasm, do you think? Will we be looking for him in every doorway?'

'We certainly need to know what he is doing,' said Bucke. 'In the simplest of terms, he is bad news for us, I am sure of that, and I would be much happier if he wasn't in the town, but it is hard to know anything about him for certain.' Bucke rubbed his eyes. 'He appeared suddenly in Swansea, about six years ago, it would be. No idea where from. Never heard of him before and then suddenly he was all we could talk about. He wasn't known to any other police force, not under the name of Riverton, anyway. If that is who he is, then it is my guess is that he had been abroad somewhere. The colonies? He has never seemed to me to be a man who suddenly discovered crime in his middle years. He has always been a criminal, I am sure; we just didn't catch him. Why he turned up in Swansea when he did, has never been explained. He's not a man for talking. For complaining, yes. But sometimes hard to talk to because he is always trying to control you. I got on quite well with him and I did wonder if that meant he had been in the army and recognised someone else who had. But I don't know. Generally, he gets very angry with anyone in a position of authority. Thinks they have ideas above their station, I imagine.' A man was shouting and Bucke turned towards the window briefly before continuing.

'I arrested him, about four years ago it would be. Series of burglaries across the town. Always choosing the very best houses. Had a glass cutter so he would take out a pane of glass silently and make away with whatever he could get. A very skilled and patient safe breaker. Claimed there was no safe he couldn't open. Very keen on silver, as I remember. He knew a man in Bristol who would take it from him. I mean, this went on for a few months. I had him after he did a house in Killay. Picked him up on the street with a sack full. Pleaded not guilty because we had confiscated his diary and didn't have a right to do so. Just nonsense. It wasn't a personal diary; it was a list of promising addresses. He said it was merely a list of residences with horses, where he could try to sell animal feed as part of a business he intended to establish. A complete fabrication, obviously. But that was the thing. He was always so very argumentative. Always complaining about something. The slight inconveniences he might have suffered in the cells were always far worse than the crimes he had committed, in his mind, at least.'

Colquhoun nodded. 'I know the type.'

'He was awaiting trial at the Assizes and he escaped from Swansea Gaol. There was a hell of a fuss. Whether someone helped him we could never ascertain. I do wonder if there was a warder involved in some way. He always said he climbed over the wall but I was not inclined to believe him then and I am not now. He'd have trouble climbing the stairs in his chains, let alone a wall and then dropping down the other side. Nonsense. Interesting actually, Isaac, that he didn't seem to know where he going. Escaped from prison and headed straight into Gower. Didn't seem to realise he was trapped in a small area with just two roads in and out, where strangers are always noted. He lived in barns, I believe, for about a week and then the Reynoldston constable apprehended him after a bit of a struggle. I went out to bring him in. Argued all the way back in the cart, of course. But that is what he does.'

'And in doing so, uses up an inordinate amount of our time, I shouldn't wonder.'

Bucke sighed. 'The judge sent him to Dartmoor. Served him right for escaping. Never been compliant when he was in there, apparently. Tried to escape from Dartmoor, too, attacked a prison officer and got ten strokes of the cat for his pains. Always claimed that whatever was done to him, he never flinched. But he invariably thinks he has been hard done by. The real lags just keep their heads down and do their time without trouble. But not Arthur. Once there is an idea in his head, you won't shift it.'

'And so now he is out. Not a good time, is it?'

'Stanley manages him pretty well. They had a few run-ins when Stan was a constable and so they know each other. And as I said, he will talk to me too, goodness knows why. But if one of the other constables says the wrong thing, he is likely to wallop them and then we have a problem. If Turner finds him there won't be a problem. Turner can talk his way out of it. If Smith finds him there will be blood, you can be sure, and it won't be Arthur Riverton's.

I had hoped he wouldn't come back here. Make a fresh start, you know. Somewhere new. Like Australia. We are not so lucky. But he is here and there has to be a reason. Why? What is the attraction? He has no family here as far as I know. He doesn't like people that much anyway. So why here? Why now?'

'There must be something, Rumsey. He doesn't sound like a man who does things casually. But the point is that he is here, and he is here now. We have to deal with it. Can't think of a worse time. But perhaps that is why he is here. He sees us distracted; he sees an opportunity. Whenever he came back, we would have to watch him. But this is certainly not the best of times for us.'

'Be handy if we knew where he was, though,' said Bucke. 'It would be a start.' There was more noise, a man was shouting again, this time it seemed from the steps of the police station.

'What the devil is going on?' asked Colquhoun.

'That is Iestyn Pugh, I am afraid. One of our regulars. Comes down most weeks and preaches loudly to anyone who is foolish enough to listen. He claims he has solved one of our older murders and that we are doing nothing about it, because we are in the pay of the killer.'

'Really? Then you will have to treat me to dinner at the Mackworth sometime, if that is the case.'

'Don't build up your hopes, Isaac. It is all about a young girl killed almost 50 years ago now. 1832, if my memory serves.'

'Before my time, then.'

'And mine, too. Pregnant and thrown down a well, out at Felindre, other side of Llangyfelach.'

'So your friend Iestyn has solved it, you say. Taken him a while then, hasn't it?'

'As I understand it, this is an argument amongst old men. Iestyn Pugh and Horace Jacques, also known as Patagonia Jacques. Quite vicious, it seems. They were banned from the Plough and Harrow in Llangyfelach last week for a few days. There is talk there will be solicitors involved, soon.'

'Patagonia Jacques? There is still so much I don't know about Swansea, isn't there?' He held up his hand. 'Please, Rumsey, tell me later.' Colquhoun went to the window and opened it quietly, better to hear the words.

'Although the savage murderer may escape for a season the detection of man, yet doubtless God hath set his mark upon him, either for time or eternity. And the cry of blood will assuredly pursue him to a terrible and righteous judgement! His time is coming! He will burn forever!'

Colquhoun closed the window. 'Quite agitated, isn't he? What do you know?'

'He claims the murderer was Horace Jacques. He killed the young woman who worked as a servant on a local farm in 1832 after she became pregnant by him. Then he threw her body down the well.'

'Not his own well, I'll wager.'

'Of course not. Why soil your own water? But it is possible, of course it is. The locals believed it was Jacques who killed her for years. Painted the road red on his wedding day and the gates of the chapel. He got paint on his hands when he pushed them open. Blood on his hands, they said. There are flowers on the girl's grave every year, that sort of thing. A local attraction, that grave, though I've not seen it myself. Calling for vengeance and justice. It's probably Iestyn's doing, I imagine. When his own wife died, Jacques disappeared to South America and came back with a fortune, they say – which is why he is called Patagonia Jacques. And now Iestyn's started again. He has reached the age when he doesn't care very much what he says or does. Every time Jacques complains, it is taken as evidence that he did it, which is exactly what happens if he says nothing. They tried to have a fist fight at the Llangyfelach Fair in September but they couldn't manage it. Waved their arms and shouted at each other, that's all.' Bucke shook his head. 'Two old men, locked in the past.'

Colquhoun opened the window again and the ageing but still powerful voice forced its way in.

'I denounce, once again, Horace Jacques for the terrible murder of Eleanor Williams! Assuredly he is guilty and will burn for all eternity in the fiercest flames of hell because of what he did. I have evidence that will prove that he killed the poor young woman. The silence of the police force is shameful and condemns them to our eternal contempt. They must act and they must act now...'

He closed the window. 'Dear me. And how often does this happen, Rumsey?'

'Every few weeks. He comes down to Swansea every month to visit the solicitors, Bellingham and Strick, to collect a small legacy left by an aunt, as I believe. Then he stands somewhere and delivers his speech. It is our turn today. I have taken the view that we don't over react. Let him carry on. Everyone ignores the poor old boy at the moment.'

'And have you spoken to him?'

'Of course, though to little purpose. He is talking about something that happened 50 years ago. Half a century. What he regards as evidence isn't evidence at all. It is conviction, it is belief and that is enough for him to demand justice. Who knows? He might be right. But he can't give me evidence. He can never tell me the whole story. He always gets distracted. I will try again, Isaac.'

'Strange, isn't it? We can't escape from our past. I don't suppose any of us can. We all carry things with us, don't we? The things that made us. You know better than anyone, you can't unmake them, Rumsey.'

'I am what I am, Isaac. Not what I was when I was in my twenties in India or when I was in my thirties and a father. I am neither of those things now. But the past is with me always. Just like Riverton and Iestyn. It is the knot you carry with you that will never be unpicked.'

'Unless that knot is a deception and someone knows how to find the truth it is trying to hide,' mused Colquhoun. 'That is the point, surely Rumsey. If your past is the truth, then there is nothing to unravel. But a lie, a fraud, can't be sustained forever.'

Five

Mr Melville had been far too optimistic in booking the Music Hall for the Swansea leg of her lecture tour. Interest in Miss Power Cobbe in Swansea was unfortunately limited and did not reflect well upon a town with pretentions to be the capital of Wales. The Music Hall was, frankly, much too large; it could not be denied. He wondered whether it would have been more politic to have booked the snug of the Queen's Head on Oxford Street. He would certainly have saved himself both bother and expenditure.

He had tried very hard, of course, to promote her visit. It wasn't often Swansea was included on a prominent lecture tour and he had invested in considerable publicity; the lecture had been advertised in the local publications for weeks, but with little discernible impact. The small audience was in danger of being lost in the generous proportions of the Music Hall. It would be best, he decided, if he moved the audience to the front few rows of the stalls. On such an occasion it didn't matter how much anyone had paid for a seat. Darken the back. Make it more intimate. But at least Miss Power Cobbe was not expensive and her requirements were happily modest. Profit might be extremely limited, but he was hopeful that if he counted the takings carefully there would be one.

It had been a strange event all round, when he thought about it. A team of men had appeared from nowhere, expressing keen support for the anti-vivisection campaign and then wandered around town getting on everyone's nerves by intimidating people to accept the leaflets they were distributing. They had come down from Mount Pleasant and spoke in heavy Irish accents of the need to support one of their own from the 'ole country.' And to the preoccupied Mr Melville, who had his own problems anyway in the Star Theatre that he could now barely keep afloat, they seemed to take over arrangements. Suddenly they were managing the evening. They showed people to their seats; they patrolled backstage to check for intruders. They became such a part of the evening, and so efficiently too, that he considered employing them on a permanent basis at the Star, except he could not afford to pay them. But they made sure everything went well, and he was grateful for that, even if the audience was disappointingly small.

Frances Power Cobbe spoke persuasively and passionately and Constance, happily relocated to the stalls by Melville, was impressed by her confidence. Her unexpected ideas were challenging certainly, but really interesting and very logical and she was very easy to listen to. She hadn't been looking forward to the evening at all, but she was glad that she had come, for it gave her plenty to think about.

Frances was a large woman who, as Emily was keen to point out, was completely disinterested in her personal appearance. She was dressed entirely in black. She had a full face which seemed to lack definition but her eyes were brimming with intelligence and, it seemed to Constance, with frustration and anger at the way the world was turning out. It was clear, when she answered questions, that Power-Cobbe was patient with others who do not have her intellectual grasp or with those who did not possess her own unswerving confidence that she was right. Constance soon realised that she had a great deal to thank her for. Her ability to argue and persuade had been in evidence in her political work, especially when campaigning to expose the domestic abuse some women experienced. She spoke about it from the stage and waved around one of her pamphlets, *Wife Torture in England*.

'We worked hard to obtain protection for unhappy wives, beaten, mangled, mutilated or trampled on by brutal husbands and because we worked tirelessly, we succeeded. Never forget what we can achieve together! Now we have the Matrimonial Causes Act, and so now abused women have the right of legal separation on the grounds of assault. Who could possibly disagree?'

Who indeed? thought Constance, for this was the means through which her solicitor Mr Strick was confident she could obtain a divorce. Not long now, she hoped.

Power Cobbe waved around another leaflet. 'But you see, the issue runs much, much, deeper than physical assault. Consider this. Who is allowed to vote in Queen Victoria's Great Britain? We know, of course we do. But let me turn that around, for a moment. I ask you, who are those who are not allowed to vote? And the answer is here in my essay. *Criminals, Idiots, Women and Minors.* And for those who rule us, it is perfectly acceptable that women – mothers, wives, sisters, daughters - are no more fit to vote than children and the insane! How is this possible?' She paused and looked around the audience, defiantly.

Constance also looked round at the audience. Emily was rapt in admiration and hero-worship, whilst Flora looked distinctly uncomfortable, as did quite a number of men. There were, she noticed a number of women smiling and nodding.

'You see, it is as obvious as the nose upon your face. Women must have economic independence from men, who otherwise will continue to enforce female suppression. And that is my point entirely. Women are beaten and excluded, as if they count for nothing! And you must therefore be able to see the obvious connection between the male brutality directed towards animals that we can see around us every day - dogs beaten, horses thrashed - and the subjection and abuse of women. It is the same thing! Both women and animals are considered irrational and inferior! Ridiculous! You see, in my view, without economic independence, women will remain subject to their husbands and fathers, in the same way that domestic animals are completely reliant on humans. And that makes us vulnerable, always vulnerable.' She looked at her audience as if challenging them to disagree. A man coughed and looked down at his lap. A reporter was scribbling furiously, thankful for the excuse to avoid her gaze. 'It has to end.' She looked down at her notes on the lectern in front of her and then suddenly stepped around it and moved to the apron of the stage, animated and gesticulating, consumed by the power of her argument.

'There are two issues here and they are indissolubly linked. The terrible practice of dissecting animals, whilst they are still alive, for the purposes of scientific study – is a stain upon our society.' She shook her head vigorously. 'And where is the church in this, I ask you? Where? It refuses to speak out on the abuse of women and its silence on cruelty to animals is equally deafening! How is it possible that our archbishops in their fancy gowns cannot see the obvious contradiction in their concept of a loving God and their acceptance of animal abuse? There must be greater protection for animals used in experiments. And that is why we have founded the Society for the Protection of Animals Liable to Vivisection and for whom I shall be asking for small donations this evening. We have made small steps and the Cruelty to Animals Act has been a start, but it does not go far enough. It does not end animal experimentation! And my point is that unless we do so, then the abuse of women will continue. You must be able to see that!'

At the end of the evening, as the speaking engagement ended, and sheepish men were led away by their energised wives, Mr Melville took Flora and Emily backstage to meet Frances as they had arranged. As they made their way along the narrow corridor, he marvelled at the efficiency of these self-appointed stewards. He wasn't sure that he could entirely understand the things they said, for their accent was at times impenetrable, but everything had run so well and even now, instead of heading for the nearest public house as the other causals he sometimes employed were wont to do, they were checking every room carefully, ensuring there were no strays in them, testing the locks and securing all external doors. He had been right, he had barely made any money from the evening at all, but at least he now knew there was a reliable team he could call upon, if he could find out how to contact them. A different team was working in the auditorium, unbolting the seats from the floor, for the Music Hall was to be the location of the Grand Ball at the end of the Prince's visit. What an occasion that would be, with a fine buffet available for such elevated guests. But these untidy and grumbling workmen were nowhere near as good at the Irish ones.

Flora had initially written to Frances on behalf of Emily, and had told her some of Emily's background. But although they had never met before, this did not seem to matter at all. Frances greeted her in the shabby dressing room backstage as if she were an old friend. She was warm and genuine, hugging Emily whilst smiling over her shoulder at Flora, who, for her part, had not been at all sure whether to permit this meeting after what she heard during the evening. However, Frances' genuine warmth and obvious humanity reassured her. So, with unusual sensitivity, thought Constance, Flora left Emily alone with her. This was Emily's occasion and she did not need to be treated as a child; she had to be allowed to re-establish her own life. She was still beautiful Emily; she was still intelligent Emily; but all those who knew her, like Constance, knew she was a damaged Emily.

So, Emily and Frances talked, though perhaps it would be better to say that Frances talked and that Emily listened, wide-eyed, trying her best to keep up with the constant flow of ideas that tumbled unchecked from this woman who was so unlike anyone she had ever met before.

Eventually, Frances said, 'Everyone gets frightened. You shouldn't be frightened of being frightened, if you see what I mean. It is completely natural. And do you know, there is something I am truly terrified of, Emily, my dear.'

'What is that?' asked Emily, bright-eyed with anticipation.

'Being buried alive. Just to say those words makes the blood rush in my ears and my throat tighten.'

She nodded vigorously. 'That nearly happened to me, you know. So I do understand. Deep underground, trapped in the deepest folds of the devil's cloak,' she said, repeating a line from one of her poems, hoping that Frances would be impressed and ask for more. She didn't.

'And how, Emily, did you find the experience?'

'Terrible, Frances. Terrible. I could not breathe; I could not see; I could not hear. I was trapped within the darkest void where all my hope had been strangled.' Another line that provoked no response. 'I wake at nights in the dark and I can taste the earth in my mouth.' She paused for a moment, whilst Frances watched her carefully. 'I remember too how it felt, believing that I would never escape. And do you know? One of the things I had forgotten but came back to me last week in a nightmare, was how wet it was.

There was water pouring down the walls, forcing out the air. That is what it felt like. That we had only moments left. I didn't know whether Connie and me were going to be crushed or drowned. Connie is a lot older than me but she is my friend. She held me. I thought we were going to die together and I didn't want to die.' She began to cry, as she often did when these memories invaded her mind. 'I am sorry.'

'It must have been a truly awful experience,' nodded Frances leaning over to squeeze her hand. 'But you describe it so well. Perhaps it is a sign you are recovering from the very worst ordeal of all. It seems to me that you are dealing with such horror admirably. And if sometimes you must weep, then so be it. I am sure I could not bear it at all. I could never be as brave as you were. I know that for a fact. You see, I have left specific instructions that when the doctor says that I am dead, my head shall be severed entirely from my body.' She laughed at the idea. 'Preferably with the sharpest knife. In this way there will be no chance that I might awake inside my coffin, deep within the ground, hammering on the lid for no one to hear me. I have written that into my will.'

'I think I shall do that too,' said Emily with determination, feeling grown up. 'The light will shine on me no more, for my soul will be in the land of the shadows.' Again, Francis made no response. 'But how can you be sure that your instructions will be carried out?'

'My wife knows this. She will ensure that my wishes are fulfilled. Have you heard of Mary? I can't remember if I have mentioned her to you. A wonderful sculptor. Extremely talented. Puts me to shame entirely. Most attractive too. Would be wasted on a man,' she laughed loudly. 'Don't tell anyone I said that, will you? Now, Emily. Do you think Aberystwyth is ready for some leaflets?'

*

'She isn't married you know,' she said to Flora later, when they had returned to their room in The Mackworth. 'Well, she is really. She doesn't have a husband. She has a wife. Isn't that interesting?'

What Constance found more interesting was that Flora seemed to be reluctant to be alone with her daughter; she wanted Constance to be with her, offering support.

'That is not what I would call it. Quite disgusting, in fact. That anyone should think it was right to parade such ideas in public.' Flora was now regretting letting her meet with Frances alone.

'Oh, Momma! Please! This is 1881! Frances' wife is a very famous sculptor. Everyone talks about her. And at least no man shall never trouble Frances, and defile her as I was defiled.'

Flora could think of a number of reasons why that might never happen, but did not pursue that idea. 'It should not be allowed. It is inhuman.'

'It isn't actually, mother. Frances told me. Did you know, Connie? There was this island where – '

'Thank you, Emily. That is quite enough. The woman is eccentric and dresses like a man. She is grotesque. What do you think, Constance?'

Emily was not ready to let Constance respond. 'I don't think she cares. She said to me that she finds no attraction in men and that no man has ever been attracted by her.'

'Hardly a surprise, Emily'

'But do you know, Momma, what else she said. 'Of course I am over-weight,' she said to me. 'But who cares? Why should that trouble anyone else?' Oh, my goodness, can you believe it? She is so brave and so confident, I think. She doesn't need a man to make her happy. She said she can always entertain herself with her knife and fork!'

'Well, that is obvious, I should think, but there are many things that are best left unsaid in my view. I am quite sure you agree, Constance.' She did not reply. It wasn't necessary.

Emily suppressed a smile. She had enjoyed shocking her mother. 'Thank you for bringing me. She is a wonderful person and I am so thrilled that I have been able to meet her. She has such fascinating ideas! Poppa would be shocked, I am sure. It is such a shame he wasn't here with us to listen to her. He might have found it very illuminating!'

'I am absolutely sure that he would not. He is quite firm on things like this. He has no time for dangerous revolutionary ideas.'

'Oh Momma! Anyway, Frances says now that we have met, I can continue to write letters and perhaps be of some help to her in her work. She doesn't think much of Aberystwyth, thinks it is stuck in the eighteenth century. How right she is, and she thinks I might be able to advance the cause in a place that is in such need of enlightenment. She speaks so well. I shall form a committee immediately we get back. Perhaps you should come and visit, Connie? I could show you the town, what there is anyway, and you could tell me what you think. You could hand out some leaflets with me.'

'I would love to, of course.' Her voice was tinged with regret. 'But I have my pupils to think of,' she continued diplomatically. 'But as soon as I can arrange something…Tell, me, Emily. Did you recognise anyone in the audience tonight? Anyone you know?' And so the gossip recommenced.

Flora sighed. What would David make of all this? He wouldn't approve. Perhaps there would be more difficult days ahead. That was not an appealing idea, at all. At that moment she did not feel she could deal with any more. 'Well Emily. I think you should say goodnight to Constance. She must have a busy day tomorrow. Lots of eager pupils, I expect. And you have had a long day too, Emily. Time for your bed, I fancy. You must rest, too. All this excitement must have quite worn you out.'

This was said with a forced smile, and not one that was welcomed. In that moment Constance saw Emily's face tighten and her dark eyes flash, the streak in her hair almost as if illuminated, the damage she carried with her uncovered. She snapped, for those scars not yet healed.

'Momma. Please do not patronise me. I will go to bed when I am ready. I am not a child anymore. All that innocence you think I still possess was stolen from me. Don't forget, ever, that I know men in ways that you do not! I am not an innocent, unknowing child anymore, who must be sent to bed when it is convenient for you! Remember, Momma. You should be so very grateful that those things did not happen to you. But they happened to me and do not ever forget that.'

Flora watched her swing angrily from the room and then fell backwards into a chair. She threw her head back against the antimacassar and soon the tears fell away, down the side of her face until they eased their way into the lace trim beneath her head. Constance knelt on the floor by her side and held her hand.

'I am so sorry you had to witness that, 'Flora said eventually. 'It is not unusual. But however familiar it might be, it is still a dagger that stabs my heart. Oh, Constance. What can I do? I don't know how I can ever help her forget.'

'She will never forget Flora; I am sure of that. But she will learn over time. It is still very fresh for her, for all of us. It is part of her. You cannot take it away, not now. You have to believe that it will eventually make her stronger. And it will, I know it will. She needs time, that is all.'

'David wouldn't come with us, you know. He has no interest in the royal family, of course. Why should he? But he didn't want to see Rumsey, you see. He blames him for not catching that man soon enough.'

'And do you blame Rumsey?' asked Constance.

Flora sat up properly. 'No I don't, Constance. He did nothing wrong. Poor man. He did not find that man soon enough, that is all. But no one did. David spent days stalking the town.' She paused. 'I have said to my husband that perhaps we should think about why Emily felt the need to join that awful church. Was it something we did ourselves? But he will not talk about it. He will not talk about anything anymore. When I told him Emily wanted to come here to see Frances, he was indifferent. That is all I can say. He didn't care. And so, we are here alone, because he would not talk to me. And I worry, Constance. I worry so much. Perhaps when we go back, he will be just as indifferent to our return.' She closed her eyes and squeezed out more tears. 'And what will that

61

mean? What will that mean, Constance? I am so frightened.'

Constance stood and went to the dressing table to pour a glass of water from a cream jug. 'Poor David. The Church of Our Lady of Mumbles made you all victims, didn't it? You are so anxious to help everyone, I know you are. But who helps you?' Constance saw in her face the bleakness of a lonely life in a strange and uninviting town, far from everything she had ever previously known.

Flora looked at Constance with raw eyes, shaking her head at the offered glass. But before she could speak the door opened and Emily returned. She said nothing to either woman, but knelt on the floor at her mother's knee and buried her face in her lap and Flora held her head and they both wept.

Constance left quietly, knowing that she was an intruder, and knowing that they had not noticed.

Six

The Gloucester Hotel was a grim place, its dismal reality nothing like the promise the word, 'hotel,' might hold for the exhausted traveller. The landlord, Fred Craven, said so often that this was a well-run establishment that served no short measures and allowed no immorality, that the traveller might form the impression that Craven was merely trying to convince himself of these attributes in the face of overwhelming evidence to the contrary.

Each of those three pitted and crumbling steps up to the door was one of the three most important moments for any traveller, exhausted or otherwise, each providing an opportunity for them to change their mind and depart unscathed. Once inside, they would be enveloped in the sickly scent of stale beer, spilled and soaking into the occasional swirls of sawdust scattered across the floor boards. The varnished walls on which condensation formed and ran, gave the saloon bar, into which daylight could rarely penetrate, the atmosphere of a used coffin.

Fred Craven, who was standing behind the bar, had once been a well-built, powerful man but those days had gone. His waistcoat, thin and torn, was tightly buttoned but could do little to contain an expanding girth, well fuelled by left-over beer. The scarf tucked into the top of the waistcoat might have been white many years ago, but nothing could ever return it to such glory, those splashes of colour upon it, that our traveller might have mistaken for whimsical decorative features, were fragments of spilled food. His short uncombed hair, its curls flat with heavy grease and dirt, could do little to distract from that grey, pipe-stained, moustache.

It would be no surprise for the traveller to learn that few visitors ever stayed here. Why would you do that? Sleeping in the street was a more attractive prospect. Thus, Craven's takings were minimal, barely enough to get by, and tonight was no different. The air in the saloon bar was stale and heavy and there was only one man sitting in the corner, partly obscured by the haze and silently brooding, Craven thought. He seemed lost in his thoughts.

He had said very little, even when Craven tried to engage him in conversation, offering him every opportunity to rage about the number of broken street lamps, or about foreign sailors spreading disease, or even about women. The man did not respond and with his hat pulled down over his brows, Craven could not get a proper look at him. Probably better to leave him alone. He certainly looked familiar but many men came into the bar; they didn't have to make an appointment; they did not have to announce themselves. But there was something about him and Craven was unsettled. The man just sat and stared from the dark shadows cast by his hat. Solitary? Threatening? Don't be fanciful, he told himself.

But that letter had unsettled him. Well, a note more like. A scrappy piece of paper with a single word on it. That was what disturbed him. He had found it pushed under the front door this morning. Who had done that? What did they know? He needed to lock up, try to think about what he was going to do.

He gave Demelza a few coins from the cashbox and sent her home. There was no point in paying her good money when there was no one to serve. He leaned on the blackened surface of the bar in the unnerving silence this man generated for a few moments, and then went into the dingy kitchen to collect a rag to wipe out some glasses, his boots squeaking and sticking briefly with every step on the unwashed floor. When he came back the man had gone.

Craven went to the door and looked up and down Gloucester Place. There was no sign of him. He knew he had seen him before, there was no question of that. But when? Not recently, he was sure, but then he didn't have a good memory for faces, especially for those he could not properly see. He assessed the street for the final time, confirmed that there was no one there and decided to shut the hotel for the night. He bolted the door and then climbed the stairs with a flickering candle in a saucer, with his cashbox under his arm and that scrap of dirty paper screwed up in the pocket of his waistcoat.

He sat on his untidy bed covered in encrusted dark blankets

whilst he burnt the note he'd received in the saucer and then took off his boots. As he always did, he then checked under the pillow. Yes, the gun was still there. It had been his habit ever since he returned to Swansea to keep a revolver there, just in case. He'd been in Swansea for a few years now, but still needed the reassurance it gave him. After all, he'd done some things in his life, here and there.

Craven stood up and stepped across to the window to look down on the Seamen's Mission to see if that man was hanging around, whilst he removed his breeches. As he pulled them down to his ankles and stepped out of them, the man from the bar slid silently and unseen, from beneath the bed and blew out the candle. As an exasperated Craven began to turn to see why the light had disappeared, the man threw an arm around his neck tightly and then pulled him close. He whispered in Craven's ear, the hissing sound of death.,

'Remember me now, Fred? Remember? You knew I'd come for you.' He flung Craven on to the bed and then sat on him.

'No! Please! Stop! You've got it wrong! You don't understand! It was never my idea…'

The man pressed his hand firmly over Craven's mouth, stifling his scream. 'There's no more to say. Fred.' He was a strong man and Craven could not move. 'It is your time.'

He stabbed Craven repeatedly and methodically until the sheets were soaked and the blood gurgled in his throat and bubbled from his wounds. He stuck the knife deep into Craven's chest for the last time and left it there.

*

Demelza found the front door of the hotel locked when she arrived the next morning. She didn't always work in the day, but a delivery from the brewery was expected and Craven had asked her to come. She didn't like the idea of leaving her mother, at a time when she was declining and they had taken in a new lodger, but Mam did seem to have improved slightly overnight. She needed the money anyway. So she went round the back, through the open gate on Burrows Place, and let herself in through the kitchen door, using the key that Fred left beneath a bucket in the small cluttered yard. There was a crash and a clatter from the railway where there was some shunting going on and it made her jump as she went inside. She noticed that the kitchen window above the sink was open and in it there were a number of broken glasses that didn't look as if they had been washed.

Where was the stupid bugger?

She went upstairs to find him. She knew where he slept. Sometimes she would do him a favour, when times were hard and she needed the money. She paused at the door. Come to think of it, things were a bit tight this week. She tidied up her hair, opened the door and went in.

*

'It is murder, Rumsey. No question about that. He's not made that mess on his own. Probably some woman, I reckon.' Inspector Flynn showed Bucke the photographs which he examined carefully but with some distaste. 'You will see the knife still in the chest, and you will see that his breeches are on the floor. An entertainment that didn't go as planned, I am thinking.'

'Still not sure I am that keen on Herr Goldman's photography. But I suppose I can see the bedroom now, as it was then, if you see what I mean. Anything in the chamber pot, James?'

'It is the way forward, I think, Rumsey. It is going to happen more and more. Have a police photographer one day, I am sure. As far as the chamber pot is concerned it was empty. No one had used it. No sign either of the cashbox that Demelza Rippon says he carried around with him. Not a nice thing for a lass to find when she turns up for work.'

'Not at all. And who is Demelza Rippon?'

'Barmaid. Old Ma Riley's eldest. From Pinkney Street in St Thomas. She is in the clear. Sick mother. Spent all the night by her side. With the priest. They did say she didn't have long left, but the old girl has rallied. Demelza arrived at the Gloucester Hotel this morning. Front door locked. Whoever did it probably got in and out through the kitchen window, as far as I can see. Stood in the sink. I found broken glass.'

'Was she working last night?'

'Yes. Everything was normal. She does say there was a stranger in the bar for quite a while. Was there when Craven sent her home. Didn't recognise him.'

'Could have been a robbery?'

'As I said, the cashbox has gone. Not that there would have been much in it.'

'Thieves always expect there will be more, we both know that, James. Any details?'

'The usual, Rumsey. A man with a hat, pulled down. Demelza said she didn't think he had eyes, never saw them. Only ever asked for ale. So ordinary voice. Ordinary clothes. Might have had a beard. Might not. That's about it. Craven is no loss to us, Rumsey.'

'No, James. To be honest, he isn't. There is a sense of justice about this, I suppose. As you sow, so shall you reap. As they say.'

Fred Craven's role in supplying lodgings to women who disappeared and were murdered by a crazed semi-religious cult had never been properly untangled and Bucke always thought that the man should have been pursued by the law with greater diligence. But now he was dead. It was more comforting to think that it was a robbery gone wrong. He didn't want to consider the possibility of a crazed lunatic; there had been far too many of them recently.

'None of our ladies of the night liked him, did they? Revenge, do you think?'

'Someone was in the bedroom with him,' said Flynn. 'We don't know how they got there, do we? Invitation? A break-in?' You are right. None of the lassies ever had any time for him. But I don't know any of 'em who I'd reckon was a murderer.'

'No. I don't either,' said Bucke. 'How long has he been there?'

'At the Gloucester? A few years. Four or five. Perhaps more. Always more than you think.'

'Long enough to make enemies then?'

'Oh yes. Not something he found difficult either, making enemies.'

'Where did he come from?'

'Don't know. Came from out of town. What I can tell you is that he bought the place with cash. I remember. I was a constable then. Everyone was talking about it. A proper cash sale. Never made the place a success though, did he?'

'So we know nothing about him? Family? Married?'

'Nothing. Except that he was a miserable, devious, unpleasant bugger, no.'

Bucke scratched his beard. 'This cash business is interesting, I suppose. How'd he come by the cash to buy a hotel? That's the question. Inheritance is one thing. And even that can be difficult. But did he come by the money legally? Or illegally? Could be that someone has come looking for him.'

'And all they got was a cash box. Or an inheritance, though that is unlikely. I reckon. Probably no will. He was never going to be one to pay a solicitor, was he?' Flynn leaned back in his chair and picked up one of the photographs again.

'Interesting to see if anyone comes forward, though from what you are saying we know very little about Fred Craven or where he came from.'

'Or who he belongs too. You wouldn't boast about it, if he was yours, but the money might bring someone out of the woodwork. Usually does. Some mysterious nephew.' Flynn put the photograph back on his desk.

'But in the meantime, we have to find a murderer. And until we find out otherwise, James, I think you are right. We have to see it as a robbery.'

'We have no choice, Rumsey. I'll take this one on. You have your hands full with royalty, I reckon. I will take Midwinter with me. See if I can get some sense out of him. You never know. He might make a good inspector, but at the moment he is a bloody awful constable. Perhaps he could start with questioning the Hat Stand Gang. Don't know yet whether they know something, or nothing. But they were all over the place like flies on a corpse. I am sure that some of the perishers had already been in the hotel before I got there, poking about, interfering, helping themselves to goodness knows what. They are really starting to get on my nerves. They always seem to know more than they should.'

There was a knock on the door and Sergeant Ball poked his head around it. 'Can I have a word, Inspector Flynn? Been a busy morning and it is likely to get busier.'

'Give me a minute, Rumsey. Be back as soon as I can.'

Bucke nodded and started to flick through the photographs. They would, to some people's eyes, appear quite gruesome. He had seen much worse in India and those pictures were imprinted in his mind. He didn't think he needed photographs; their appearance in his nightmares was more than enough.

He hadn't liked Craven, but someone must have disliked him even more than he did, to do what had been done. There were multiple stab wounds. A frenzied attack? Looked like it. But there were no signs of struggle, even in a room that was so dismal and untidy.

Flynn came back in. 'Got another body, Rumsey. Just been brought in.'

'Another one in the dock, James? Goodness knows what we would find if we drained them all.'

No, Rumsey. A bit more public than that. But it is not all bad news. We have found Simeon Simons' cart.'

'And the body was in the cart?'

'Indeed it was, Rumsey. On the Strand.'

'And who is it?'

'Now that is a question. We have no idea. No one who has looked at him recognises the body. Nothing to identify him at all. They have put him in the stables, but no one knows who he is. Just been out to look myself.'

'Do we know anything at all?'

'Dr Reynolds has had a look at him,' said Flynn. 'To be honest, even Evan Davies could have done it. The victim had been beaten around the head – black eyes, lips bashed in, teeth missing. A proper beating by someone who knew what they were doing, I would say. And then they shot him.'

'Shot him?' This suddenly made it a very different incident.

'Yes. A single bullet in the chest. Not even Reynolds could have missed that. Scorch marks on the shirt front and so he was shot at close range. He is in the stables, as I said, Rumsey. You better take a look.'

'Who found him?' asked Bucke as they walked briskly across the small untidy yard.

'Constable Gill. Been there a while. Left there in the night. Looked as if he had gone to sleep and someone had stolen his horse. People didn't trouble him, didn't look too closely. Thought he'd dropped off, so left him sleeping. Gill was only worried because the horse had gone. Of course, no one heard a sound or saw anything – or if they did, they are not saying.'

'But he had been left there, that's the point isn't it. Deliberately.' He put his hand on the door to the stable. 'They could have thrown him in the dock. But they left him there. Someone is sending a message to us, I am sure of it.' Grey had arrived in town, so Bucke's head was ready to churn out conspiracies.

'There is a lot going on in the town at the moment,' said Flynn. 'You know that more than I do. I might be getting a bit out of my depth, but if it is a message, Rumsey, it might not be a message for us.' Together, they pulled open the worn door of the stables, which scraped on the cobbles. 'Need a new door,' he said.

'If we keep finding bodies, I reckon we'll need a proper mortuary,' said Evan Davies from the gloom. 'You know, a place for dead bodies. Been thinking about that.' He was beyond the body on the table, at the back of the stable, stroking the neck of a horse.

'I believe Sergeant Ball was looking for you,' said Bucke briskly.

'Stanley, eh?' he said conspiratorially. 'Poor old bugger. Getting old, see. Can't deny it. Too much for him. What's he want now, do you think?'

'I reckon you best go and found out, laddie. Now,' said Flynn ominously.

'He's always fussing, Inspector. I can deal with him. Probably needs help.' He was a professional, ready for promotion, relaxed amongst colleagues who valued him, and he nodded wisely in acknowledgement of this shared moment.

'Now,' said Bucke. 'Go to him now.'

Davies was about to reply when he suddenly sensed the concept of seniority that was hanging over him. 'Tarrah, Waterloo,' he said to the horse and then scurried out of the stable with his eyes averted. He stumbled into the door and Bucke and Flynn watched him. 'I'd rather deal with the Hat Stand Gang, you know. It is a wonder I haven't laid hands on him.'

'I have,' said Bucke. 'It made no difference, just made me feel guilty.'

They turned to look at the body on the trestle table. The man probably once possessed an anonymous face, though it was hard to see past his injuries. He was dressed as a working man, in an old jacket, an open, dirty waistcoat and a thin pallid muffler of undistinguished colour folded around his neck, the end of it suddenly red and damp where it had rested against his wound. The burn from the gunshot on his grey, collarless shirt was clear to see, in spite of the blood stains. Bucke looked at his brown sightless eyes. Was there still a hint of defiance in them? Or was he just dead? 'His pockets been searched?' he asked. 'Any distinguishing features that I can't see?'

'Nothing there,' said Flynn. 'Absolutely nothing on him. As if everything had been cleaned out before the body was left on the Strand. No marks on him. If he had been a sailor you'd like to think he had tattoos. But no. Nothing.'

'A stranger, do you think?

As I always say, someone knows him. But it isn't Simeon Simons, and so how come he was sitting in his cart?' Flynn looked down on him, chewing his lip. 'Definitely one for you, Rumsey.

71

Not normal at all, this. Seems to be carrying with it too many messages. It would have been easier to put him in the dock. But they didn't.'

'Thank you very much, James.' Bucke walked around the table, examining the clothes, checking pockets. 'Someone has removed a label from his jacket pocket. Why? And was that after he bought it? Or before? He looks normal, doesn't he? Or looked normal, we must assume. But perhaps that was the point.'

'Much rather be dealing with a proper villain, Rumsey. You know what you are up against.'

Seven

He had always liked his walking cane. It had always made him feel prosperous when he clicked along in his expensive coat and shiny shoes, through the well-paved streets of St Thomas. Emlyn Burrows was, after all, a respected member of the Watch Committee, overseeing the efficiency of the police force and keeping his gimlet eye on public expenditure. He was a man of the people; his self-appointed duty to ensure that the ratepayers got value for money. He knew that his job was to doubt, to ask the awkward questions, to challenge everything, particularly so in these days of excessive expenditure prompted by the Royal Visit. He knew, inevitably, that everything could always be done much more cheaply, and he enjoyed every petty fulfilment of his obligation to protect the ratepayer from indulgence and excess. He was, he knew, a lion of probity in the untidy landscape of public finances, feared by the profligate. If it had made him unpopular? Well, such was the consequence of duty, observed and performed. But why should that bother him? He was a confident man, comforted by the knowledge that he appealed to discerning ladies of maturity and sophistication, for such was the inevitable consequence of undoubted civic influence.

Others, oddly, did not see him in the same way. They would have noted that he was short, with a pugnacious face and a large neck that seemed forever to be fighting to escape from his starched shirt collar. Elwyn was stocky, but with a frame that suggested latent strength, at least in his own mind. He was sure that his role as a member of the Watch Committee was such that it meant the attributes of a policeman had somehow transferred themselves to him, so he knew that he could be athletic when called upon, a man who could soothe a rabid lion at a moment's notice and then disarm a rabid killer to general acclaim. He always dressed formally in black, for sobriety emphasised his quiet strength, he believed. His only habitual concession to frivolity an elaborately embroidered waistcoat, which he was sure received much whispered admiration.

But as he walked those streets, unusually on a Sunday, so close to the arrival of the royals and with a foolscap envelope clamped beneath his arm, Emlyn Burrows was not a happy councillor, doubly so because it was all his fault. But he recognised now that there was something inside him, some need, previously unacknowledged, that had led him to the top of Inkerman Street on that warm Wednesday night in September, just a few frantic weeks ago.

He had been on his way home after yet another fractious council meeting when he saw those men standing around a small folding table. He had seen them before, when he had looked wistfully in their direction for too long. He knew what they were doing and he knew it was illegal. But he could not stop himself. When he thought about it, and he thought about it constantly, there must have been a devil hiding deep within him, ready to emerge. Emlyn also knew that if he hadn't stopped that night, eventually he would have done so on another night. It was inevitable. And so very soon and so very quickly, he had been trapped.

He remembered clearly standing at the back of the group of untidy working men, watching the game. It seemed so easy. The girl with the cards was a comely girl indeed; bright eyes, a happy smile and Emlyn was sure she had winked at him. She had deft elegant hands that moved sinuously, like co-ordinating eels. The way she shuffled the cards and laid them face down on the table was so graceful. Emlyn watched the men at the front gambling, guessing which one of the three was the Queen of Hearts, finding the lady, while a taller man stood behind the girl, on the look-out for constables.

Emlyn could not understand it at all. It seemed to him to be impossible to lose. He knew where the queen was every time. But the men at the front, playing and laying down small piles of coins always got it wrong. How was that possible? This was easy money, surely.

Then he realised he had brought some money with him. He

74

didn't usually leave the house with money in the evening, for fear of footpads, but this must have been an unconscious but deliberate act. He hadn't planned anything like this, not so far as he was aware. But he had money, just a few shillings, and he could earn some more; it was so ridiculously easy. The girl was smiling at him and it was a warm evening and if he raised himself ever so slightly on to his toes, he could see down her blouse. She had a lovely soft Irish voice too, a proper colleen. They called her Aoife, which had a lovely sound and, as he watched the cards slip and slide around the table, there was an unexpected voice in his ear. A man was standing next to him, whispering, commentating on the game. He was Irish, too.

'Sure, this is easy. Easiest thing I ever saw. These clowns in front don't know what they are doing, that's a fact. Look! It was the one on the right! Obvious that was, wasn't it? I can't believe it. I'd play myself but I haven't got no money at all. You wouldn't lend me a few coins by any chance? I shouldn't have asked. But I can't believe it. This is easy, honest to God. I'll pay you back, with interest, I promise.'

Emlyn said nothing, watching the cards. He wasn't sure how to say yes, even though he wanted to.

'I got a better idea,' said the man. 'I tell you what. I'll watch the cards for you. You put the money down and when you win, because you are bound to, you split the winnings with me. That's fair, I think. Just to get me started. Then I am on my own and I will pay you back from the money I will surely win.' He dropped his voice further. 'We can take these buggers apart, so help me.'

Emlyn looked at him with contempt. No money? Whose fault was that? But it occurred to him them that with two of them watching the cards, working as a team, they were certain to win. It would cost him hardly anything in the long run when they triumphed, as they surely must.

Aoife banged on the table forcefully. 'Now you boys,' she said in her seductive voice, 'you ugly bastards have had your turn. Stand aside now and make way for the distinguished gentleman at the back. Come through, sir. It is good to see you. You're going to show this lot how it's done, am I right?'

'I am not an expert, my dear. But I believe I have a carefully thought-out system of my own.' He smiled knowingly. 'Gentlemen, if I may?'

She shuffled the cards and then suddenly they were on the table. Emlyn realised how different it was when you were at the front. It was all so quick and he lost track of them. He looked at his new friend, who winked at him. 'On the left, without a doubt. Your left, not hers, mind.'

He put his bet down and Aoife turned over the card with a dramatic flourish. The Queen of Hearts. He had won! There were cheers and backslapping. 'Congratulations, sir,' said Aoife. ''Tis a pleasure to do business with a proper gent. And I won't have you telling this gentleman lies, Irvine Sellars! None of your tricks. He is more than capable of sorting this out for himself. Isn't that right?'

Burrows, smiled in acknowledgement. This attractive woman had recognised his qualities. She could see he was a man of his word when he split his winnings with his friend, Irvine. Then the game started again and it was mesmeric; everything was so quick that he didn't have a moment to think and he lost track of the cards again. But Irvine bet on the one in the middle and so he followed and they won again and his new friend paid him back. This was easy and the people in charge of the game were very stupid and there was no reason to stop now. He knew he was too clever for these people; they couldn't trick him.

But the next game he lost. He wasn't sure how. He'd stared at the cards and was sure he was right. He lost the next game too and he couldn't understand that either. But he would get his money back. You just had to increase your wager. But he still kept on losing. And there was this new rule. There were two occasions when he had followed the queen like an eagle. He knew he couldn't be wrong. But his friend, who had been much more successful than him, bet on the same card and Aoife said that she would only pay out to the person who had wagered the largest amount. And his friend's stake always seemed to be a little higher than his own.

Oddly, although he had won, it seemed that he had lost. So next time he let the other man bet first and then put down a higher stake himself, but somehow it was the wrong card. So he lost that one too. Emlyn was angry. How could this be happening?

Aoife dealt the cards once more and Emlyn could see quite clearly where the queen was. Perhaps Aoife was getting tired but she hadn't done much to disguise where it was. So, he put all the money he had left on the card in the middle. They waited for the other man to put down his stake…and then the tall man on look-out suddenly spat out a single word. 'Guards!'

Emlyn stood still, suddenly returned to reality. He realised that he was penniless at the very moment when he was going to start a winning streak. There were swift movements around him and everything suddenly disappeared. The cards and the bets were swept off the table, which was quickly collapsed and thrust under his friend Irvine's arm, which he thought was odd, and everyone started to walk away in different directions.

Aoife came to him, took his hand and rested it between her breasts. 'Oh sure, you have been so unlucky tonight.' She leaned across and kissed him on the cheek. 'Come back tomorrow night and see me. Promise?' Then she too drifted away.

Certainly, someone in his position didn't need to meet a constable in such circumstances but as he walked down Inkerman Street, there was no sign of one anywhere.

This set the pattern for Emlyn for the next few weeks. The card players seemed to be waiting for him, checking that he had brought more money than the previous night, for this was the night when everything would change. So, he would play and Aoife, such a pretty name, would pull his hand to her chest again and tell him that she really wanted him to win, which did make it hard to concentrate. And sometimes he did win. But most of the time he didn't and after just a few nights they were lending him money to play and so very, very quickly he owed them a great deal of money indeed. He hadn't noticed how quickly it had grown. But really, he told himself, it wasn't a problem. All he needed was one big win and that would change everything. Except it didn't happen.

When he went home, he wasn't sure who looked back at him from the mirror. He no longer recognised that reflection. He wasn't sure whether Mrs Burrows did either. She had gone very quiet.

But Emlyn kept on going and he kept on losing until the night when his losses were suddenly stretching further and further into the hundreds of pounds, more than he could ever comprehend. That was the moment when Michael, the Lookout, decided that it was time to take Emlyn on one side and offer him a simple solution to all his difficulties.

This had been an exemplary operation and he was really proud of his team. The key to success was to make your victim – your mark – think you were the stupid ones. Surround the mark with shills to encourage him, find yourself a dextrous dealer like Aoife and you couldn't lose. And they hadn't. And now Emlyn Burrows was theirs.

'You have been a really good customer of mine. A proper Welsh gentleman, without a doubt. Myself and Aoife have been thinking a lot about your troubles. She is a lovely girl and she holds you in high regard. She told me so.' He smoothed back his neatly parted hair and offered Burrows a wink from the dark depths of his hooded eyes.

Emlyn looked up at the stars, considering his own stupidity, wondering too, where he could find just a little more cash. He'd be fine, then; soon get his money back. Had a new system now. The lady was always the middle card every fourth game. He knew that for certain now.

'Listen to me, Emlyn. We've got a plan, see. Sort out all this for you in a twinkling. You see, I am not important in this game. I am just a Watcher. This Find the Lady game belongs to the Big Boys. And they get angry with us and with Aoife. And you like Aoife, I know that. It is in the way you look at her. But anyway, they get angry if we don't hand over the cash. You wouldn't want her to get into no trouble, now would you? If it was up to us, of course we would let you off. Course we would. But the Big Boys are likely to come looking for you. And you never know who the buggers

78

might do their blabbing to, an' that's a fact.' He shook his head sorrowfully.

Emlyn closed his haunted eyes, as if he could dispel the reality into which he had stumbled. But he couldn't.

Michael smiled and touched Emlyn's shoulder. 'But I think I can stop it,' he said brightly. 'I will be able to let you win, once we have sorted this little difficulty. You will get all your money back and The Big Boys need never know. It is no skin off my nose, to be sure. And Aoife would be so pleased.'

Emlyn looked at him like a drowning dog pulled from a lake. This man could save his life; he would do whatever he asked.

'Now as I understand things, Emlyn, and I am only a simple Watcher, I know, but you are a proper watcher, as they say, cus you are on the Watch Committee, are you not? A very distinguished position.' Emlyn nodded. 'And you are making yourself busy appointing a whole bunch of temporary constables for these royal shenanigans. Am I right?' Emlyn nodded again. 'And you are part of that? Choosing these people?' Another nod. 'Couldn't be better, Emlyn. That's perfect.'

Perhaps the right-hand card would be better. They would expect him to wager on the middle one. Keep the element of surprise. Wrong-foot them.

'Now, Emlyn. I have a piece of paper here.' He took it from his pocket. 'These are the details of six of my cousins. Lovely boys. As honest as the day is long. All of them. My grandmother is very proud. And they are all wanting to be constables. They live in different parts of the country if you look at the addresses. Chester, Sheffield, London, Maidstone. Working on this royal visit would be a good place to start for them. Experience. Help them get a proper job, when the time is right. I wouldn't normally ask but it would make my grandmother very happy. You got nothing to worry about. These boys are the best. Ask anyone.'

Emlyn said nothing. He still thought right was better than left, but it might be better if he slept on it.

'I want you to fill in the forms for them. All six of them. Then stamp them as approved. There isn't much point interviewing them, not when they live at different ends of the country as you can see from the addresses. But then you come back to me with all the permissions and all the passes that they need. Badges. Everything. Do you understand, Emlyn? Bring them and all your problems will be over. Emlyn? Are you listening?'

It was only when he sat down in the Town Hall to complete the forms the next morning that he wondered how Michael knew who he was or, indeed, what he did. It could not possibly have been a guess but it was of little importance now, given the difficulties he had created for himself. So that was why Emlyn was returning to Inkerman Street on a blustery evening in early October with that foolscap envelop beneath his arm. Tonight though, he was determined to drive a hard bargain. He'd been distracted last time. He would demand that they provide him with sufficient stake money to start him off, now he'd filled in the forms. He wouldn't need that much, not now he had a plan to double it every five games. It was definitely left he should be choosing, he was sure of it. He had flirted with right but that was a passing infatuation. He knew it had to be left. His left, obviously. Not hers. Because that would be his right and that would be wrong, wouldn't it?

Michael was waiting for him beneath the street lamp, for once shining brightly. Emlyn was disappointed to see him alone. No table. No Aoife. He was hoping to resume his game, now that he had a plan for guaranteed success.

''Tis true. You are a gent, sir,' said Michael, after he had examined the documents and the passes very carefully. Emlyn was slightly offended. Did this man really think that Emlyn Burrows made careless mistakes? 'All appears to be in perfect order.' Those deep-set eyes appeared to be gleaming.

'I was hoping you would have your table with you. I have, after all, kept my side of the bargain.'

Michael looked at him and smiled. 'Let us not forget that you still owe me over eight hundred pounds, Emlyn. Don't forget the interest. Mounts up. But let's leave that for another day, shall we?

80

Let's go and celebrate, shall we? Down at the Cuba Hotel.'
Another figure emerged from the shadows and gripped his elbow
fiercely. It was his old Find the Lady friend, Irvine, the one to
whom he had lent some money. He looked different tonight. Less
approachable, more irritable.

'I don't think that is such a good idea. It is not the sort of place
in which someone like me should be seen. I have a reputation and
it is very different from the reputation of the Cuba Hotel.' He
blustered but he began to realise that he had no choice.

Michael took his other arm, though he didn't squeeze it as hard
as Irvine did, which was a relief. 'We are going to the Cuba Hotel,
Emlyn. It is all arranged. Aoife is there. She is waiting for you.'

Eight

John Jones-Jenkins, the Lord Mayor of Swansea, was not just an industrialist and speculator; he was also someone with an eye to social advancement. He was the owner of the Swansea Tinplate works and his life amongst the noise and the heat and the smells of his factory, and the inevitably unsophisticated nature of industrial relations there had, as a consequence, done little to prepare him for the subtleties and protocols of civic duty. He was bewildered at times by the world for which he had previously craved acceptance, for he was perpetually anxious when separated from the smells of industry, and his ability to manage a meeting properly had never been regarded as one of his more polished mayoral attributes. But the impending visit of Edward, the Prince of Wales, seemed to have been deliberately designed to test these imperfectly understood skills. Preparations had involved long meetings and continued to demand them; an awful lot of meetings.

He had long since accepted that that he was not a bureaucratically gifted man, acknowledging that he lacked the mental agility of the men he admired most. But he also recognised that his personal reputation, and, moreover, his place in history, would be forever defined by the events of this single day in October. Therefore, he was determined that all should go well.

'I am sure you understand that I am most anxious to present the town at its very best. I am absolutely sure you agree with that ambition. There is so much to do but we shall do it and I know everything will be an enormous success. Just think. A week today their Royal Highnesses will be arriving. I cannot wait.' He looked at the preparatory notes he had made for this meeting with Buckingham Palace's security officers and realised that what was written there, either did not make sense, or was entirely irrelevant. He decided to improvise. 'I would just like to remind you, Chief Constable, that all the vagrants, tramps and pedlars, indeed anyone undesirable, must be removed from the streets before the arrival of the Royal Party.' He turned down his mouth and nodded firmly for emphasis.

'Of course, Lord Mayor,' replied the Chief Constable, pretending to place a neat reminder in his notebook. They had discussed this three times already during the last week.

'Good god,' muttered Colonel Grey. 'There will be no one left. Like a ghost town.'

Bucke had already formed the impression that Colonel Grey was not taking the meeting too seriously and looked down at his own notes, as if considering an important point of his own that he soon intended to proffer.

Jenkins smiled at the elite group sitting around the small, highly polished table in the mayoral study. This was how great events were managed; by like-minded men of influence, sitting together in mutual respect, in quiet rooms and being decisive. He looked at his notes again but they still did not make any sense. He cleared his throat.

'As you may be aware, Colonel Pollard, we have had a committee working all hours on this. Vital work, of course. But as I always say, it is attention to the little things that make the big things happen. Nothing is beneath the attention of powerful men such as ourselves, I am sure you will agree. So, I have instructed that the streets will be cleaned. All front doors, anywhere, and certainly any adjacent to the royal route, will be freshly painted. Indeed, we designated September as Painting Month, just to show how seriously we are taking this occasion. If you would like to assess the route, of course we can – '

Colonel Pollard smiled. 'Fret not, your honour. Grey and myself have already done so. I hope you are not offended, but we can't afford to leave things to chance, you see.' Pollard was a patient man; as a senior official within the palace, he was experienced in dealing with civic dignitaries whilst smiling benignly. His leisure time often involved shooting rats in a barn. Any barn; anywhere.

'Admirable work, Lord Mayor. No one could have done better,' said Grey. Bucke noticed that the pause that came after 'no one,' gave his words a slightly different emphasis. He wondered if anyone else noticed. The mayor didn't.

'Thank you, Colonel. The whole of Walters Road will be decorated for their procession. We have ordered new flags. There will be trophies, venetian masts, everything. The Prince will be singularly impressed, I am confident of that. The Lady Mayoress has always been eager that there should be a theme to our arrangements. Her small but dedicated committee has been working on it for months. They have decided on the colours of the Prince of Wales, red and white. I am sure the Prince and the gracious Princess will be impressed.'

'How tasteful,' muttered Grey. 'The Prince of Wales's own colours? Astonishing. It must have been an agonising decision'

'There were some sleepless nights,' agreed the mayor, and everyone laughed dutifully. 'But it will look so attractive. We have a number of triumphal arches, of which one, particularly I think, will be worthy of your special attentions. Naturally, we shall illuminate them all in the evening. We want to do our very best to honour our Prince.'

'Indeed,' said Pollard, nodding his approval.

Grey smiled too and appeared to be making extensive notes, but as Bucke, sitting opposite him could see, he was merely drawing complicated geometrical designs. 'Nothing, will impressive him more.' That pause again.

'Thank you, Colonel Grey. We do our best here in Swansea. After all, we are already regarded by most right-thinking people as the true capital of Wales. I am confident that will be noted by gentlemen of good sense and influence. In fact, I am sure that the Prince will not find it difficult to express a preference, once he has seen what we can do. Here in Swansea, we are always eager to perform our duty.' He tapped some papers together to form a neat pile. 'You must remember, we are very familiar with our responsibilities towards honoured guests, gentlemen. Please don't forget that a little over a year ago we welcomed the great Monsieur De Lesseps to our town. A fine man, a great occasion. It could not have gone better.'

The mayor saw Grey raise his eyebrows and exchange a glance with Bucke.

'Well, there may have been a slight disturbance, I grant you, but nothing that we couldn't handle. We are very experienced in such things, Colonel. Ready for anything.' He tapped his papers together again and they slipped from his fingers to the floor.

Bucke wondered whether experience in dealing with assassination attempts was something that should be acknowledged at that particular moment. The mayor sat upright once again after picking up most of his documents.

'Everyone is so enthusiastic,' went on Jones-Jenkins, urgently searching through the rest of the untidy sprawl of escaping papers that had spread out in front of him, apparently of their own volition. 'We have a colliers band performing somewhere, I am sure.' He could not find what he was looking for, but something else distracted him. 'Ah yes. Yes, indeed. We have a sub-committee drawing up a list of persons for the presentation to the Royal Party at the Reception Pavilion. I have that list here, I believe.'

Colonel Grey stopped his doodling for a moment and smiled again at Bucke. 'I hope you haven't forgotten the Chief Constable, Lord Mayor.'

Jenkins was increasingly flustered, turning over papers rapidly. 'Oh yes, here you are,' he smiled with relief. 'Never fear. There he is. Captain and Mrs Colquhoun. Just before Mr Williams, the Public Analyst'

'And what are you doing about the weather, Lord Mayor? Important issue, of course.' Grey was clearly bored and Pollard gave him a significant look.

He began shuffling through his papers again. 'I am sorry – 'then he realised that it wasn't serious a question. 'Well, of course, we are hoping. Praying, even.'

'That's the spirit.'

'I do apologise for my colleague,' said Pollard. 'He has, on occasion, a tendency to be frivolous.' Grey smirked at him and

Colonel Pollard felt it was time to take a little more control. 'Shall we review the arrangements, as we have them at the moment. So that we can see how the day will unfold, as they say.'

'Please,' muttered Grey. 'Not an early start, for heaven's sake. Just remember, Bertie doesn't do mornings.'

'The Prince and Princess are staying at Singleton Abbey with Mr Hussey - Vivian on the night of Monday 17 October. They will have arrived at a temporary station erected by the London and North Western Railway Company in Singleton.' The Mayor smiled. 'No call upon civic funds there, gentlemen. Then, after the most comfortable of nights, on Tuesday at noon they will leave the abbey grounds where there will be a massed choir of Sunday school children to greet the Prince in song.' He shuffled some of his papers again. 'Not sure what they are singing but they will all have practised it separately in their schools, so I can't see a problem.'

'Ah yes. Wales, the Land of Song.' There was a sharp noise and Bucke was sure that Pollard had kicked Grey beneath the table.

'The party will then proceed to the Reception Pavilion at the top of Walters Road.' The mayor could not now contain himself. He was very excited. 'Wonderful structure, Colonel. Sixty feet long, fifty-one feet wide. Two hundred and fifty chairs. Of course, everyone will be standing when the royal party arrive, but they will be able sit down afterwards.' The look that Pollard gave Grey was sufficient and he remained silent. 'It will be marvellous. Raised dais, steps. No expense spared, you can be sure of that. Armorial arms, plumes of feathers for the Prince. Flags everywhere.' The mayor turned over a piece of paper in triumph; it was evidently something he has been looking for. 'And I don't want you to worry about security, Colonel Grey. Obviously important to you, in your position. But really, no need. The Watch Committee have authorised the appointment of six hundred extra policemen. Temporary policemen, of course. Just for the day.'

Colonel Grey put his pencil down loudly. 'Six hundred, you say?'

'Impressive, I know. We will be using the Agricultural Hall as a barracks for them. Bedding, catering, everything that you can think of.'

Grey's manner had changed. 'And you will have the opportunity, before next week, to check all these temporary policemen of yours?'

'Of course.' The mayor continued confidently, assured by what he interpreted as the encouraging tone of the royal officials. 'Never a difficulty in finding six hundred stout and true officers here in Swansea. Never fear, Colonel. Expecting hundreds of thousands of visitors from all over Wales. These temporary officers will keep the crowds under control, that's all, though we won't put any of them on horseback. The horses might run away with them.' He laughed. No one else did. 'We will also have the Militia lining the route, of course.' Bucke sighed and looked down at the papers in front of him.

'Mr Jenkins, if I may. It is these constables who trouble me, and they trouble me quite considerably, if I can speak frankly.' Grey was clearly alarmed. 'Do you really need six hundred of them? What do you know about these people? Who are they? What do you think, Chief Constable?'

'I believe most of the appointments have already been made, Colonel,' said Colquhoun, diplomatically. He had a plan to deploy them, but he did not want the mayor to know what it was.

'Oh yes,' said Jenkins. 'All appointments have been in the hands of Elwyn Burrows, member of the Watch Committee. Very good man, very efficient. No cause for alarm there. I believe we can serve as an example to other civic authorities who might find themselves blessed with a royal visit.' He nodded confidently.

'Shall we return to the ceremonial route, gentlemen? said Pollard, conscious of the time and of his own temper.

This was something that was clearly close to the Lord Mayor's heart. 'We have arranged what I am sure will be an impressive opportunity for our Masonic Lodge to greet the Grand Master of England in appropriate circumstances. We will have an impressive marquee. Tickets only, of course.'

'His attendance will shed fresh lustre upon an ancient and honourable institution, Lord Mayor,' said Grey, doodling once more, though this time a little more aggressively,

'I believe so. Here Princess Alexandra will name our new street – Alexandra Road, naturally. And there will be a rousing rendition of the *Men of Harlech.*'

'A highlight for so many, Lord Mayor.' Bucke, watching him carefully, was sure that if a chicken were to have wandered into the meeting, Grey would have picked it up and wrung its neck viciously in his frustration.

'As I hope very much. So, from there we proceed down High Street and Wind Street, past some of our most venerable financial institutions, to the new dock. We are very hopeful that the weather conditions will permit a brief cruise around the bay on the Lord Lieutenant's steam paddle yacht, *The Lynx.* A fine vessel.'

'All at sea, Lord Mayor. All at sea.'

'We do hope so. His royal Highness will then inspect the machinery in the dock, that sort of thing. Lift the sluice, let the water in for a moment. We shall have a stand for 2000 singers under the direction of Doctor Joseph Parry, who will perform his march '*Hail! Prince of Wales!*' followed by his second new piece, '*With Loyal Hearts.*' If I may be so bold, may I refer you to the words of Dr Parry, words which I hope will touch the Prince, because they express so well the depth of our affection and loyalty.' He read the verse slowly and loudly, obviously impressed by the rhymes to which he gave particular emphasis.

We loyal Britons ever pray,
That both our Prince and Princess may
Enjoy a long unclouded day,
Of happiness and peace
And then ascend, Oh, blessed flight,
Adorned with crowns forever bright,
To regions of eternal light,
Where life will never cease.

'There is always a song in the Prince's heart,' murmured Pollard. Even he was staring at the wall opposite, as if mesmerised.

'I am so looking forward,' added Grey. 'How I share such a fervent wish for his immortality.'

'I did wipe away a tear when I first heard it,' admitted Jones-Jenkins.

'As I did, also,' said Grey.

'And then, of course, there is a luncheon arranged. We have engaged one hundred and twenty-five London waiters, fifty cooks and servants. We shall not be embarrassed at the table, you can be assured of that. Mr Bath, the Vice Chairman of the Library Committee has assumed responsibility for this element. Very efficient.'

Grey put his hands briefly to his head. 'Is there anyone in the kingdom who you have not actually employed? Have you considered, Mr Jones-Jenkins, releasing burglars from Swansea Gaol? Footpads? Highwaymen? Anyone facing execution for a failed assassination attempt on a minor member of the royal family?'

'No one, as far as I am aware, but I can make enquiries on your behalf, Colonel Grey, if you wish,' said the mayor diligently, writing himself a note on small piece of paper which then fluttered to the floor, caught in a breeze caused by more nervous rummaging.

'Please Colonel Grey, I would be obliged if you could control your excitement.' Pollard glared at him.

The mayor went on regardless, not really understanding Grey's comments. 'We have ensured value for money, of course, with all the catering staff. They must decamp from the dock and then conduct the arrangements for the buffet at the Mayor's Ball in the Music Hall. We drive a hard bargain, here in Swansea.' He looked around the table, nodding in approval of his own acumen. No one responded so he carried on. 'There is the military march past at the Guildhall of the Volunteer troops, and then in the evening we have the Grand Ball. Over five hundred dancers invited and I am sure they will dance joyfully, with unflagging spirit into the early hours. A full day indeed.' He picked up the paper from the floor. 'Ah yes, one last thing. There will also be a grand display of fireworks in the evening. And we have ordered twenty thousand commemorative medals, at 6d each.'

'Such impressive municipal largesse does you credit, Mr Jones - Jenkins.'

'No, Colonel Grey. We will be selling them,' said the mayor proudly.

'How impressive. Swansea has lessons for us in so many different ways. I shall buy at least two, said Grey.

'Oh please, no. Allow the town to present you with one as a gift in recognition of all this hard work. '

'Your sense of generosity goes before you, Lord Mayor,' said Colonel Grey. 'All this work, indeed. Unmatched in its quality.'

'Thank you.' The mayor smiled proudly in response to what he regarded as praise. 'All of Wales is in a state of excitement, Colonel, and I know that we are best placed to deliver a wonderful day that will live long in the memory of all those involved. I am led to believe that the Cowbridge Rifles will form a guard of honour on the platform of Bridgend Station as the train goes through. Such exciting times…'

Afterwards, when the mayor had taken Colonel Pollard to meet with the rest of the corporation, and Captain Colquhoun had left to update the Lord Lieutenant, Bucke and Grey met in the mayor's office.

'To be frank, Inspector Bucke, the whole thing is an absolute nightmare. You may as well place an advertisement in *The Times* inviting all anarchists to attend Swansea next week, preferably with explosives. Why not? We have already got the Fenians here. How in God's name can this be managed? Ask me which part is the most disturbing and I will be unable to tell you. It is all disturbing. Temporary constables? Waiters from across Europe leaning over the shoulders of the great and the good? And, in the middle of it all, we have a boat trip. Has anyone actually checked out this boat?

So, what do you think? Will Bertie be shot, poisoned or drowned? Difficult to make an informed judgement at the moment, I'd say. All of them? Why not? I knew I should have come down here sooner, Inspector. We have work to do to control the arrangements, let alone offer the Royal Party even the semblance of protection.'

'You are a better judge of these things than I am, Colonel,' said Bucke trying to calm him. 'But it seems to me that ensuring adequate protection for the royal party across the whole of an untidy town like Swansea is impossible. Too much is left to chance, I would say.'

'In normal circumstances it does have its challenges. But in these circumstances, when we know there is a significant risk of hostile action by a group of fanatics, then it becomes a vision from a lunatic's nightmare. Esteemed civic gentlemen like your Mayor have no understanding at all of what is involved and what might unfold. They are too obsessed with painting doors and masonic greetings. And I do understand, Bucke, that you don't have the space to lock everyone up who might be a threat. And they would be merely those we know about. But this visit cannot be cancelled, no matter how much one would wish it were possible,' He shook his head and sighed.

'We can work together. I am sure our knowledge of the town and its characters will be useful to you,' said Bucke blandly, trying to sooth him.

'Oh yes, there are still things that we can do, Bucke, and we will have to work together undoubtedly. We can clear the streets as soon as the procession has processed, as it were. Get them home or into the public houses. But get them off the street at the very earliest opportunity. If they attack the Masonic Lodge we would have to accept that as a bonus – we have to accept anything as a bonus, as long as it doesn't harm the Prince of Wales.'

'Yours must be such a difficult job, Colonel. So many different things to consider. My employment seems so much simpler to me.'

'Possibly, Inspector. One gets used to it. But since the nature of your job has come up,' he said rather too brightly, 'I understand you have found a body.'

'Yes,' said Bucke warily. 'On the Strand.'

'Terrible really. Most distressing. But you are not to worry about it. It is a job for me.'

'But, Colonel. I am – '

'Yes, I know you are. But I can assure you that this is well within my own range of responsibilities. So I would be immensely grateful if you would back away from this. Don't want you getting involved. Would be a complication I don't need at the moment, and nor do you. Don't worry about the victim and we know who did it. And it will be dealt with. But it is mine. I can be quite insistent about this, but I am sure I do not need to say anymore.'

*

Bucke had almost completed his reluctant walk home to Fisher Street, still seething about what Grey had said. His professional status had been comprehensively undermined. There had been a murder in his own town but he was not permitted to investigate. He was expected to turn a blind eye, to pretend that it had never happened. And also, that additional meeting with Grey which had left him so angry, had prevented him from going to visit Constance. What an unpleasant afternoon. Then, as he crossed Temple Street, a figure appeared from the shadows and walked briefly by his side.

'He's in the Mermaid but I never said nothing.'

It was Lizzie Thomas and she slipped quickly away. It was good to have eyes and ears on the street and he would find her tomorrow, give her a coin. At least someone understood what his job was about. He cut across the square and went down Castle Lane.

The Mermaid was quiet, with a couple of sailors already staring sightlessly across their beer, sitting upon stools that seemed ready to collapse. If they did, it was unlikely that the seamen would notice. Their smoke had gathered against the ceiling above them like a blanket, their minds also clouded and smothered. A woman, who might have been Eunice Grimshaw, left immediately, clearly not keen to be seen by the Inspector. Bucke had little reason to pay attention to her, for he saw Arthur Riverton sitting in the corner, leaning back against the peeling varnish of the panelling. If he was surprised, he did not show it and gestured to Bucke, an invitation to join him. He was older and more worn, his skin rutted as if ploughed, but still recognisable and still someone to be watched very carefully.

'Evening, Inspector, still got your informants then?' He was a small man, but powerful, determined. It is a pity he is on the wrong side, thought Bucke. He could be really useful as a constable.

'Evening, Arthur. Must feel good to be out.'

Riverton nodded and indicated a battered chair. 'Care to join me? I am sure this isn't a social call. I won't be buying you a drink. Not good for my reputation. I am sure you understand.' He looked into his beer. 'Mind you, I would have to say, this filth is not likely to inspire your liver.'

Bucke looked suspiciously at the chair.

'It is one of the best ones in here, Inspector. Nothing but the best for you,' he said with a smile. He scratched his long sideburns that had spread downwards, had met on his chin and then pushed upwards in defiance of gravity. The hair framed his face, holding it in place as if it was still imprisoned, Bucke thought. His was a pugnacious face, with a nose that carried reminders of the numerous blows he had received, blows which had always persuaded him that he was right, in whatever circumstances he found himself. Riverton remained neat and self-contained, thought Bucke, just as he remembered him. But there was an undeniable, brooding intensity about him, an indication that his life could only ever be validated if it was in turmoil and conflict.

Bucke sat down and tested its strength of the chair. It didn't seem ready to fall apart; it might even last another week. It was clearly the best chair in the tavern. He waited for Riverton to speak.

'Been busy since I been inside, Inspector, or so I am told. And

I was sorry to hear about your missus. That sort of thing isn't easy. I know all too well.'

Bucke remembered that Riverton's wife had died of typhoid. He nodded his thanks. He knew that was sincere. Everything else he said might prove to be a tangled web, but that was sincere. 'How was Dartmoor, Arthur?'

'As always. It doesn't change.'

'I hope you have decided to change, Arthur. I hope you have decided that you are not going back there. Some say it is your second home.'

Riverton took a sip of his beer, not taking his eyes off Bucke. 'That's up to you, isn't it? You are the one that catches me.'

'There is no need for catching, Arthur, if you don't do anything wrong. It's your choice whether you decide to break the law or not. Not a decision that I can make, now is it?'

'Depends who is deciding what is right and wrong, doesn't it? You are not seriously telling me that you agree with all the laws you have to enforce, are you? A ridiculous idea. Makes you a hypocrite, to my mind.'

'It is not my place to question those things, Arthur. I have a job, you know that.' He paused, briefly, to indicate a change in the conversation. 'I understand you found yourself in difficulties when you were inside. Read a report.'

'They tried to bend me to their will. I was never going to let them break me, you know that, Bucke.' He looked at him defiantly. 'And they didn't. They beat me, but I was never broken. And one day soon, I shall go back for them.'

'Perhaps that isn't always a good idea, Arthur. There are some battles that do not need to be fought. You know as well as I do. Some things are best left in the past.'

Riverton shook his head. 'You can never ignore the past, Inspector. It never goes away. There is always a price to be paid.' He paused, then smirked. 'Speaking of Price, I understand one of your constables managed to catch a train the other week.' He nodded at his own cleverness.

94

Bucke was neither shocked nor surprised. This vindictive streak could never be concealed for long. He looked back at him. 'You never know what is inside someone's head. Things that people keep to themselves can eat them up. Can happen to anyone. You know that, I am sure.'

'Don't I know it.' Riverton leaned across the table and gripped Bucke's forearm. His eyes were suddenly very bright. 'There are some things you can't forget, no matter how hard you try.'

'There is not one of us can change the past, Arthur. You can't make things unhappen. We all have to accept what has happened and try to deal with it as best we can.'

Riverton shook his head again and sat back, unexpectedly reflective. 'My problem, isn't it? I haven't changed. Always too worried about what was right and wrong. Doesn't seem to count for much with some people. But for me, there is nothing more important. You understand that, Inspector. Not everyone does. Something is right or something is wrong. There isn't a different choice. But there are plenty of those who think there is, who do wrong things and then they get away with it because constables let them. Burns me up, that does, Bucke. We've all got the past inside us, all of us and yes, as you say, there is always a price to be paid for the hurt you have done, for the harm you have caused. No one should be allowed to escape, whether they are rich or poor.'

'Tell me something, Arthur. Why are you here? Why have you come back to Swansea?'

'Shall we say for old times' sake? Would you believe that? There are things that need to be done. Loose ends, you might say. You know that, there always are.'

'I hope those things won't involve me. I have never understood the Swansea connection, Arthur. You are not from Swansea as I understand it. Why come all the way back from Dartmoor?'

Riverton paused, as if deciding how much he was prepared to say. 'Was born here. Not many people know this. I was here with my mother until I was about two years old. My earliest memory? My mother holding me tight, watching my grandmother being hanged.'

Bucke said nothing, waiting for Riverton to say more.

'I remember a man frying bacon, selling sandwiches from a cart. Whenever I smell bacon now it takes me back to a crossroads somewhere in Gower, watching my grandmother being dragged across a field. Didn't know what was going on, did I? I just knew it was terrifying, feeling my mother shaking like that. And some things never leave you, do they?'

'And this would have been in the 1840s, would it?'

'More like 1836 or something I think, and out in Gower, near Oxwich I reckon. You know, where they make their own laws. She had done nothing wrong. Not my grandmother. Accused of burning down hayricks. Three of them. It wasn't her. A year later they wouldn't have done it, not for arson, they changed the law, but the Mansell's wouldn't have cared one way or another, even then. Just a bit of entertainment to them, wasn't it? Not much else to do out there in Gower is there? Other than stealing sheep and incest.

'My grandmother was arrested with a girl called Annie Pugh. She was the one who did it. She was the one with the motive. Being evicted from her cottage, I think, or a Mansell had been interfering with her. Don't know, but she went after the landlord's hayricks. And then she turns Kings Evidence, tells the magistrate that it was my gran, Catherine Harris, who had arranged it all. That was the lie. She had just met her on the road that night, had a chat about what a waste it was for someone to burn down a hayrick. My gran was totally innocent. But they hanged her the next day, all the same. Older than Pugh, so they said she had led the young girl astray.' He shook his head and took another drink. 'Do you know? The Pugh girl was transported. How is any of that right? Tell me, Bucke. You know the law. It is supposed to be for everyone, not just the rich bastards. You will have heard that old lie, just as I have.'

'It is in the past, Arthur. It happened and you can't change it, however wrong it seems.'

'Yes, well we shouldn't forget either. There is no running away. I will find the Pugh family, don't you worry. Eventually I will find them. That is why I am here. They owe me. And I don't forget Catherine Harris, my grandmother, because she was wronged, and neither do I forget them.' He took another drink. 'And if you do know them, drop them a word. Tell them I am on my way.'

'That isn't how it works, Arthur. If the Pugh family are still around, what happened then has got nothing to do with them now. This Annie Pugh might have died in Australia. Might have married out there. You can't unpick this. No one, specifically you, should be doing something that I might have to get involved in.'

'Choose not to get involved then; it isn't difficult.'

'I think that is up to you, Arthur. This is no longer the time for revenge. Those days are gone. Long gone. It is a modern world now,' he said hopefully. 'There are basic things you can do that could keep you out of trouble. Found somewhere to live? Found yourself a job? They are always looking for men in the copperworks.'

'You will never find me in the copper, copper and that's a fact. Taking orders from someone's stupid uncle who had been in the works for thirty years, man and boy? Don't be dull. I have heard it all before, Bucke. Little men, getting on my nerves. Wouldn't make for a contented labourer, now would it?'

'You need to be doing something, Arthur. To keep yourself out of trouble. Rebuild your life. Stop punishing yourself. Be normal. Most of us manage it. It isn't that bad.'

'If you are worried about me, then perhaps you need to stop trouble coming to me. You won't have any cause to arrest me, then.'

'Just behave yourself, Arthur. It is all I ask. These are busy days. We have a great deal to do and if I thought it would give me peace of mind, I would bang you up until all this royal business was over.'

'You can't do that. You have no right.'

Bucke laughed hollowly. 'Oh yes I have, Arthur. In fact, I have been invited to do that very thing. And I might accept that invitation. You just need to behave; keep your nose clean. It isn't much to ask, after all.'

'And by so doing, show proper respect for the royals? My god, have you any idea what you are saying, Bucke? You are being ridiculous. You want me to turn myself into a petty criminal who lives on the very edge of society, but underneath it all is a loving monarchist who will rush to shake a cheery cap as they pass along the street? He broke into a cockney accent. "Gawd luv 'er! Int she bootiful, guvnor!" Is that what you expect? What do you think I am? You need medication, Bucke. We shall have to find you some in the newspaper. Plenty of advertisements.'

'Stay out of my sight, that is my advice to you,' said Bucke firmly. 'You are here for a reason, Arthur, and it is unlikely to be an honourable one.' Riverton began to speak, but Bucke held up his hand firmly to stop him. 'You went down the wrong path in your life. I don't know when and I don't know why, but I can't do anything about it now. But if you as much as walk on the wrong side of the pavement, I will lock you up. Understand?'

Riverton smiled, unbowed. 'As we used to say when we were children, Inspector Bucke. Catch me if you can. But you see, we are really on the same side, don't you think? Punishing those who have done wrong? You should be pleased.'

'Leave the punishment to me, Arthur. That is not a request, by the way,'

Riverton stared at him and then smiled thinly. He went back to his beer.

As Bucke walked back to his cold room, he wondered if he had given him a strong enough warning. He doubted it very much, for Riverton was not a man who would listen. He had known that there had to be a reason why he was in Swansea and Bucke was expected to believe that the reason was revenge. But was he telling the truth, or was he playing games? Was it really about the Pugh family? That seemed so far-fetched. Who it was and why they deserved it, were not questions that he needed at this time. He would have to be detained and locked up. He was distraction they didn't need.

But the following day when Bucke sent three constables to bring Riverton in, he could not be found anywhere.

Nine

'My God! This is a dismal place. Please don't tell me you haven't noticed. Look at it. Look at the buildings. See how black they are? You'd think someone had tried to set them on fire. There is a pile of rubble at the top of this dreadful street. I thought it was a consignment of coal awaiting a tradesman. But no. It is the castle. And this hotel? I mean, they say that this is the very best they have. I very nearly got back on the train.' Therese D'Auch placed the back of her hand against her forehead in an exaggerated fashion. 'You do realise, don't you, Charles? They have absolutely no champagne. I asked and the waiter, the one with boils on his face, you know the one, said he couldn't open a bottle, but they had some on draught. Oh, God! Where have you brought me, Charles? I shall have one of my attacks. I can feel it coming on.'

'Therese, don't be so dramatic. You are working. I am working. We don't have choices about what we have to do. Don't forget, I have been here for a few days already, and I can assure you it doesn't get any better. You must, like the rest of us, learn to accept it.' He picked up a pair of bloomers from a chair with exaggerated disgust and threw them on the floor, before sitting down. 'I find slovenly habits so tiresome.'

Grey smiled at her, for he knew her better than anyone else. He valued her essential compassion and her mind, and she always had the capacity to make him laugh. They had been on many difficult assignments together and they each owed the other their life, not something that was easily forgotten. It was her company that he always sought above all others, and though he would never tell her so, he was honoured to know her.

Therese was, after all, a woman of considerable beauty and it was a daily entertainment for him to see how others responded to that. It was the first thing they saw, but then how could they not? A face finely sculptured, as if an artist had been trying to represent an impossible perfection. It always amused Grey because the impression they then formed of Therese, based upon her flawless appearance, was wrong and it was usually men, though not always, who soon found that Therese was untouchable. Like so many beautiful things she was damaged, and deeply so, but the damage was unseen, for it lay within her heart.

She had intense blue eyes, which were remarkably expressive and always alert. Her nose was straight and thin, in perfect proportion with the rest of a remarkable face. Her blonde hair was ridiculously short and shockingly unconventional, cropped closely around her ears. It was casually untidy, and appeared as a stylish choice, but one that others would never be able to emulate. Every gesture she made was elegant and precise and she displayed effortless poise and confidence.

But those eyes were trained to see threats and were often cold and ruthless and her hair had been slashed to facilitate the many different wigs she wore for the disguises behind which she hid. She had created many enemies who wished her dead, for Therese was a killer, trained, decisive and ruthless.

'Anything else you feel I should know?'

'Have you seen the sanitary arrangements? I cannot tell you. What are those Scottish hovels called? A bothy? They could not be any worse. And the food? Did you know, Charles, that earlier tonight they offered me seaweed? Tell me, Charles. Do I look like a seal?'

'Difficult question, Therese. Allow me to consider my answer for a moment.'

She shook her head and smiled at him. 'Yes, Charles. I am working. But you know as well as I do, that it never stops being personal. Not for me. That I should have sunk so far.' She shook her head and then laughed. 'Oh, Charles. The things we do.' She poured herself a glass of murky sherry from the chipped carafe on the dressing table and sniffed it suspiciously.

He made a conciliatory gesture with his outspread hands. 'No, Therese. It can never stop being personal. I know you well enough, and I would be disappointed if you ceased to care.' He offered her a sympathetic smile. 'It has been six years now, Therese. But I could never expect you to forget. You would not be the person who I think you are, if you could forget, if you could turn off your memories.'

Therese turned away and closed her eyes, as if there was much more to see within them than without. 'Six very long years, Charles. Painful years. I can't forget. I won't forget.' She paused. 'And is Duggan here in Swansea? Do you think?' She went across the room and poured her sherry out of the window.

'He would appear to be, though no one has reported actually seeing him. But all the intelligence would say that he is here, Therese.'

'I suspected as much.' She gazed out of the grimy window, seeing nothing at all.

'Therese, I understand how you feel but – '

'Yes I know, Charles. I know all too well. I have a duty as a member of the Royal Protection Brigade. Those responsibilities come first. Princess Alexandra must be protected at all times. You don't have to tell me that, I know.' She turned to face him. 'I won't go looking for him. How would I know where to look in this desolate hellhole?' She turned around and leaned against the window. 'I often wondered what I would feel like if I was ever to come across him. And suddenly I am in the same town. He could be anywhere around me. It is curious. I feel quite numb, I suppose. After all this time. Does he have children, do you think? He stole that possibility from me.' She rubbed the back of her neck vigorously with both hands. 'I think he would prefer it if he had children, since I do not. More scorn. I have always imagined him as a father. He would do it just to spite me. Does he have children, Charles? Do you know?'

'Don't ask yourself that question. Don't make him real. We know little about him, nothing about his background that amounts to anything. Keep it like that, Therese. Don't turn him into a human being. You are one of his few enemies who has ever seen him face to face. Do you think you can recognise him? He might have changed over the years.'

'I cannot describe him, Charles. But I will know him when I see him. I see him every day in my mind. When I go to sleep, when I wake, he is there. He walked out of a doorway on an empty street in Dublin. He stood in front of us, shot my husband once in the chest, looked at me, smiled, tipped his hat and walked casually away. You know all this, Charles. It was over in an instant, but every detail had been scratched clearly on the insides of my eyelids.' She closed her eyes. 'There he is. I can see him. The man who destroyed my life. I look for him every day. And one day, that day will come and I will find him. Whenever, wherever, I shall be ready. If I have a destiny, Charles, then Michael Duggan is my destiny. And I am ready. Here in this town, in this inner circle of hell, I am ready.'

Grey stood and took her hand, because he knew she would let him. She let very few people come close, let alone touch her. She smiled at him. 'I am sorry, Charles. It has been an unhappy day. I have too many of them.' She sighed. 'And I will not rest until I have found him, you know that. But tell me about your day. You have had meetings. You adore meetings, I know you do. If it was with the mayor then your joy will have been unconfined. What did you learn of this dark and filthy town?'

'That the police force is like a fruit cake, Therese. A couple of cherries but too many nuts. The Chief Constable is sensible, the two inspectors you can rely on in different ways. One of them, Rumsey Bucke, is wasted down here. We ought to have him in London. One of the constables seems to have a brain, so I suppose he won't be a constable for long. The rest of them? You wouldn't trust them to take a fish for a walk. And the Mayor? For God's sake keep that man away from me. Bertie skewered in Swansea? At least the commemorative medallion will be a collector's piece. So, I think it could be worse, Therese, though please do not press me for details.'

'Perhaps you should entertain the idea that we might actually have to live here. But it is much easier for you, is it not? You can be out and about. I am part of the royal party, walking behind the princess. You just don't understand how difficult it is to find a clasp which is both fashionable and large enough in which to conceal a revolver.'

Grey sighed, shaking his head in what he hoped looked like sympathy. 'Such a burden.'

She picked up a wig from a stand and put it on, then thought better of it and threw it on the bed. 'And another thing, Charles. I ought to have a maid.'

'We have talked about this before. If there was a maid, you might be distracted. She might get in the way.'

'But that is entirely the point, Charles. Surely you can see that? And however tiresome it may be, if I may remind you, we have indeed had this conversation before. Remember, a maid would be an additional person behind me, someone a malcontent would have to get past to get to me. It would buy me time. Precious seconds to turn round or to get the Princess to the floor.'

'I will consider it. See if I can find anyone. It won't be easy in Swansea, I can assure you.'

Therese was persistent, 'All they have to do is to stay two dainty steps behind me. We know that the Fenians are in town. A maid is an obstacle. Dress her in Welsh costume- the locals would be so excited they would have seizure, and that awful Welsh flannel is so thick it would be like a suit of armour. You know as well I do, that the most important person is not me or this maid, is it? It is Princess Alexandra. I am her protection. So find me a maid, Charles. But remember, she will be my maid, so please, no cross-eyed seaweed seller. Not that I am choosy in any way.'

Grey looked at her, recognising the strength - and the cynicism - of her argument. 'Leave it in my hands, Therese. I shall see what I can do.' He held up his hands to stop her reply. 'I will do it, I promise. But this is proving to be a challenging operation. There are more holes in the town's arrangements than you will find in a sieve. How many waiters are coming from London? Don't ask. Do we know who any of them are? Don't ask that question either. We should have come down sooner. What the Fenian's plans are we don't know but they are certainly planning something and obviously it is something to do with the Prince. And we can both imagine what it is. Poor old Eli Feeney has been returned to us. His body was left sitting on a cart in the middle of town. The Fenians are not here for the festivities, you can be sure of that.'

'Eli! Oh no! I thought he was well concealed amongst them.'

'So did I. But we have to revaluate what we think we know. Perhaps they have known about him all along and they have been using him to feed us false information. That is why they have left us his body. To sow confusion. Badly beaten he was, poor man. Then they shot him. Even if Duggan has one of his men placed in the police station that was never going to help them in these circumstances, since the police didn't know a damned thing about Eli. But I have sent Joshua Burton back to London. He was Eli's contact and there is no way of knowing if they are now looking for him, so I didn't want to take a chance. The police have Eli. I suppose I ought to have another word with Bucke. Who knows who did it? Does it matter? Well, we know, and yes it does matter. We can add it to the list, it is long enough.'

'A good man. We can't afford to lose men like Eli. I shall miss him. He always made me laugh and not many men can do that these days. His wife will be looked after, I hope.'

'Of course. I shall make sure of that. The last message he passed on to Joshua suggested there was some link between the Power Cobbe woman and their plans. He wasn't sure what it was but he would find out. If that is what has triggered his murder then we need to be concerned about the mad woman as well, on top of everything else.'

'You shouldn't worry about Frances Power Cobbe, Charles. I know you think she has some unusual ideas but she is a peaceful person and I know of no suggestion that she might be harbouring nationalist sympathies. She is from Irish stock, of course, but not all Irish people support the Fenians. I don't see her as a problem and anyway she has moved on, hasn't she? A lecture in Bristol or somewhere equally drab. No, she isn't a problem. I would wonder though, whether she provided some kind of distraction. A screen? If I was a Fenian I would have thought of her visit as an opportunity. Now Eli is dead, we don't know. But remember Charles, they killed him. They knew he was one of ours but they killed him. They could have kept him alive and fed us with all sorts of lies. But they didn't, did they? He knew something and that made him dangerous. Poor Eli was, as a result, more useful to them dead, than alive passing on falsehoods.'

'Yes, I know. He was getting too close, I should think.' Grey pushed at his teeth with his thumb, thoughtfully.

'But we have to do something, Charles. We can't let them think they are untouchable.'

Grey smiled. 'When the time is right. We owe it to Eli. I am going down to the lounge. See if I can find a cup of tea. There is a waiter there, too. Don't like the look of him. Bit uncomfortable with the idea of any waiter at the moment.'

'And if I was Duggan, I would have placed someone here in the hotel. And so would you,' said Therese.

Grey nodded. 'That I would. But I would like to think our agent would be better than the one they have downstairs.'

*

Constance couldn't remember seeing Rumsey quite as cross as he was when he called to see her. She decided to let him talk, though she was not sure how she could have stopped him, even if she had tried. She sat on the piano stool as he paced around the small room in rapid circles.

'This is absolutely ridiculous. I can't understand it. A man is found dead in the middle of the town. In my town, in the one which I am supposed to police, and I am told I must ignore it. Mustn't investigate it. The word has been given and I am to pretend it didn't happen. People saw it, of course. They saw the body in the cart on the Strand but I am supposed to say they saw nothing? Is that it? Someone went to see the newspapers too. Told them not to report it. A man has died but we must pretend that he didn't. Ridiculous.'

'Why, Rumsey? What possible reason – '

'It is all to do with Colonel Grey. All to do with 'security,'

106

whatever that is supposed to mean. Obviously the man was an agent of some sort. But it isn't to be my concern. Isaac isn't too happy about it either, but we are told it is all in hand; it will be dealt with. But it is a murder. In our town and I am expected to ignore it. And if it happens a second time? Or a third? It is madness!' He paused, as if to take breath.

'You were in the army, Rumsey. I didn't know you, of course I didn't, but I imagine you were an extremely good officer.' She smiled. 'You must have been, they promoted you.'

He watched her and Constance could see that he recognised what was coming next.

'You followed orders. You had to. And perhaps you have to do so now.' He didn't respond. 'You have a good relationship with the Colonel. I am sure he will confide in you when it is prudent, in his eyes. And, so it seems to me, at the moment you don't know anything.'

His eyes flashed and Constance was briefly worried that she had upset him, but the squall passed and his face became less set, more relaxed. He sighed. 'You are right, Constance. Of course you are. When the Prince is here, for that one day, we are at the centre of the Empire. There are others who I have never met or even heard of who are in control of all this. I am sorry, Constance. Professional pride, I suppose.' She stood up and gathered him to her. 'I have dealt with too many murders recently. I am concerned that one will lead to another. It is what has happened before and I am supposed to stop them. But I am very sorry for venting my anger on you.'

She kissed him. 'And if not on me, who else would you choose?'

'Only one other, Constance. Myself. I am planning to go out to Felindre to see Iestyn Pugh. I need to decide whether I should lock him up before the royals come. I would have complained about Grey to myself all the way, out loud. I might still do that,' he smiled.

'Here,' she said. 'I have this. It might cheer you up.'

It was a letter, not very well folded. He opened it and then read it carefully

'Deer Constant mummy and me are living in New York it is a nice place and we like it we have two rooms and they are very nice mummy works in a shop we have nice Food I go to school everyday I have lots of frends my Best frend is Helga please write to me I like letters from Amy Rigby

'Rumsey, I have cried all morning. This is so touching!'

He looked at the letter carefully and then smiled. 'I need to sit down.' He read it again. 'Oh my. Look at the words she uses, Constance. 'Mummy' and she calls herself 'Rigby.' Two lives saved.'

'And I can't write back! She hasn't given me an address.'

'Perhaps she will next time.' Bucke smiled. It was a tonic they needed.

'Look how neat the writing is. All she ever needed was a chance – and love. And look what happens. I hope she does write again. It is what we need ourselves, too. We just need the chance.'

'That will come, Constance. If Amy's life can be changed, then so can ours. But like her and her mother, we might have to leave Swansea to achieve that.'

Constance sighed. 'I wish I had her address.'

But it was a less angry walk than it otherwise might have been and Constable Midwinter was lucky that Bucke's mood had improved to the extent that he was ready to overlook a constable without helmet or boots, sitting under the only tree in Brynhyfryd and rubbing his feet. Idle bugger, thought Bucke.

But it felt good to get out of the town into the cleaner air and, as he walked along through the narrow country lanes, he felt miles away from anywhere, out in another world, back in a different time. It seemed to him a place that had never changed, away from the chaos of town life. People were just as poor, out here. He knew that; it was a different type of poverty, that was all. But he knew that it had just as many dark secrets as anywhere else.

It was a small but neat cottage on the hillside above the village of Felindre, beyond the farm where Eleanor Williams had worked and where she had died. It had belonged to Catrin Pugh's family for longer than anyone knew and now her husband, Iestyn, lived there with her, seeing out his days by the fireside, reliant upon a monthly payment from his aunt's legacy, Catrin's cooking, and regular visits to the Plough and Harrow in Llangyfelach, which had left permanent reminders in his reddened cheeks and nose.

'Why should I stop?' asked Iestyn. 'He killed a young woman, an innocent young woman. And then he threw her down that well. It was a long way down. Still is. And she was at the bottom of it. It burns me up, Inspector, every time I think about it.' There was a pile of small square pieces of paper torn from the Cambrian newspaper next to him. He took one, coughed into it, screwed it up and threw it on the fire. It hissed briefly and his wife shook her head in distaste.

Catrin was a comfortable-looking woman, happy, it seemed, in her domestic tasks - sweeping, boiling, baking. Today she was at the ancient table with her granddaughter, making Welsh cakes. Bucke enjoyed the air, full of the warm scent of grated orange peel, and the little girl would sometimes lift her large eyes from her stirring, to look at him suspiciously. Catrin stuck her finger in the mix and popped it into the child's mouth to draw her attention back to her task and away from the two men sitting either side of the fire. There was a planc balanced on the grate, ready to receive the small soft cakes, and Bucke hoped he would be offered one, though neither husband nor wife appeared very keen to see him.

'You cannot be surprised that I have called, Iestyn. I have a duty. I can't allow you to either withhold information about a crime, or indeed make false accusations about – '

'They are not false. I tell you now, as I have told so many constables. Horace Jacques murdered her. Brutally. And the girl was innocent of any wrong doing. He shouldn't be allowed to get away with it.'

'Perhaps the best way for us to deal with this is to start with what you believe is evidence, don't you think? So that I can decide

109

what we should do about all this.' Bucke knew he was opening the flood gates. Asking an old man to talk about the past could suck the life out of the room.

Iestyn leaned back in his chair. 'You see, I remember the evening well. Catrin and I, well, we were bundling, nice and cosy like. Not a care for anyone else.'

'Bundling?' As an outsider there were still Welsh words that caught Bucke unawares.

'Old Welsh custom, inspector. Out in the country,' said Catrin, turning away and wiping dough from the child's cheek.

Iestyn smirked at him and winked. 'Courting in bed, that is what it is, fully dressed, of course.'

'I am sure I have never heard of that. It sounds, well, like something the local vicar wouldn't approve of. Not the vicars I have met.'

'You see, Inspector. It rains a lot in Wales. And it is a bit more congenial than a barn, if there are things you want to discuss, like, privately. Not unusual. Everyone did it. And if you go even further west, well. You wouldn't want to be marrying someone who was barren, now would you? Stands to reason. Had to make sure, didn't you? Put everyone's mind at rest, see. Not wasting your time.'

'That is enough, Iestyn,' said Catrin sharply. 'Remember our Edith.'

'And where was this, Iestyn?' Bucke dropped his voice slightly. 'This bundling business.'

'Here. In the back bedroom. Black night. Heavy rain. Me and Catrin weren't going to be standing outside, were we? We have been married a long time now, so it doesn't matter anymore. Catrin let me in through the window. I looked back out as I closed it. And I could see a figure going down the hill towards the farm. I knew it was Horace. From the way he walked. It was him, no question.'

'Even out here, Iestyn? With no light? And on a stormy night, like you said. There would be no moon. Must have been dark as

110

pitch.'

'Oh aye. But you get used to it, out here in the country. I could tell it were him. Knew for certain. He was on his way to see her. I didn't have no doubt. And, then the next day, when Old Ma Simkins went out to the well, she couldn't get her bucket in the water on account of Eleanor's body. I knew then.' He looked angrily at Bucke. 'Of course, there were no constable then. But we all knew and we told old Llewellyn, because it was his land, but he wouldn't do nothing. But we couldn't let it lie. Why should we? We knew it was Jacques. His father was French. No one liked him anyway.'

'And you told everyone? On the basis of what you saw on the darkest of nights? And so that is when you painted the road and the gate of the chapel? And as a result another man has lived his life in the shadow of that accusation?'

'Feelings were running high, Inspector. You had to deal with things yourself out here in those days. Not so different today either, sometimes.' He looked at Bucke defiantly. 'No one would talk to him. Or to her. His wife didn't last long, either. Died of shame, she did. No one went to her funeral.'

Bucke looked up and saw that Catrin was staring at her husband. There was the light of something in her eyes, but Bucke could not be sure what it was.

'And then of course, Horace cleared off somewhere, didn't he? Guilty as hell, he was. And he knew that everyone knew. Made his fortune, so he says, but he still lives like a tramp. And so when he comes back, well, we had to let him know we hadn't forgotten, didn't we? We old un's have never forgotten, not for a minute, not even when he was off on his travels. We'd had her gravestone done as soon as she was buried, like, and we take flowers on the anniversary. We put another stone in front of hers, a smaller one, to remember that poor unborn child who died with her. Have you seen her grave, Inspector? It was right and proper that we did it, to remember the poor lass. We collected money and had a stone carved. Folk come from all over to see it, you know. Very popular. We did use some of the words from the Murder Stone in

111

Cadoxton, of course we did. It saved a bit of time. Have you seen that one, Inspector?'

'Yes, I have. A servant girl murdered. In the twenties. A very large stone. Says 'To Record Murder' or something like that in large letters at the top.'

'That's the one! You see! Ours was the same. This was a murder and we knew it. It says at the top of Eleanor's stone - '1832 To Record Murder' - and that is what it is. We had to make sure that Jacques couldn't wipe away history. The people of Felindre were not minded to forget what had happened. So we have been waiting for justice but it has been a long time coming. We stood together in that regard. Jacques shouldn't get away with it, everyone hereabouts thinks that. We don't forget in Felindre. Not our way. She might have been a servant girl from down Carmarthen, but it made no difference to us. She was one of our own and he murdered her.'

'And so, to be absolutely clear, this man who you say is a murderer, is Horace Jacques, also known as Patagonia Jacques?'

'Call him what you like, it makes no difference to me. I know him as a murderer. And he is not getting away with it. Not whilst ever I am alive.' Iestyn started to declaim loudly, as if he was outside Swansea market. 'There cannot be forgiveness for him, ever. He may think he can escape the detection of man for the brief season of his miserable life, yet God hath set his mark upon him. God has singled him out and he will be pursued until that moment of terrible and righteous judgement that awaits him.'

'Hush, Iestyn', said Catrin. 'Edith is here.' She stared at him, unblinking, willing him to be quiet.

'And so,' said Bucke. 'All this happened almost half a century ago. And the only evidence you have is that you might have seen him. It is an awfully long time to remember details with any accuracy.'

'I did see him, Inspector. I know it was him. Stands to reason, doesn't it? He needed to get rid of her. Her being expecting and his making promises to Betty Wheel. He would have got away with

112

it too, if I hadn't seen him.'

'You see, Iestyn, it seems to me that this is all rather flimsy. A tissue of assumptions and complete guesswork.'

'I know what I saw, Inspector Bucke.'

'And I know that there isn't enough to proceed with any of it. You do not have any evidence.'

'I do! I saw him! And if you won't act, then I shall speak to people who will! I accuse Horace Jacques!'

'Hush your noise, Iestyn! For goodness sake!' said Catrin loudly. 'Think of your granddaughter! She doesn't need to listen to this! Stop it now!'

'I will not stop! I cannot!' He stared back at his wife but her gaze was unflinching and the room fell silent. After a long moment, Iestyn looked away and then spoke more quietly. 'That man murdered Eleanor Williams and I shall continue to demand justice.'

'I have to tell you, Iestyn, that you need to think very carefully about what you have said. In normal circumstances you would be charged with making a public nuisance of yourself but – '

'Aye, well enough. And then I would get my time in court and it would all come out and there would be nothing you could do to stop me.'

'As I was saying. Iestyn. In normal circumstances. But these are not normal circumstances. We have the Royal visit shortly and if I thought – '

'I shall stand in front of the Royal carriage and the whole of Swansea will – '

'You will not. Because if I thought you were going to do that, then you will be in Cox's Farm until the visit is over.'

Pugh began to bluster pompously about injustice, but Bucke stopped him. 'I have the power to do so. I have been given the power. Anyone, no matter who they are, if there is the potential for any sort of disturbance, then I can take what we call precautionary measures. I can bang you up, Iestyn, until the prince and his entourage have left.'

'Outrageous!'

'Possibly so. But I can do it. I don't have to ask permission. My decision. And so you have to convince me that you are going to behave yourself.' Bucke turned to Catrin. 'I am sorry you have to hear this, Mrs Pugh. But pleased, nonetheless that someone else, who may have more influence than I have, can speak to him and urge upon him the need for common sense. I am not taking Iestyn in today. If I decide to, then I will come back with the police cart so everyone knows what is happening. But I would strongly suggest that you have a serious word with your husband before he finds himself in more trouble than he would like.'

'And all this in front of our Edith, for shame, Iestyn Pugh.'

Bucke walked down the hill towards the mill then stopped. He had to go and see it. So he went into the grounds of the Nebo chapel to find the gravestone, and saw a swirling desire for revenge that had taken physical form, angular and hard, etched and unrelenting. It was grey, close to a grey wall, below a grey sky. But a fire burned in the words that had been carved on to it. This stone wasn't something you could ever forget – and in its silence it seemed more powerful than the words of Pugh's repeated declamation could ever be.

These things didn't happen on their own, Bucke knew that. Iestyn must have collected the donations and organised the stone to keep his rage alive. Those angry words were a copy, as he knew, of those on the similar gravestone in Cadoxton, though the details of Eleanor's death had been recorded – *'with marks of violence upon her person she was found dead in a well by Llwyngwenno Farmhouse.'*

Something about it didn't sit right with Bucke – not the crime of course; that was real enough. It was the response it had provoked which was standing silently in front of him, as it had been standing there for almost fifty years. As he stood looking at the gravestone and the initial shock faded, he started to feel that there was something not quite right, almost as if the emotion in the stone wasn't entirely genuine. Perhaps it was because he knew that it had been copied, but he wasn't completely convinced.

'*God hath set his mark upon him*'...'*terrible and righteous judgement*' and because he had heard the speech that contained these words so many times, it didn't impress him quite as much as it should have done.

He pressed down the grass at the base of the stone with his boot where there were more words, this time from the Bible. '*Vengeance is mine. I will repay says the Lord.*' There was no writing on the small stone in front, but he knew it remembered the unborn child. He looked around him at the peaceful green hills, white sheep dotted across a distant field. Lives were still lived here as they had been lived for so many generations, still ruled by the seasons, by the weather, by the darkness of unlit nights. Yet here, even here, there was death and suffering and a need for vengeance.

And that gravestone? He turned at the gate of the chapel as he left and looked back at it. What a thing to find in a quiet country graveyard. And he wondered. Yes, it told the truth.; It wasn't lying about Eleanor Williams. But had it been designed to deceive? To point the reader in the wrong direction? Did it actually represent a lie?

How would anyone ever know? After all this time?

Ten

When Bucke arrived in the police station the following morning, freshened after his walk into what he had previously believed was the untroubled countryside beyond Llangyfelach, Sergeant Ball was waiting for him with information.

'That pal of yours, Emlyn Burrows.' Ball shook his head. 'Who would have thought it, eh?'

'What's he done now?' asked Bucke wearily. 'A complaint about the extreme expense of truncheons or something. Have whistles gone up in price? Are policemen's children too well-fed?'

'Drowned himself in the North Dock. Leastways, that is where they found him.'

Bucke was immediately alert, regretting his cynicism. 'When was this, Stanley?' This was so unexpected. What possible reason could a man like Burrows have for being down there? He was a pompous committee man, squeezed tightly into a misshapen suit, not a docker. Quite a few dockers themselves were unwilling to go to the North Dock when they weren't working. And yet Burrows had died there.

'They pulled him out of the water at first light. The nightwatchman saw his hat, floating. Mrs Burrows, bless her, reported him missing yesterday morning. Hadn't come home, she said. They are saying that large amounts of money have gone missing from his bank account in recent weeks. So it looks as if he had financial difficulties. The old story, isn't it? Did he fall? Was he pushed? Did he jump?' Ball consulted the ledger. 'Bashed his head on the side of the dock as he went in, they say. Hell of a mess.'

'I am really surprised, Stan. They did a search, I assume?' His mind was racing. There were a number of ways in which a head wound could have been sustained; bashing your head on the side of the dock as you fell into the water was only one of them.

'Yes, they dragged it for a while. Didn't find anything else

116

pertaining to Burrows. But they did find what was left of another body. Been in there a long time. Some rags, might have been child's clothes, and a couple of bones. No one has missed the poor soul, whoever they are, as far as I can see anyway and I have gone through the records in the ledger for most of this year,' he said, tapping the cover with his finger, 'but it doesn't tell me anything.' He shook his head. 'Awful, Inspector. Such a sorry place, the dock. Full of grief and sorrow. We both know it could be a child. There are too many kids wandering around this town. And this one has died and no one has missed them.'

'This job is grim sometimes, Stanley. Our job is always to pick up the pieces, it seems. But Burrows? He had money issues so serious that he'd rather be dead? That is a shock. I always thought he was a bit mean.'

'Hidden depths, Inspector. A bit like the dock, I'd say. I have sent Evan Davies down to the Mayor's office. Important he knows as soon as possible. I just hope Davies remembers the message properly. You know, at times like this, I think this new-fangled idea of the telephone will be better. At least if I am shouting down them wires, I know I will have sent the right message. Davies is capable of saying anything.'

'It is the bit about the missing money that is interesting, Stanley. He has always come across as a miser. If he has lost money, what has happened to it? Where has he been spending it? Making unwise investments?' Bucke scratched his cheek firmly. 'From what I understand, the only way to describe his life would be 'frugal.' Hard to say what is really going on though, isn't it?'

'A woman, Inspector? Can't dismiss it, you know that.'

'That's true. I can't, no matter how unlikely it sounds. I will see if Eliza Keast has heard anything. If he has been troubling the girls, she will know.' Bucke was already making a list in his mind of things that needed to be done. 'Someone will have to go to speak to Mrs Burrows. It must have been an awful shock, particularly if she didn't know about the finances.'

'Perhaps the Chief Constable would be best, Inspector, him

being a member of the Watch Committee. Respect for his position and all that. I am sure he would speak to her. Though he better do that afore the newspapers. They never do their best to make things better, do they?'

'You are probably right, Stanley. I am sure he will want to go to see Mrs Burrows. I'll go down and check with him. Watch Committee meetings won't be the same without him.'

'Aye. You might get something done.' Ball wrote something in the ledger and then blew on it to dry the ink. 'I reckon Evan Davies has had my blotting paper again.'

'Probably trying to read what it says. He would struggle if it was the right way round.' Bucke sighed. 'We've got a doctor going to look at the body have we? Please tell me it isn't Dr Rowlands.'

'It is Dr Rowlands.'

Bucke rubbed his eyes with his fingers. 'That is it, then. Emlyn Burrows died of a verruca. If Rowlands is doing it, that is the best we can hope for.'

'This job is full of surprises, isn't it, Inspector? When you think about it.'

'Yes, you are right, Stanley. And most of it is because there are so many people who have secrets. And then they emerge from where ever they have been hidden.' He thought of his unsatisfactory meeting with Pugh yesterday, not noticing how uncomfortably Ball fiddled with the ledger. 'But those secrets will always emerge. Always. No matter how deep you try to bury them.' He sighed. This was a distraction no one needed, just before the Royal visit, that was hanging over all of them like the darkest storm cloud. 'I will go and see the Chief Constable now, Stanley, and I should be grateful if you could stop finding bodies. There will be no one left to wave at the Prince at this rate.'

Bucke went towards the door, then turned back to the counter. 'Tell me something, Stanley,' he asked. 'Heard a story the other day. Something new to me. Wondered what you knew. It is a long time ago, now. A woman called Catherine Harris. Before the Queen. 1830s, something like that.'

118

'Oh, that old story,' said Ball. 'Haven't heard anyone mention that one for years. Hanged she was, poor old dear, out near Penrice, I think. A crossroads. Hangman's Cross, some call it. There was a gibbet there.'

'Oh dear. Not familiar with it. What's the story, then?'

'Shocking it is, inspector. They reckon Catherine Harris was innocent, see. She spoke to a woman she met on the road. Called Pugh, as I heard it. Annie Pugh, that's it. She was out in the night setting fire to hayricks. Unlucky in love, they say. Betrayed by one of the Mansells. Wouldn't be the first. Anyway, the local farmer arrested them both because they were gossiping by the side of the road when there was a fire in the field next to them. And the Pugh woman then turns King's Evidence and claims that they were setting fire to the hay but that she was the accomplice. It was all Catherine Harris' idea. She was much older than Annie. A grandmother. So Pugh is sent to be transported and Harris is hanged, even though it had nothing to do with her. Big crowd turns up, all a bit agitated because they reckon she is innocent. So they drop her quick from the gallows, but the rope breaks. They pick her up and they keep Granny Harries waiting for an hour whilst they go to the Mansells for another rope. Then they have another go but they botch it good and proper again and she was hanging there for a good few minutes, they reckon, before she stopped struggling. A lot of stones thrown at Oxwich Castle that weekend, they say.'

'I don't think I have seen a gibbet. Where is it?'

'Someone pulled it down some years ago. Always looking for firewood in Gower. About the same time as Old Man Mansell fell off his horse and broke his neck. You must remember, Inspector. We were chasing that pest Riverton all round Gower at the time.'

Bucke said nothing for a moment. 'That is a terrible story, Stanley. Any of the families still around?'

'Don't know anything about the Harris family. Could be anywhere. Plenty of Harrises round here, as you know. As I said, the Pugh woman was transported. Don't know whether she ever came back. Might have had a brother at Felindre, so I heard once. That is where the family came from. Might be that friend of yours, Iestyn, if that matters. But poor old Granny Harris is why it was remembered, at least for a while. There were a lot of very unhappy people back then and there was damn near a riot. But it is a long time ago. The town was full of it at the time, though I don't remember myself. I was a nipper. But it was one of those things. A big fuss at the time and then everyone forgets about it.'

'Not everyone, though'. He could see Riverton's face in front of him, with those piercing eyes, that sense of outrage and that need for revenge. A riding accident? A disappearing gibbet? More old history, stalking the streets of Swansea? Wasn't there enough of that already?

*

Later in the day, whilst Ball was re-arranging the lost property and items confiscated by the constables, which included a rather grubby revolver, Nick the Holly turned up in the police station. This was peculiar, because he wasn't under arrest.

'I am telling you now, Sergeant Ball. I swear on my mother's life. There is something going on in the Plume o' Feathers. I have heard noises. Loud noises, as I live and breathe.'

'Have you now?' said Ball, wrapping the revolver hurriedly in a yellow duster to make sure that Nick could not see it. You never knew with Nick the Holly; he was as trustworthy as a scorpion.

'Oh yes. Noises. In the dark, like.' He paused. 'Was that a gun you was wrapping then, by any chance?'

'Gun? No, Nick. A new-fangled potato peeler, that's all.'

Nick the Holly shook his head wisely. 'Complicated things, potato peelers, as far as I can tell, anyway. Never had no cause to have one.'

'So tell me, Holly. These noises you have been hearing. What were you doing round The Plume of Feathers, then? Been shut up for quite a time now.'

'You know. Just having a look. Like to keep an eye open. Always ready to help the constabulary.'

'For something you can nick, more like, I'll be bound.'

'You can be very hurtful, Sergeant Ball, and there is no cause for it. All I am saying is that there is something going on. It should be quiet, shouldn't it? Now it is empty. But I heard hammering. Honest I did. Not a word of a lie. There were hammering. Something's going off, I'm telling you.'

Ball quietly closed the drawer beneath the counter that now contained the gun. He looked at Holly carefully. His head was always thrown back, so that he seemed to be looking at the world along his nose. It was a face so full of deceit that his eyes could have been his nostrils, and his yellow teeth merely the toenails he had stolen from an unconscious tramp. There had never been a moment in his life when anything about Nick the Holly could be trusted.

'So what is going on here, Nick? Are you confessing to something so that you can get back into prison? Or are you now my new best informer, so that you can stay out of prison? I am confused.' Ball scratched his head and then spoke in a more conciliatory tone. 'Poison Ivy being difficult, is she?'

'She can be a difficult woman, I grant you, especially since she lost her baby. But I is trying my best to stay out of Cox's Farm. Too much like hard work when you are in there and I have never liked being hungry. Even if I do live with Poison Ivy, but please don't tell her I said that. But I am telling you now, Sergeant. You can ignore me if you want, but I will allus know that I have told you. There is something going off at the Plume o' Feathers. I told constable Morris but he told me to bugger off but that is his habit. You see, I thought, what with the king coming, that I had a duty, like.'

'Nick, listen to me,' said Ball, the irritation clear in his voice. 'I can understand what Constable Morris said and I am inclined to say the same, except I go to chapel more than he does. You heard nothing in The Plume of Feathers. Nothing at all, I am sure o' that. And anyway, we haven't got a king and it is the Prince of Wales coming, so you clear off or I'll shut you in the cells for getting on everyone's nerves before you know what's happened. And that'll

121

be before the Prince has ever even heard of Swansea. So get out of my police station, if you will.'

*

It became a busy and unhappy day, as Bucke attempted, and failed, to tidy up the business of Burrows' death. It appeared to be a complete mystery. But two questions hung over the incident like a cloud and they tantalised Bucke. What was Burrows doing with the money that he had removed from his bank account? He lived a careful life, tight-fisted, spartan. But what was he buying? Who was he buying? And why? Eliza Keast had not been able to offer any clues. All the street girls exchanged information with each other about their clients. It was in their interests to do so. No one had had any dealings with him. They did not seem to know who he was.

And then there was the other question. What reason did he have to be down at the docks during the night? It was completely out of character. It was hardly a place he would go unaccompanied. It was a place that someone like him would normally avoid. And no one had seen him, which might suggest that he didn't want anyone to know he was there. This was all guess work, and Bucke knew it. But it was a very unwelcome distraction just before the Royal visit. He tried to remember what they thought about before they knew that their fragrant and respected guests were coming and he realised that he could not remember. It seemed to have been going on forever.

Bucke sat on a crate on the side of the North Dock, close to where they had pulled out Burrows, thinking about the ugly head wound he had sustained. He had slipped and fallen in to the dock, tripped over a rope or something and has possibly bashed his head on an iron stanchion on the way into the water. It was what they told Mrs Burrows and it was definitely a possibility. In fact, it could be a probability. It was certainly convenient, with all the pressures they were experiencing with the Royal visit. They could believe that it was an unfortunate accident, then forget about it and concentrate on other things. It was seductive idea and certainly much less work than the alternative.

Because someone could have hit him – and hit him hard - and that was what was troubling Bucke. And if he had been struck, then that changed the whole nature of his death. It couldn't be dismissed, could it? Not if it was murder.

But why? The same old question. Why? Why would you feel it was necessary to kill someone like Emlyn Burrows? For what he had? Or for what he knew?

It was quiet down on the dock today. No new boats to be unloaded. Just a few heavy-booted men standing around in desultory groups, talking. Seagulls were sitting untroubled on gunwales and masts as the grey, stained ships rocked occasionally. The faint but unmistakable scent of coal and oil had infiltrated the breeze that ruffled the scummy water slopping against hulls. A distant shout. A sudden bang and a clatter from the railway line that ran alongside the dock. Everything seemed rather dismal and forgotten today, truly a stale backwater, though he knew it wasn't always like this. It had never been a life that appealed to him, he had never felt the call of the sea. It always looked so cold and uninviting. And yet some men spent their lives upon it and missed it when they were separated from the surging grey waves. They had bad trips, saw awful things, lost friends and companions and yet still returned to do it again and again.

He looked at the resting ship in front of him, seemingly deserted. The rigging was neat and ordered, creating attractive and complex shapes, but supporting no sails. He wondered briefly about going on board to have a look around. He was a police inspector after all, and so he had every right to do so, in his own mind at least. He wondered what it would be like to spend weeks at sea on a boat like this, unable to get off. Bucke had sailed to India, of course, but that was different. The troops had nothing to do, other than playing shooting games with objects floated off the stern. Eventually they would get off. But it was different for sailors. They were working; they were trapped with strangers, unable to meet anyone else. Cold mountainous seas, danger, everything wet – that was their life. Bucke couldn't imagine it.

He stood up and walked over to the ship. *The Drimnagh Castle*, it said, in faded lettering on the salted prow. Irish, he thought. A place in Dublin, he thought. He was sure he remembered it. He had been to Dublin once, when he was a young soldier. Some disturbances or something. Food riots, now he thought about it. They had been required to fire a volley to disperse the crowds, who were pushing and protesting. Very frightening for a young soldier, to face all those angry people. He remembered how he felt very clearly. There were men, women and children in the crowd. They seemed to have a point, too. There was not enough to eat. To be honest, the soldiers didn't have much to eat either and they felt very vulnerable, for they were just a uniform away from being on the other side of the disturbance. These were people who were no different to his relatives and neighbours. He had recognised their faces; their clothes; their grievance. But as a young soldier it was his duty not to think. His duty had always been to obey.

A woman had died, apparently. He remembered it quite clearly now. The pushing, the shouting, the fear. He remembered the shouted order to fire over the heads of the protesters, the looks the soldiers exchanged when they heard the fear in the captain's voice. And then a woman died, shot in that first volley. It had troubled him for quite a long time afterwards. The woman had died accidentally, there was no doubt in his mind. No one aimed at her, he was sure of that. Why would they do that? But the bullet came from someone's gun. He was sure that it hadn't been his gun. But then, how would he ever know? Someone pulled the trigger and fired it. For quite a few months afterwards, he had done his best to persuade himself that he would have known if he had done it. But he realised then, and realised now, that all he could ever say with any certainty was that he was there when it happened, and that he had been holding a rifle which he had been told to fire into the sky. And when he squeezed the trigger, whatever control had over the destiny of the bullet, had been abandoned.

There was an unexpected movement on deck and so he slipped out of sight behind a pile of empty crates, as if a sense of guilt from something long ago could be seen upon his face. It was a ridiculous thing to do, and he knew it would make him look suspicious, if someone saw him hiding there. So he banged on the crates as if checking their contents and then emerged into view, stumbling over a canvas sack full of rubble that was propped against the crates and which then fell noisily to the ground. He touched his cap to the two men descending the short gangway. They looked at him suspiciously but recognised his uniform and nodded in reply.

They were dark, unexceptional men, weather-beaten, dressed in shapeless, working clothes, so stained, it was impossible to believe they had ever been clean. Dirty faces, unshaven, mufflers pulled tight against the wind. They were heading for the town. The taller of the two men, the one with a dirty rope acting as a belt, turned on the quayside as an after-thought, it seemed, and appraised Bucke carefully.

'You's a guard, is it?' He asked in a clear Irish accent.

Bucke nodded. 'Inspector Bucke, Swansea Police.'

'Well, yous make sure none of your buggers tries to steal my boat. I have been here before. I got your name and I shall be looking for you if they does.' He smiled thinly. 'Good afternoon to you, sir.' He looked Bucke in the eyes for a fraction longer than was polite and then the two men turned and walked along the quayside.

An interesting encounter, thought Bucke. One with a little more edge to it than he had anticipated. He was pleased that he had not replied; it kept them at a distance. He watched them walk away together. He would not be surprised if he were to arrive at Tontine Street to find them in the cells, shouting and hammering futilely on the door. The shorter one leaned into the other and said something conspiratorially. They both laughed, and the taller man looked back at Bucke over his shoulder, grinning.

'We'll meet again,' Bucke whispered to himself, as he raised his police cap to them. 'I have no doubt about that.'

*

Mrs Harrison came in, of course. It was an arrangement that worked well for Lemuel, for the life of a constable was unpredictable and there were attentions Alice required which he could never have provided as her son. So Mrs Harrison came to dress Alice, to talk to her, to carry out all those more personal duties that featured infrequently in polite discourse. Lemuel was naturally relieved and accepted the need to arrange for the house to be kept clean and for his mother to be well-fed, without question, so that she could spend her days comforted by Vasco and re-living her rich and varied life.

Alice had once been completely independent woman, who had travelled the world with her husband and was now, somehow, unexpectedly, reduced to this –to a single room within a small world enclosed by the four walls of Lisbon Cottage in Sketty.

Lemuel was her only child – the pride of her life, the lasting connection with the husband she had loved so deeply and with whom she had experienced so much. Maynard had been a railway engineer in Portugal and elsewhere and, until Lemuel was born, she had gone everywhere with him. Alice was proud of their son, of his intelligence and his compassion. She worried most of all that her needs were a burden that Lemuel did not need as he tried to build his own life. But life had been cruel and she could barely move now. Her hip seemed to have fused, as if it had been welded to her legs in the tinplate works by one of the more assiduous employees.

They lived in devoted tranquillity and, though Alice believed that her son needed to move on from life with his mother, Lemuel did not appear to be ready for that step. Alice loved him with all her heart, and their quiet evenings together were the best part of her restricted life.

It was his habit now, once Mrs Harrison had helped Alice into bed and then left for the night, to tell her stories and so together they could explore an exciting, colourful world. For those moments he could set her free and travel with her to the places she had once known and, in such a way, create the gentle, happy images that became her dreams.

Tonight, he gave his mother a small glass of port and then watched its warmth relax her painful body. She reached out a hand

and laid it gently between the dog's ears. Then her son murmured gently to her, whilst she closed her eyes and lived within a world created by those softly spoken words.

'We have been a long time on the ship, but that matters not at all for, as we sail into the estuary, the sun is shining and the small fishing boats with their colourful sails scud past us on the wind. This is the Douro and this is Oporto. We see the river has widened into an expanse as large as a great lake, opposite the old seaport. We cannot wait to land and we find that the quay side is lined with the happy wives of the fisherman behind their stalls, heavy with those bright, shiny, silver fish. Vasco is delighted to be ashore and wags his tail so happily and so furiously, it is as if he is sweeping the street. Not that he needs too, for the streets around the beautiful cathedral are so clean. We have good friends in Foz and we may see them tomorrow, but today we are here for the harvest. The women are carrying baskets of purple grapes to the presses and some of the juice runs out at the bottom, forced through by the weight of the grapes above. This is the choicest wine. Not to be sold, but to be shared, and the men soon jump into the vats of grapes and place their hands on each other's shoulders and they dance to the music of bagpipes for hours and hours. Then when they are exhausted, they invite you and father to join them and so you dance on the grapes until every grape skin is dry, like forgotten paper. There is laughter and there is food on long tables in the bright warm sunshine and you watch Vasco running and chasing on the grass and soon you go to him and together with father you throw and chase and roll and laugh and a gentle wind catches your hair….'

When he judged that she was asleep, he gently took the glass from her and blew out the candle before retiring to his own room and his copy of *Fullerton's Gazetteer of the World* to continue his search for Aucaman.

Eleven

'I think I have found someone. Therese. Well actually two people, who could both help us.'

'Really? In Swansea? Let joy be unconfined. Please tell me more, Charles. Your news may well be worth a reviving glass of sherry.'

'Well, you see, sitting in the lounge and keeping it under observation is not the waste of time you think it might be. As a result of my work I have discovered that the Fenian amongst us is called Keane.'

'I should have guessed,' said Therese, rolling her eyes melodramatically. 'I am sure he is.'

'Collects information and thinks he is being very discreet, as you might expect. He is always confirming the names of guests and which room they are in. I wasn't happy about that at all. So very second rate. He thinks my name is Crawley, as I told him when he brought me my Darjeeling. I watched him go out to a doorway opposite to speak to someone. Seemed to be receive instructions. Then he came back inside. Quite amateurish. Very disappointed. You would have been embarrassed, Therese.'

'Perpetually Charles. I am in Swansea, after all. Isn't that enough?' She briefly resumed combing a wig resting on its stand.

'Possibly, but one does expect better. Hardly a challenge. Not even trying. We will wait a day or two. Don't let them think we are too hasty. But he is merely a detail to be disposed of. Let's us make a point. Show proper respect towards Eli. But more importantly, Therese, I believe I have found you a maid.'

'How exciting, Charles. And is she reasonably presentable? Or is she in-bred? Does she dribble?'

'Therese, she will fit the role perfectly, trust me. Young, attractive, innocent. Will do as she is asked, I am sure of it. Bucke knows her. She is currently living in Aberystwyth. Intelligent, I think. Mother is of a particularly nervous disposition, but I think she can be managed. Think you will like her, actually. Got talking over a cup of tea. Never deny the importance of tea, Therese.'

'If only that were permissible,' she sighed. 'But in your honest opinion the girl will suffice, you think?'

'Oh yes, and in the long term too, perhaps. Quite spirited, I would say. But you can mould her.'

'Mould? Have you seen my bathroom, Charles? Let's just get out of Swansea first, shall we?'

'Meet her, Therese, and recruit her into enticing the waiter. As we did in Birmingham. See how she manages that. Not too demanding and we should be able to make a judgement. I have arranged a meeting with her. If she does her work well, she will be ours. She and her mother are staying in the hotel. They now believe that you are aristocracy and are very excited about meeting you.'

'As they should be.'

'You are a member of the English aristocracy, Therese, after all. They cannot fail to be impressed.'

'There is always a sting in the tail, isn't there, Charles? That's no fun. Can't I be Spanish again? As I was in the frightful north? Even the sound of the word Leeds makes me shudder.'

'No, Therese. We will keep it simple. The truth. Therese.'

She pouted. 'You know I always enjoy being the show-girl, best of all.'

'The truth, Therese. Please.'

You are such a bore, Charles.'

Grey raised his eyebrows. 'Arrange a treat for the waiter. See how Miss Emily manages that. You can't mistake him. He is the one with acne.'

'Already I am repelled.'

*

When they met later that afternoon, Therese was surprised at how much of Emily she could recognise. She wasn't a copy of

Therese at all. But she could see a significant part of herself, that latent recklessness that made her both foolish and brave. She knew that something had happened to both of them, something cataclysmic, which meant that neither of them seemed to put any value on themselves. They both seemed to care so little, for life had lost its meaning for them. And when she saw Emily and realised how sorry she felt for her, she suddenly wondered if that was how others saw her. A chill passed down her. She wanted sympathy from no one; what Therese wanted more than anything else was revenge. Nothing else mattered. She wondered whether Emily felt the same.

She appraised Emily very carefully, wondering how honest she should be. 'My dear child. You are perfect for my requirements. I could not ask for better. You are a very pretty young woman. You'll become a beauty, though that is not all it is believed to be, let me tell you. Tell me about yourself.'

She listened to Emily's story without commentary, without shock. Therese wondered whether this in itself shocked her. When she had finished, she nodded at her.

'I can see all this in your face, Emily. It is a terrible story, but it makes you strong, I can sense it. Of course, it was abominable. Absolutely. But don't worry. I will find you a man.' She smiled at Emily's shock. 'Oh please, Emily. What sort of woman do you think I am? I will find you a man, and then you can kill the bastard.' She smiled, but Emily, wide-eyed, was sure that she meant it. 'So let's get down to business, shall we?'

Emily gulped and nodded.

'Now you must call me Therese in private. You will be my friend and there will be no secrets between us. Can you manage that, do you think? In public of course, as my maid, you must call me 'My lady' or 'Madame' or 'Lady D'Auch. It is vital you don't forget that or you could put everyone in danger. In public you are my maid; privately you are my accomplice. Clear?'

Emily nodded at her again, wondering what exactly was being planned for her.

Therese smiled reassuringly. 'There is no need to be shy. You pronounce it like douche, my dear, though it is not nearly so racy as it sounds. Means shower in French, though finding one of those in Swansea is like trying to find feathers on a frog. I have to ask you, Emily. Do relatives come round to see people wash? Is it an occasion? Some kind of festival? Is there an announcement in the paper?'

Emily smiled, though she was not sure that this was the correct response. Therese spoke so quickly and so confidently she was struggling to keep up.

'You will be an absolutely splendid maid. I am so pleased. I would have offered you the position even if we were doing this in London, so I wouldn't want you to think you are second-best. I think you are perfect. You shall be my ever-watchful magpie - that splash of white in your hair is quite remarkable. I am insanely jealous.' She ran her hands through her own hair to spike it up. 'I am extremely pleased. A beautiful young woman who has elevated herself above her dismal surroundings would always have been my choice. But it is only for a day. To begin with, I would say. You do have a basic grasp of personal hygiene, don't you? Even though you live in Swansea?'

Emily nodded.

'Excellent. There might be an opportunity for you, a resourceful, intelligent young woman. Always looking for someone like that to join us. Let's see how we get on, shall we? Would you like London, do you think? It isn't Swansea.'

'Actually, I am no longer from Swansea. I now live in Aberystwyth.'

'There are limits to my compassion, Emily. Shall we move on? Let us talk about your dress. I am sure that you may have entertained a fancy for something of elegant lace with a high bodice and sculptured hem that will float softly above the ground.' She shook her head. 'A ridiculous fantasy, though I have something like that which will be perfect for tonight. We will make it fit. No, let us turn our attention instead to the Royal procession, of which you will now be an integral part. You will wear traditional Welsh costume. It will work a treat. Like chain mail, should the bullets ever start to fly. But think of the attention you will have. It's always a crowd pleaser. They will look at you, rather than the princess, I am confident of that. The perfect expression of all those traditional virtues that they so admire. But you will not need the basket of cockles that is apparently regarded as the traditional accessory. It would get in the way. You are being employed to walk behind me at a distance of, perhaps, no more than three feet and alert me of anything untoward that you might notice. We can rehearse this tomorrow. As I said, you will, of course, be a member of the royal party. I will introduce you to the Princess, who will remember you and may well write you a letter, but I will endeavour not to introduce you to the Prince, for he may remember you all too well.' She smiled.

Emily was bewildered. 'I wonder what arrangements – '

'Your mother? Will she worry? Is she neurotic at all, do you think? Mine was, God knows. What shall we do with her? Should we just stick her with the Lady Mayoress and have done with it, do you think?'

'She has a friend.' Emily was thinking of Constance. 'They will be watching the procession together.'

'We put both of them with the Lady Mayoress then, if you think that is a good idea. You don't think she will faint, do you? Most tiresome. Can't come with us. Don't want too many people crowding around the Princess. She doesn't like it and it obscures my view. My gun isn't fond of bystanders. Not as choosy as it should be. See what Charles says about your mother. And, whilst we are talking about the royal party,' and Emily wasn't sure that they had been, 'Sir William Gull. One of the queen's doctors. If he turns up keep a respectable distance from him, Emily. All hands, that man. But personally it is his eyes I don't like. Slices your clothes open with them. Sees every woman as a specimen. Any trouble then either stamp on his feet – I am sure you will be wearing boots given the nature of the pavements – or call for me. He knows that I can get cross.'

132

'The only other thing you need to know is the most important thing of all, and that is, that if you see me open my purse then turn around and stand with your back to me and watch for anything I should know about. Don't wait to see the gun. As soon as I open my purse, you turn. It is never opened for any other reason. And of course, the other point I must make, and I don't want you to be alarmed but I must make this absolutely clear. Our task is to protect Her Royal Highness Princess Alexandra. And as such therefore, we are expendable. She must go home safely, even if that means we do not. I hope this does not shock you.'

Emily was not sure what to say. Suddenly the wigs on their stands scattered around the room looked like trophies, like a collection of scalps.

'We have our information, of course, and that tells us to expect trouble from the Fenians. Serious trouble. That is why we are here, because they are here already. They are clever, they are cunning and they are foolhardy. But then, so are we. They always think they are one step ahead, but in truth they are one step behind. But dangerous? Oh yes. And they are our enemy and they would like to kill me. It is the sort of thing that can make a lady quite irritated.'

Emily's heart was beating rapidly. Have conversations like this ever happened in Aberystwyth, she wondered?

'There we are. Knew you would understand. Now you are a member of the secret service. Not as exciting as it sounds. A great deal of hanging around and smiling at local worthies. There will be lots of speeches. Imagine the worst speech you have ever heard and then double it. Never-ending. Just smile and nod, if you think it will help. Your obligation is to stay upright, that's all. No fainting, please. We all need to concentrate and there will be so much going on. These temporary areas we will have to work in are always so difficult. Always a chair in the wrong place or something unexpected on the floor. Of course, you are unable to tell anyone about your role or indeed our arrangements.' Therese smiled.

'Of course, though Connie is the secret lover of Inspector Bucke and so I could tell her I…'

'I know all about Constance White so it isn't that much of a secret, but you do not mention it to her at all. I need to be quite firm about that. Oh yes, and if you have agreed to meet anyone to watch the occasion, well...' She paused. 'Have you? A young gentleman perhaps?'

'Only Harriet.'

'Poor Only Harriet. You must tell her you have an attack of the vapours. Of course, if she recognises you in the Royal Carriage she will be consumed with jealousy. She may never speak to you again. Which may, or may not, be an advantage. That is for you to decide.' She smiled. 'Are we clear, Emily?'

'May I ask a question, Therese?'

'Of course you may. I assume we are quite clear on babies and what causes them?' Therese smiled.

Emily blushed. 'Of course I am.'

'Thank goodness. It wouldn't be right if I were to usurp your mother's duties.'

Emily rolled her eyes. 'No, Therese. I think it might be a bit more complicated. Why do these Fenian people want to murder the Prince? Momma says I shouldn't trouble myself with the Fenians, but I do. I saw something in the paper.'

'You have newspapers in Aberystwyth? How very modern. The reason they want to kill the Prince is the same reason why the buggers tried to invade Canada. They are dangerous and stupid and they must die. Every one of them.' She paused. 'Perhaps I am being unkind. You see, for me, if these people want Ireland to be its own country and everyone agrees, well, why shouldn't they? To be frank what use is that god-forsaken bog to anyone? None whatsoever. They play violins loudly and badly and call them fiddles and they stamp their feet a great deal. Leave them to it, if you ask me. But apparently we can't, so I have to risk my life. Put some women in charge on both sides and it would be sorted before lunch time. But I am told that wouldn't be good enough. We have to shoot at each other for two or three generations before we can even think of talking about it. About anything.' Her tone shifted

134

again. 'It is madness. The Fenians won't surrender. They will keep on, even if it takes centuries. Because it is what they believe in. It keeps them going. We all need a reason for getting up in the morning. I have mine; they have theirs. If you can give those things up so readily, then they were never important. So when it comes down to it, our job, yours and mine is to protect the Princess. Because we will never defeat the Fenians. They will simply change into something else, but their cause won't disappear.'

'But why don't we ask the people what they want?'

'Because they don't know. It often depends entirely upon whoever spoke to them last. I have ceased worrying about it, Emily. I just perform my duties because to doubt them makes you vulnerable.' She looked away for a moment and bit her lip. 'So tonight at dinner,' she said more brightly, 'I want you to flirt with one of the waiters. I will show you which one. Smile at him. Blush if you can. No harm will come of you, I promise. But encourage him. A discreet wave always helps.'

'You mean, like in chapel?'

'Well a girl has to do something during a sermon, hasn't she?'

'They do if its Vicar Cyrus Bishop. He's dead now though.'

'Probably bored himself to death. A vicar called Bishop? Only in Swansea.'

*

When Constance called to see her and her mother the following morning, she found Emily excited and energised.

'Oh Connie! I think she is the most beautiful woman I have ever seen. Oh my goodness.'

'Even more beautiful than your own mother, Em?'

'Well, apart from my mother, obviously. But my mother does not carry a revolver in her clasp.'

'I am not aware that many women do, Em.' Constance was shocked, but realised that she should listen carefully. She could always speak to Rumsey about it later.

'I have met such interesting women here in Swansea. Frances

135

Power Cobbe, Therese d'Auch – so much more interesting than wet Aberystwyth. They are all rather dull chapel-goers up there who smell of camphor and speak Welsh very quickly.'

'Perhaps you need to be more patient. You never know what passions lurk behind heavy velvet curtains. I am sure there are fascinating stories waiting for you. Be positive. You just need to look more carefully, that's all.'

Emily wasn't properly listening. 'Hers is such a romantic story. Did you know? Well, how could you? I don't suppose you have met her, but her grandfather fought with Napoleon at Waterloo and he was killed. Think of that! And then her own father, a Hussar, was killed by the Prussians at the Siege of Paris just before she was born. And then her English husband was shot to death by a Fenian in Dublin! Whilst she was watching! And now she wants her revenge. Well, I can't blame her. It is so romantic. She wears a black garter at all times to remember him. I mean, it is so sad, obviously, and she has had lots of troubles. And so now she works as a spy and has to protect the Princess. I mean, I am not supposed to tell anyone but I think it is alright to tell you because of Inspector Bucke. I am sure I will be able to help her and offer her advice. But she is ready for anything.'

'Yes, it sounds very sad. She must feel that all the men in her life are destined to die. That must be a hard thing to live with.' Constance watched Emily's eyes, surprised by this sudden change in her.

Emily's hand covered her mouth briefly. 'Oh my goodness! I hadn't thought of that. You would think she is English, I imagine, but really, she is French. I knew straight away.' Emily was excited pacing around the small room. 'Do you know, Connie? Her own hair is really short. I mean, Connie, it looks absolutely wonderful and I am so jealous, but when she goes out she wears a wig so that if anyone grabs her hair it comes off and she can fight back. She thinks of everything.'

'It makes sense I suppose, if you are travelling around looking for fights, Emily. Though if you think about it, most of us don't.'

'Oh I know that, but it is so exciting. It is because she has such an important job. Mostly it is just men who get jobs like that, but she is as good as any man and she keeps a gun in her handbag! It is so thrilling. I am sure she has killed endless numbers of agitators.' She paused. 'I think I would like to be a spy. Obviously, we have to protect Princess Alexandra and watch everything so carefully. We might get killed but that is the price we have to pay.' Emily nodded bravely.

Constance wondered if she had fully considered the consequences of what she was saying. Was she actually frightened, she wondered or completely reckless? 'She has made quite an impression on you, Emily,' she said. 'I worry that she has persuaded you that you are worth so little that your life can be thoughtlessly thrown away.'

'What do you mean, Connie? She said no such thing, at all. I have a duty to perform now. You should be proud. What I had to do at dinner last night was to wink at a waiter. I don't know why, but Therese was so insistent. I felt quite daring! I have to do the same tonight. To the same waiter, apparently. I have to make sure he can see this stripe in my hair so he knows I am the same one. Therese didn't tell me anything about it but there has to be a good reason, doesn't there? I didn't tell momma, of course. She would have been shocked but I am old enough to have secrets now, aren't I, Em? It was quite funny actually. The waiter smiled back but momma thought he was smiling at her! Golly, Connie! It was so thrilling!'

'You shouldn't be making fun of your mother, Emily,' said Constance severely.

'Oh I wasn't, not really. But she doesn't know that I am involved now in work of such importance that I might actually have to speak to Princess Alexandra! Think of that! You are not allowed to say anything, Connie. Obviously.'

'I can't imagine that your friend is a great deal different from the rest of us, Emily. She is a woman. She has the same body as the rest of us. Underneath all that finery she wears.'

'Oh yes, I realise all that.'

'But Emily, if your friend Therese is there to shoot at people, she must also have to accept that those people might be very keen to shoot at her. And the same will apply to you, Emily. By doing this work, whatever it is, you are agreeing to allow people to shoot at you. And your mother doesn't know any of this?'

'No. She is a worrier.'

'Really? And that justifies not telling her the truth, does it?' asked Constance.

'Why don't you want me to have excitements? Why do you think I haven't thought of her? That is the reason I haven't told her. To save her the worry. Surely you can see that? I have been asked to do an important job. Vital for the security of the realm. That is what Therese said. And I am old enough to make my own decision about that. At least, I thought I was. I had hoped that you might have supported me in this but obviously I was wrong.' She flashed Constance a scornful look.

'Em. I am entitled to have a different opinion. On this. On anything. We can disagree, but it doesn't mean we cannot be friends, does it?'

The door opened, and Flora entered tentatively. 'Good morning, Constance. I thought I heard a voice in here and wondered who Emily was talking to.'

Emily snapped back. 'Am I not allowed to have conversations, Momma? Or must I always ask your permission?'

'Please Emily. I meant nothing of it. You are looking lovely today, so bright, so much better. A proper young lady.'

But Emily's face had changed and Constance knew that there was about to be another storm.

Twelve

This sudden and unexpected influx of healthy young men into the Irish community in Greenhill had caused huge excitement, for they brought with them lusty new blood to reinvigorate a weary world of poverty, where lives were lived in dirty streets, where well-used privies and wells were side by side. Their devoted commitment to refreshing the Swansea gene pool – an urgent necessity indeed - hardly endeared them to an established male population, ground down and emasculated by the constant struggle for survival in a dark town suffocated by smoke. The community's quietly acknowledged leader, Jimmy Giblin, was sympathetic to their concerns, for he knew, without a doubt, that the indigenous young males could not compete with these brave and robust outsiders who, everyone suspected, had arrived on an exciting and secret mission from a healthy and more vigorous place. He watched sympathetically as their anger and frustration at the way their rightful place at the heart of a libidinous, if incestuous, world was usurped, though there was little he could do about it. Jimmy, for whom such disappointments in life had always been his daily expectation, was anxious to prevent any fights that would otherwise arise, in order to avoid attracting unwelcome police attention. He was not completely aware of the Fenian's intentions but understood that it was best not to know anything at all, for then he could neither inadvertently reveal nor betray his countrymen. But maintaining the fragile peace was not easy and it took a great deal of his thin reserves of patience to do so.

There were incessant mutterings, of course, amongst the young, and in normal circumstances these intruders would have been suitably bruised and then shown their place without delay. Giblin was adamant, however, that these visitors were here for a reason, and that reason necessitated unquestioning discretion. And it was obvious too, that their presence could not be acknowledged. Giblin made his position perfectly clear, on many occasions. No one would ever know that these priapic new boys were here, as long as nothing was said and that nothing stupid took place. He reminded everyone he met that they had known these boys for a long time. They had always been here in Swansea, of course they had. Good boys they were, without a doubt. Never in trouble, that is why you have never come across them before, officer. Such a thing was highly unlikely of course, but it was the best argument they had. A strong word, a heavy hand upon a shoulder that was a little firmer than it had a right to be, were the ways in which he ensured compliance.

The young women were harder to manage however; habitual, uninspiring encounters had unexpectedly been transformed, and consequently so had their own enthusiasm. And this, as Duggan noted, was the problem. His troops, as he liked to call them, had every reason not to stay hidden. How could they when such a range of delights were presented to them on every corner, on every street? Like Giblin, he knew that enthusiasm, opportunity and willing consent made a dangerous cocktail.

The giggling and the fluttering eyes and the hurried liaisons added to the tension that the boys of Greenhill had to manage, torn, as they were, between loyalty and anger. However, things became particularly difficult as a grey dusk settled on Croft Street on Wednesday afternoon. In the gloom an incident occurred, one which could never have been kept out of either the police station or the newspaper, not once a doctor was called to deal with the consequences of Declan grabbing hold of Kathleen Connor.

'We've had 'em all in here today,' said Sergeant Ball, when Bucke returned to the police station from a meeting with the Chief Constable. 'It is a wonder there is anyone left in Little Ireland this afternoon. And all because one of the lads was larking about, someone called Declan Murray, apparently. Never heard of him myself.'

'Nor me,' added Bucke thoughtfully.

'Byron Midwinter came in with the news. He had never heard of this Declan Murray either, he said. But he was told that Murray grabbed hold of Kathleen Connor when she was going home after work. You have probably seen her. Big girl, if you see what I mean.

140

I am sorry, Inspector. Perhaps you haven't. Anyway, the lass works in Clutterbucks doing alterations – dresses, trousers, that sort of thing. She was on her way home. Problem was, young Declan was a bit too eager. Doctor reckons there was a needle left from work, stuck in her dress. He grabbed her, she squealed by all accounts and then this needle went straight into his heart and then broke off.'

'Are you making this up, Stanley?'

'Not according to the Doctor, I am not. Doctor Green it was, not Dr Rowlands, heavens be praised. Sent his assistant to tell me. That's how I know. They took Murray to the Infirmary straight away. He decided that he had to get the rest of the needle out before his heart got inflamed. So he opened him up, got down to the heart, found the end of the needle and pulled it out. They reckon he will probably die, which is why the assistant was sent up here to tell me. Oh aye, clever enough getting it out. But what was the point?'

'Very amusing, Stanley.'

'Please Inspector. You know what I mean. Be warned. Be careful what you are grabbing up there in Little Ireland. Always said the same.'

'A cautionary tale, without a doubt – and a warning for those who lack discernment, I would say. But tell me something, Stanley. This poor boy. Do we know who he is? Have I heard of Declan Murray? Don't think so. But I can't believe there is a boy up there who we have had nothing to do with over the years.'

'I haven't heard of him, either. I will ask the constables when they come in. See if they know anything.'

'He is not a visitor, is he? Newly arrived? Ask them, Stanley. Are there any new young men up there? Boys we have never seen before. It is important.'

Constable Midwinter suddenly spoke. In truth, Sergeant Ball had forgotten that he was there, brooding in the shadows, dabbing at his ulcerated lips with a dirty rag. 'Should have let it be, if you want my opinion. There was no cause to go fiddling with the lad's heart, just to pull out a needle. Why bother? We have all got one of those stuck in our hearts.' And he walked out of the station, wrapped in his dark cloak of loneliness.

Bucke looked at Ball and raised his eyebrows.

'Yes, I know,' said Ball. 'I am keeping an eye on him, as best I can. There is something not quite right there. Iago Morris is supposed to be keeping a look out too, but he hasn't been right himself since Dai Price...well, you know.' He shook his head. 'There's a deal of unhappiness around, Inspector and I can't say that a royal visit is going to do much to change that.'

*

Jimmy Giblin was concerned enough to call a meeting. That idiot child. The absolute idiot.

'You told me he was one of your best. Really? Is that the case, Mickey? One of your best? What does that say for the others you have brought here, eh? For the love of Christ, I would have thought that at least he would have known to keep his hands to himself. He was here for a reason, not to chase girls, though from what I have heard young Kathleen has never needed much chasing. What are we going to do now then? What do you think? Is this the end of all your plans, Mickey?'

'No. We brazen it out,' said Duggan after a moment. 'It will be in the papers. We can't stop that. So we make a noise, we make a fuss. No point trying to cover it up, so we don't try to avoid it. Who is that newspaper seller of yours? Paul Roe? Get him to shout about it when he is selling – make it sound like a music hall story. If you want to hide something there are times it is best to make a commotion. Hide it in full view of everyone. Can you trust Roe?'

'Certainly. He is no royalist, you can be sure of that. Let me have a word. He is almost like blood now, see. Walking out with my Shelagh.'

*

'Heartless doctor in death experiment! Read all about it!... Only a little prick says Doctor. Boy dies!... Needle used to mend Lady Vivian's knickerbockers kills Irish boy!... Toff's shop sells cheap

142

needles!... Poor to be burnt at breakfast to keep Bertie warm!'

Very quickly, the unexpected death of the apparently self-effacing Declan Murray became an entertainment. Questions about him provoked merely an amused version of his unusual death, one that had the advantage of happening to a stranger, so it didn't matter much.

But not everyone forgot – it was, as James Flynn frequently observed, a policeman's job never to forget. And the death of this unknown young man troubled Inspector Flynn greatly. The community seemed to him to have moved on very quickly. There was no protracted mourning, there was no wake, which was very unusual. But if there was something going on up in Greenhill, Flynn didn't want to take his big policeman's boots and trample all over everything and obscure important evidence, when what he really needed to do was to find out quietly and methodically what was going on. And he was sure something was going on. And then he remembered; he had a legitimate reason for visiting the streets of Little Ireland, one that would not draw undue attention to himself, or so he hoped.

And so, on a grey and breezy Thursday afternoon, Inspector Flynn went up the hill to talk to Josiah Padley. Flynn knew him as an odd and very intense man, a fish dealer, behind whose dark and crumbling house there was a ruined shed in which he smoked herrings, with a grumbling chorus of neighbours regularly complaining about the smell, although Flynn didn't think it was the worst element in the permanent, poisoned, haze that hung over Greenhill on most days. But that smell clung to Josiah like a cloak.

Two scabby tomcats, their territorial rivalries suspended for the moment, watched Padley from the top of a damp, moss covered wall, with expectations. They watched Flynn enter the yard, apprehensive that this police inspector would serve as an unnecessary distraction from vital fish gutting.

Padley was sitting on a stool, slitting open herrings from a dirty barrel and scraping their insides into a bucket before he threaded them on to a thin pole, bent through constant use. He paused in his work and waved his bloody knife casually at the Inspector. 'I am telling ye now, Flynn. April and the bitch dies. Don't say ye haven't been warned.' He picked up another fish.

'Stop your nonsense, Josiah. I have heard it before. We have had this for years now.'

'Well, this time I means it. Been going behind my back with the Ley brothers. No man should be expected to tolerate that. Her a mother too.'

'You shouldn't plan to take a mother from her children either, should you? You two have got plenty of them.'

'And she should know better than going with other men then, shouldn't she? She can't say she hasn't been warned either.' He disembowelled a fish with a flourish and then spat into the bucket of entrails.

'I am telling you, Josiah, like I have told you before, if you carry on with this nonsense of yours round the town, I shall have you locked up. You are trying to make us look foolish and you need to understand that I am not prepared to tolerate it.'

Josiah snorted and pulled a liver from a fish and flicked it with his knife towards the two cats. Their armistice ended in jealous snarls and a sharp claw swipe of victory. 'It's not me ye should be worrying about anyway, Mr Flynn. There is something going on, here in Little Ireland. Don't know what it is. Nobody is saying. But there is a lot of strangers up here at present.'

'There are always strangers in Swansea, Jos. You know that. Come here for the work, don't they? In some parts there is not much work at all, so they come here. Then they find they can't do it or they don't earn enough, so they move on. You know that.'

'And ye have found a body in a cart, ain't ye? Someone ye have never seen before? Didn't that strike ye as funny? Christ Almighty, if it didn't, then I should be doing your bloody job for ye. I am telling ye. Something is going on. Clear as the nose on your face. I don't rightly know what it is. No one talks to me. But I reckon he was left there as some sort of message to ye. Not up to me to work it out, now is it?'

144

'Cut out your nonsense, Jos. or I shall do you for wasting police time.'

Padley shrugged. 'Well, if that is all ye can say, then I shall see ye in April, like as not. But for God's sake don't ye go round saying ye haven't been warned.' He pulled out an unidentifiable organ from a fish and watched one of the cats jump in the air to catch it. 'Clever bugger, that one,' he said, nodding his approval.

*

'What's going on, Jimmy? Tell me. Tell me now.'

Giblin raised his eyebrows. He was starting to find Duggan a little obsessive. Sure, he had been asked – ordered even – to offer him every assistance and he would do it. But not to the detriment of his own fragile and impoverished community. But here was the light of fanaticism in those penetrating eyes that hid beneath that heavy brow, and there had been occasions in these recent weeks when Giblin had found him difficult and aggressive. He was a tall man, with neat hair, parted precisely and brushed back and a presence that suggested wrongly a privileged background. But it was those lips Giblin didn't like – thin and tight that gave him an almost permanent sneer.

'Tell you what, Mickey?'

'Why was that policeman up here? I saw him down at the corner. Wasn't a constable either. An Inspector. Not the sort of thing that I like, at all.'

'This is normal, Mickey. This is where we live. This is what happens. Policemen come up here all the time. We learn to get on with them as best we can. That was Inspector Flynn. Here to see Josiah Padley, I shouldn't wonder. A strange bugger he is.'

Duggan shook his head. 'I didn't much like the way he was looking around. I think he might be suspecting something. I think that was why he was here. He was checking up. And I didn't like the way he looked at me. Because he didn't speak. He watched. And then he looked at some of my boys and I didn't like that either.'

'Perhaps your boys should have buggered off when they saw

him, then. You don't get anywhere staring at Inspector Flynn. He is not going to wet his breeches because a couple of yous gave him a hard stare, I can tell you that for a fact.'

'We are going to have to deal with him,' said Duggan decisively.

Jimmy Giblin shook his head. 'No, you are not, Mickey. You'll leave him be.'

'He might interfere with our plans Jimmy, and I can't allow that.'

'You listen to me, Mickey. He is an honest rozzer and there are few of those around, to be sure. He looks after the people up here and we can trust him. Who knows who would replace him. You will come and you will go. The rest of us have to live here and I like to keep things nice and calm. Important to everyone.'

Duggan snorted derisively. 'You shouldn't worry about that. The worse they are the better for us. It'll drive more people to the Brotherhood.'

'And do you know what? I don't much care.' He held up his hand decisively. 'No, don't interrupt me, Mickey. You'll listen to me. We all live here. This is our place, our home, not yours and we have to do what we can. We make the best of it. It is not a good place sometimes and it stinks and most days there are old man coughing in the street until they can't breathe. But this is all we've got. This is our life and the lives of our children. Oh for sure, Mickey. You have a job and you are eaten up by it. Nothing is more important to you, I know that, truly I do. But when you has gone, this will still our world and I shall be obliged if you would do your very best not to turn it upside down, because there will always be our wean to be fed, and that's something you'll not be interfering with.'

Duggan stared back at him. Giblin's failure to accept the overwhelming importance of their mission was troubling. He wondered whether he should argue with him and then wondered whether it would have any purpose. Giblin, he recognised, was too wrapped up the trivial concerns of the here and now. He needed to look beyond the detail; if people were hurt, then it was merely an unfortunate consequence of the route to their triumph. Sacrifices would have to be made and each sacrifice would be just one minor detail – and their ultimate success would show that all those troubles were worthwhile. He looked back at Jimmy and ran his hand under his chin and round his neck, as if he was practising strangulation. He always found it hard to work with people who lacked the proper vision.

'Listen to me, Jimmy. I am a man down, now, because of that hedge creeper of yours. Kathleen, wasn't it? So find me someone. I'll need them immediately.'

'And what are you looking for Mickey? A safe cracker, for goodness sake?'

'Safe cracking? What are you talking about, Jimmy? We don't need that anymore. You don't need explosives to get into a safe or a man with a set of picks. All you need is paper. That is how you get rich. Words on paper. You don't need to see the cash anymore. Just have the right numbers on a banker's draft. So there is no noise, no sacks of coins, no chasing through the streets. We just get an old man to sign some papers, though the cold hard cash doesn't complain quite as much. All we need. So find me someone, Jimmy. No special skills, just a lad who knows how to do what he is told, though they are rare enough here, from what I can see. But we had six and now it is five. I need another.'

Giblin shook his head. 'I won't be doing that. You will have to cope with what you've got, I think. We don't provide cannon fodder, Mickey.'

'What do you mean?'

'He will be the first in line, we both know that. You haven't got time to train him properly, so whatever it is you are here to do, if I give you one of our boys, they will be the first to go. And when there is a body that they can recognise, when there is a funeral, when the priest is collecting donations - there will be questions. We can handle this business of yours, Mickey, if we can say afterwards that we knew nothing about what happened. That none of us was involved at all. But when they have one of our own, dead on the street, their questions will get a little more urgent. Can't you see that? We've got our lives, our ordinary lives. We are not part of this grand plan of yours. Oh, we all support you, don't misunderstand me and there's none here that will snitch to the guards. But don't push us. We live here. You don't.'

Duggan sighed, loudly. 'Listen to me, Jimmy. There is nothing, and no one, more important than our mission. We came here to carry out a task, an important job for the Brotherhood. And the Brotherhood is far more important than any one of us here. Any of us, and I am surprised that I have to make this point as strongly as I do, but any of us, must be ready to make sacrifices in order to ensure the success of why we are here. It is not for us to question the purpose, Jimmy.' He paused, wondering how far he should go. 'For the cause to triumph, then people have to die. And we have to be ready for that. It might be the death of the person most dear to us. And we all have to understand that. Each of us is just a flake of snow. But when we gather together then each flake of snow finds the power of an avalanche.'

Giblin snorted. This was far too fanciful for him. 'Explain that to the child with no shoes or no food. You know, Mickey, the one whose father has been arrested by a dishonest inspector because some Irish bastard shot the only decent rozzer we had. Is that what you want?'

'There will be some casualties. You can't pretend that there won't. It is what happens and we have to be ready for that. You have to be ready for that. But this is part of the struggle and we can't be blamed for that, Jimmy. That is the fault of the British. They drove us to it. Remember that, Jimmy. Tell our people, The British are making us behave in this way. It isn't our choosing. They don't listen and so they don't give us a choice. Remember that.' Duggan looked aggressively at Giblin from beneath his dark brow, unflinching, unblinking.

Giblin held his gaze. 'All I will say to you, Mickey, is that if you harm any one of my people, as you call them, by anything that you do, you have my word as a gentleman of honour, that I'll kill you. I hope that I am making myself clear.' There was no menacing smile; this was no empty threat. This was a statement of fact.

Duggan did not react. 'And I will tell you, Jimmy. If anyone-anyone at all – interferes with my work here, I'll kill you.'

'Glad we have reached an understanding, Mickey. I shall be wishing you a good afternoon.'

Thirteen

The anger came to him suddenly, when he was least expecting it. It had been a day with little comfort, a day when the grit of the world seemed to creep up his cheeks and scratch away at his eyes. Today was the day when they examined arrangements in the Masonic Tent, erected for the inauguration of Alexandra Road. It was immediately obvious that, of the two hundred or so masons who would gather beneath the canvas, no more than two hundred of them believed that they should be in the front row and thus presented to her Royal Highness. Many had practised their respectful bows before a mirror and were unwilling to renounce the progress they had made through such rigorous rehearsals.

Bucke surprised himself by how quickly he managed to move from mild irritation to impatience, exasperation and then on to serious annoyance. He had slammed his hand upon the unstable desk, informed the Grand Master or whatever he called himself, to sort it and to return tomorrow with a definitive list and then swept out dramatically. Let them argue about it for the rest of the day, he decided, for he did not care.

He stood outside staring at an unexpectedly blue sky, and wandered off towards the tannery on Gower Street. This was not something he would normally do, but it had been closed down, to prevent the vile stink of its work troubling the visitors, who naturally had more refined sensibilities than Swansea residents, who had long been obliged to accept it.

There were weeds pushing out of the small, uneven, wall opposite the large wooden gates of the Tannery where he sat, feeling uncomfortable and irritated. Behind those substantial gates Bucke had found the bloodstained sawdust which had shown him where Patrick Connor had been murdered. How long ago? Six months? Seven? If he hadn't been killed, would he still be selling newspapers on Temple Street? Probably, for despite his young age, his had been a vital support for an impoverished family. And what purpose had been served by the poor boy's death?

He saw Byron Midwinter in the distance, sliding along the road, then watched him disappear down Horton Street. He shouldn't have been there, that wasn't his beat, but everything felt upside in these strange days before the royal visit and Midwinter was always ready to take liberties, even in normal times. After it was over, Sergeant Ball will have to deal with the constables, thought Bucke. This sort of laxness needs to be addressed urgently; it put too much pressure on people like Gill and Turner who tried so hard to do their jobs properly.

Iago Morris came round the corner from Bellevue Street just a few yards away – someone else who shouldn't have been there. He knew that Bucke was looking straight at him and Morris had no choice but to brazen it out; retracing his steps was not an option.

'Afternoon, Inspector.'

'Yes, it is, Iago. I am surprised to see you here.'

'Following a lead, Inspector.'

'Really? I thought you were a constable? Thought you had a beat, Iago.'

Morris shrugged and seemed unsure about what to say. 'I can see what you are thinking, Inspector. And I can understand. I would have brought it to you, once I was sure.' He looked around him. 'There is something else going on in the town, Inspector. Not just the royals. Something else. Craven murdered, see. Makes the town unsettled. Heard a rumour, but I wanted to be sure.'

'And what rumour was that, Iago? You just said you were going to bring it to me. Now is your chance.' Bucke didn't think he would lie.

'It were Nick the Holly who told me. Heard noises coming from the Plume of Feathers on Wind Street. He's not the sort you would believe, ever, I admit that, but it troubled me, except I did not want it to trouble you, Inspector. I am being honest here. Believe me if you want, I don't care. But I thought I would go and have a look for myself. In case someone had a grievance against public houses,' he added lamely.

'And?'

He shrugged again. 'All locked up. Dark. No signs of a break-in. I asked around. No one else had heard anything. Some hammering the other day but no one could be sure where it came from. Could have been from any of the buildings out the back. I heard nothing but it don't mean to say there were no one inside.'

'Thank you for that. It was worth looking into, though you should have spoken to someone first. We do need to know where our constables are, no matter how unusual our current circumstances

We need to ask ourselves how reliable is Nicholas Holly and then, of course, what was he trying to hide? Had someone seen him trying to break in and he was covering his own tracks? If you have ambitions to become an inspector, then these are the questions you should be asking yourself.'

'Inspector? Me? Ridiculous idea. If you pardon my saying, Inspector, I have heard more sense from Nick the Holly. I am on the beat and I shall stay on the beat. I was told there were intruders at the Plume. I went there, saw nothing. Heard nothing. But with the royals here, turning the town upside down, I thought it best to check it out. That is all there was to it.'

'When the Prince has gone, perhaps you would like to accompany me? We can get in and see if anything untoward has been occurring. The bank is next door. They would say if they heard anything unusual.'

'If you like,' he said, diffidently.

'Thank you for your efforts, Iago. But remember. Sergeant Ball assigns you to a beat for a reason. It is not for you to decide that you know better.'

Morris grunted and turned away, and Bucke watched him slouching towards Castle Square, weighed down by whatever burden he was carrying. It was obviously a very heavy one. As he watched him, Bucke felt a sense of dread wash through his mind. There was something seriously wrong with Morris and he was fearful of how it would unfold. But there had always been a wall around Morris and now that wall seemed even taller than before.

He sighed and decided to go and look at the Plume of Feathers. Wouldn't do any harm.

*

He saw nothing that could alarm him on Wind Street, other than the remarkable absence of litter. It really did seem very unnatural. He wondered why it couldn't be like that every day. The walls, though, were still black and soot engrained. Perhaps the buildings beneath the grime were quite striking, but he had never seen them without that despairing overcoat. He walked back towards Castle Square and saw Constable Turner admiring a large ornamental clock that Mr Hennessy, the watchmaker, was hanging on a silver chain outside his premises.

'Correct to the second, that clock,' he said proudly. 'Their Royal Highnesses are bound to be impressed. They could set their own watches by that. Anyone could.'

Turner nodded his agreement as Bucke took him away, saying over his shoulder, 'I do apologise, Mr Hennessy. Important work and the Constable is required urgently.'

'Thank you, Inspector. He had so much to show me that it was likely I would be there until after the Royal party had departed. Sergeant Ball sent me to check the security of the Plume of Feathers public house but I found no signs of intrusion.'

That was interesting, thought Bucke. Stanley had sent Turner, not Morris. So why was he there? He said nothing about his own brief reconnoitre.

Bucke and Turner walked slowly down the narrow cobbles of Temple Street, which held that unwelcome memory of Patrick Connor. It was a pleasant afternoon and Bucke enjoyed the autumn sunshine that managed to penetrate the small gap between the closely packed buildings, whose roofs leaned towards each other alarmingly. It would be a relief if the royal visit could deliver such weather, though it seemed highly unlikely to him. Bucke knew it would be more realistic to expect wind, rain and a very tetchy crowd poking each other with umbrellas and expecting temporary constables to sort it all out. Temporary constables?

153

That was something he really didn't want to think about at the moment. His own constables were more deserving of his attention. When they stopped to allow a man with a handcart full of vegetables to rattle noisily down towards the market, he turned towards Turner.

'How long have you been with us now, Lemuel?'

'It isn't a quite a year yet, Inspector. I commenced my employment in December 1880, just before we had to find the camel. I have always been pleased that I started my career on a successful note. Of sorts, anyway.'

'My goodness. Is it only a year? That was quite an evening. It is not every constable that can say that they started their career in pursuit of a camel.'

Turner smiled in acknowledgement. 'I am still very grateful for the opportunity I was given that Christmas Eve. I still find the work most illuminating, Inspector. Most of the time. The occasional haunting is always welcome, too. A camel and a ghost? I had no right to expect such excitements and regretfully accept that I might never experience them again.'

'I am pleased to hear that you have found such interest in our work. A constable can be a difficult job, physically and mentally, as we both know when we consider some of our colleagues. I am sure you have seen some awful things since you began.'

Turner nodded. 'Yes. I think the worse has been when we have to pull bodies from the docks. I never like that. Seems so disrespectful to pull them from the water with a hook or a grappling iron. Many of them had enough trouble in their lives, didn't they? That is why they ended up in the dock. And then you have to drag them out, like a wooden duck in a pool at the fair. But yes, the drownings I find the worst, though I have never been that close when we have had to pull people from beneath the trains.'

'Often that is just a mess. It doesn't look like a person sometimes. It could be the body of an animal, until you see a detail like a hand or a foot. But I do know what you mean, constable.

154

There is something very undignified about pulling a body from the water. All the colour seems to have seeped out of them.' Bucke remembered the young woman whose head had been minced between propeller blades a year ago in the Swansea canal. That really was the worst of both worlds. They continued to walk along Oxford Street, nodding in response to the people who raised their hats to them. 'Always try to be positive, Lemuel, no matter how grim things might become. Always look for something that you can learn.' Bucke suddenly held his arm. 'This man here. Coming towards us. Have you met him? Patagonia Jacques? Spent his time all over the world, or so he claims. He certainly lived in South America during his travels, obviously, though he doesn't talk in any great detail about his time overseas. He is far more interested in what might once have taken place in Swansea centuries ago.'

'I don't believe I have met him up to now. I am sure I would not forget a name like that. Why do you ask, Inspector?'

'He is a very interesting man, Constable Turner. Extremely unusual, actually. Let me introduce you.'

He was using an old stick for support, for his rheumatism was insistent today. His movement was ungainly but determined. He might be impaired but he was not immobile. There was, thought Turner, a mission in his eyes, though at the moment he did not know what it might be. He was accompanied by a powerful looking man, a silent, watchful, figure who Bucke did not recognise.

'Good afternoon, Pat. How goes it?'

He looked up, his eyes wide and bright, beneath his fiercely pulled-down cap. 'Steady. Very steady, Inspector Bucke. Very close to a break-through. I can sense it. I have narrowed it down to Gower, in my own mind. It's got to be right. They didn't have no time to get it further west. Not in them days. Hardly any proper roads. Must be in Gower. I am sure of it.' He clenched his free fist with determination. It appeared leathered by hard work.

'I wish you luck, Pat. It will be a remarkable achievement, if you can find it.'

'I told you. Very close. Couple of places in Gower look very promising, Course, there is nothing written down. If it was on paper it has all gone, rotted. But someone knew. They must have said something. That is how I shall find it. You can see that, can't you? There is a family out there that knows for certain, I am sure of it. Been telling each other the story on them dark winter's nights ever since, I shouldn't wonder, and it is all piled up at the back of a barn or beneath the roof. No reports anywhere of it ever being seen, are there, Inspector? You'd tell me, wouldn't you?'

'Pat. This is a new constable of ours. Constable Turner,' said Bucke. Turner nodded respectfully. 'I am sure he will be most fascinated to learn of your work.' He turned to the constable. 'This is Mr Horace Jacques. He is busy most days in the library, carrying out research. It is an unexpected hobby but one with enormous potential.'

'More than a hobby, inspector,' said Jacques. 'It has become my life's work.' He looked over his shoulder to check that no one was listening to him on the busy street. 'You might not know this, constable, but the treasure of Edward II, King of England, went missing in Swansea over five hundred years ago and I intend to find it. And I am almost there. I am sure of it.'

'*Buenos tardes, Senor Jacques. ¿Cómo estás hoy?*'

Jacques looked at him suspiciously. 'Fair to middling, sonny. Why do you ask?'

Turner ignored his question. 'Your work sounds very interesting, Mr Jacques. I have studied the fourteenth century, though very briefly, and I have certainly not given it the attention that it deserves, unlike yourself. If I can be of any help, I would be only too pleased. You see, as far as I am concerned, the mistake Edward II made was sending his treasure ahead to Swansea without adequate protection. Asking for trouble, I should say, at any time in history. No wonder it went missing. There is a lesson here for us all, I think, Mr Jacques, isn't there? Royal visits to Swansea never seem to go very well, do they?' he said brightly. 'We must hope for better. But what do you think, Mr Jacques? Did Edward II die at the hands of torturers with a red-hot poker? Or

156

are you a supporter of the notion that he escaped and died in a monastery in northern Italy? Not quite so dramatic, is it?'

He chose not to answer straight away, assessing Turner very carefully. 'I did think for a long time that it might be Cilibion I should be looking at,' he said. Then there was another long pause. 'But then I started to wonder about Landimore.'

'Hmm,' said Turner thoughtfully. 'Landimore? Could make sense. You see, Inspector, that's another great puzzle, as Mr Jacques will know. Who actually built the grand house at Landimore? Where did that family's wealth come from? A significant question that one. You could be on to something. Mr Jacques. The treasure of Edward II? A fascinating mystery. I wish I had the time.'

Jacques looked at him. 'Your eyes good enough? I reckon they must be better than mine. You'll do. If you want to help, come down to the library. I am there most afternoons. Give the lad some time off, Inspector. He needs to be helping me, not following enquiries about unfit meat, or whatever it is you make him do.' He took a few steps and then leaned on his stick and turned back to Turner. 'It is out there somewhere. I am sure of it. Hoping to start digging soon, if the weather gets better.'

'I would be happy to help in any way I can, though, naturally, my duties as a constable take up most of my time. Perhaps we can arrange something once the royal visit has successfully concluded? I would look forward to it.'

Jacques grunted and then nodded at Bucke. He appraised Turner again for a moment.

'Just one thing Mr Jacques, if I may,' asked Turner politely. 'Perhaps you can help me. You are a very well-travelled man, as I understand it and you obviously speak Spanish. But I wonder whether, during your time overseas, you have ever come across a place called Aucaman? Might be a river, or a volcano or...'

'Never heard of it,' he said abruptly. 'Look. Here is Irvine's cousin, Aoife, come to fetch us home, I'll be bound.' He pointed at the smiling young woman walking towards them.

'Uncle Horace, 'tis time for your tea,' she said. 'Time to be home for a rest after all that learning.'

'Whatever you say,' said Jacques.

She smiled brightly at the other men. 'Sorry, constable for the interruption and yourself, sir…'

'Constable Turner, miss,' he said. 'And this is Inspector Bucke of the Swansea Constabulary.'

Aoife looked at Bucke a little longer than politeness allowed. 'I am pleased to meet you, sir. The world speaks very highly of you.' She smiled pleasantly.

'These buggers is seeing me home,' announced Jacques abruptly. He looked hard into Turner's eyes. Then his nephew, the silent man, took his arm and hurried him away. He did not seem ready to accommodate Jacques's limp. After a few yards Aoife turned and smiled at them both once more.

Bucke watched, curious about this apparently unsympathetic relative that Jacques had produced. Something to think about, he thought. He looked at Turner, impressed. 'You handled that well, Lemuel. You could have made a friend for life there.'

He nodded thoughtfully. 'He certainly understood what I asked him in Spanish, so he does have some experience of the language, though we don't know how much. It doesn't prove anything, I know that, but it was important to know. I don't think we can doubt that he has been overseas, though there are many languages in use in Patagonia as I understand it, even Welsh, so the Spanish isn't conclusive evidence of residency there.'

They saw Jacques stumble and then the rough handling he received from his nephew that kept him upright. They were walking much too briskly, for the nephew seemed very eager to put a distance between himself and the police. That was interesting, thought Bucke.

'The thing is, Horace is a lonely old man and there are plenty of people who would like to help him spend his money, after either discovering or deciding that they are so happily related. Like that nephew of his we have just met. Who is he? Who knows?'

Turner looked at Bucke quizzically. 'Is there something else I should know, Inspector?'

Bucke nodded. 'You might not realise it, Constable Turner, but you have been speaking to probably the richest man in Swansea.'

'Really? But he dresses like a tramp.'

'That's Horace Jacques for you, though everyone calls him Patagonia Jacques. Made a fortune building railroads in South America, they say. Horace lives frugally, I think that is the word, in a small damp house up on Mount Pleasant. And pleasant it certainly isn't. He eats yesterday's bread because it is cheaper and regards butter as a waste of money. He wears old clothes, as you can see, and only buys a chop for his tea if he can haggle about the price. Oh yes, Horace is a miserable old miser, and yet he has far more money than anyone you are ever likely to meet. And he spends all day reading things he does not understand in the Free Library because he believes that untold wealth lies buried in Gower. Soon it will be within his grasp, or so he thinks.'

'If the treasure of the king did ever get as far as Swansea, it will never have survived. They would have melted it down. No different then, than they are today, Inspector. It is foolish to think otherwise. Although I think it is important to Mr Jacques that you always agree with what he says. I don't expect he allows people to disagree with him, not when he is as clearly fixated as he is.'

Bucke smiled. 'I am sure that yours is the most likely explanation, But I can tell you now, that Horace will never accept it.'

'Oh yes, I can see that. He is an obsessive old man and that is a very difficult species for anyone to deal with, whoever they are. But to acquire a fortune in South America in general and Patagonia in particular isn't impossible. It has a reputation as a very lawless place.'

'It would be interesting to learn where his money came from, and where it is. Left Swansea under a bit of a cloud they say. But Horace does concern me, because I think he is a felony waiting to happen and without more information there isn't much I can do to prevent it.'

'There is that old man, what is he called? Iestyn? The one who rants in the street. Isn't he shouting about a man called Horace? Accusing him of murder?'

'That's the one, Lemuel. It is all a long time ago, though. Not sure how we can ever unravel it. But he won't let it go. I have warned him, but there is no knowing what he might do when the Prince is here.'

Turner paused for a moment. 'You can't escape what has happened in the past, can you? It is always there.' He thought of his mother. 'You will always have it with you. It has made us what we are. For better, and for worse.'

*

At home on the other side of town, the evening was calm and peaceful and Turner was able to spend some time examining maps and his gazetteer, although with no success.

He could find no place - village, town, province - called Aucaman, no trace at all. Of course, that didn't mean anything really, he knew that. It could be a small insignificant village, somewhere on a sand bank on a mosquito-ridden Malaysian delta, where no one would linger. He didn't think that was likely, when he thought about it a bit more. He could not dismiss the idea, but he felt he was looking on the wrong continent. South America? Why not? That is what the sound of the word suggested to him. And so in the absence of any evidence at all, he constructed a picture in his own head, like an illustration in one of Ballantyne's Tales of Adventure that he had loved so much as a boy. Life had been so much simpler then, with nothing to interrupt those immersive imaginative games and dreams that had sustained him. And now? He used those bright images in his head to sustain his mother, an adventurer and a beauty, suddenly washed up and exhausted on the beach of old age.

This evening, when he helped her into bed, he realised how tired she was. She smiled at him wearily and then took his hand. 'Where are we going today. Lemuel? Take me away from the dirty

160

smoke and the endless rain and the cold that prevents me from moving. Please. Lemuel.' She patted the eiderdown and Vasco jumped on to the bed. He loved story time as much as she did.

Lemuel Turner looked at her with gentle love. 'Tonight we are in our boat again, travelling somewhere far, far away. We have done it before, of course we have. It is calm, peaceful, beautiful. Father loves this place. Who could be surprised? We would have lived her forever, too, if it wasn't for father's trains. But no matter where we went, Aucaman would always call us back.' He leaned closer to his mother, dropping his voice and watching her eyes close and that dream of a lost time of happiness, embrace her as a smile flickered across her lips.

'Look, Momma. The sky is blue, the sea is blue and the sails on our boat are perfectly white. Vasco is sitting in the bow, looking at the small village at the heart of the bay in front of us. It is surrounded by palm trees swaying gently in that refreshing breeze. Can you feel it? It cools us after a long day in the sun. To the left there is a large green mountain. It might once have been a volcano. But all is quiet and peaceful now. We can see a small wooden jetty and Vasco can see it too. He barks and you smooth his ears back, so he wags his tail vigorously. You know he is ready to jump into the sea and swim to the shore. But not yet, Vasco. Not yet. Let us get a little closer.' He gently raised the blanket up to his mother's chin. 'Look at those white houses,' he said. 'They are so bright. Look at the birds swooping and crying. People are coming out on to the jetty to see us. You mustn't worry, they speak Portuguese here. Father waves to them because he is happy to be here. They know him and are pleased that he has returned. But of course he has, for this is one of his favourite places and these are his friends. This is Aucaman. It is so beautiful. Can you see it, Momma? Can you hear the water slapping gently against the hull?'

'Where is Aucaman, Lemuel? Tell me.' His mother was drifting elegantly, as always, towards a distant shore.

'It is the most beautiful village in Brazil and we are there, just the three of us and Vasco, and we have never been anywhere like it. The people here are your friends and they love you. This is paradise. And it is ours. No one else knows about it and you and father can stay here in our own simple house on the shore and every day I will sit beneath the trees and write and you and father will walk up into the green forest on the mountain to pick wild fruit and to play with Vasco beneath waterfalls. Here you know that you are free; you can do anything.' And as the imaginary sun soothed her ancient limbs, Turner watched his mother drift effortlessly into these invented memories.

Turner sat back and looked at his beautiful mother trapped in a damaged shell, sleeping calmly, regretting that his mind could not relax in the same sort of way. He was driven to find things out; he could never rest if he didn't know. And he didn't know about Aucamen and it was troubling him greatly.

Why did Aucamen have to be a place, he wondered? It could be anything. A mountain, a river, anything. A person, even. But that didn't matter a great deal tonight. Tomorrow he would take his mother on a walk through this paradise and he would lead the way and then turn to see her and his father holding hands. He smiled. She would like that, he knew she would.

Fourteen

Constable Turner came away from his afternoon in the library, both puzzled and excited. Inspector Bucke had released him temporarily from his duties so that he could help Patagonia Jacques, in the hope that he might then find out a little more about the accusations being levelled at him by Iestyn Pugh. It had been a futile exercise.

Try as he might, and credit to him, he had tried, all Turner had seen was the dismal sadness of old age. Later, he viewed it with an intense and surprising sense of relief, for it was from all this that his father had been spared when he died suddenly and too soon. He missed his father most days, his calm demeanour, his intelligence and his considerable practical skills, but perhaps it had been for the best. There had been no long decline, neither confusion nor obsession, and his mother would always remember him in his prime, for she never saw anything else. He never became an old man and was never thus a danger to those around him or to himself.

Turner saw with absolute clarity that poor Patagonia Jacques was obsessed, desperate to untangle lost secrets from the past, as if the past could solve the present, to ensure for himself a famous future and simplify the complex world in which he now lived. But this fixation would never make him young again. Nothing could do that; and nothing would ever uncover the lost treasure of Edward II. It had left no discernible trace in the Swansea historical record and it was likely that any trail had already disappeared by the time someone noticed that chest full of jewels wasn't where they had left it.

Turner had tried to help Jacques but help wasn't what he wanted; all he required was nothing other than agreement and blind obedience. Jacques certainly had no intention of permitting his assumptions to be questioned. His research methods, Turner could see, were haphazard and illogical. On the basis of a sketchy eighteenth century map of an ordinary boggy field at the far end of Gower called Bessie's Meadow, he told his nephew Sellars, his constant companion and, it seemed, his guardian, to buy a shovel. Sellars clearly had an antipathy to policemen but even he took time out from his hostility to roll his eyes and shake his head in Turner's direction in a search for sympathy. For his part, Turner had no clue at all why Jacques had reached this sudden decision, but then neither did Patagonia Jacques.

Constable Turner knew he was wasting his time, even though he was still hopeful that some useful information might emerge, but his mind was wandering and he started to give half his attention to volumes that he discreetly pulled from the shelves. And that is when he found it. A simple thing. A fact, that was all; not a guess or a supposition, but a fact, the sort of thing that eluded Patagonia Jacques on a daily basis - and it changed everything.

*

Back at the police station, Bucke sat down with James Flynn in the quiet of one of the cells. They were confident that they would not be disturbed for a while, and confident too, that they could not be overheard. Flynn was unhappy because he was making no progress at all with the murder of Fred Craven but, as he said, everything relied upon someone seeing something and no one had, as far as he knew. But now Colonel Grey had managed to unsettle them both by a suggestion that there was probably an informer somewhere in the police station. It was how these people worked, he said, gathering trivial details and then putting them together to make something important. It was presented to them as if this was a radical and dangerous idea, but Bucke certainly knew that this was exactly how Grey's own team operated, for he had seen the body from the cart on the Strand.

They quickly dismissed the idea that the informer might be Evan Davies. He couldn't carry a hand-written message in a bucket from one end of the street to another. But the other constables? It came as some surprise that they realised it could be any one of them, though they both felt it was unlikely to be Turner, and, if it was, they had no hope of catching him out.

'I shall be glad when this royal palaver is over,' said Flynn, 'and we can get back to some proper police work. It is all a bit too underhand for me. Not trusting anyone, thinking everything you have been told is a lie.' He scratched his scalp vigorously.

'I know what you mean, James. But there is something going on. We both know that.'

'Aye, Rumsey. Hard to fathom. And there are too many strangers in Little Ireland and that's a fact. And what are they doing? That is the question.'

'There is only one thing that could have brought them here. That is this visit. And I can't imagine they are here to wave an adoring handkerchief at the noble Prince,' said Bucke.

'Identifying them is the problem. Rumsey. I spoke to Josiah Padley, as you know. He has seen them but then so have I. Hanging round in groups and then scurrying away. But there are too many places for them to hide and too many folk ready to hide them.'

'Without more information there isn't much we can do, James. I can't lock up everyone on Greenhill. It is not as if we have many of our own informers up there, is it?'

'Only Padley, and he is as trustworthy as a rat in a sack.'

Bucke sighed and leaned his head back against the wall. 'Something is up. Something is happening. And it has to be that they are planning to do harm in one way or another. It is obvious. That is why Grey is here, that's obvious. But we can't police the streets and the visit and launch a raid on Greenhill. We don't have the constables to do everything. But I will tell you something, James. Colonel Grey knows all this. And it doesn't seem to trouble him in any way. And so I think, between the two of us, that Grey wants something to happen, so that he can flush out the Fenians.'

Flynn sucked in his teeth. 'Dangerous, to my way of thinking. You can never tell who will get hurt.'

'It bothers me, too. All we can do is make sure the constables are visiting Greenhill so that it all appears normal and then I need to have a word with Jimmy Giblin.'

'Don't do it on the hill, Rumsey. Wait until he comes down

165

into town. It feels a bit dangerous up there right now.'

Flynn was called to deal with two boys who had been stealing carrots in the market and so Bucke stayed in the cell on his own for a little longer, trying to clear his head, as much as he could. There were so many things in there, and as fast as he removed something so that he could concentrate more clearly on the royal visit, another concern would push to the front of the lengthy queue in his mind, demanding attention.

He tried as hard as he could, but he couldn't get Rhys Price, Dai as they called him, out of his mind. He had, all too briefly, been a colleague who had never had enough time to establish proper relationships with the rest of the police station, apart from Morris who already knew him. But Bucke had always thought that something wasn't quite right, even from the start, when he thought about it. Price had naturally been nervous, starting a new job, but it had been more than that. There was something unspoken, he was sure of it. If he had known him better he could have asked and, well, who could say what might have been avoided? There was something else, too. He couldn't say what it was, but he had an instinctive feeling that something important was hiding inside that terrible tragedy. How often does a young and devoted father thrown himself at a speeding train?

Sergeant Ball pushed open the door of the cell. 'Had a message from the Dock superintendent. That pal of yours brought it. Jack Dawes. He told me that there is another sailor in Swansea who was on the *Para* with Rhys Price. Dai Hughes, but known as Dai Lingo. Thought you'd want to know.'

'Do we know him, Stanley?'

'Not a sailor who has come our way, as I can remember.'

'A collector's item then.'

'He's on the *Maidstone Lily*, South Dock. Sailing tomorrow, so you best be quick.'

Bucke nodded. 'I will find him. Dai Hughes, you say?'

'Ask for Dai Lingo. That is how they all know him, I am told. Speaks English, Welsh and Spanish, see.

'Obviously.'

Evan Davies had already propped himself against the counter and nodded cheerfully at Bucke as he left the station. Most evenings, when Sergeant Ball took his long walk home, he would reflect on how it could be that Evan Davies always managed to be there, his elbow leaning on the counter, appearing, so it seemed, as if from nowhere. Stanley Ball would think, 'I haven't seen Davies for a while. Perhaps he is doing some work.' And then, instantly, he would be there. It was unsettling but Ball realised why, for his mother's ambition for her son was what she saw as the clean and unthreatening position of desk sergeant. If it was the job that he wanted, then why shouldn't it be his? As a dutiful son, he understood without a doubt that the job would inevitably, one day, be his alone, as his mother had ordained. Thus the counter in Tontine Street was the magnet to which he was always drawn, by a force which he could not resist, so that he could rehearse his future glory..

'Shouldn't you be out on your beat then, Constable Davies?'

'All quiet, Stanley. Think I have got the place under control.'

Ball was thinking seriously about putting Davies on duty further away from Tontine Street. 'The Roe shouting anything interesting today? Anything I should know about?'

Davies shook his head. 'Very quiet today. Well, when I say quiet, he was shouting. About that Prince of Wales fella. But I told him straight. Soon shut him up then, didn't I? No one is harpooning the Prince on my beat, so Roe had best look out. Doesn't know what he is talking about. Harpooning Wales? I ask you. It is a wonder he sells any newspapers at all. Quiet here, today, Stanley,' he added, looking around him wisely, assessing his future domain.

Ball started to search haphazardly in the drawer beneath the counter.

'Me bowels are grutching something terrible today, Stan.' He screwed up his face. 'Worms.'

Ball opened another drawer, paying as little attention to Davies as he could get away with. 'Make sure your mother cooks your pork properly, that's my advice.'

'Mothers, eh?' He enjoyed sharing conversations like this with Sergeant Ball. He looked around the empty police station and nodded again. 'Inspector Bucke's gone to look for a Dai then, has he? Lot of Dai's about, if you ask me. You see, it is what I don't understand, like. See, my cousin is called Dai Killapig because that is what he does. You lives up Bonymaen, you wants your pig killing, you sends for our Dai. Everyone knows. Collects all the blood in one of them buckets. No waste. And his brother is called Byron Bacon, see. Don't understand that.'

'What don't you understand?' asked Sergeant Ball, against his better judgement.

'Well like, Byron is called Byron Bacon because my mam says he cures the pig. But how can you cure a pig, that's dead? I mean all its blood is in a tin bath with a fire underneath it. To be honest, Stan, I do worry about Mam sometimes. And I shall watch her with the pork from now on, as you said.'

*

'You were in the army, I've heard.' Hughes was a confident man because, as Bucke realised, he had nothing to hide. He'd never had any dealings with the police and so had no occasion to lie to them or, indeed, to anyone. He was sitting on a barrel on the deck, working carefully on a length of rope. A weathered man, a leathered man, with skin stained by sun and wind, but with bright blue eyes. A seagull squawked in the rigging above and then flapped away when Hughes waved his hand casually towards it. There was a controlled strength about him, a reassurance. His confident hands, calloused and worn, seemed to have a skilled strength as he manipulated the stiff, recalcitrant, rope. If Bucke was ever going to be cast adrift in a rowing boat in the open sea, he would want Dai Lingo with him, he thought. He hadn't been difficult to find; everyone seemed to know him; everyone seemed to smile when they heard his name. 'Where did you serve?' he asked, gently unkinking twists in the rope.

168

'In India, Mr Hughes. Northwest Frontier.'

Dai Lingo nodded. 'And so you saw action? Fighting? Death? Of course you did. You don't look like a pen-pusher to me.'

'I saw some difficult things. Had some bad experiences, but that is life as a soldier. Had some good times too.'

'But you don't talk about some of it, do you? Left that behind in India, didn't you? Don't like to remind yourself, let alone tell folk about it. We all do it.' Bucke said nothing. 'You see, Inspector. I've been a sailor for thirty years now. Started when I was a lad. And I seen lots of things I don't talk about. Just between me and the sea, they are. Same for you, same for all of us. Folk don't need to know some of the things you saw, or what I saw. That's ours. No business of anyone else. And so we leave it be.' He worked the stiff rope between his hands. 'But some things we have to remember, don't we? Can't not remember them, if you see what I mean. Especially if it involves someone else. And sometimes we have to talk about things that have happened, don't we? To the right person.'

Hughes now put the end of the rope under his foot and stretched it. 'So sometimes we do talk, if we are troubled, if it is eating away at us. And I reckon that is why you are here.' He stretched the rope once more. 'But you see, if folk start asking me about a Sailor's Law or the Custom of the Sea and they do, don't doubt it, I never reply. Cus I don't have to. Because they have not been there and they do not know what it is like. And that means they might not understand.' Hughes lay the rope across his thighs. He shrugged, 'But you are a copper and you have a right to ask questions. So, yes, I was with Rhys Price. There were others there, but we were the only two from Swansea, see, and at a time like that on the ice? Well, it creates a bond. It has to. You go through a lot together. Can't pretend it never happened, any of it. And there are always times when it wakes you up in the night.'

Bucke didn't interrupt, ready to let him talk. He watched Hughes produce a sharp knife and trim threads from the rope. The boat shifted slightly on its mooring and Bucke heard it creak.

169

'But I can tell you something. There was no crime. I 'd swear on the Bible. Fetch me one and I will do it now, if it is important to you. Yes, a man died. Poor bugger fell through the ice and we pulled him out – almost lost Dai Price too, he nearly got pulled in. Oh yes, we got the man out. But we couldn't warm him up. Couldn't keep him awake. So we lost him and we were still stuck on the ice. That was all we could see. Just ice. No mountains or hills or anything. Just ice, no matter which way you looked. Flat. No people, no houses, no nothing. Just ice. Hard and sharp and evil. It hated us. All of us. That is what I will always remember. There was nothing to look at, nothing at all, apart from the birds circling and calling, waiting for you to fall. Everything looking flat, but it wasn't, and white and heartless, stretching out away from us, forever. And we wanted to get off. My god, we wanted to get off. We had to walk. But we had nothing to eat. What are you to do? How can you get off that ice if you have nothing to eat? You can't light a fire; you can't dry your clothes. You crawl under the boat that you have dragged forever and you hold on to each other tight for the warmth and you feel ashamed and you want to be dead but you know you have to stay alive. And so there is something you have to do.' Hughes stared at the rope and then slapped it loudly against the deck. 'We didn't kill him. He was our shipmate. But he gave himself to us, to help us get home. It is called The Custom of the Sea.' He paused again. 'Shall we leave it like that, Inspector? There was no crime. But it is a story from the ice and that is where it stays. Not going off to see his wife am I and tell her? Why would she need to know? Your husband? He's dead, but we enjoyed a nice bit of shoulder?' Hughes shook his head and then he pulled his hands down over his face, as it drawing a curtain in front of those memories. 'That is why it was his last trip. That is why he went for to be a police constable.'

'And this was a man, was it? This man who fell through the ice. Not a boy?'

'A grown man. Bosun. Bristol he was from. We crewed together, drank together. But no, he wasn't a boy.'

'I see.'

170

'First time for most of us – and the last, please God. But Price reckoned he'd done it before. He didn't explain, just said he'd been trapped before. Reckoned he was unlucky like that. Took it badly. Very quiet, even when we were picked up. Couldn't shake it off.' Hughes sighed and closed his eyes briefly. 'You see, there is all them old stories. You know, if your body is destroyed you'll never get into heaven. That is why they dissected them who'd they'd hanged in the old days. No body, no afterlife. Some still dwell on that. But to be honest, it doesn't trouble you much when you are already living in hell.'

'And so when Price said he'd done it before, he didn't say when or where?'

'On the ice somewhere.' He shrugged. 'Could be north, could be south. He never said, properly. There is ice everywhere. There was one day I remember when I thought he were going to say something important. You see, I asked, why he was called Dai. Didn't make no sense to me that his mates called him Dai. I mean, I am Dai because I am David.'

Bucke raised his eyebrows, encouraging Hughes to go on. 'He told me other people had started to call him Dai, it weren't his choice but it isn't short for David. As I remember it, he started to tell me and then stopped. Backed away from it, so I thought I'd give him time. Tell me when he was ready. But that never happened, did it? But I have always thought that were important to him. That there was something he needed to say. But he didn't.' He started to coil the rope, inspecting it as he went along its length. 'He was a good shipmate. One of the best. Was doing everything for his wife and his kids. Proper bloke. But troubled, yes. But I never thought he would do what they've said he did. The Rhys Price I knew when we were out on the ice wouldn't have done what he did to his wife. and you get to know a man out there, and he was not that kind. He talked about her all the time. So yes, Inspector. I was shocked. That's not the man I knew, and I knew him better than most, as I said.' He paused and looked out to sea. He didn't speak for a while and Bucke thought it best to leave. Suddenly he spoke. 'When you eat with a man, you get to know him,' and he laughed hollowly and seagulls cried on the wind.

'Tell me something, Mr Hughes. 'Aucaman.' Does that mean anything to you?'

Hughes shook his head. 'Should it?'

'It doesn't mean anything to you? You sure?' persisted Bucke.

'Name of a place, is it? Not a place I ever heard of and I've been a few places in my time.' He shrugged. 'What language is it? If it is Spanish, then I have never heard it. Is it Portuguese? I have had no reason to learn Portuguese. Or Italian for that matter.'

'Wondered if you knew of some kind of connection, that's all.'

Hughes shook his head, then stood up and put the coiled rope into a wooden chest. 'I think about poor Rhys quite a lot. There is a deal of thinking time when you are in the harbour. Find out what happened, Inspector. Put poor Rhys to rest. He was a good sort. If he had some trouble in his mind that meant only killing his wife could set him free, well I just wished he had said something. I didn't know about it. We had bad times together but I don't understand what he did. He told me when we were out on the ice that he loved his wife, and a man don't often say that to another man unless he means it.'

Bucke walked away from the dock lost in his thoughts, barely acknowledging those who wished him a good afternoon. He hadn't known Rhys Price particularly well, but he couldn't get him out of his mind. Eventually he stopped at the bottom of the Strand and stood against the reassuring stone of the large Colonial Buildings. He really didn't have time for this. He should be concentrating on the Royal visit. But there were things that were troubling him.

Storms happened inside other people's heads. He knew this. He had had his own dark times, and he knew that he had been trapped in terrifying, dark cellars of loneliness, but he could never have spoken about it. Not to anyone. It wasn't what you did. You were a man and so you remained silent and suffered. And he knew that it was only through speech that someone else would ever know what was inside your head. There was no window, other

172

than words.

Rhys Price had said nothing at all as far as he knew. Everyone said they were shocked when he murdered the wife he loved and then took his own life. But why should he say anything at all? He might have believed that he had finally discovered the truth about the pointlessness of his life. Why should he feel the need to share that with someone else? Particularly if it was the truest idea he had ever had.

But Bucke was not convinced. It didn't add up. Oh yes, it was convenient to say that the balance of Price's mind had been disturbed. It might be convenient, but that did not make it true. Why had he killed Molly? Why? Bucke could not let it go. Something wasn't right, he knew it. And, they said, his spirit had been unable to find the peace he sought.

Instinct wasn't enough; it never was, and he had work to do. There was the heir to the throne to protect and that was far more important than an unquiet grave.

He pushed himself away from the solid permanence of the stone wall, and surveyed The Strand. It was quiet, too early to be a problem. The door of the Troubadour was open and Marie Matthews was brushing the old stained sawdust on to the street. She waved at him cheerily and he saw a once-pretty face now lined by unforgiving work and poverty. Would the Prince see the same thing when he arrived at Singleton Abbey, he wondered?

There was a dry screech of metal against metal and he turned to see a dirty, leaking steam engine roll slowly and breathlessly along the long curve that led from Quay Parade onto the North Dock, a childish but patriotic plume of feathers attached to the side of the cab. And a young man he knew had chosen a monstrous machine like that, massive and hard and sightless, under which to end his life, surrounded, as he remembered the reports, by fragments from a splintered wheel barrow. It was a mundane, inconsequential detail, but one which, for Bucke, seemed to be mocking a terrible crisis of life and death in this dark and indifferent town.

At the other end of the Strand, Iago Morris was also leaning against a wall, thinking. But he was waiting for someone, a man he hadn't seen for a few years now. An old colleague with whom he had shared the sort of experiences that brought men together, for things had happened that no one could ever be expected to forget.

'What's going on, Arthur?' There were no pleasantries. They were not needed.

'Pleased to see you, too. I have just got out of Dartmoor. Least you could do is ask me how I am.'

Fifteen

'Morning, Lardy!' shouted the workmen on the other side of Neath Road, laughing and waving. They always waved; they always laughed. What a card he was!

Hamish waved back and laughed dutifully as, it seemed, he was always required to do and then carried on walking to the copper works. It was one of the consequences of being a character, always being expected to behave in exactly the same way, no matter what the circumstances. It was his duty to be predictable, to be 'good old Lardy,' even when he didn't feel like it. And how had this happened, he asked himself? It was simple, of course. He had a past full of different experiences which had brought him no benefits at all. How were the mighty fallen, indeed. He knew he would never be regarded as anything other than a comic figure to those who knew him. Hamish Darr, the son of a Scottish Equerry to Prince Albert, forever known as 'Lardy' Darr, who had indeed fallen so very, very far.

A rebellious, wandering life had brought him to Swansea and his new circumstances had then taken him to the copper works as a labourer. His colleagues knew the barest details of his background, but all that really mattered was that once he had been posh and now he was not, just one of them. Not a foreman; not a puddler; just a labourer. His life, his fall from wealth and comfort, was a joke that never ever wore thin for those who had been born poor and would forever remain so, and he had played along, for what choice did he have? If he knew a way out of this complete mess his life had become, then he would have taken it already. But until such an exit turned up, he laughed and joked, and sang music hall songs for his workmates.

He didn't feel much like laughing today, though. There had been a noted pushed under the draughty door of his room on Martin Street in Morriston. It was in his pocket and he wasn't sure whether he wanted to read it again. He could throw it in the canal on the way to work and never see it again, if he wanted. But could

175

he do that without reading it one last time? He wasn't sure, but he was alongside the canal for the next few hundred yards so he had time to decide.

Where had the message come from? How did they know? Had someone talked? He did not think that was likely. The note was like a weight in his pocket, heavy with guilt and remorse, banging against his long leg.

He was a tall man, much taller than most others in the Vivian Copper Works. He had short and carefully parted hair that was fair - when it was clean – and wide blue eyes and a permanent smirk, it seemed. Sometimes, at the end of a shift or after a particularly tiresome joke, the contempt that flashed across his face, showed that he was brought up in very different circumstances. Not everyone saw it, but it unsettled those who did.

Lardy Darr. One of the few people in the history of Swansea to lose money running a pub. Like everything else in his life, it had been a disaster. All the money he had, all the money he had brought back with him, had been invested in the purchase of the Plume of Feathers on Wind Street and he had watched his investment drain away like stale beer emptied on to grass. He hadn't known that the ownership of the pub was a matter of some dispute within the family who had managed it previously, or that the man who sold it to him for cash had no right to do so. When Hamish heard that he had disappeared with the money, he laughed and laughed. It was what he would have done himself. It was just another moment to go alongside his mother disowning him, his disinheritance by his father and the myriad smaller miseries that pursued him wherever he went.

His leg had started to ache again so he paused on the bank of the canal, its black water carrying a film of grease or oil, and there was a smell of rotten wood rising from it. Hamish remembered that a man had drowned in here last week. Fell in when drunk. He shook his head at the idea of submerging in that liquid filth. He decided that if he were to throw the note in the water it was very likely to float and stare at him every time he passed. He'd burn it in the furnace, that would be safer.

He was compelled to look at it again. He pulled it from his pocket. It was an unremarkable piece of brown paper. He turned it around in his hand. Perhaps it had been torn from a paper bag. It was coarse but, because of that, the pencil had found purchase on the rough surface and left a clear and unmistakeable mark. He spoke the word aloud, for there was no one to hear him.

'*Aucaman.*'

That is all it said. Just that one word. But what a word, one that carried enormous significance. Who knew? And why had they sent it to him? He wasn't a fanciful person, but as he stood there by the side of that poisonous canal, he wondered if, in some way, he was haunted, whether this, in fact, was a message from beyond the grave. A ridiculous idea. But he had to acknowledge that it had unsettled him. Who could he talk to about it? Eliza? She would listen, but she wouldn't pretend to understand. Couldn't go and see Fred Craven anymore, could he? Just showed you how dangerous the life of a publican could be. And he couldn't go and see Dai Price either. The life of a policeman was dangerous too, when you thought about it.

And then the implications of those thoughts suddenly struck home. Fred Craven was dead. Dai was dead. A coincidence? Did coincidences like that really happen? He didn't think so. And so he had to speak to someone else. It might be a risk, when you considered what had happened, but in the circumstances did he have a choice?

He'd think about it at work, make a decision later. He rubbed his thigh vigorously. Sometimes the old wound ached terribly. Today wasn't a good day, but there was nothing he could do to ease it.

It was a hard morning. Hamish was unsettled and anxious and all he could hear between the infernal hissing and the hammering was 'Lardy this' and 'Lardy that' and he could feel that his permanent smirk was wearing particularly thin. It was hot and the other men seemed to move around in the orange light like demons, their leather waistcoats, dripping with the sweat not captured by those dirty scarves tied around their necks, shining like polished breast plates. Would this be his life, for eternity? Don't be stupid, he said to himself. Another couple of weeks. Something will turn up; it always does.

There seemed to be a new man there. He wasn't part of the shift as far as he knew, but men came and went all the time. That was normal. But there was something about him that he was sure he recognised. He didn't know where from and it irritated Hamish because he never managed to get a proper look at him. He was always moving around, not doing much if truth be told, but never still long enough for Hamish to get a proper look. A short man, powerful-looking, apparently silent.

The men took a break in the corner next to one of the furnaces. The overseer wasn't there and they needed water anyway. This was hot work and some of the men habitually put salt in their water. Made them feel better, they said. He thought he might try it, but not today. Hamish was unsettled, uneasy. This had not been a good day at all. He couldn't see the new man and took his jug of water with him as he wandered around, trying to find the unsettling stranger. There was something about him he didn't like. Might be something. Might be nothing. But this stranger fitted well into this very worrying day he was experiencing. At least it was an early shift. When it was over he could go down to the Strand, see if he could find Eliza. Or Lizzie. She was quite nice, too.

'Come on. Lardy! Sing us a song!' called one of the men over by the furnace.

Hamish pretended not to hear him and walked around by the side of a vat of copper. He needed to sit quietly and rest his leg for a moment. He felt the puckered skin on his thigh and looked at a plank someone had laid across the vat, along which some of them would run, allegedly to save time, but really as an act of bravado. Stupid idea. Why would you do that? He ought to move it. It was a couple of feet above the molten metal and if it wasn't moved soon, it would burst into flames. They always did. Perhaps he should let someone else do that. He couldn't face it. No matter how long you worked here, you never properly adjusted to the ferocious heat. When you went outside, whatever the weather, you shivered. He took a drink of water. Lizzie Thomas was the best idea he had had today.

Suddenly he received a tremendous blow to the side of the head from behind. He was confused and disorientated and a strong hand pushed a rag deep into his mouth. He tried to spit it out but it seemed to have been already tied in place. He couldn't focus; everything seemed to be spinning around. He wasn't sure whether he was standing up or sitting down and he couldn't move his arms at all. And then there was a voice, a vicious disembodied whisper in his ear, that seemed to come from nowhere.

'Yes. Come on, Lardy! Sing us a song! Oh, sorry. You can't, can you? Never mind.'

He tried to push out the gag with his tongue but he couldn't and he realised that there was now a rope around him that pinioned his arms to his side. He couldn't manage to turn his head to see who it was, but suddenly Hamish knew; without a doubt, he knew who was behind him and who was dragging him roughly to the hoist at the side of the vat of molten copper.

'Told you I would come for you, didn't I? Well, I am here.'

And Hamish knew what was going to happen and there was nothing that he could do. He was struggling frantically now, desperately trying to scream. His terror had destroyed any semblance of co-ordination. All, however, was futile. Those screams coming from the very centre of his soul remained unheard. In spite of his panic and his terror, he saw the iron beam, he saw the pulley, he saw the chain, each with terrible clarity.

The man pushed the hook at the end of the iron chain through the rope that pinioned him and then hoisted Hamish into the air and swung the beam to which it was attached, over the copper and its vicious volcanic turmoil.

Slowly, methodically, he lowered Hamish Darr into it and the sight of his incinerating body was immediately hidden by the spitting horror of the erupting copper as it consumed him. As soon as he judged the rope had burnt away, he pulled up the empty hook, now cruelly misshapen, and returned the beam to rest.

Then he screamed, as loudly as he could, as the flames subsided. The men by the furnace stopped and peered into the gloom but they were unable to see anything.

Then he shouted loudly. 'Oh my God! Come quickly! There is a man in the copper!'

They dropped their water and ran straight to the side of the vat but of course it was much too late; it was always going to be too late. All they could see, if they looked, and some of them chose not to look, was just a carbonised shape, vaguely human, rapidly diminishing in the agitated, bubbling liquid metal. They looked at each other in horror, not really sure what to do, for there was nothing that could be done.

This man they had never seen before was saying something and some of them were grateful for the chance to turn their heads away from the terrible scene and listen to him.

'It was that plank. He climbed up on it and said he was going to sing you all a song. I told him not to but he wouldn't listen and then he fell in. Stupid bugger. I will have to go outside for a minute. I think I am going to be sick.'

It was later on that the furnace men realised that they didn't know who that man was, the one who went outside to be sick. They had never seen him before. Perhaps he was new, but he never came back. Perhaps it had all been too much for him. You couldn't blame him, really.

They would miss Lardy; they knew they would. He'd been a laugh, and the fact that he had fallen into molten copper just showed what a stupid-born bugger he was. Terrible accident, mind. But still, something to remember him by. That and the fact that he was the man who wrecked the Plume of Feathers. Hell of a boy. Mind you, a bit of a cold fish at times but he would sing a song if you asked him. In the end though, they knew he wasn't like them at all. Not really. Didn't come from the Hafod or from Morriston or anywhere like that. Much too posh, not cut out for this sort of work. A bit Lardy Darr really. But yes, they would miss him. Life went on, though. Someone though would have to replace the hook beneath the hoist. It seemed to have taken a battering recently.

The bosses decided that there was no need to bother the police with this. Just another accident, after all. But they sent the works manager to Martin Street with a sovereign for Lardy Darr's family. Except he didn't have one and he realised that they had never really known that much about him. Still, his landlady took the sovereign in lieu of rent, so it wasn't wasted.

*

In his macabre death, Lardy Darr briefly became a news item. His story, fractured and lacking in any great detail, focused on the rich boy who had fallen so far that he had laboured and sweated in the copper works, where his clownish behaviour had killed him, when he had fallen for the last time.

When Sergeant Ball read out his name from the paper in the police station, Colonel Grey was suddenly very interested.

'Hamish Darr? Well, I never. Have always wondered what happened to him. Not that he deserved my attention of course, even when he was alive. He always most unpleasant, actually. Perhaps he had mellowed, though I find that hard to believe. And here in Swansea? How could that be?'

'I don't think people knew his history in any detail, Colonel,' said Bucke. 'He was regarded as a bit of a card, as far as I can work out. The others workers loved it, having a toff they could boss around. I came across him when he came here and took over one of our public houses. His tenancy was a particularly short one and he lost, they say, a very large amount of money.'

Grey nodded. 'He was a difficult boy. He and his father, Major Darr, never saw eye to eye – which was very difficult for everyone, principally because his father was a royal equerry to Prince Albert. Thrashed weekly at Harrow apparently, though that made no difference. Attacked his father with a table knife at a dinner for the Earl of Dundee, was rusticated for attacking a professor of Archaeology. Got on everyone's nerves in town with his drinking and there were all manner of problems with money which generally was not his own and, in the end, his father disinherited him. Not a happy castle, in spite of splendid views across the loch. Mother enjoyed too many sherries and too many guardsmen, you see. Lots of difficulties. Briefly our Hamish was a scandal and then everyone happily forgot about him.' Grey shook his head. 'Didn't know he was in Swansea. Last I heard, and you must understand that I have not followed his career with any interest, I heard he had gone to make his fortune in America. That doesn't appear to have worked either.'

Bucke picked up the newspaper and scanned the news item for himself. 'I can't add anything, about him, Colonel Grey. The failure of the Plume of Feathers was a bit of a news item for a while but I don't suppose him falling into a vat of molten copper will stay in the news any longer than that. Everything about him appears to be yesterday's news.' He put the newspaper down.

'And had he been here long, do you know, Inspector?'

Sergeant Ball offered the information, folding the newspaper neatly and placing it precisely on the counter. 'I think he arrived about two years ago. As the inspector said, he bought a public house but was unable to make it pay. Lots of creditors. And then he discovered that the man he had bought it off, for cash, was not the rightful owner and that he had disappeared with his money. He was left owning a failing public house that wasn't his anyway.'

'And he bought the Plume of Feathers with cash you say?' asked Bucke. 'I don't think I knew that.'

'That's the story. No one has said how he got it, but it might be because he was a toff, as everyone knows.'

'So there were two of them did that? Bought public houses at the same time with cash? How odd.' Bucke scratched his beard.

'You mean Fred Craven?' asked Ball. 'Yes, that would be right. They both arrived at the same time as I remember it.'

'And they have both died this week?' Bucke looked at Colonel Grey.

'Coincidences do happen, Bucke. I have no reason to believe that Darr would be of interest to me in my current work. No matter when or how he died.'

Bucke raised his eyebrows. 'And so you think it is nothing more than a coincidence, Colonel?'

Grey smiled. 'I didn't say that, Inspector. It is very interesting. But we have more important issues to deal with in the short term.'

'Can't help thinking it is strange, though. Where did he live, Stanley?' Bucke asked.

'Martin Street, they say. Morriston.'

'Reduced circumstances, indeed,' said Grey, shaking his head. 'Still, must dash. Things to do.'

*

Grey stood on the opposite side of Wind Street watching the entrance of the Mackworth Hotel, waiting in the shadows until Keane appeared, looking as fresh as an off-duty waiter can, but wary. He looked professionally up and down the street, assessing it for possible dangers. He didn't see Grey, but then it was Grey's job not to be seen. 'There he is, Jack. That's the man. Now do your job. Remember your lines?'

'Of course, sir. You have no cause to worry. There are many tasks I can perform that are far more complicated than this.' He stepped out of the shadows and walked confidently across the street, casually patting the flank of a horse as he passed.

'Good afternoon,' he said to the man who had been identified for him.

'What do you want?'

Jack sighed. 'To help you, sir. To find a little relaxation, perhaps?'

'What are you on about then? Clear off, you urchin.'

'Would you like to come and see my sister, sir?' he asked. 'She is very obliging.'

'And this is going to cost me how much, do you reckon? To spend time with your sister, as you call her,' said Keane dismissively.

183

'Sir, you misunderstand me. There is no suggestion at all that any money will change hands. She told me that she is a lonely young woman, bored beyond measure. That is what she told me. She is in Room 4 at the Castle Hotel, ground floor, and is very keen to see you. Very sophisticated lady, is my sister.'

Keane looked at him sceptically. 'Bugger off, you little liar.' He paused. 'What's her name then?'

'Sir, I can only pass on the message that Muriel asked me to deliver,' Jack said smoothly. 'Surely you can see that I am not old enough to be anything other than a messenger? You can make your own decision, of course. But it is a genuine offer. She saw you last night when you were serving at table at the Mackworth. That is what she told me.'

Keane looked more thoughtful. He had been serving last night. And there had been a pretty young lady who looked at him more often than women usually did. Was it her? In the high-necked cream brocade dress? A handsome girl, not too old, but old enough, and with that peculiar white stripe in her hair. Was that sort of thing fashionable in Swansea, he wondered? But he remembered too, that he thought she had smiled at him. He was sure she was a guest at the Mackworth, with her mother. It might be, he thought quickly, that she had taken a room away from her mother at the Castle Hotel to facilitate such a liaison. How exciting that would be. But this irritating little urchin couldn't really be her brother, could it? But then, when he thought about it, he realised he had a couple of hours before Sellars wanted to see him.

He knew that he was supposed to tell someone about his movements. Sellars was very particular about that. Someone should always know where he was, for everyone's safety. But he had plenty of time, and this was no one's business but his own.

And did it really matter? A little deception never hurt anyone. It was very quiet here, not half as exciting as he'd been promised. Police were incompetent, easily outwitted. No London agents or anything. This was proving to be a simple mission. So yes, he could spare a couple of hours. She was clearly a young woman who needed discretion, and surely, she should be able to rely upon him

– and, so he imagined, she would then reward him appropriately. As long as she didn't ask for any money. No, she would be paying him. He grinned. It was good to know he could still do it though, that he still had the gift. Keane looked down at the small boy with that defiant look in his eyes and took a couple of coins from his pocket. 'Room Four, you say? Ground floor?'

'I did, indeed. But please, I don't need the money. Very kind of you sir, but my sister has already paid me and if you should indeed seek entertainment with her, then she will reward me further.' He knew that a refusal added veracity to his proposal.

'Please yourself.' He shrugged his shoulders and dropped the coins back into his waistcoat. Keane was keen. He nodded at Jack and then walked off towards the Castle Hotel, avoiding walking under a ladder, at the top of which a man was wrestling with a length of bunting. His luck seemed to be in, but even so, no need to take chances.

Jack watched him go. He took a coin from his waistcoat pocket, flicked it into the air with his left hand and caught it with his right without looking, 'You stupid bugger,' he said softly. 'You are dead.' He turned to look for the Colonel but he wasn't there. This was what he had expected; the man was a professional. He was a man of quality, and he looked at the confident back of Keane striding away and hoped for further employment.

Keane stood on the street outside the Castle Hotel for a few minutes, waiting for the grubby entrance hall to empty. He could see the dark oak door, battered and chipped, that led to the rooms. He wondered how the boy had identified him. His sister, if that who she was, and he doubted that very much, must have described him well. He nodded. Never underestimate your appeal, he smirked.

Mayhew the manager, grey, spare and irritable, eventually went into the back and Keane quickly slipped inside and was instantly through the door. Room 4 was at the end of the short corridor, opposite the lavatory. Very modern, he thought.

He knocked discreetly. She needed to know that he was

sophisticated and understanding, a man she could trust. Not a man who would blunder in, panting, with his tongue hanging out.

The door opened slowly and he smiled. She had been waiting for him, that was clear. He couldn't see her because she was behind the door, but he found the idea of such bashfulness quite thrilling. Keane stepped inside and waited for the door to close, to reveal this woman who he had so excited.

But it wasn't a woman. It was a man who grabbed him and pushed him against the wall. He was so surprised that he struggled to say anything sensible. He heard his voice and realised how ridiculous it sounded. 'What do you think you are doing?' he said, and 'Stop this immediately,' and other things equally nonsensical filled his head. As he was pinioned, a woman appeared from within the room, carrying a gun. His mind, working at high speed, recognised her as that very attractive single woman from the Mackworth. Which room was she in? It wasn't the woman from the dining room. And then the man he did not think he had seen before hit him, expertly, in the stomach and he doubled over, seeking for breath. His body seemed to enter a spasm and he reared up again, which allowed the woman from room 19 – that is who it was- to prod him viciously in the eye with the revolver. The blood roared in his ears and he was dragged further into the room. He was writhing and his eye seemed about to explode. If there had been any breath in his body he would have screamed but he was gasping, making guttural sounds like a maimed dog,

Then, up against the bed, they pushed his head into a large bucket of soiled water and held it there until he drowned. He had never expected to die so quickly. Minutes ago, just a few minutes ago, he had a future, entertaining thoughts of pleasure. And now? He was falling head first, gasping, into a breathless, bottomless, darkness.

Therese sat on the bed and looked at Rhodes, who released his hand from the back of the man's neck. 'You see" she said. 'I told you. The old magic is still there. We make a good team. Always have. We should do it more often.'

'Always ready, ma'am.'

'Good to know. Quick is always best, Mr Rhodes. Just a few short minutes ago he was forever young. And now? Well, there is a body to dispose of.' She removed her wig and scratched her scalp, as Rhodes opened the window of the bedroom. Outside two colleagues were waiting and they took the body as he passed it through to them.

'What happens to him now. Do you know, Mr Rhodes?'

'The colonel wants him displayed somewhere. But I don't know Swansea well enough to know. A warning, I suppose.' Therese nodded her approval. 'They killed Eli. We can't let them think they can get away with it, can we?'

'Indeed no, Mr Rhodes. I just have a reluctance to accept staff shortages at the Mackworth Hotel. Where will they find any kind of competent replacement in this filthy backwater?'

Rhodes shrugged sympathetically. 'It is only for a few more days now, ma'am. Then we are either dead or moving on to whatever fetid slum the prince is visiting next.' Rhodes emptied the bucket out of the window.

'It is never a straightforward choice, is it? Best make our excuses and leave. Shouldn't take long to sort out the room. We haven't made too much of a mess, have we?'

'The carpet is damp, ma'am. Otherwise adequate.'

'Such is the perfect Swansea hotel room, Mr Rhodes.'

Sixteen

'Inspector Bucke. Good morning. Please forgive the intrusion but I wanted to see you urgently, so I delayed my departure to my beat. Sergeant Ball also felt that it was important that I saw you.'

'Good morning, Lemuel. I am sure your people can wait a little longer for you today. And how are things on Powell Street?' Bucke smiled. It was always a relief to be talking to Lemuel Turner, who had been waiting by the counter for the Inspector to arrive. It was highly unlikely that he had remained behind simply to express his unhappiness at a policeman's lot.

'The residents of Powell Street are as well as you might expect, Inspector, although I am not quite as assiduous to their needs as I should be. I must confess that I do try to avoid the previously haunted Mrs Lambrick as much as I can. She is always asking me to bring Vasco with me so that she can pet him, though privately I do question her motives.'

'Really?' asked Bucke.

'Well, a woman has to start somewhere, Page,' said Sergeant Ball, as he tapped and squared a sheaf of papers.

'This is, indeed, my problem, Sergeant. I fear Mrs Lambrick has great expectations, and they seem to include the more uncomfortable elements of a romantic novel published in weekly instalments. I may be turning to mature gentlemen of experience like yourselves for advice very soon,' said Turner with mock solemnity.

'She is so dismissive of your duties! How can that be?' asked Bucke.

'I cannot answer, Inspector. Except she appears to believe that Vasco can carry out all of my duties on his own. And whilst I have considerable faith in the abilities of a dog like Vasco, this is hardly flattering.'

'Well, I agree with the Lambrick woman that your dog is better than some of the constables we have, Page,' said Ball. 'But come on now, sonny. Your beat is waiting for you, so have a word with the Inspector and then you can commence your duties. You will just have to walk a bit faster, that's all. Imagine Mrs Lambrick is behind you and you will be fine.'

'You would be surprised to learn how quickly a man can run, Sergeant,' said Turner over his shoulder as Bucke took him into his office.

'Settling in nicely,' said Ball to himself. 'Always knew he would.' He smiled as the door was closed and he returned to his quiet searching of the drawers and cupboards around him. He didn't want to mention it, but that revolver had gone missing, the one Constable Gill had taken from a boy in The Hatstand Gang, who claimed to have found it on the South Dock. Whether it was loaded or whether it was capable of firing he could not be sure, but Ball did not want to admit that it had been misplaced. It must be somewhere and perhaps, soon, he would be able to have a proper look for it. But there was no need to worry anyone else about it, not at the moment. He just could not remember where it was, that was all. He remembered wrapping it in a yellow duster and hiding it away from the calculating eyes of Nick the Holly. He remembered that clearly. The public were always very firmly kept on the other side of the counter, so he didn't think anyone had stolen it. He was absolutely sure he had put it in a drawer, but he couldn't find it.

Inside the office, Bucke was surprised to feel an apprehension about what the constable might say unexpectedly wash over him. He braced himself. 'So Lemuel, what is it?' asked Bucke.

'My research, Inspector. Into the significance of the word, Aucaman.'

'And has it reached a dead end?' he asked, fearing the worst.

'Well no, Inspector, though to be honest I am not sure where this is leading us. But I have found a possibility. No more than that, but perhaps something for us to work with.'

'And?'

'Aucaman? It isn't a place, not as far as I can see. Not a village

189

nor a mountain nor a river. It is a South American word. It comes from the Mapuche language, down in the southern Andes. Chile, the border with Patagonia, that sort of area.' He pulled out his notebook and flipped through the pages. 'It is the name for a bird. A condor. Something like a vulture, I suppose. But it is a bird. A very large bird. Here, Inspector. I have done a sketch for you. It isn't entirely accurate, but it will give you an idea of the size and nature of the bird.'

Bucke looked at the sketch carefully. It was very impressive. 'An ugly thing, Lemuel. And what is the significance of this, do you think?'

'I have been thinking about this, naturally, Inspector. And I have started to believe that the warning on the note concealed in the pocket of the apron that we extracted from the garden on Powell Street, is not about a bird. Even though it is the name of a bird. The note I saw did not say 'an aucaman' or 'the aucaman.' It was just the single word. Which encourages me in my belief that it is a name. Not necessarily of a bird, but, perhaps, of a person. You understand, Inspector. Just as we use the word Robin as a name? The name of a bird and of a man? So if I am right, then 'Remember Aucaman' might be a reference to a person. Of course, who that person is and what they did and why they did it, are harder things to know. I found a reference in the library whilst I was with Mr Jacques, you see. And I did find it peculiar, because when I asked him about the condor, he professed never to have heard of it, which I did find rather unusual. I would have expected him not only to have noticed the birds when he was in Patagonia, but also to know what they were called. They are the largest birds that fly over land in the western hemisphere, Inspector, which I thought was quite interesting. They eat carrion, apparently. Dead things,' he added for clarity. 'So it is my considered opinion, Inspector, that Mr Jacques is lying. The logical path is quite clear. If he was in the Andes, as he says he was, then he knows about condors, or aucaman, as the natives call them. He must know about them. So what profit is there for him in lying like this? Is he just being awkward, which I accept is an integral part of his personality? Or

190

he is trying to hide something?'

'You are making an assumption, about him knowing about the bird, but is a fair assumption, I think. If you fell and broke your leg, they would come and eat you, from what you say, if you were out in the country. They might wait until you were dead, but they might not. It is the sort of detail you should know, whether you are interested in birds or not. So yes, your argument is persuasive. Unless he knew them only by the word 'condor,' of course. But there is merit in your logic, Lemuel.'

'You see, he didn't say, 'Oh, it's just a bird,' which would have closed off the conversation. In reality, by denying he knows anything, he has effectively opened the conversation up. In my opinion.'

'That is very interesting, Lemuel. Well done. That is very helpful. If we make that leap and say that Aucaman is a person, then Patagonia Jacques doesn't want to talk about him. Or her.'

'As you have told me before, Inspector. The important question in police work, is why. That must be our next step.'

'It could be just a coincidence, couldn't it, Lemuel? It doesn't mean he is involved in the death of Rhys Price. That happened in Swansea. It might just mean that he doesn't understand South American languages.'

'I find it hard to believe that he knew nothing of the bird, Inspector. My opinion is that he is hiding something, or avoiding something.'

'I think we should make that assumption and see where it leads us, constable.'

*

It was later that evening, when Bucke was walking to Constance's rooms after a detour to ensure that the Music Hall was under vigilant observation, that Lizzie Thomas once again emerged from a dark doorway on Cradock Street and briefly walked alongside him.

'Don't ask me where he is, Inspector, because I don't know. But what I have heard is that he is after Patagonia Jacques. That's

191

why he is here and he won't rest until he has done a job on him. All I have got. If I find out more, I shall let you know.' And then she was gone, making less impact than a breeze as she drifted away, back to her night in the shadows.

Why did Riverton have a problem with Patagonia Jacques? But then, everyone seemed to have a problem with Patagonia Jacques. Had something once linked them all? What was it that was now trying to pull them apart? There was a sense of disruption about Jacques. There was certainly an element of tension surrounding him, but it might be that this was the way he liked to live his life, pulling the strings, playing one off against another. Or it might be the inevitable consequence of having money with no apparent interest in spending any. Was it as simple as that? Bucke knew he needed more information, and though Constable Turner's work was not conclusive, it was certainly interesting. But did this link to Rhys Price? And if so, how? He sighed and looked along the dark streets. There was a familiar-looking figure in front of him in the shadows on Union Street. Some of the gas lights were out again; they were out far too often. He peered through the gloom but couldn't be sure who he was looking at so he turned to his right and walked more briskly towards Constance's rooms. When the prince had gone, he might have the time to investigate Jacques properly.

*

Iago Morris was leaning against a cold brick wall on Union Street, thinking about Arthur Riverton, too, about the meeting they had had which troubled him greatly. He needed to tell someone about it - he knew it was his duty - but he wasn't sure that he could.

It had been largely affable; their conversations usually were, though Arthur had always regarded himself as the dominant one, as the leader. But they had gone through so much together, seen things and done things that could never been forgotten. They had learned to trust each other, even if their lives had taken different paths, even if they were now operating on different sides of the law. But they had different ways of dealing with problems; Iago did not have the same rage, the same anger, the same need for revenge. The experiences that fuelled Arthur's anger had scarred Morris too, but he was different; he didn't want those wounds re-opened.

Riverton had been as forceful as always. 'You can see what's going on, can't you?' He had said. 'For Christ's sake, you are a policeman. It is obvious. A man turns up out of nowhere. From Ireland? Says he is a nephew of Patagonia Jacques and has come over to look after him? And the police believe that bucket of hog swill? Of course he is not. It is obvious. He is after his money.'

Morris had shaken his head. 'So what? We have bigger issues to deal with at the moment.'

'No, you haven't. For God's sake, someone down at the police station needs to do some serious thinking. How much more obvious does it have to be, before one of you buggers sits up and take notice? They are Irish and they want his money. And you know, and I know, that the money isn't his. It is ours. And in truth, we can't let the money get into Irish hands, can we? They will buy guns with it. We both know that our duty is to stop it.'

'Duty? You? Don't make me laugh, Arthur. And anyway, Pat reckons we gave him that money. As a gift. He is not obliged, he said.'

'He is such a ridiculous man. I am not talking about Jacques's buried treasure here, am I? This is the real thing, not a stupid dream. We worked for it and we went through a lot and now he thinks we just gave it to him, like a gift? That is madness. That money is ours and you know it. Are you with me or not?'

Morris felt the cold stones on his back and remembered how insistent he had been and the angry fire in his eyes that seemed ready to light up a street. He had always known that Riverton was not a man ever to forgive. Or forget. Injustice stayed alive within him; it didn't ever fade. There was disaster looming, Morris was sure of it, and it worried him greatly. He recalled that he tried to be light-hearted, but that it hadn't worked. 'And so this money, it's in a sock under his bed, is it? Is that what you want me to believe,

Arthur? In money bags? Or neatly bundled notes, all counted out?'

'With Pat you wouldn't ever ignore that possibility. But no. It is in the bank. In the cellar. I know that for a fact.'

'He is hardly going to give it to us, is he? But we can't just take it, Arthur. That is theft. They will put you inside again.'

'Think about it, Iago,' Riverton had told him. 'It can't be theft if it was ours in the first place. Where is the justice? We can't get near him anyway, as far as I can see. The Irish have got him. They are not relatives, that's ridiculous. Ask yourself why they've got him. Money, Iago. They will smuggle him back to Dublin, you can be sure of that. Then the money will follow. But we can stop it.' He had heard a dangerous exasperated tone in his voice, one that he had heard before. 'It couldn't be theft anyway, Iago. Think about it. That money is ours. It never belonged to Patagonia Jacques. So we do our duty and stop the money disappearing to Ireland, and then we get back what is rightly ours, and what has always been ours. He stole it from us, that is what happened and you know it, don't you?" He remembered Riverton smiling and nodding.

Morris knew he was being outmanoeuvred and that his responses had sounded weak and insubstantial. Riverton was mentally quicker and had always been able to defeat him in an argument. But he felt he had a duty to resist. 'And so you expect me to keep quiet about this do you? Me, a constable? I am supposed to be better than that.'

'Iago. I told you before. Why on God's earth have you become a policeman? A ridiculous idea, Iago. Do something for yourself, for once. You have thrown your life away.'

'Oh yes, and you haven't then? Spending all these years locked up. Is that making the most of your life, then?

'I have made mistakes, Iago, although not as many as some other people. But I am out now. You lot won't catch me again; you can be sure of that. I am here because I have things I must do and you have to decide which side you are on. Because nobody, nobody at all, is going to get in my way.'

There had been a challenging look in Riverton's eyes when he said this but Morris didn't respond immediately and held his gaze. 'There has been some trouble recently, Arthur,' he said finally.

'Your job, isn't it? Bringing trouble to people.'

It was at this point in the conversation that Morris had been aware of a change in Riverton's face. It was more set, more aggressive. It was as if he had opened a door on to something much more dangerous. He felt compelled to protect his colleagues, and his occupation, from Riverton's contempt. 'Except those who have brought it on themselves, Arthur. Dai Price killed his wife then threw himself under a train. He was a decent lad, Arthur. But he was troubled.'

Riverton's face had remained impassive. 'I heard. A judgement on him, Iago. What do they say? You reap as you sow? In the Bible that is, so it must be true. That is your answer. It is what he deserved, as a result of what he had done.'

'But not his wife, Arthur. Not Molly.'

'She was riding the same horse, Iago. Sorry to hear it. But she was part of his punishment, I reckon. It is what happens. No mercy.'

His reply had chilled Morris more than anything else he heard. 'But that don't make it right, does it? And then we have Fred Craven, don't we? He was stabbed too.' He had watched Riverton carefully and, once again, he was a little too dismissive.

'Dangerous occupation, running a pub,' Arthur had said. 'Never know who is coming through the doors, do you? And anyway, you know what our Fred was like. Enemies everywhere. Could make enemies quicker than you can make a fire.'

Morris knew there was truth in what Arthur said but the conversation had become deeply alarming, confirming those deep fears that he had been unwilling to confront. Yes, Dai Price seemed to be carrying a lot of trouble and Fred seemed to cause a lot of trouble without making a great deal of effort. He couldn't argue with that. But why now? That was the point, for these deaths had happened so close together. So the conversation had limped on for a while, until they had finished their beer and Riverton had disappeared into the night, leaving Morris to chew his knuckle and to brood, first in the pub and then through a largely sleepless night.

And now, today, Lardy was dead. And that changed everything. He had never believed in coincidences. Nobody, in Swansea at least, really knew who Lardy was, did they? But someone did and they had killed him. It was all too obvious. And if he was right, then what did that mean about the deaths of Dai and Molly? What forced the troubled young man to do the awful thing that he did. Or who?

But however conflicted his feelings were, he was still, by choice and experience, a policeman. And that experience made him question the story, the one that everyone believed because it was simpler and neater. That Dai Price had killed Mollie and then that Dai Price took his own life. Except what if he didn't? And that would mean that someone else was involved. And Morris could no longer believe it was suicide. Neither did he think Lardy had died in a careless accident.

There was a sudden noise that pulled Morris back from his troubling memories. There was an argument and two drunken miners were trying to fight, urged on by a semi-circle of equally drunk spectators beneath the one gas light that was working tonight. He pushed himself away from the wall and slipped off quietly in the opposite direction. This was certainly not something that he wanted to deal with at the moment.

Seventeen

Keane 's body, an unpleasant, grey, hollow shell, was left slumped against the door of the Running Deer where he had been dumped in the night. The eyes were empty, even of reflection. They would never see again, but the body was left for everyone else to view, outside a pub naturally selected for its largely Irish clientele.

It was a message, and Duggan recognised it immediately. He and Sellars withdrew to a quiet room at the back of the Full Moon public house where they could assess their options. How much did the British agents know? Something? Or nothing? This was obviously a response to the killing of Eli Feeney. But did it mean they had to change their plans? Or was it designed to unsettle them?

It certainly was unsettling, there was no doubt about that. Displaying the body of Feeney in a cart on the Strand now seemed like a foolish act of bravado, for they had not anticipated this kind of response. They had not expected to be out-played at their own game, and it unsettled them, for they thought it was wrong and underhand.

The gesture, however, had made Bucke angry. The official response to the crime of killing a man and leaving his body on display on the Strand, had not been to find who had done it and bring them to justice, but rather to murder someone in retaliation. How was he expected to deliver justice in the face of an anarchy he was not permitted to confront? And yet the clear expectation was that even though they were not privy to what had been done, nonetheless the Swansea Police were expected to sort out the consequences of it all. Little Ireland had its own way of dealing with things and the story that circulated with the help of The Roe, was that a visitor from (an unspecified) afar, had drunk too much and had been visited by God in the early hours. Wry sighs, and everyone was ready to think about issues more pressing.

Inspector Bucke, however, was not ready to move on at all. He spoke to the Chief Constable quite forcibly; he had to, for his professional world had been inverted. Captain Colquhoun listened, sympathised and then confirmed that there was nothing he could do. He would raise the issue of uninvestigated murders on the streets of Swansea, but he was under instructions from the very highest levels to offer Grey and his men full cooperation – in the national interest, of course, which meant, in effect, that Colonel Grey could act with complete impunity. The casual contempt in which they viewed other people's lives as they played their own game appeared breath-taking.

Bucke remained insulted of course, but he also realised that he too, was no less of a pawn in this absurd, deadly, entertainment than either Feeney or Keane. Their deaths were nothing more than unavoidable damage amongst the minor pieces, preparatory encounters to test out the opposition, whilst the bigger pieces were moved around the board. And if other pawns had to be sacrificed? Well, it was all part of the sport.

He wondered who ultimately made the decision about which side had won, and which one lost? Because from his perspective it was hard to judge. Was it determined by nothing more complicated than the final body count? There was another more chilling conclusion to be drawn, however. That it would never end. That it would continue in this way forever, and the cheap pieces would be discarded or exchanged, whilst the principals plotted, schemed and avoided attacking each other to preserve themselves.

Back in the real world, the traditional life of Swansea continued as it always did. Several women came to the police station, claiming to be in a relationship of sorts with Keane. Bucke knew they were either there to elicit information or, more likely, to eagerly submit a fraudulent claim for any unpaid wages he had left behind. In fact, so many women turned up that, had they been genuine, Keane would have had neither the time nor the energy to do any waitering at all. Then, inevitably, the sly, twisted features of Frankie Starr were dragged into the police station by Constable Smith and he was warned about trespassing around the rear of the stables at Singleton Abbey. Bucke wondered why it had taken him so long.

Ellen Sweeny was in the cells for smashing windows at the Willow Tree public house on High Street when they refused to serve her because she was drunk and Jack Dawes still stopped people on Wind Street and tried to sell them binoculars.

Bucke watched it all and sighed. Everything had become frenzied in these final few days before the visit and yet nothing in Swansea ever changed. Sometimes that was useful; certainly his informants hadn't changed and they continued to provide him with an insight he would never otherwise have. And so it was time to see what he could discover about Riverton and Patagonia Jacques. They were both beginning to dominate his thoughts rather too much, particularly since he did not know where Riverton was or indeed why he was in Swansea. Revenge for his grandmother's unjust and horrible death? Did that really make any sense?

It was easy to intercept Patagonia Jacques, for he was a creature of limited habits. Bucke stopped him at the end of Tontine Street as he walked home from another session in the library, his nephew, that constant companion, walking rather too closely behind him.

'I have to tell you, Pat, that I have received certain information, information that I regard as credible, that Arthur Riverton is in town and may be intending to pay you a visit.'

'Coming to visit, you say? Is that a fact? And what does the stupid bugger want with me?'

'As far as I understand things, Pat, he feels hard done by, for some reason.'

'Arthur always feels like that. Heard he was out. You don't need to tell me; I can guess what he wants. Like everyone. They all want some of my hard-earned. Every one of them.' He glared over his shoulder at Sellars. 'They think I don't know.' Sellars' eyes flashed, though he said nothing; talking loudly to a police officer was clearly not something about which he approved. 'As it happens, I had heard that Riverton is back in town. There are them that says he has been seen and they are the same ones who are wondering why he is still on the streets. I hope you are going to arrest the

199

bastard. Sooner the better.'

'He might be a changed man, Horace.'

'Pigs will nest in trees before he is a changed man. I tell you now, you would be best advised to do something about him.'

'Time to go home, uncle,' said Sellars suddenly. He glared at Bucke, as if frustrated by being unable to attack an obvious enemy.

For his part, Bucke didn't like Sellars either, this man who had suddenly become Patagonia Jacques's constant companion, who never let him out of his sight.

'This is my nephew Irvine. Come to Swansea to look after me. Not that I need any looking after, you understand. I don't want you getting no notions about me being incapable or any nonsense like that. Irvine is here to help me handle the King's treasure once I have found it. I shall need protection from all the evil thieving bastards that the Swansea police won't do anything about, Inspector.'

'You will always be offered the very best of our protection whenever you require our services, Horace. You are no different from anyone else.' Bucke smiled at him. 'You know that.'

'There will be no need for your help, Inspector,' said Sellars quietly. 'I am here to protect my uncle. I can assure you that no harm will come to him. I watch him night and day. I thank you for the offer.' But his voice carried no sense of gratitude.

Bucke appraised Sellars carefully. His cold eyes; his tension; his aggression.

'Family, see,' said Jacques. 'Makes no difference, though. Buggers think they is having my money. But they are not having any of it.'

'Uncle, please. Calm yourself.' Sellars laid a firm hand upon Jacques's shoulder.

Jacques took no notice. 'And another thing, Bucke. Since I has got you here. That bloody Iestyn Pugh. You best shut him up. Still making baseless accusations everywhere round the place. I shall not be responsible for my actions, I am telling you, if he carries on as he is doing. I have every right, it seems to me, every right. If he is not careful, I shall have him sorted out. Once and for all.' He shrugged away Sellars' hand from his shoulder. 'There we are. You have been told. I am not wasting good money on lawyers and the like when it is much easier to deal with him, once and for all. Do everyone a favour. Spends all his days in the Plough and Harrow, banging on about this and that and me. Getting on everyone's nerves. No one should listen to him. And one day soon they won't be able to listen to him.'

'I have spoken to Mr Pugh, Horace. About causing a public nuisance.'

'Well, it hasn't done much good, has it?'

'I have threatened to take him in, so I am hoping that will be the end of it.' Bucke paused and then spoke very carefully. 'But I will tell you now, in front of your nephew. You are not to consider, even for the briefest instance, taking the law into your own hand. It is my job – or your solicitor's job – to deal with this. I don't think I can be any clearer. Are you listening to this, Horace?'

'Iestyn Pugh? Listening to sense? What has got into you, Inspector? He is a boil that needs to be lanced. It has got to happen and it will. Who knows that? You and me both know that. There is a reckoning coming, don't you doubt it. I'd take him to court but I don't want to waste my money. So I am telling you, Inspector. Be prepared, because he will be dealt with and that will do everyone a favour. You wait, Inspector. You will be coming to me to say thank you.'

'Horace. Please. It is very clear. You do the research into the missing treasure. I will do the policing.'

Jacques glared at him from beneath his crusted eyebrows. 'Listen to me, Bucke. I could be doing with another couple of hours with that constable of yours. Sensible lad. Intelligent. Jesus knows why he is a policeman. But he understands what I am doing, so I would be grateful, Bucke, if you would release him for another afternoon.'

'I am glad he has helped you. He is, indeed, a capable young man. But I am afraid that his duties, in light of the impending royal visit, are more important.'

'More important? What sort of nonsense are you spouting now, Bucke?'

Bucke sighed. 'You have to understand, Horace, that in these times in which we live, when we are anticipating all the complications of a royal visit, that it is important he carries out the duties that the town expects of him. And for which they pay him.'

'Well, the town should be concentrating on finding this royal treasure, not slobbering all over the royal arse.'

'Horace, please.'

'No, Bucke. There are secrets locked in the past and if we look often enough and hard enough, we will unlock them.'

Bucke appraised him carefully. 'I am glad you think like that, Horace. Because there is something you can help me with, I think. And perhaps if you do that- you do understand, don't you, Horace? Your civic duty, that sort of thing? - If you do that, I might just be in a position to get you the kind of help your research so rightly deserves.'

Jacques was surprised. He had not expected this. 'Oh aye?'

'Yes. One more session I can offer you. But you will have to come down to the police station just along the road here,' he gestured to the front door behind him, 'and you can help me with some enquiries I have in relation to something that happened some years ago. Pop in tomorrow morning, on your way to the library. Alone, if you please.'

'That won't be possible,' said Sellars abruptly.

'Oh, but it will,' said Bucke.

Sellars sneered. 'I am telling you, that – '

'And I am telling you, Mr Sellars, that it is happening tomorrow. And I can also tell you that I can take you into custody right now. Special dispensation. From the Home Office. At my own discretion.' He gestured across the High Street, where Constable Gill had been waiting and watching in front of the railway station.

He stepped forward, ready to assist. 'But do not worry, Mr Sellars, if I do place you in detention, it will only be for a week or so. You will be perfectly comfortable, just so long as we don't have a cold snap. And our catering arrangements are regarded by some as almost adequate.' He smiled. 'Shall we say 10.30 am, Mr Jacques?'

*

Of course, Sellars had to make a point. He accompanied Jacques to the police station and waited morosely on the bench under the window opposite the counter, glaring when the busy Sergeant Ball occasionally glanced at him, staring whilst the seconds clicked their noisy way around the clock.

Bucke had taken Jacques into his office. He still wasn't sure that he was doing the right thing. There was so much to do and the death of Eleanor Williams happened such a long time ago. In the time since her death, some had been born, lived useful lives, loved, had children and died. And Eleanor could have been one of those people. And a crime – a murder - still deserved to be investigated. They – he – owed it to her. And perhaps, it was a way of pushing the royal visit to the back of his mind for a while. If it was, then at least, he felt, he was doing something useful.

Jacques sat opposite him, stiffly upright. He was using his stick today and he rested both hands on its smooth top, looking defiant.

'I am sorry to say it, Horace, but you really do seem to have got yourself into a bit of a difficulty. You seem to inspire a surprising measure of hostility. I have two men in the town who appear to have serious issues with you.'

'Small town. Small men. Small minds. You tell me that you are supposed to deal with it. So deal with it. It is not as if you don't know who they are, is it?'

'But you need to help me. Why is it rumoured that Arthur Riverton is out to get you? What is this grudge that he bears towards you?'

'Find the bugger and then you can ask him.'

'What do you think is making him angry?'

'Everything makes Arthur angry, Bucke. Everything. He has

203

been in prison for a long time. It does things to a man. He has lost his senses. What he thinks I have done, I do not know. Probably best if you ask him yourself. Once you have caught him. The one you need to deal with is Iestyn Pugh, because I shall go looking for him again if you don't shut him up. Everyone knows where to find him, don't they? The Plough and Harrow. So you shut him up or you deal with the consequences, Bucke. And they will not be pretty. Do it or it will be on your head.'

'It won't be very pretty if I decide to lock you up. Doesn't matter how old you are, if you carry on making these threats then you will be inside for a week at least. I told your nephew last night and I am telling you today, Horace. Read your books and let things lie. That is my advice.'

Jacques looked away, as if weighing up the advantages of free police accommodation, and Bucke waited for him. 'A long time ago, it was. So many wasted years since then,' he said reflectively. 'You know, Bucke. He was the reason I ended up in South America. I couldn't bear it any longer. Being called a murderer every single day. And it wasn't right, Bucke. Not at all. They hounded me and poor old Betty, the girl I married. Killed her it did, I am sure of it. Because Pugh just wouldn't leave it alone. And it wasn't me that killed little Eleanor. It couldn't have been me. I was nowhere near Llywngwenno that night.'

'And so you remember where you were?' asked Bucke.

'Of course. How could I forget. I was bundling with Catrin Norris.'

'Norris? Catrin Norris?'

'Yes. Was always sweet on her. The best. Always the best, was Catrin.'

'And you didn't tell anyone?'

'How could I? Not fair on the girl, was it? She was she already promised to that evil bastard, Iestyn Pugh. Given away to him for beer money by her father. Pugh probably told you he was bundling with Catrin.'

'I am not in a position to – '

'Yes, all legal. Banns to be called soon. Heard all that. He's told that story so often. But it was me was with her. It always was me and Catrin. I loved her. I love her still. And that is why he makes all this fuss, after all this time. He is after me and he wants me charged, because he knows as well as I do who did it.'

'And who is that then, Horace?'

'Obvious, isn't it? Even to a policeman. Pugh murdered Eleanor Williams. Not me. He is the one who killed her. He was the one going behind Catrin's back. She was always too good for him.' He spat on the floor, clearing his throat. 'Her bloody father. He is the one who is to blame. He sold her. I know that for a fact. Pugh give him money for his drinking. And I didn't have no money. Not then.' He shook his head at a memory of the thing that appeared to have defined his whole future. 'Ask yourself this, Bucke. Why would I kill Eleanor Williams? She was nothing to me. She wasn't Catrin. But it was Catrin's father, Ianto, who promised her to Pugh, after that money changed hands. That was why I left in the end.' He sighed. 'I mean, Bucke, yes I got married. To poor old Betty. Nice enough girl, but I did it in haste. I was lost because Catrin had gone. Don't get me wrong, Betty and me were happy enough, it wasn't that we wasn't happy at all. But she wasn't Catrin and she found it hard, nobody in the village talking to her, for a start. But it was Iestyn Pugh who did all the poisoning, bit by bit. Drop by drop. There was all that nonsense at the Nebo Chapel when we were wed. Then that ridiculous gravestone. A millstone, more like. Became too much for her. Visitation of God they said when she died. What the bloody hell he was doing visiting Felindre, I have no idea. Never been there before, to the best of my knowledge, nor since. A Godless murderer poisoning minds and God done nothing about it? So I went. Got a boat to America. Make myself a fortune. Show Catrin I was good enough,' He paused, wiping his eyes as if they were wet. 'Thought I was heading north. But the boat was going south. That's how it all started. And now I am Patagonia Jacques.'

Bucke considered all these old passions. Still alive after almost 50 years. Two burnt-out old men, unable to leave the past behind.

Both accusing each other, both believing that there was no evidence to implicate them. Jacques, however, had not finished.

'Catrin? She is why I come back to Swansea. I hoped Iestyn was dead and that she would be a widow and we could be together. But he will be dead soon enough, if he's not careful – and don't worry, Bucke, you'll never pin it on me. I got friends. I won't be anywhere near him. But I have not done for him yet because of Catrin. I know she won't say no to me. It has been a long time - too long – but it's not too late. Never too late for me. She won't say no, I am certain of that. What we have been waiting for. To be together, I'd marry her on my death bed if I have to. I'll leave all my money to her once I am sure that bastard won't get his hands on it. All I have to do is ask her. Catrin won't say no, not to me.'

It did matter, thought Bucke as he studied the old man carefully. He couldn't ignore any of this, could he? It was because there were two old men involved, that now made it seem so ridiculous. But it hadn't been ridiculous. Not then. Not now. It was wrong and it was cruel and a young woman had been thrown down a well, murdered on the darkest of nights, thrown away as if she counted for nothing.

Jacques stood up and opened the door of the office. 'I haven't killed him yet, Bucke. You might have noticed that. But I could have done and I might do it yet. All this shouting out on the streets using my name, it's got to stop. He was the murderer, not me.' Sellars pushed himself away from the wall against which his head had been resting and stood up quickly. He crossed the foyer to Jacques.

'I made my fortune, that's what happened and now everyone wants a piece of it,' he said, looking at Sellars. 'And you, Inspector. Shut the bastard up or it will be on your head, I am telling you.'

'But what you are not telling me, is why Riverton so unhappy with you.'

Sellars took Jacques's elbow. 'Come on, Uncle. You are getting overwrought again.' He started to lead him towards the door.

'I am no such thing. And keep your hands off me, you villain.

It is only my money that you wants. I tell you, it is not for you.' Sellars pulled him to the door of the police station and dragged him down the steps on to Tontine Street. Bucke followed and watched them struggling along the pavement and Jacques occasionally waved his stick in an angry fashion.

He knew that there was only one other person he could talk to and that, of course, was Catrin. She was effectively being used by both men as their alibi. Bucke wasn't sure what he made of her. Her reactions to his visit seemed complicated. He had formed the impression that she had something to say. But would she say it to him? Would she say it if Iestyn was there, sitting by the stove? But a plan had started to emerge when he remembered that Iestyn Pugh spent his lunchtimes in the Plough and Harrow in Llangyfelach.

Eighteen

It was Grey's habit to take a morning constitutional, as he called it with an ironic smile, around the streets of Swansea. In truth, it would never improve his constitution, but it might enable him to understand the layout of the town and provide an opportunity to look at worn and battered faces, to search for clues, to search for enemies.

In these last few days before the visit, the streets had been frenetic. Grey knew that normality had disappeared some days earlier. There now appeared to be constant and fruitless sweeping, for no amount of brushwork could master the black soot that flaked incessantly from the walls above. He stopped and looked up into the grey sky at the upper storeys. The soot will be a long time failing, he could see that. Banners displayed too early in an excess of patriotic eagerness, were already starting to look battered and torn by the wind. A similar fervour had moved shopkeepers to improve their window displays and incorporate royal details that would never be noticed, even by the most keenly eyed observers. Messages of devotion for the Prince and Princess, however inspired and lyrical, were far too small to be seen. A clean window, thought Grey, was the key, but so very difficult to achieve amongst such neglected and stained buildings.

He was constantly alert. He accepted that the killing of Keane might be seen as a serious provocation but he was never one to back away from confronting his enemies. If they wished to respond, then that was their choice. He was ready and he was not alone. His trained eyes scanned the shadows, assessing threats and opportunities. Looking for those who looked at him for a moment too long, for faces that seemed to reappear at intervals. Such things, he knew, were never accidental.

On Oxford Street, so different from the street he knew with the same name in London, he met the Welsh-costumed attendant who they now called Lady Emily (for a while, at least) and her mother, bright eyed and excited amongst a stream of people heading towards the market. They were talking to a woman with a pram – a nanny, he imagined. Unless the wealthy of Swansea pushed their own prams, but that was an unthinkable idea. He heard the nanny say, 'Young master George will always be able to tell his own children that he was here on this momentous day! He may not remember, though I shall try my best to keep him awake, but that is less important than actually breathing the same air as our future king!' Her round face was illuminated by a devotional smile. 'You must excuse me, Flora. It has been such a pleasant surprise to see you. I was not expecting such a treat! And I shall look out for you, Emily, on the big day. How lucky you are to be so involved. I am consumed with envy.'

Emily, so pleased with herself, smiled in embarrassment, Flora Beynon nodded approvingly and then turned towards him, having decided that a colonel was more important to speak to than the wife of the manager of the Bristol and West of England Bank.

'Isn't everything looking so perfectly splendid, Colonel Grey? How beautiful is the town today! How much more beautiful it will be when the Prince and Princess arrive.'

'Without doubt, Mrs Beynon. Only the very finest of our poets could do it justice.' He looked around him and caught the eye of his newly-constant companion. Jack Dawes was always just close enough. Grey nodded at two men loitering by the market entrance. Jack knew what he had to do but made no visible response. He would follow them and then report to the colonel as soon as he could.

'The shops are so glorious that they quite take your breath away. I am sure that not even the traders of London can match the quality and the arrangement of the goods on offer.'

'They have much to learn, Mrs Beynon,' he nodded.

'So do the shopkeepers of Aberystwyth,' muttered Emily, a comment Flora chose to ignore.

Grey watched as one of the constables dragged away a man who had been found sleeping in an alley surrounded by a dark pool of beer-ladened vomit. 'You are nothing more than a walking beer barrel, Ebenezer Lewis!' shouted the constable.

'Gawd bless yer majesty,' he slurred as he staggered into a wall, dragging the constable with him. Lewis started to sway, looking queasy.

'I am warning you, Ebenezer Lewis! My uniform is clean on today. You puke on it and you'll be feeling the weight of my truncheon.'

'Such patriotic fervour is quite inspiring, don't you find, Mrs Beynon?'

'Dear me, Colonel Grey. I suppose we must all celebrate this remarkable day in our own fashion, but even so, there must be some limits to our national pride.'

'I believe that it is a bottomless well, Mrs Beynon.' He turned to Emily. 'And I hope you are in good health today, Lady Emily. I know of no one who deserves such a title more than you.' He looked over her shoulder. There was a woman in a head scarf, avoiding his eye. He had already seen her earlier. Black shawl, skirt and boots. Too young for the clothes. In mourning for Keane, he wondered? He returned his attention to Emily and smiled. 'I hope you are excited, though naturally not too excited, not when you have important duties to perform.' He raised a discreet eyebrow. Flora had not been told the extent of Emily's involvement, for Grey was not sure he could rely upon her discretion or her approval. All Flora had been allowed to focus upon was Emily's proximity to the royal party and Grey judged that this was an honour that would serve to out-weigh every other consideration.

'It is so very good of you to allow Lady Emily to be part of the ceremonial elements of the visit. I know that her appearance in a vibrant Welsh clothing will set hearts aflutter across the entire town, if not across the whole of the Principality.'

'If only her father could be here to see it, said Flora, but alas the duties he must perform prevent...'

'I quite understand. But whilst he may not witness it at first hand, he will know instantly from the acclaim she will receive, as the perfect embodiment of the true spirit of Wales. I am confident that the respect in which she will be held by all, will warm his heart forever.'

Emily rolled her eyes.

Grey smiled again and looked beyond Emily. The woman he had been watching was still there. She hadn't moved on. He could not see her face because the scarf around her head was creating dark shadows. Not an accident. Perhaps he had sent Jack Dawes after the wrong people. Damn.

He raised his hat and bid Flora and Emily a good morning. 'I look forward with anticipation to our meeting in the Town Hall. Is that tomorrow? I do lose track of time, overwhelmed as I am by the glories of Swansea's architecture.' He brushed soot from his shoulder and shook his head amiably. The shadowy woman was still there. Perhaps he shouldn't have mentioned the rehearsal, though he was not sure how much Flora understood. 'Nothing to worry about, Mrs Beynon. Just some tiresome arrangements to go through so that we can ensure all are properly prepared for the ineffable glories of the regal presence.' He bowed slightly more than necessary and turned away.

Flora felt properly respected now. A cheerful conversation with an important man from London, whoever he was, was a recognition of her proper status. It was such a pity that Constance hadn't been here too, to see her natural social position acknowledged, but she had gone elsewhere, carrying out duties for Rumsey. Such a ridiculous idea. What possible use could she be to him in his work?

Grey had a plan, and it was the sort of game he enjoyed. He needed to confirm whether the woman he now called The Black Shadow was following him and so walked casually into the market, shaking his head sorrowfully and tapping his midriff at the loud lady shouting something in Welsh, trying to sell him cockles in a bag.

He moved on, to look at a butcher's stall that had upon it the worst and most unappetising sausages he had ever seen. They were grey and misshapen, distorted by prominent lumps that were

211

certainly not meat, sitting on the wooden stall dripping thin blood on to the floor below. The badly written sign hanging above said, 'Mabe's Meats.' Maybe not, thought Grey, smiling affably at the large, dirty, dark-haired man with thin eyes standing beneath the sign. He was sure he could see a rat's tail protruding from beneath a tattered sack on the floor. The woman who interested him had, rather clumsily, drifted behind a stall selling second-hand clothes. What did she think she was going to achieve, for goodness sake?

He continued further into the market, stopping next to admire a display of handkerchiefs and then crossed over to Powe's Boiled Sweet Stall, where he bought a bag of humbugs. He wandered towards the handkerchiefs again and turned suddenly and doubled back towards the cockles. There she was, turning away from him. She was good; but not good enough.

Grey smiled as this time he did buy cockles, whilst the woman busied herself with a length of curtaining material. Suddenly, Jack Dawes was by his side, although unseen, behind a cart.

'Nothing doing, Colonel. They went off into the King's Arms. Decoys I reckon. They were the ones you were expected to see. To make you think it was them who were going to follow you. There must be someone else tailing you.' He sniffed. 'Not the cleverest idea I have come across, but I can see it's attractions.'

'Oh yes. I know all about it, old boy. She is over there. Don't stare, if you don't mind.'

'Don't need to. That's Aoife.'

'Do you know her, Jack?'

'Best card dealer I have ever seen. A real expert. Been in Swansea, I would say, for about a month or so. Was doing the three-card trick with a team in St Thomas but I haven't seen her for a few days now. A real professional, Colonel.'

'How splendid, Jack! Here. Have some cockles, old chap. Then make yourself scarce. Pop into the hotel later if you will. Always a pleasure, Jack.' He watched the boy melt away almost immediately, as if he had never been there. What a talent, he thought. And still only a boy.

He put the humbugs into his trouser pocket and then loudly shouted across the market. 'Aoife! Aoife! Over here! How are you? Lovely to see you! Hope all is well, don't you know!' How he enjoyed a moment of mischief. The market traders and their customers barely gave Grey a glance. Such was life in the market – loud and inconsequential. Some of the stall holders joined in, chanting her name haphazardly: it was a welcome entertainment that, if only for a moment, interrupted the tedium of not selling anything. But not so for Aoife. Grey was thrilled at how horrified she looked as he watched her walk away hurriedly, with her head down towards the door, trying and failing, not to draw attention to herself. This was exactly what he had planned. She would be so confused, for the man she was supposed to be following not only had seen her, but also, knew her name. How had that happened? And perhaps more importantly, what did it mean? How much of their mission was compromised? He knew exactly what apprehensions he had created in her mind. But then, there was the biggest question of all, the one that he had left for her consideration. Was someone controlling what was happening here in Swansea? And who was it?

Grey smiled. He had enjoyed that.

*

Constance sat down in front of the range, watching Catrin making tea. It wasn't a large cottage – but it was certainly larger than her own modest rooms. It was warm and comfortable and very traditional. Homely, thought Constance. Naturally, the black range was the heart of the cottage. This was where jam was boiled, where bread was baked, where batter was beaten, where dinners were made. This had become the whole of Catrin's life.

They talked inconsequentially for a while – about the royal visit, whether Catrin would be able to find somewhere to stand, indeed if she could actually stand still for the length of time required, about how the coal had been difficult to light this year, about how much easier it was in the village now that the Brynafon store had opened. They drank their tea and Constance waited patiently.

Eventually, Catrin took their teacups and saucers away and put them on the old, solid, worn family table that had seen so much. Then she came back and sat down opposite her visitor. She seemed calm, but almost defiant, thought Constance.

Catrin looked at her silently for a few moments. 'I know why you are here, Miss White,' she said eventually. 'I know what it is. The inspector sent a message saying you would come.' She arranged her hands neatly on her lap and settled against the stiff back of the chair. 'From what I have heard, you have had some difficult times, Miss White. Ups and downs, they say.'

'Oh yes, Mrs Pugh. Life hasn't always run smoothly for me.'

'Does it ever? For anyone?'

'Some say that it does, Mrs Pugh, though I have no evidence that it is true.' Constance watched her closely.

There was a pause, as if Catrin was arranging her thoughts. 'It is all these things from such a long time ago, isn't it? You might think it was all nigh-on fifty years ago, but it seems like yesterday to me, and then our Edith comes into the kitchen chirping away and I will suddenly realise that she is not my daughter, Rachel. She is my granddaughter. Look at me, Miss White. What happened? If this life of mine is a book, then I am in the last chapter. So much unfinished. All these loose ends that don't matter much to anyone else.'

'I think that is probably the same for everyone. Any of us could be in our last chapter, or even our last paragraph. Sentence, even. You don't book an appointment, like you do with a solicitor. No one tells you your time is up a week next Thursday.' She smiled. 'I suppose it is a good thing. And you look well enough to me, Mrs Pugh. Plenty of years left, I would say. That is the only way any of us have to live our lives, thinking we have still got time.'

'As you said, you can never tell. I'm still here. Other people I have known are not. But why? Is it just an accident? Because if it isn't an accident, then there is a plan. Except no one knows what it is.' She checked that her hair was still contained neatly in the bun on top of her head. 'I still think of poor old Betty. She and Horace deserved so much more than they had. Especially Betty. And I do wonder sometimes…'She left her sentence unfinished.

'What happened, Mrs Pugh?'

'With Betty?'

'No,' said Constance gently. 'With you.'

'Me?' She looked down at her lap. 'No one ever asks, Miss White. I am just Old Ma Pugh. You know, she sits at the back of the Nebo every Sunday without fail. She makes Welsh cakes. She walks past the gravestone.' She looked at the small curtained window. 'That's all I am. But I have been in love, you know. Proper love. The sort that turns you inside out. Me, just ordinary Old Ma Pugh. But I knew passion. I knew love. But not with my husband, that's the shame of it.'

Constance laughed. She couldn't stop herself.

Catrin looked affronted and Constance leaned forward and put her hand on her knee. 'Please, please forgive me, Mrs Pugh. You might be speaking of me.'

Catrin smiled faintly. 'I used to think I was alone.' She touched the corner of her eye and might have pushed away a hidden tear. 'Even after we were both married, Horace used to come and see me. In the afternoons, when Iestyn was out. Horace would always find the time.' She became animated. 'What I don't understand, is why that happened. All that passion.' She leaned forward a little more. 'You see, I have never told anyone this, but I don't rightly know who is the father of my own child. That is terrible, isn't it? Please don't say. But then, of course, Horace went away, didn't he? Driven away. And poor Betty. She'd done nothing wrong. She didn't deserve any of it. But Horace went away after she died and I was left here. So you make the most of it. You have to. Not done too badly, really.'

'And what about Eleanor? What about the night she died?'

'It is a long time ago, but some things live with you. Ellie was a good girl, she was pretty, she was happy. Always made you smile. A bit young it seemed to me, if I am honest. Said she was seventeen, but I thought she was younger. We were friends. I was a bit older, not a great deal, but Ellie was not much more than a child. But old enough to get herself into trouble. Came from down west somewhere. Worked in Llwyngwenno Farm. Met someone, not that there were many young men in Felindre, then. I was tied up in my own life at the time, lots of difficult days, lots of trouble. But for some reason, I always worried about her. It was like she was a rabbit that found itself in a yard full of foxhounds.' Catrin closed her eyes for a moment then looked straight back at Constance. 'Might have been a stranger. Who knows? And then they found her down the well. Pulled her out with ropes, in the end.'

'And on the night that she died, you were with someone, weren't you?'

Catrin didn't say anything and returned to staring at the window again.

'Who were you with, Mrs Pugh? That night.'

'I don't remember. It was dark. Couldn't see.'

'Please, Catrin. Who did you let into your room? Through the window? Was it Iestyn? Is that who it was? He says he watched Horace going down the track towards the well.'

'I don't remember. It was a different world, Miss White. Half a century, near as, they say. I was nineteen, you know. Edith will be here soon. If I remember I shall let you know.' She stood up decisively. And then she blurted out, as if, Constance thought, it was involuntary, uncontrollable. 'He wanted to punish us both, but he wanted my money more. I should have used the arsenic.' She gathered her apron and used it to cover her face. 'I think you should leave now, Miss White. Barometer's falling. There's a storm coming. You best be home.'

The storm clouds were indeed gathering and she really needed to get home as soon as she could but Constance stopped at the Nebo Chapel, as Rumsey had done before her, and stood briefly in front of the gravestone in an act of respect, and of curiosity. She had heard of a similar sort of thing in Cadoxton and another one that was smaller in Gower at Penrice but she hadn't seen them herself. This, however faded, was still a shock. She was amazed by

Eleanor's grave and what it represented – the anger, the outrage, the need for justice. Constance reached out, for her touch would connect her directly with this tragedy, still apparently alive in the minds of the old. And there was the small stone in front of it, emerging from between strands of wet grass, the stone that represented an unborn child. A silent permanent accusation, impossible to ignore or to forget. As cold as only a grave can be, demanding justice, never changing, never blinking. Waiting.

She looked at the words, the statement of fact that came first and then the righteous words beneath, with the Biblical intensity she had heard once in chapel and that memory made her shudder. She felt a terrible power contained here, a power that would wait forever until it could draw the killer into its dark, cold oblivion. How could Horace Jacques have looked at that every day? It was no wonder Betty, tainted by association, couldn't live with it.

And of course Catrin still did live with it. A reminder, just like the well at the entrance to the farm, past which she would walk every day. She could never forget or ignore what had happened there. It was her fate to be permanently reminded by a harsh cold grave, of shocking cruelty, of a life discarded, so that the unworthy might live. And all this, so close to where she had lived her life for almost half a century; an indestructible demand for vengeance, one which could never be ignored.

Quite suddenly Constance felt an overwhelming need to leave. The wind had suddenly decided to drive her away, swirling leaves, bending branches. She found the graveyard threatening and the stone a sinister presence. It seemed empty, an obsessive place where humanity and love had rotted. She could sense no God here, just hatred and indifference. But there was a hunger in that gravestone, that must one day be sated; a need to consume a life. It chilled her and, although she did not regard herself as fanciful, she felt an imminent death and she hoped desperately that it wasn't Rumsey's. She had never felt like this before, but she knew.

There would be a death, no question.

As she hurried away along the wind-rattled lanes towards Llangyfelach, Constance came across two men standing by a stream. They appeared to be waiting for someone. Perhaps they were working. It was what happened in the countryside, she believed. Men working away at tasks that townsfolk did not understand. Clearing a drain, perhaps, or maintaining the simple bridge. They seemed reluctant to acknowledge her, but she was too wrapped up in her own thoughts to give it any attention. All the way along she had been puzzling about the conversation she had just had, that probably said more than the words did themselves.

Constance was sure that Catrin had spent that evening with Horace and she tried very hard to work out the implications of what she said. Did the things that happened so long ago really matter that much? Obviously they did, as the impassive gravestone showed. There would be more deaths until the price, whatever it was, had been paid. No one would know when that would be.

Some people went to great lengths either to keep memories alive or to deny them. But their efforts were futile. What happened in the past controlled the present and the future. From that there could never be an escape.

She could see Llangyfelach ahead of her as thin rain, sharp as needles, was thrashed into her face by the strengthening wind. There might be a policeman there with a cart who would take her back into town. Or there might not. The rain was making her eyes water – at least she hoped it was the rain. She had not had a premonition of death before and she didn't want to have one again. She tried to think about something else, anything else, but could not manage it and that cold, unresponsive gravestone filled her mind. Then something else occurred to her. She realised that she was unable to decide who it was that Catrin Pugh was protecting. Her husband? Or Horace? It could be either of them. She must have lived those moments every day of her life and those memories will never have lost their power, not in the aura of that stone. It created daily torture, a daily nightmare, but one Catrin had never been ready to confront. And then, when a sudden gust of wind almost blew her over, it came to her. Catrin was protecting herself, perhaps more than anything else, from having to confront the reality that she had spent the only life she would have, married to a murderer.

Nineteen

Iestyn was smiling to himself as he walked down the steep narrow lane from Llangyfelach, towards the quiet mill. The high hedges sheltered him from the worst of the wind and that pleasant hour or so in the Plough and Harrow had left him in good spirits. He knew exactly what he had to do. Very simple. Keep his head down, that was all. Keep quiet and behave himself. Let Bucke think that he was going to do as he was told. This was such a clever plan and he knew without a doubt that it would work. Because on the day of the Royal visit, when everyone was busy with whatever they had to do, he would leap out of the crowd on Walters Road and run alongside the Royal Coach denouncing Horace Jacques. They would have to take notice of him then, wouldn't they? He was never going to stand in front of the plumed horses. That would be stupid, wouldn't it? Much too dangerous. No, he would run alongside. They wouldn't be expecting him to do that. They would never catch him out, he was sure. He was too clever for them. Always would be.

He kicked up some leaves in pleasure at his own cleverness. 'God hath set his mark upon him;' yes he had, God had chosen him because he was a cunning man. He nodded proudly, and realised he loved those words, loved the sound, loved the feel of them in his mouth. He spoke them aloud as his boots crunched through the dry leaves; it mattered little that there was no one else to hear them; he could hear them.

'Although the savage murderer may escape for a season the detection of man, yet doubtless God hath set his mark upon him, either for time or eternity. And the cry of blood will assuredly pursue him to a terrible and righteous judgement!'

Something scurried away in the hedgerow. That hadn't escaped the detection of man, had it? No matter how much it tried. But then, nothing much got past him, did it? Iestyn picked up a twig blown off in the winds and threw it to where the noise had been. What was it? A fox?

He hoped Catrin had been baking. She was good at it. Everyone knew. He'd enjoy a couple of Welsh cakes when he got home. There was another sound. A mouse? Could be a rat. He'd keep a look out. Then there was the crack of a twig breaking. Definitely a rat. Unless he was being followed. He stopped and looked around, carefully. No sign of anyone. Must surely have been a rat. He'd have to ask someone to turn up with a dog. Not such a bad idea. A bit of sport, perhaps.

He turned right at the mill and went up the hill, past the Nebo Chapel. Now that had been a good day, hadn't it? Painting the gates red on Horace's wedding day. Horace the Murderer. That always made him laugh when he thought about it. He had watched his anger; he had watched a man looking frantically for someone to blame, with paint on his hands. And not knowing who had done it, that was the best. He almost felt sorry for Horace. Almost.

It was a steep pull up the track. And to the left was Llwyngwenno and the well, down which Eleanor Williams had been thrown. All those years ago, eh? Who would have thought that time could pass so quickly? He paused to catch his breath. He remembered a time when he didn't have to do that. He looked at the sky. Dark and ominous. It had rained once already, a viciously sharp squall; it would rain again soon, he knew that. Didn't matter much really, did it? Not once he was sitting in front of the fire in the kitchen.

What was that noise? The wind catching something? A branch? Leaves? Someone had talked about a storm. He looked around. Was there someone there? He looked more intently but could see nothing. Why should there be? Ridiculous idea. Why would anyone be hiding in a hedge on a cold autumn afternoon with that storm on the way? Time for a Welsh cake.

*

She stood by the fire, rubbing the small of her back. Iestyn had gone. Life was full of surprises, in the end. It wasn't as if she had any warning. One minute she was kneading bread at the table and then the door was flung open loudly and her daughter, Rachel, was standing there, breathless, her face the colour of ashes, her voice

221

speaking of a life-changing moment that she struggled to process.

'Mother you must come! Now.' She bent down and scooped up Edith and held her tight. 'It is father. They have found him in the well at Llwyngwenno. He must have fallen in! They are trying to get him out...'

Catrin remembered clearly that she couldn't quite understand what Rachel was saying. She knew she would always remember the moment when she was told of her husband's death, not because of her emotions, but because of her sticky, dough-filled hands hanging motionless in front of her, and for the feeling that none of it seemed to make any sense. 'Iestyn?'

'Yes! Father is in the well. He must have fallen. Quickly! You must come!'

'But I have bread to make,' she said, bemused by what Rachel was saying. 'In time for your father's tea. He will be here soon. He will be expecting it.'

'Mother! He is at the bottom of the Llwyngwenno well.'

'How did he get there then? Stupid man. Edith is going to make a bara planc for him, isn't it that so, my darling?'

Catrin remembered how exasperated Rachel became. 'I am here to take her, Mother. Your husband is at the bottom of the well.'

'Your father? Iestyn?'

'Yes. There are men with ropes! I will take Edith. You have got to go to Llwyngwenno!'

So she did, and he was. Iestyn was found dead at the bottom of the well. Was this God's work, she asked herself quietly? Divine justice? If that was the case, then it had taken him an awfully long time to get on with it. But even so, now it was done. Fifty years later perhaps, but it was done. All that remained was the gnawing anger that God had allowed her to live with a murderer for all that time. She shook her head. But really, when you thought about it, he wasn't making such a good job of the rest of creation either. There must be a lot to do.

But now she was a widow, her husband having somehow managed to fall into a well, knocking his face, or so it appeared, on every brick on the way down and his arms and legs contorted into strange shapes. He was a frightful mess and no one was going to be able to use the well for quite some time, which was very inconvenient.

Of course, no one could explain what he was doing there. Given his obsession, the best guess was that he was looking for evidence –although since the murder of Eleanor Williams had happened so many years ago, there was never a chance that he would find anything at all. No one had seen him there; no one had seen anyone else there, either. But the fact remained he had fallen in and was discovered when old Mrs Trehearne couldn't drop the bucket in the water because something was in the way. No one could be sure how long he had been there. The wooden cover had been removed and was propped against the worn brickwork. Must have been leaning over the side, looking for something or other and slipped. Stupid bugger. And so now he was lying on a rough table in the shed at the bottom of the garden, waiting to be buried in the Nebo chapel where Eleanor Williams was, a dead girl who appeared to have dominated his life for so many years. Catrin had always thought he should have taken more concern for the living, rather than those long-dead, but at least it meant that he had ignored her most of the time.

Catrin sighed. And now all those wasted years of indifference were over. Now, at last, the coldness of his body matched the coldness of his heart. Catrin had entered her marriage with trepidation and sorrow and this eventual freedom must be some kind of reward for her fortitude over so many bleak years. But it had taken such a long time to achieve that freedom. Why now? For God's sake, why hadn't it happened sooner?

It was far too late now. The family Bible, in which all births, marriages and deaths were recorded, said that Catrin Norris was born in 1812. She was 69 years old. Some days she felt it, too. She sat in the chair where Iestyn had always sat. She hadn't been allowed to, but it was her chair now. She didn't really know how she felt about his death, though she was pleased about the chair. She hadn't been upset; shocked at the suddenness of it, yes, though not distressed. But she hadn't been pleased either. What she felt more than anything else was a weariness, a feeling that her life had slipped through her fingers with so little of consequence to hold on to, apart from Edith. And the reward? A freedom she could never use. What a waste. Perhaps she ought to cry, she thought. It would be expected of her. And she might well cry later, she thought. But if she did, it wouldn't be for Iestyn.

When she looked up, Horace Jacques was there. She had been so lost in her thoughts that she had not heard him enter. But she wasn't surprised to see him. Perhaps he had to be there, if the circle was finally to be closed; if she was finally to be set free.

'Good evening, Horace. I wasn't expecting you. You should be home. There is going to be a storm tonight, they say.'

'I came as soon as I heard, Pugh in the well? Seems right to me.'

She watched him carefully, his eyes unexpectedly bright. He appeared agitated, excited. Horace seemed to her to find it difficult to form his words and she was curious about that. So she watched him lick his lips nervously, until he found the courage he needed.

'Come away with me, Catrin,' he said abruptly.

'Pardon, Horace?'

'You have no reason to stay, not now. We can marry, now he has gone. Be together. It is not too late. I have a deal of money. Enough for the both of us. We won't want for nothing. I'll make sure of that.'

Catrin shook her head, faintly. 'It is too late, Horace, too late. What about Rachel? And Edith? You are asking me to abandon them and go on some wild adventure with you? Is that what you are saying? After all these years? No, Horace.' He was about to speak but she interrupted him. 'No. You listen to me. What we had, all those years ago, was all we were ever going to have. It was beautiful and wonderful. The best moments of my life. But it is too late now. It has gone. I am Old Ma Pugh, that is who I am.

224

No one's secret lover.' She laughed at the idea.

'You are more than that. You always were. We were meant to be together. You know that. You know how we both felt. What we said.'

'And I can never forget what we had. Never. The rest of my life since then has been nothing but an after-thought. An endless counting of lonely, rainy days. Never doubt it. But it is too late. You have your family now. They want to look after you.'

'If that is who they are. But I want you to have my money. Not them, not a man who calls himself my nephew, who I have never heard of before.' He screwed up his hands, his knuckles white. 'I have taken you with me wherever I have been. Never a night has gone by, without me speaking to you. Even on the coldest and harshest of nights. Everything I have ever done has been for you. And we know who killed Eleanor Williams. We both do. It was a truth that we shared. It couldn't be me. We both know that. It was Iestyn, of course it was, The father of her child. That is why he made such a noise about it, because he was the one. But he has gone. You don't need to worry about him anymore. It is all about us now. Let's have that happiness. We owe it to each other.'

Catrin could see a desperation about him, an old man trying to deny the inevitable progress of the years, persuading himself that the clock could be turned back. But he could never persuade her, not now. 'Horace. You are three score years and ten? Doesn't that tell you something? Are you familiar with the Bible? It is too late.' She paused for a moment. 'Did you kill Iestyn? Did you, Horace?'

'It wasn't me. I had every reason to do it, but it wasn't me.'

'And did you pay someone else to do it?'

He looked away. 'No money changed hands, Catrin.'

'And that makes a difference, does it?'

Horace looked into the fire, as if he could see Iestyn burning for eternity. 'To me it does,' he said. 'Come on, Catrin. You and me. Let's run. Together. While we still can.'

There was a movement outside and Catrin looked towards the dark window, but could see nothing. She turned back towards him, her eyes unflinching. 'No, Horace. No. Those days are gone now. I have my life. I got my daughter, Rachel.' Her eyes flickered towards the window again and then she continued. 'Got my precious granddaughter, Edith. Whatever I had in the past is less important now than the future. I want to be there for our Edith. Yes, we had our time, Horace. And I would not have missed it for anything. But it has gone now. I am too old, too tired. I think about the two of us, of course I do. But I sometimes wonder what is real and what isn't. I dream, Horace. I still dream. I still remember. But which parts are real? I can't tell you now.'

The light in Horace's eyes started to fade. He said nothing.

'Eleanor is dead. Betty is dead. There is nothing we can do to change that. What happened can't be undone. Ellie can't climb out of the well. Neither can Iestyn. And there is nothing you can do that will ever make Betty's life any happier, is there? So stop pretending, Horace. I haven't been waiting for you. How could I know that you would ever come back? Not a word from you for all those years. And the life I have had – the life I have – is the only one I will ever have. I have got Rachel. I have got Edith. And you expect me to throw it all away, at my age too, and disappear somewhere with you?'

'But there is nothing to stop you now! Iestyn Pugh has gone! He isn't poisoning your life anymore. We can be together! At last! What I always wanted.'

'And it's probably what Betty wanted too, Horace,' said Catrin severely. 'Yes, my husband has gone and it is a release for me, of course it is. I once thought about poisoning him, you know. Bought the arsenic too, from Moses Davies in Swansea. For the rats, I told him. I was going to slip it into a Welsh cake. But I wasn't brave enough. What if they had looked into it? Examined him? I would have hanged. Oh yes, I am not going to lie to you, Horace. I wish he had gone sooner. But my own life has been a mess and I don't want my Edith to make the mistakes I made. I need to be here to make sure that doesn't happen. As much as I can, anyway. I am not much of an example to her, am I?' She looked through the dark window again. 'There is someone out there, Horace. Is that your nephew waiting for you?'

She saw Horace with his head bowed, a single tear dripping from his cheek. He said nothing.

'I loved you, Horace. Of course I did. I have never loved anyone else like that. Madly. Completely. But I love Edith now. She is what matters. I am sorry if this upsets you, Horace. I have my family and you have one now, one you didn't know you had. It is a blessing for you. You are not alone anymore. Something else in your life, apart from old books in the Free Library. You mustn't forget what we had. I won't ever forget the wonder of it. But it lives in the past now. It has to.' Horace still said nothing. 'I am so sorry, Horace but I had to tell you how I feel. It is only fair. We are the sheep at the back of the flock that no one is interested in, not even the dogs. We had our time, but that was a long time ago.'

Horace stood up. 'You are wrong, Catrin. Terribly wrong. And I will give you time to think about it. I will be back tomorrow. Alone this time. We'll get it sorted. I have got a plan.' He left the cottage without a backward glance, the door slamming. She heard the trees outside shaking as the wind increased.

She wondered whether he had been listening to anything she had said. Poor Horace. Did he really believe that he had the power to change her mind, to persuade her to leave with him in elated contentment? She had experienced joy and happiness, but had paid a terrible price. And she cried; for the first time in that completely unexpected day, sitting in front of a dwindling fire in Iestyn's chair, she cried. Time never healed anything. It just blurred the memories a little. But they were always there, waiting, and she was still their victim.

*

Sellars grabbed him by his greasy waistcoat and threw Jacques into a chair. It slid backwards and clattered into the table behind, loudly.

'I am telling you now, Mickey. I 've had enough of him. It is a wonder I brought him home, the stupid old bugger. What the hell do you think you are playing at?' Sellars screwed up Jacques's muffler in his fist and pushed his head back. 'You are getting very close to a proper baytin, and you will not be waking up, I can promise you that.' He gave the muffler a final twist and then snarled.

Jacques tried to respond but could not muster the spittle. He coughed and wheezed.

'I tell you, Mickey. He was talking to that old Nanna of his. And before yous says anything, I was listening right outside the window.'

'Shocking mistake, Irvine. Leaving him alone like that. You need to have a word with yourself.'

'Too right, Mickey. And it will not be happening again. He told me he had to express his condolences on account of her now being a widow woman. Which I know about, because I did our Horace a favour, didn't I? By throwing his mate down the bloody well.' He turned and pointed viciously at Jacques's face. 'Just to stop him drawing attention to you by shouting out about you in the street when all you is wanting is a peaceful life. And then this bugger starts on about running away with the auld Nanna – as if he would be of any use to her. You can't even raise a smile. That's it now. Had a belly full of yous and your bloody library. Did you seriously think I was going to dig up some bloody barn for you in the middle of the bloody night? And I will tell you something else! I am fed up of all these bloody kids hammering on the door, asking me where you are. I have had to give them coppers to keep them away. I tell you, Mickey, if it goes on, we'll have to move him somewhere else. He is a liability, no question at all.'

Duggan shook his head regretfully. 'You see, Horace. Families can be tricky things, don't you think? Always arguments. But also there is always forgiveness. And so we will forgive your little lapse away from the obligations of family loyalty. Because that's the sort of people we are. Family, like I said.' He looked at Jacques darkly and laid a firm hand upon his forearm. 'But there has to be trust, now doesn't there? And at present it seems to me, that what your loving nephew is saying, cannot be ignored.'

'He is not my bloody nephew!'

'As I said, you are getting a little confused. And so you can't be allowed outside. Not now. We might lose you. You might wander off. We would never forgive ourselves. Am I right, Irvine?'

'Yes indeed, Mickey. We would never be able to live with ourselves if he fell into the bloody dock.'

'We would be letting the family down. Couldn't have that, could we? We'd never sleep, for sure.'

'You are not my family. I know what you want You want my money, but you ain't never having it. I am going nowhere with you. Not nowhere. You can't force me.'

'Ahh, you see, Pat. This is a little difficulty, as you might be knowing. As we have explained, patiently in my opinion, you're coming home to your family in Dublin. I thought that was clear. We have mentioned this before, haven't we, Irvine?'

'Well, I am not. I am staying here.' Jacques set his face in an attitude of defiance.

'See, you are not,' said Duggan with exaggerated patience, as if he was speaking to a recalcitrant child. 'You're coming with me. All the arrangements are made.' Duggan leaned forward and squeezed Jacques's thigh extremely hard, looking into his eyes with a smile that could cut throats. Jacques put his hand down and tried to pull Duggan's away but he didn't have the strength. 'We agreed. Home to your family. For them to look after you. Remember? For your own good. So those that love you can look after you. It will be a joy everyone can share. The happiest of days.'

'These people I have never met? Is that who you mean? I am not going, Duggan. How many times do I have to tell you?'

'Well, don't tell me again because it is getting tiresome, Pat. You are coming with us and that is because you have to. Why are you finding this difficult to understand? I am not sure I can speak more slowly than this.'

'I shall go to the police, Duggan. I will tell Bucke about you and you don't want that. They will be on to you straight away.'

Duggan snorted. 'Poor old Pat. It's all a little complicated for you, as I see it.' He removed his hand from Jacques's leg and took a pinch of the old man's cheek, working it roughly between his fingers. 'We got a man in the police station. We got a man in most places, Pat. We are not amateurs.' He released his cheek and pushed him firmly in the forehead with his finger. 'You are getting a little bit boring, to be sure. Must be your age.'

'I will tell them that you killed Iestyn Pugh. You see if I don't.'

'Ah well, you won't, see. In the first place, you are not going anywhere. Not now. Not tomorrow. Not the day after. And then, you see, in the second place, our very own constable in the police station will tell them that he heard two men arguing and that he saw you at the well, throwing someone down it. He shouted and you shuffled away. He could never tell them that you had run away, now could he? You are just an old man with damp trousers, these day. Everyone knows. That will have the constables searching long before you could ever get down to the station to tell them anything at all, even if you could. What with all the shouting and arguing you two have done, you will be number one suspect, anyway. And to think it was your loving nephew Irvine who got you away from the scene, isn't that right, Irvine? You are hardly being fair to him, Pat. Not when he has done you a favour.'

Sellars nodded impassively.

'That is not true. Sellars did it. He just said so. You know that he threw Pugh down the well.'

'It doesn't matter what I know. It is all about what the police believe. And they will believe one of their own. They are out there now, looking for you, I shouldn't wonder. We can always tell them where you are, you know?'

'You wouldn't do that. But I will tell 'em. Tell 'em everything. You lot are up to something.'

'Not even the Swansea police are going to listen to the ravings of an obsessive old man, Pat. Think about it, for God's sake. Looking for ancient treasure that someone has in their barn but doesn't know what it is? Are you mad?' Duggan paused. 'Well, yes. Probably you are. So you are not going to speak to anyone. And

230

you are coming to Ireland with your dear nephew, Irvine. Because I will tell you this. If you stay, you will be hanged. They will love it in Swansea. Nothing better. A rich old man dancing at the end of a rope? And you see, a policeman saw you do it. And you slipped away because it is your village and you knew where to hide. Too easy, Pat. You do not have a prayer.'

'I will tell them that Irvine Sellars did it. He's no nephew of mine.'

'For goodness sake, Pat. You just haven't been listening, have you? You haven't a hope. You're coming back to Dublin for your own safety. You can settle down then with your loving family. Get a dog. Take it for walks along the Liffey. Go to church. Find yourself a young wife. I'll find you one, got just the right person in mind, Pat. Look after your money, she will. You'll be fine.'

'I tell you now, Duggan. I am not going.'

'In the name of God, shut up,' said Duggan calmly, before he slapped Patagonia Jacques viciously across the face. 'Irvine, you better take your uncle for a lie down. He is looking tired today. Not himself. Not thinking straight. And we couldn't have him sleep-walking, now could we? So best if you tie the stupid old bugger to the bed. And another thing too. I don't think he has been sleeping all too well. Excited about going to Ireland, which we can understand. But he is not sleeping and he is getting overwrought. That explains everything. We can't have him getting out and about, and upsetting all these royals who we all love, by shouting off his mouth, can we? So perhaps a sleeping draught will help him. What do you think?'

Twenty

Turner was unexpectedly relieved when he went to the library for another meeting with Jacques. He didn't feel that the research – if that is what it could be called – was going anywhere and hoped that this would be the last time Inspector Bucke would ask him to do it. However, Patagonia Jacques did not arrive. He waited, assiduously exploring old newspapers, for Turner was sure that he would not willingly miss his moment in the library unless, of course, he had dragged his nephew away to dig in a field in Gower. Best use you could make of him, thought Turner. But eventually, he thought he had better check that there was no issue he should know about, so he went up on to Mount Pleasant to the dirty untidy terrace where Jacques lived. The storm had blown down two trees, the exposed roots snaking and jumbled, like the story he was sure he had discovered. At least the storm had happened before the day of the royals, but there was now a great deal to put right before they came.

He knocked, the door was opened almost immediately, and Sellars pushed his head into the small gap that he permitted. 'In the back, he is. He's got a fever. I thought you were those bloody kids again. I will tell him you called.' He began to close the door and then stopped and pushed his head out once again. 'And constable. I would be obliged if you could have a word with those brats over there.' He gestured towards two boys who Turner recognised as members of the Hatstand Gang and who appeared to be watching the house. 'Tell them to bugger off. They are getting on my nerves,' then the door was closed decisively.

How interesting, thought Turner. And perhaps convenient. It might be true that Jacques was unwell. It was that time of year and he was an elderly man. He walked slowly down Mount Pleasant Hill, stopping at Belle Vue just before Bishop Gore's School, where workers from the corporation were chopping up the fallen trees, to look at the bay.

It was a handsome view, one that inspired reflection, he

thought. It was unusually clear today. The stiff breeze was blowing the smoke from the works away across to Neath and he could see Devon clearly. There were ships busy in the channel. It was like a child's drawing, bright with detail that was spread out, not crammed together. All those journeys, heading who knew where. And then coming back. And coming back with what? Goods to trade? Or experiences? Memories?

The Royal Visit wasn't very interesting, he thought. A lot of plans and organisation, but all designed to ensure that everything happened smoothly and without surprises. That would be how you would know that it had been a success; because nothing happened. It was this other business that intrigued him, the death of Price and the note about a South American bird. There was something going on but it was all far too elusive. There had to be something, somewhere, that would make it all clear. He didn't like existing in this indistinct half-world, full of mystery and guesswork.

He ought to return to his beat, but he still had time and something was nagging away at him and wouldn't leave him alone. Those ships out in the Bay had brought it home to him. Ships bringing something home. And so he went to speak to Demelza Rippon, the bar maid at the Gloucester Hotel.

*

'I tell you now, Mickey, like I have told you before. I shall not rest until I have Bucke's liver dangling on the end of my knife.'

'And I am telling you, Irvine. Just like I have told you before. You are to leave it be. What is important here and now, is our mission. Not our personal vendettas. There will be sufficient time for such things later. But for now you concentrate. We have been sent here to do job and we will do it.'

'We don't know how much they know about us, Mickey. You tell me we have a man in the local guards passing on information. But tell me something. Just how important is he? What has he told us that we didn't know? That Flynn the Inspector has two sugars in his tea. Is that it? We need to get rid of him, Mickey. What bloody use is he? He is laughing at us.'

'He has told us many things, Irvine. He is very useful. How the constables are deployed, what their beats are. Who to watch, who can be disregarded.'

'Which is of no use at all, since they have changed everything because of the royals. For all you know, he is passing information about us to the guards. He is their agent, not ours. So deal with him.'

'You are worrying too much, Irvine. Every piece of information is important eventually, you know that. You are being too anxious, I know it. The things he doesn't tell us are just as important as the things that he does. Use your brain, for God's sake. The guards are not concerning themselves with anything other than the arrangements for the prince. Which is just what we need. They are not talking about us, which means, Irvine, that they don't know about us.'

'But that other man does,' said Aoife, twisting her hair. 'The one who shouted after me in the market. He knew my name.' Aoife closed her eyes tightly. She was pale, her face lined by anxiety and a lack of sleep.

'He is not the police, Aoife. He is from London. He is very different from the guards. His name is Grey and he has been sent here to protect their Royal parasites.'

'Exactly, Michael, and he is the one who knows my name. And if he does, then something has gone wrong. You just told me. He is from bloody London and someone has told him about me. And then on top of that there is Bucke. He knows things too, far too much. Irvine's right. We have to deal with him sooner, not later.'

'Please. It was always possible that something like this would happen. He is a professional, is Colonel Grey. He is our enemy and he is not to be underestimated. But he is only as strong as their weakest part, and that is the local guards. The inspector is a threat to us, I grant you, but the others...'

'The constable who has been with me in the library is no fool. We should never have let Jacques pull him in like he did. I didn't need him and whilst I am about it, Mickey, I didn't need the library either. Jacques was wasting his time but so was I.'

'But it took the attention away from anything else we were doing. You must see that, Irvine. It is a complicated game we have been asked to play. And you have done your part very well.'

'You are not listening to me, Michael. This Colonel knew my name. Don't you understand what that means, Michael? Something has gone wrong.' Aoife felt she had been waiting too long to repeat her anxieties.

'No, it hasn't. His purpose is nothing more than to unsettle you, to provoke you. If he thought you were going to kill the Prince then he would have detained you there and then. He didn't and that shows he doesn't know the details of our plans. Take encouragement from that, Aoife. They do not know anything. His role is intelligence, in knowing things. Perhaps he has heard your name around the town. Perhaps the man just wanted to play cards.' He tried to lighten the mood but it didn't work. 'They are all bluffing, I am sure of it. They have no substance and we will destroy them. We have been sent here with a plan, we have the talent and we have the numbers. Our movement is just and our time has come.'

'You are being ridiculous, Mickey. I am with her. We should stop now. We have been found out. I just want a moment to deal with the policeman before we go.'

'No, Irvine. No. We follow instructions. That means all of us. You, Aoife and me. And no one has told us any different. Your job is still with Jacques. You have to get him back to Dublin. Concentrate on that. Keep moving him around – we have both had enough of those library shenanigans but no one is going to trouble about his absence when there are so many other things to deal with.'

'The guards will know.'

'And the guards will be busy. And then we can deal with the informer who troubles you. But at the moment he is still useful to us and he will be useful to you. His moment will come, you know that, Irvine. All of us just have to believe in our mission and do the things we have been prepared for at such a time as this. It is all any of us can do.' He looked at the other two significantly. 'We have to be together on this. We cannot allow the others to share any doubts or fears. We need them to be confident because a moment's hesitation could be deadly. We are all going home, I promise you, and we will be heroes.'

*

At the police station, Bucke was making notes on a scrap of paper he had pulled from the waste basket, trying to find the connections that eluded him. He had drawn lines connecting circles in which he had written names. The paper was a mess, and the more he wrote on it, the less helpful it became.

All this falling, that was what was troubling him at that moment. It was becoming very difficult to believe in it, unless it was an unacknowledged epidemic. Price fell under a train? Burrows fell into the dock? That man Hamish Darr fell into a copper vat? And then Iestyn Pugh fell into a well? Did he? Did he, really? Because if he did, what was Iestyn doing? What were any of them doing? How could you know that they weren't pushed? That was the problem. Bucke knew that under pressure, constables – and some inspectors – would take the easy way out. They fell. Oh dear. Case closed. But it was too easy and in each of those recent cases, he had a doubt scratching away at his mind.

He thought about Pugh again. If he fell, then he must have had to bend over an awfully long way inside the well to lose his balance. If he was thrown into the well, then who had a motive? Patagonia Jacques appeared to have reasons for doing such a thing, but he didn't seem strong enough, as far as the Inspector was concerned. Men can find a strength within themselves that they did not know was there in extreme circumstances. But even so, Jacques didn't seem capable. The interesting possibility, of course, was Riverton. His motive was much more obscure. Could it really be revenge for the cruel execution of his grandmother so long ago? It was clear that such things were kept alive inside his mind for decades. Was he strong enough? Certainly. But it would be impossible to find any proof at the moment. It undoubtedly needed more attention, but he had none to spare, not until the Prince and his entourage had departed. At present there seemed to be no time for anything.

Constable Turner was standing in front of him. He must have knocked but he hadn't heard him. He would never have just walked in.

'I do apologise for disturbing your deliberations, Inspector Bucke. But I have given all this a great deal of thought. It would be wrong for you to have to do it, since your priorities are far more elevated. But of course, I do not have to concern myself with the royal visit. And so on my beat, which has been quiet of late, I have puzzled over the issue of Constable Price's death. And I am, I believe, entirely objective you see, Inspector. Please do not think that I am emotionally involved, I barely spoke to him when he was a colleague, which I regret for he appears to have had many and varied life experiences in which I would have been interested. But his death has so many unanswered questions, doesn't it? Not in the how, of course. But in the why. So I have walked my beat and that has rather suited my deliberations. Because my own investigations, Inspector Bucke have taken on another dimension.'

Bucke rather wished his language was sometimes less pompous, though he had to admit that he sounded quite systematic. 'Go on, Lemuel,' he said, leaning forward across the desk with interest.

'I went to speak to Demelza Rippon. She was, you may recall, Inspector, the barmaid at the Gloucester Hotel. A rather shallow young woman in my opinion, but she is important because she was probably the last person to see Craven alive, apart from his assailant.'

'And, constable?'

'Yes, well, you see. When I was in the library a few days ago with Mr Jacques, otherwise known as Patagonia, I became a little bored. As I have told you, his research methods, if that is what you can call them, are ridiculous. Guesswork informed by assumption, to be honest. So I used the opportunity to consult a number of volumes from the open shelves which resulted in my happy discovery of the word '*aucaman*.' But at one point, I removed a volume of bound copies of the Cambrian newspaper, our very own august journal, dating from 1879.'

'It would probably be better if it was only published in August, constable. Then perhaps fewer people would read it and believe it was telling the truth.'

'I had a memory of something I saw in it, which at the time seemed of little significance, but I went back today to check on what I had seen. I was not a Swansea resident in 1879 and so the reported items were all new to me, though not necessarily of any greater interest. However, Inspector. It was this one particular news item, hidden away beneath an advertisement extolling the virtues of Mrs Winston's Elixir of Youth, that I remembered. It was church news and it caught my eye for some reason. I could have missed it, but I didn't. And so I went back today, as I said, and confirmed what I had seen. A short piece written to use up a bit of space, of very little importance, and hidden away by the editor. But in it, the journalist, if indeed he should be worthy of such a name, compares the chapels of Chubut in the Welsh settlement in Patagonia with arrangements here in Swansea. And who does he refer to in that piece? Which Swansea resident does he consult for their expertise? None other than Frederick Craven, proprietor of the Gloucester Hotel, who we are told, '*has recently returned from South America.*'

'And this is true, Lemuel?'

'I think we have to assume that it is. I can certainly vouch for what I have told you referring to myself and my work in the library. If I had made it up it would have made it more interesting. But that is why I went urgently to see Demelza Rippon. To question her. Did she know anything of this? Well, it seems that she does. She said that Craven was forever talking about his time in South America, about his great successes as an adventurer and bandit, apparently. Made his fortune he told her, though if the Gloucester Hotel was the summit of his ambitions, one could be tempted to suggest that he should have offered more effort and commitment whilst he was overseas.'

Bucke said nothing, carefully processing this information.

'But consider this, Inspector,' continued Turner, 'we have our own Rhys Price himself, who worked on the copper ships between Swansea and Chile, according to our own Constable Morris, and received a note referring to the name of a south American vulture bird, which we presume was not welcome. And then we have Fred Craven, who spent time there. And, of course, we have Patagonia Jacques. There is a clue in his name, isn't there? And so it seems to me, that there is some kind of connection, however slight, that brings together Price, Craven and Patagonia Jacques and it involves South America, the land of the condor, of the aucaman, about which Patagonia Jacques professes no knowledge.'

Bucke had stopped fiddling with his pencil. The more Turner said, the more concentrated he became. 'Interesting, Constable. Very interesting. And just for the avoidance of doubt, the conclusion you have reached is that the connection between this odd collection of men can be found in South America.'

'Or in the south American experience, I would suggest. We don't know whether they were all there at the same time, though it seems likely. Something happened there. I am sure of it.'

'Excellent work, Lemuel. Very well done. And so now, what would propose that I should do? Now that I have received this compelling information from you?'

Turner nodded. 'I anticipated this question, of course I did. There has to be a way forward towards the truth. So it would seem the most sensible thing to do would be to ask Constable Morris for his thoughts, since he spent some parts of his earlier life on ships sailing between Swansea and Chile and was certainly acquainted with Rhys Price. Perhaps such a conversation will be productive, Inspector, who can say? I should not dismiss the possibility of coincidence, but at the moment I am not inclined to do so.'

*

As he walked through the dark streets of the town, the blackened walls swallowing what little light there was, Bucke realised that every part of the town held a memory of a crime or an unhappiness for him now. Swansea was a small place and each street corner seemed imprinted with sorrow. Perhaps he had been here too long, because those layers were building up, one unhappiness on top of an earlier crime, itself on top of a previous tragedy, and he knew most of them. And he had a terrible apprehension that something new and grim was about to be revealed.

He had always known that events had been leading to this. He had always known that at some point he would find himself in a conversation with the brooding Iago Morris. He had been too busy, too preoccupied. He should not have had to rely upon a junior constable like Turner, no matter how intelligent he was. Turner had done the job that was asked of him and found a solution in ways that would have taken Bucke himself much longer to uncover. But he had known that Morris was preoccupied, that he had been so ever since Price had died, and that he should have given it greater attention.

Turner had given him the information that he needed and he had a duty to follow that information and find out where it would lead, and then use that information either to dispense justice or to stop another person from being harmed, because something, whatever it was, had been set in motion. He knew where to find Morris, who had withdrawn into himself even more in recent days and so Bucke walked down to the cold pier, beneath which the sea surged and churned, like the mind of a preoccupied man. He saw that the slouched figure of Morris was hanging over the rail and staring at the water. Bucke stood next to him and waited for a few moments before he spoke.

'Funny thing the sea, isn't it? Never been a sailor myself, but I have sailed, of course. Spent those long days on it when I went out to India. Endless days, with nothing to look at. And I remember thinking to myself then, that it is nothing more than an enormous road that leads wherever you want to go. You can stand here in Swansea and start your journey to anywhere in the whole world. Like those migrant ships we get. We have roads that lead merely from Swansea to Carmarthen. The passengers on a ship are on a road that leads to America. North or south.'

Morris turned to look at him but said nothing. Then slowly returned to look out at the dark restless sea again.

'A man might sail across the sea and he could do all a manner of things, a very long way from home, amongst strangers, and think that no one will ever know. But whatever that man does, he can never leave it behind him. He might try, but whatever he has done, he will always bring it home with him. Because it is inside. He cannot escape from it. He will have memories, scars, sorrow. He can't drop those overboard and then imagine he will never see them again. It isn't possible. I know that. Look at my ear. Look at your knuckles.'

Still Morris did not speak.

'Dark tonight, isn't it? The sea looks endless. And cold and cruel. Unwelcoming. Unforgiving. And full of so many secrets.'

Then, he realised that Morris was speaking towards the sea, softly, as if a door on a broken hinge had suddenly sagged open, untouched, in his mind.

'There are things happening in your life, things you don't expect. They become normal to you but they isn't normal to no one else. And so you deal with it. It is what you do. But later on when you think about it, you think it is bloody mad. Well, that happened to me, Inspector. Can't explain it, I suppose. But one thing led to another and, after a while, what you do seems normal; It is only later, when you think about it, you understand that no living person would ever say it was normal.'

Morris seemed to be rambling, Bucke knew that. But he knew it was best not to interrupt him. Whatever he wanted to say wasn't going to be easy for him. He needed to give him time. So Bucke touched him gently on the arm but said nothing. Let him talk. Didn't matter what he said, it was better than saying nothing at all.

'Arthur is a crook. I know that, but our lives took different paths for no reason I can ever explain. He went down one path and became a villain. I went down another one and became a copper. But it could have been the other way round. I don't know why it turned out as it did. Probably no one does. Arthur has been inside, has served his time, but that could have been me. It is me you could have been looking for. It is Arthur who could have been a copper. What we have is how it turned out, and it turned out like this because it was chance. I can't tell you why it did.' Morris stopped and seized his face with both hands, as if trying to mould it into an alternative shape. 'I can't get away from that, you see. That could have been me. Why was I lucky and he was not? No reason I know why not. Except he is cleverer than me. Always known that.'

Morris fell silent, his head pushed back, his eyes closed as if travelling back through time. If he told Bucke these things perhaps he would feel better, perhaps the demons that haunted his nights would leave him alone if he spoke to Bucke. The Inspector would understand, he was sure that he would.

'I mean, when we first met he needed me, I knew that. I was a sailor, knew my way around a boat. Someone was after Arthur, that was why he was on a boat. Don't know what he had done. Didn't want to know. And we were friends, like. You need friends on a boat. Nowhere to go, is there? You can't get off if you are in the middle of the Atlantic if you don't like the company, can you? You make the most of it. But he is here now in Swansea, because in his own mind he has unfinished business. And he has come out of prison and come to Swansea because there is something he has to do.'

'And do you know what that is?'

'Why should I know what is going on inside his head?'

'Anything to do with his grandmother, you think?'

'Grandmother? What are you talking about, Inspector? Whatever he has said about the injustice of her execution, that is not why he is here. He might stick a few flowers on the doors of Cox's Farm but that is his way. No. that is not why he is here. There is another injustice that is eating away at him, I know that. And it is not finished.'

Twenty One

'We were shipping out on the *Caswell*. That's the long and the short of it. That's how it started. You might have heard of it, Inspector. Not a happy ship and the captain was Bully Best, a right villain. We couldn't take it – we signed off as soon as we could, when it docked in Buenos Aires, before all the trouble started. You must have heard about it. There was a mutiny. Hanged a poor sod in Dublin for it. Like as not he were innocent, but that is how things are. Your life don't count for much if you are a deckhand.'

'But there were three of us. Me and Pricey and Arthur had teamed up on the *Caswell* and once we had signed off, we scratched around looking for work. Lots down there, if you are ready to turn your hand to it. We drifted further south, no reason not to. Plenty of Welsh people there, if you know where to look. We ended up in a place called Chubut. You could tell it was Welsh, it was full of chapels. Mind, you could sometimes get a decent cup of tea, so it wasn't all bad. But Pricey and I did a bit of building. Bit of farm work, digging ditches, that sort of thing. Proper cowboys we were for a while, too. Arthur was happier using his head, though as far as we could see, it didn't mean he ate any better than us. And to be honest we didn't have much money. Everything happened down there on barter. Do a job, get fed. Which is fine, but it stops you looking much beyond tomorrow.

'Then we met Patagonia Jacques. He was already there, with Lardy and Fred. Suddenly we were the Six Jacks, even if Lardy was more Scots than Welsh. Everyone knew us. Pat was the man, see, we followed him. Always full of big ideas and he had a way of finding work for us. Not that he did much himself, as I come to think about it. But people knew us and they could rely on us and that sort of kept us busy. The Six Jacks. Stupid name, really, but for lots of them it was easy to say.'

'Darr? He was part of this, was he?' asked Bucke. Someone else dead. Just like Price and Craven. 'Why were the others in South America? I mean, you've told me why you ended up there. But

243

why the others?' Bucke wondered if it was just a place for fugitives, nothing more.

'As far as I could work out, I reckon Lardy was there cus he owed someone serious money in New York and it was a lot less complicated if he did a runner. Fred? Followed some woman or other, I think, though you could never be sure with Fred. But anyway, we sort of fell in together, went on an adventure across the Andes and down into Chile.' Morris looked away for a moment. 'Good times they were. Saw lots of things no one else in Swansea has seen. But after a while, Arthur and me worked our passage back from Valparaiso. I only did a couple more trips before it was time to settle down. Although, if I am honest, Arthur never settled down one bit. He was very quick to give up the sea. Had enough, he said. Too many rules and he was expected to do as he was told straight away and that was never going to suit him. And so, well, Arthur and me, we took different paths, didn't we?'

'When Dai turned up a year or so later, I used to see him around. Have a drink, a talk about the old times – though there were things we didn't talk about, like. Don't get me wrong, I liked Dai. We got on well, even if he was a lot younger than me. Then he gives up the sailing. Gets a job in the works, gets a bad chest, gets married. You know the rest. Nice old girl was Molly. Never no trouble between them, as far as I know. Then he ups and kills her. Knocked the wind out of me, that did. Didn't seem right, to me. Why would he do it? Even if he was wrong in the head, surely he would never have done a thing like that.'

Bucke watched him carefully. 'Funny that, isn't it? Three of those people you talked about are now dead. Price, Craven and Darr. Within weeks of each other. And Molly murdered. Makes you think, doesn't it?' he asked.

'If you say so,' said Morris evasively.

'And there is nothing in what you have told me that explains why they have all died. You see, Iago, I think that there is more that you have to say, if you want to do your best by Molly. She was murdered by her husband. And none of this, any of it, judging by your reactions, has been a coincidence. For me, the reason why

244

she was murdered must lie in Patagonia, and you know what it is.'

There was a long pause whilst Morris looked at the floor between his feet. And then he began.

'It was a big idea, you see. Make a fortune, that was what Pat said. I remember. Made it sound so easy. It couldn't go wrong. And we believed him because we wanted to, because it sounded good, you see. I have sailed round the Horn. You know that, Inspector. Seen friends lost overboard. Some days I believed I would never get home. Surrounded by those enormous waves, with huge towers of freezing grey water hanging over us, like being at the bottom of a well, just waiting for the sides to fall in on you. Waiting, just waiting. Battered and cold and without hope. So when Pat pipes up with his idea, then to be honest, it sounded perfect.

'Build a railway, says Pat. Right across Argentina and through a pass in the mountains to Chile. Bring all the copper to the ships, don't take the ships to the copper when there is no need. And no more Cape Horn. Simple, isn't it? And he reckons there are some natives who can show him a route through the mountains. Tells us that he has these wealthy backers who will stump up some cash, but only when we've made a start, shown willing, he said. And the thing was, Pat always knew people. Not just the Welsh, but English, Italians. So we believed him. But we didn't have enough money for much more than a bloody shovel between us. And we didn't know either, that Pat had collected creditors all across South America, like a naturalist collects butterflies. He owed a lot of money and we didn't know. But everything he said made perfect sense. That is what Pat always does, as we soon found out.'

Bucke nodded, not wishing to interrupt him.

'One of the problems was that the people in Chubut weren't that interested in having any kind of station at the top of the length of mud they called Stryd Fawr, if I am honest. That is Welsh for High Street, Inspector. Pat was irritated by the fact that they were more concerned with their houses being washed away, rather than with making money. They were far too worried about their chapels too, mainly the ones they didn't like and didn't go to. Typical

Welsh. But all the other ranchers in Argentina were dead keen. Ready to let us run a railway through their land in exchange for a station where they could load their cattle on to the train and have them down to the sea for export within hours. Easy money, Pat said. The stations didn't have to be grand, not like Swansea High Street. Just a platform, a pile of concrete, that is all. It sounded so easy and so right.

'So all we needed to do was some hard work – and get some money in, too. That was how we were going to make our fortune – be in it from the beginning. But how were we going to get enough money? Because we had nothing to invest, did we? Digging a few ditches was not going to do it, was it? Just a set of tramps, that is all we were, when all's said and done. The Six Jacks. The Patagonia Jacks.' Morris scratched his cheek, thoughtfully. 'And that was when Pat come up with another bright idea. He's always been a boy for ideas, has Pat.

'It wasn't my idea, it was Pat and Arthur probably, but it wasn't me or Pricey, though we went along with it, we didn't say no. It was Pat who always had the good ideas. It was never me.'

Bucke raised his eyebrows and Morris looked away again.

'Lots of bandits down there in them days. Probably still is. But Pat reckoned we could rob a silver mine or something and the Jacks wouldn't get the blame. It would be these American outlaws or someone. Not us. Not the Patagonia Jacks. Do the job and then drop down the other side into Chile. No one would know. Then we could start the railway line from there and no one back in Chubut would ask where the money came from. Typical Pat. Made everything sound so easy. So we headed west, like he said.'

Morris chewed at a fingernail, briefly. 'We had a guide. Guzman he was called. Lars Guzman. German I think, I don't know. Danish? Doesn't matter. And we had an Indian lad too, who looked after the donkeys. Guzman used to talk to him because he spoke the lingo, but we didn't have a clue.' Morris looked out at the dark waves. 'It took us a while, following the rivers that came down from the mountains, until they were nothing but tiny trickles under the stones. But it was up there that the mines are, see. We were looking for a silver mine where Pat had worked once before. It was so dry, and cold too. Never known cold like that and I've been a Cape Horner. And there was this terrible wind that never left you alone, and it was like it was blowing the air away. Never enough to breathe on. And rocks like teeth everywhere. No one knows what it is like down there in Patagonia. No one. No matter what you imagine, Inspector, it was so much worse. A desert, high in the mountains. But cold. And somewhere that hates you.'

He seemed to shudder at the memories that were wandering freely across his mind. Perhaps, thought Bucke, they had been locked away for too long.

'But Pat was right. There was a mine. And so we waited a day, for a couple of days I suppose, trying to keep warm and then, sure enough, there comes this mule train, about a dozen of them, all carrying the silver. We had guns. There was some shooting. It didn't last long.'

'Anyone killed?' asked Bucke?

There was a silence. 'Robbery isn't straightforward, Inspector. There were four or five Indians and three guards. They weren't expecting us but, anyway, they were rubbish guards. One of them managed to get a shot off that hit Lardy in the leg. But it didn't take long and so we left them there. Indian lad was upset when he saw these other natives were dead and so we had to watch him in case he ran off, but suddenly we had a mule train and a pile of silver ore. All very easy. So off we went, with Guzman leading the way, and with Lardy strapped to a horse. He always walked with a limp since then. Did you know that? He was lucky – the bullet went in and came out so we didn't have to dig for it.

'But everything was fine, just go down the mountain and we would be in another country. But we couldn't. There was no down that we could find and so we kept going up. Guzman said it wasn't a problem but it was getting colder and we were high and the path wasn't there. Just rocks and shale and scree, little bits of stone stretching for miles. And that is where it happened. We stopped and put Lardy on the ground to put another rag on his wound. One of the mules slipped and started to fall down this long slope of shale. There was nothing to stop it and it took the other mules too, because they were tied together. Guzman was caught up in it and he went as well. They just slid and slid until we couldn't see him no more. We could hear him screaming but we couldn't do nothing. We tried to get to him but we couldn't see him anyway and we couldn't get down the slope. Too steep. Too long. Too unstable. We managed to pick up a couple of bags but everything else had disappeared. Gone over the edge into the valley below.'

There was another extended pause.

'You have to remember,' said Morris emphatically, 'that without Guzman we were lost and the Indian lad wasn't saying much anyway. So we were trapped and we had lost everything. What should we do? Go back? Could we ever find the way? Or carry on going west? And how were we going to manage Lardy? Pat was all for shooting him there and then, but Arthur wouldn't do it. Said it was wrong. So after a while we decided to go on a bit further. Indian boy started waving and saying something and so we went where he said. It was hard going, because Lardy could hardly walk and in the end we had to take it in turns to carry him. Pat wasn't happy but the lad seemed to know where he was going and after a bit we found this small lake. A pond really. So we had water. But we didn't have anything to eat. That had gone down the shale with the mules. Pat and Craven went through the two bags we hadn't lost, but there was no food in them.'

Morris stopped talking and Bucke waited, wondering whether he would continue, but also sensing that there were still things that he needed to say. He watched as Morris pushed against the side of his head with his hands, as if trying to keep everything in place. Eventually he started to speak again, but softly.

'We had to eat, didn't we? But there was nothing. Just moss and little blue flowers. Not enough. We watched the lad. He was clever. He chewed the flowers and made a paste and put it on Lardy's leg and it seemed to soothe him. But we had to eat. So we drew lots.'

Bucke's mouth went dry as he realised how the story would unfold. 'You drew lots?'

'Yeah, but to be honest there could only ever be one loser. It was not as if he was a good Welsh boy, now was it?'

'And that made a difference, did it?'

'To us it did. He died hard, he did. Poor bugger. There wasn't much of him but he was strong. And Fred Craven didn't have much idea what he was doing. Had to strangle him you see, on account of us not wanting to lose any of the blood. Took ages. You have to understand, Inspector. We had no choice.'

'He was a boy, Iago. You said so yourself. Do you think he had a mother? Or a father, perhaps?'

He shifted uncomfortably. 'You don't know what it was like. Nobody does. He was a native. Just another native, that's all.'

'Still going to chapel, Iago?'

'It is expected.'

'By whom? God, do you think?'

'It is easy for you. You weren't ever lost in the Andes, Inspector. And anyway, I never did eat him. Me and Arthur, we never touched him. The others did. I remember them fighting over the liver. Fred would have eaten his mother if he had a need to – wouldn't have shared her, either. They took long strips from the lad's body and let them dry on the rocks. We didn't, we ate the moss and tried to catch the birds that came to steal the meat. Argued about that, we did. The others tried to keep the birds away, to stop them stealing the meat. We wanted them to come so we could catch them. But we had no fire – there is nothing to burn up there. So it was all raw. I have never been as cold in my life as I was then.' He paused again and rubbed his eyes. 'You can say what you like about Arthur, and he is a difficult bugger, but he does have very fixed ideas about what is right and wrong and you can't shift him. You can't change his mind, ever. We were never going to eat the boy. Can't say that it made the others stronger than us, if I am honest.'

He rubbed his eyes again, as if trying to erase the pictures imprinted upon them and when he removed his hands, Bucke could see that with those agitated eyes, Morris was watching for

249

birds with cruel beaks circling around them, seeking meat amongst the sharp rocks.

'We were there for a couple of weeks. Everything had changed, too. There wasn't a lot of talking. Just a lot of watching. What was going to happen next? So it was hard to sleep. Always worried that you were next, that one of the others would kill you in the night and that soon strips of your body would spread out on the rocks, drying in the wind. And every morning Fred Craven would go to each of us in turn and offer us a piece of meat. But only Arthur and me said no. The others had made that step and for them there was no going back. But that was our choice, see, and we had a pact, didn't we? We all had the same pictures in our minds. We were all blood brothers and we agreed that whatever we did, it was all to stay on the mountain. Mountain business, that's all it was. I mean, we all went through the same things. But the others broke that bond, they destroyed the pact, except we didn't know until much later.'

'And how did they do that, Iago?'

He didn't seem ready to reply. 'Every day the two of us would go out a short distance. See if we could find a possible way out. And then when we had just about given up, me and Arthur found a trickle of water that was heading north. Water trickling from the pond under some rocks. Not much but it was moving, so we tracked it, shifting rocks, ripping our hands. First thing we had found that could be any use at all, but it seemed to be heading in the wrong direction. But if we followed it, we knew it would take us somewhere and at that time we didn't care where. And then after a couple of days we found where came out from under the rocks and it turned west. We had to trust the water. We didn't have a choice. Lardy was moving better but he was still slowing us down and Fred Craven wanted to leave him behind but the rest of us said no. Mind you, the rest of us were suffering too, limping, stumbling, moving slowly. It was only Arthur and me who seemed strong enough so we had to help them all along. It was only much later that we started to think that was a bit strange.'

'And there was no one else around? You saw no one?'

'Pretty soon we did. Indians. The Mapuche, they were called. They had been looking for us because of their mates we had shot in the ambush, I think. And then they saw the lad spread all over the rocks. They couldn't have missed it. When they saw that, there wasn't much point in us hanging around. We still had a couple of guns and we fired a few shots and held them off. Their guns were old but they were frightened of us too, I think. Thought we were evil spirits or something. They wanted revenge, don't doubt it. But they kept their distance.

'We were exhausted by the time we came out of the mountains and we suddenly found ourselves in a green valley and this farmer took us in and fed us. Beautiful place. Lakes, green hills, forests. Suddenly everything seemed to be better. Never forget, we got them out, me and Arthur. We saved the buggers. The nightmare was over, we thought. After that, well, we had Lardy seen to proper in Puerto Varas, but we had all had enough by then. The others stayed on in Chile, saying they were getting a job on the railways or something but Arthur and me came home. We gave Pat what little money we had. An investment, we called it, in case he ever cracked on with his railway plans. We worked our passage from Valparaiso and then took different paths, as you know. But you see, Inspector. We didn't know. The bastards lied to us. We hadn't a clue. We trusted them. But they lied to us.' Morris shrugged and shook his head.

'I always wondered about it. Why no one came after us once we had ambushed the mule train. But they had. They had sent the army out looking for us. You see, that mule train only belonged to the President of bloody Argentina. Avell something or other. They were always talking about him in Chubut. And what those mules had wasn't just silver ore. Oh no. They were also carrying diamonds for the President from the mines in Bolivia. His secret treasure and he was anxious to find it. Very anxious. And when they found that Guzman had fallen down that mountain side and his body was torn and battered, well they believed we had all died too. They spent all their time looking for the diamonds and didn't bother looking for us. And do you know? Those two bags Pat found? They were full of diamonds and the bastards never told us. That is why they couldn't walk. Weighed down by diamonds they were, but not ones they were ready to tell me and Arthur about. And once that lie had been created there was no backing away from it. They all had to keep it going. So they didn't say. Couldn't suddenly announce it, could they? Oh by the way, been meaning to tell you…' He shook his head. 'We trusted them, why shouldn't we? But whilst we were out searching for a way out of the mountains for all of us, they were dividing up the proceeds and keeping it a secret. That is why they were happy to see us go. I mean, I shouldn't be surprised. Fred Craven had no idea of right and wrong and Dai Price was just a young lad but I reckon that Patagonia Jacques was at the root of it. I am sure of that.'

'You must have felt betrayed.'

Morris nodded. 'When Pricey came back to Swansea, he told me eventually. Leastways as much of it as he knew. He had lost his own share, he said, but really Patagonia Jacques had swindled him. Well, he would. Invested it all in a railway going into Santiago and then said that Dai's bit had gone bust. He had to come home anyway. It was getting too difficult for him. Everyone had all started to call him Dai.'

'I have wondered about that.'

Morris snorted and laughed bitterly. 'Poor Rhys. It was Spanish, see. Short for Diablo. The Devil. There were rumours about our journey across the Andes, and Pat told anyone who asked that it was all down to him. Bastard. They used to shout after Pricey in the streets,' he said bitterly, then went on quickly. 'Pat swindled Lardy and Fred Craven, too. They came back, bought pubs with what they had after Pat had bought them out. But as Arthur used to say, never let stupid people have money. They will waste it. And they did. He fleeced us all. Arthur ended up in prison and I now work as a constable all hours of the day and night. So you can't be surprised if Arthur is agitated. And I can't blame him. We deserved our rightful share. And we never had it.'

'Quite a story, Iago. So Arthur Riverton came out of prison, looking for revenge. That explains why he is in Swansea. I have been wondering about that. In the time he has been here, in whatever way, Price and Molly, Craven, and Darr have all died. Does that mean I have to look at the death of Price differently, do you think? Molly too? Are you next, I wonder?'

'No, not me. He has no problem with me. The one he really wants is Patagonia Jacques. He is at the root of all this. A liar, a cheat and as far as Arthur is concerned, living on borrowed time.'

'And where is Riverton? Where do I find him? We've got enough to do without worrying about Arthur Riverton. I would be much happier if we had him locked up.'

'I have no idea, Inspector, but I will bring him in. He knows places, but he can't stay hidden forever, not if he is after Patagonia Jacques. I went to see the old bugger, myself, last year. Asked about our investments. He denied it. Said they had been gifts. That is not going to sit too happy with Arthur, is it?"

'And have you seen Riverton, Iago? In the past few days? Have you been talking to him? He is a murderer, you know.'

'No I haven't,' lied Morris.

'But how can I trust you? You are a criminal too, Iago. You have told me about murder and robbery. Cannibalism. How can I trust a constable who has done such things?'

'You can't prove any of it, Inspector. No witnesses. Just the stupid story from a miserable old sailor. You know you have no evidence. The robbery, the shooting, what happened in the mountains....' There was a hollowness in his eyes. 'But I will square things with Arthur Riverton. That is for me to do. If he is responsible in some way for the death of Molly Price then he will pay. Rhys Price was young and stupid, but Molly did nothing. I will find him. Leave him to me.'

Bucke raised his eyebrows and shook his head. 'No, Iago. I can't do that. We enforce the law, but we don't make it.'

Morris held his gaze and said nothing.

'One thing puzzles me, Iago. You have been working in the same town as these people with whom you shared all these difficult times. How did you feel when you realised they had come back?'

He shrugged again. 'Stayed out of their way. That was all gone. I thought we had left it all on the mountain. Never liked Lardy very much anyway. Very sly, if my opinion is important to you. Craven? I stayed right out of his way. Reckoned he would have blabbed if I had tried to run him in. Never had too, thankfully. And Pat? Well, I always thought he was a bit mad, you know, a bit obsessive. Suddenly turns up, pretending to be a tramp. Looking for treasure but we all know he is not going to have any more success than the Argentine President.'

He screwed up his eyes. 'But you see, I had no reason to think they had done anything wrong. They'd just come back, that's all. People do. Pricey told me what had happened a couple of weeks before he died. Until then I hadn't a clue. Perhaps I would have felt a bit different if I had found out sooner. But Arthur knew. Arthur knew before I did. Found out in prison somehow. He has his ways. Locking him up has never stopped that. That is why he turned up here. We never left anything on the mountain, did we? Brought it all with us. Apart from the lad.'

There was a pause. 'And that boy?' asked Bucke softly. 'The one who died in the mountains. His name was Aucaman, wasn't it?'

'I never killed him,' said Morris, quickly. 'On my mother's life. I never ate him.'

Twenty Two

That had changed everything, though Bucke wasn't very sure what to do about it. Morris had confessed to a number of crimes, crimes without witnesses it seemed, and crimes that were impossible to investigate. He knew that he had to concentrate on the here and now, which was complicated enough. Everything else was a distraction that would, or would not, eventually fall into place. But he was as sure as he could be that the death of Hamish Darr had been murder, just like the death of Fred Craven. If Morris had planned to kill these men, he would have done it sooner. He had had every opportunity to carry out murder quietly and probably undiscovered. No, Riverton was the man he wanted. And he was as sure as he could be, that in some way that he had not yet identified, Riverton was involved in the death of Rhys Price, though how he had done it he wasn't sure. The pattern was there, and he was sure that Morris had identified that, too.

But where was Riverton? And did he have the time to find him? He knew that the answer to the second question was that he hadn't. No one would let him, because the Royal visit was the most important thing of all. He really ought to put Horace Jacques under police protection since Riverton was after him. He was unlikely to accept it – and neither would those who had gathered around him, though that was irrelevant. He should lock him up until the Prince had departed. He hadn't the men to spare to do anything else.

There was a meeting planned for the morning; more plans and rehearsals and he knew that he would only be told a fraction of what was intended. He had a right to know what was going on, but no one else felt he actually needed to know much at all. Not long, he told himself. Then he could return to proper police work. He decided that he would send Turner up into Greenhill to see what he could find out about Patagonia Jacques. This ridiculous research of his gave him good reason to inquire after his health and then they could spare a couple of constables to bring Jacques down to Tontine Street to ask him questions about Iestyn Pugh's death and accommodate him until the visit was over. Constance had told him about the men hanging around by a bridge. He could not ignore that. Perhaps it was the start that he needed.

But when Turner, along with Vasco, went back to the house it was empty. The Hatstand gang who had been watching were nowhere to be seen and the house was dark and locked. No one had seen Jacques for a while but that was because he had been ill, the neighbours said. Turner looked around at the narrow houses on the narrow streets, uneven, unmatched, untidy. Where could he be? And why had he gone? Was he being hidden? If that was the case, then the next question was obvious. Why?

*

Disquiet had been simmering for some days now. The poorest in Swansea, those who had been sent to the workhouse or lived an itinerant life in hovels and sheds and abandoned premises, knew that they were not wanted in the town. They were regarded as an inconvenience, a reservoir of infection, an affront, a stain on the town, a filthy pit of crime. These opinions had been magnified by the imminent visit of the Prince of Wales and they were now a shameful embarrassment that should be removed from sight as soon as possible. Bucke could understand their feelings; their hard lives were being made harder by the abuse they were receiving from those more fortunate than themselves; these people were not poor by choice, they were the casualties of town life. However, he also had an obligation to carry out the wishes of the town and so he moved the beggars and the vagrants on and ensured that the constables directed them to the soup kitchen on Back Lane, which was some way away from the ceremonial route.

However, Alexander Fredericks did not take this change in the atmosphere very well. He was a notorious and professional beggar who had, once again, absconded from the Workhouse. He had previously threatened to jump in front of the Prince's carriage and prevent it from moving, though Bucke was sure that the royal coachman would merely ride all over him and had told Fredericks so. Today, he asked for money from Father Wade from St. David's

Presbytery on Union Street, and then screamed at him when he refused to give him any but, instead, invited him to the church for food and shelter.

'I course you! May yew rot in hell for eternity! And den anudder day on toppo dat!'

He then said much the same to Mrs Crapper on Oxford Street but with the addition of 'yew fat awld bitch !' She had tried to move him away from her door and, in response, Fredericks threw stones and mud at the recently cleaned windows of her china shop. She feared for her glass, and for her splendid display of commemorative teacups in the window, and shouted for a constable. PC Smith appeared and Fredericks ran. For a man who was generally fuelled by beer rather than food, he was surprisingly quick as he scampered away towards Goat Street, but it was his considerable misfortune that the cry for help was also heard by PC Turner, returning from Mount Pleasant, who had with him his dog.

This was one of the best moments Vasco had experienced for quite a while. He was immediately released in pursuit, barking in excitement, with Turner in his wake. He raced down Goat Street, up Caer Street to Castle Square and eventually ran Fredericks to ground in a narrow passage between the Plume of Feathers public house and the bank next door. Vasco was delighted and wanted to play some more, but Smith pulled the man away, who was not so breathless that he could not swear loudly, put handcuffs on him and dragged him back to the Workhouse.

Turner had been called to the meeting at the Town Hall where plans for the Royal procession were being discussed and he had also been asked to bring Vasco with him to check the bandstand on the side of the new dock for signs of rats. So this chase would not delay him, for it had not taken him off his route. But Vasco was reluctant to depart. He was scratching at the door of the pub, as if he wanted to go inside. As far as Turner knew, the place had been empty for a while, but he thought he heard something– a hammer, perhaps, or a brick falling. But there were so many noises happening around him as those essential final arrangements were being made, that he could not be sure where it had come from. He would have to come back after the visit, he decided, for Vasco was very interested in the door, but time was getting on and they had to go.

He met Bucke on the steps of the Townhall and they went in together. Bucke had been asked to bring a constable with him who could trust and of course, Turner was the best of them all. In fact, thought Bucke, Stanley Ball was right; Vasco was more use than some of the more underachieving constables. It would be a valuable experience for Turner to see how an important event was organised, and if he was given a role, he knew it would be done properly.

Bucke looked around the chamber. He nodded at Flora Beynon, then Colonel Grey; he saw a woman he assumed was Therese D'Auch and a number of unidentified men, equipped with hard, unsympathetic stares. Turner's attention however was somewhere else entirely. Standing away from the others, looking rather nervous, was the most beautiful young woman he had ever seen. She had shining black hair that was pulled into neat bun with a remarkable white stripe running through it and he found himself trying to decide whether she was short or of average height? And why was that important? He didn't know but he could not decide since his attention was fixed on her large mesmerising dark eyes. There seemed to be full and beautifully shaped lips below but all he could see were those eyes. Her head seemed to be on one side, looking at him quizzically, and then at Vasco, and whilst the older people moved around amongst each other to gossip, she came across the room to him. He could not believe it was happening.

'What a beautiful dog, Constable…'

'Turner, ma'am. Though for tiresome reasons some of my colleagues call me Page.' He realised he was bumbling but he could not stop himself. 'It is what passes for humorous discourse in the police station. My proper name is Lemuel.'

'That is a very fine name, Constable Turner,' she said smiling. 'And have you travelled as far as Mr Gulliver did?' She stroked Vasco gently between the ears.

'How perceptive of you. ma'am. My mother tells me that is why I received that name. Because my parents travelled widely throughout the world. In fact, was born in Lisbon. I spent my earliest years in Portugal.'

'Oh my goodness, how exciting!'

'It was. I remember it as a beautiful place, Miss...'

'Beynon.' She bent down to stroke Vasco more firmly, who responded to her touch and curled himself around her hand, his tail wagging. 'You have told me your name, constable. What is the name of your dog?' She rubbed the dog's ears between her fingers.

'This, Miss Beynon, is Vasco, named, of course, after the great Portuguese explorer. Vasco da Gama.'

She shrugged, as if this was an unimportant detail. 'And is it appropriate, as a name? Does he actually explore? '

'Most certainly. When he is allowed to do so.'

'And is he obedient?'

'Generally. Particularly if you speak to him in Portuguese.'

She laughed. 'Don't worry Vasco,' she said, patting his flank. 'I shall not be issuing you with any instructions.'

'Miss Beynon, I am sure that Vasco would do whatever you ask. I can see that you have made quite an impression on him already. He has had a particularly entertaining morning,' he said and told her of the pursuit of Fredericks through the streets. 'It was nothing more than a fox hunt brought into the town and was not much of a challenge for a dog of his talents.'

Her eyes narrowed slightly. 'And do you approve of foxhunting, Constable?'

'I regard it as unnecessary cruelty, Miss Beynon,' he said, hoping fervently that she was not a member of a local hunt. 'To pursue an animal which has more integrity that those who chase it, and then to kill so cruelly, seems to me to be wicked. I don't understand why it is permitted. I do apologise if this shocks you.' He instantly regretted being so forthright but it was too late now and a silence hung in the air between them. 'Oh my goodness,' he thought. 'What kind of stupid thing have I done?'

'And what, Constable, do you think of vegetarianism, if you are so moved by the hunting of animals?'

'I think it is an interesting concept, Miss Beynon, which flourishes in many parts of the world. I have often considered the virtues of a vegetarian diet on my travels. Local people appear to thrive, so why shouldn't I?' Why did he feel the need to say such things?

'Perhaps you should think more carefully about it, Constable. Then you might feel less hypocritical when you stroke Vasco,' and she bent down to ruffle his ears once more.

'What an interesting point, Miss Beynon. I have not considered this before.'

'Please, Constable. I would be honoured if you would call me, Emily.'

Turner blushed 'That is one of my very favourite names. No, honestly, it is. It reminds me of Emily Bronte, of course. Please call me Lemuel. It would be an honour.'

She looked at him closely and then smiled. 'If you are such a reader perhaps I, too, will call you Page.'

Turner realised that he was perfectly happy for her to do so. He looked at her in awe. That someone like her should want to speak to him…

Bucke called to him across the room. 'Constable Turner, if I may…'

He nodded. 'I must attend to my duties, Miss Beynon.'

'As must I,' she replied. 'I am an attendant to Lady Therese D'Auch. The elegant lady over there. She is terribly exciting.'

'Oh,' said Turner, downcast. 'I thought you were from Swansea,' his dreams suddenly in shreds at his feet.

She laughed. 'I am really. I am just a maid for the day. We both have work to do, it seems. But perhaps I can offer you a pamphlet to read by the great Frances Power-Cobbe? She is my mentor on all things, particularly animals. And on the persecution of women, of course.'

'I would be delighted to do so. It is my great regret that I was unable to listen to her on her recent visit to Swansea, Miss Beynon.'

'Emily!' She laughed, with a face so open and honest that Turner could feel his heart melting. 'My name is Emily, Page! Don't forget!'

Flora, her mother, who was sitting in the shadows at the back of the council chamber, was completely shocked. She had not seen Emily speak to a male so comfortably before. She couldn't hear what she said but she could see her reactions and Emily seemed at ease in his presence, relaxed, normal. In fact, more normal than, in truth, she was happy with. What had happened to her? This was only a constable, after all. She appeared to have forgotten all her obligations. Bringing her to Swansea was clearly a mistake. But that wasn't all she was now worried about. What was this performance in the Town Hall about? They had started rehearsing something with extremely peculiar movements.

As the morning went on, Turner found it hard take his eyes away from Emily, watching carefully as she practised a number of choreographed movements that seemed to involve her moving at a precise position in relation to Lady Therese. Emily seemed to stay behind her, apparently watchful, then on a signal, which he couldn't see, she would turn to look to the rear as if, thought Turner, she was protecting Lady Therese from someone.

He was forced to drag himself away to be introduced to a man called Rhodes. Bucke's acquaintance, the well-spoken and confident Colonel Grey, told him of the part he was expected to play.

'Now Turner, there is much you do not know and which you do not need to know. And, to be frank, such is my life, too. But the day will end with a grand ball in the Music Hall. I do not know who is responsible for this completely ridiculous idea, but this is what we have to deal with, in a particularly unsuitable venue. It is a security nightmare and you would have thought this would be perfectly obvious. But what, apparently, do I know?' he said with a dramatic flourish. 'There are always photographers around these days to record such prestigious events for an excited future. What a thrill it is for us to have ourselves thus preserved.' He yawned in an exaggerated way. 'There will be photographers and their assistants everywhere. And this will now include you, Constable Turner. Rhodes here – a fine, trustworthy man – will be an additional photographer and you will be his assistant. Your job is not to take photographs. You have merely to pretend to take photographs. You are there to watch the crowds and to provide an additional level of security. You will follow Mr Rhodes' instructions who will, in his turn, be following mine. In such a way we cannot possibly get things wrong, can we, Mr Rhodes?'

'Absolutely not, Colonel Grey,' said Rhodes, winking at Turner.

'Just keep a watchful eye, Report anything you don't like the look of, and if there is shooting, keep your head well down. There may be a couple of shots fired but nothing to alarm yourself about, in my estimation.'

Turner's eyes widened in fear at that idea. Emily Beynon would be there? With the royal party, it seemed. And there might be shooting? How could they possibly place someone as radiant as her in danger like this?

*

Bucke had another meeting in the afternoon.

Following protracted negotiations involving a number of intermediaries, they met in the Welcome Coffee Tavern on High Street, chosen as a convenient location for both of them and perceived as neutral territory. Bucke and Giblin knew each other well, both aware of the status of the other and were occasionally ready to meet, to manage issues in the Irish community together.

Jimmy was not comfortable in the Welcome Coffee Tavern, surrounded by the paraphernalia of temperance. He approached the coffee that Bucke had bought for him suspiciously. He added sugar generously to the cup that sat in front of him, sniffed it, and then sweetened it some more.

He sighed. 'This is not as good for you as a nice cup of tea. You can see that, for sure. 'Tis a strange world indeed when there are people who want to drink this.' He put his cup down. 'The world is a mad place. That never changes. So inspector, you wanted to see me.'

Bucke drank from his coffee cup, making him wait. 'You see, Jimmy,' he said eventually, 'it is always a pleasure to share moments like this with you. But I must not lie, I have a problem that needs the attention of both of us.'

'More than one, likely enough. That is your job, as I see it. Dealing with other people's problems. A wonder you are not worn out completely.' He shook his head sympathetically. 'And how is Miss White? A bonny lass and much too good for you,' he said with a smile. 'So they say.'

'She is very well thank you, Jimmy. It is kind of you to ask.'

'You'll be wanting that divorce, I'll be bound, so that she can make an honest man of you.'

'Her greatest wish, you can be sure of that. But let's not trouble ourselves too much with domestic issues. Let's talk about your problems, shall we?'

'My problems? It must be this coffee that has turned your mind,' he said, moving his own cup further away with exaggerated distaste. 'I don't have problems. You are the one with problems, you told me so, unless you are talking about our Shelagh and there is no man alive can do much about her. Reminds me a lot of her old mother, god bless her.'

'Jimmy. Please. People are saying that you've got a lot of visitors up on the Hill at the moment. New people. Ones we have never seen before.'

'Ah sure,' he said, waving a dismissive hand. 'It is this royal visit business, Inspector Bucke, sir. All ready to wave the large flags, these lads. Very patriotic, you know. They can't hardly wait for the big day.'

Bucke raised his eyebrows. 'Of course.'

'It will be good to be able to show the royals the sort of respect they deserve, always thought so.'

'You see, Jimmy, I will not lie to you. These newcomers of yours? The ones who you say are eager to cheer the future King? Well, I believe they are deceiving you. I am sorry to have to report that I have received unfortunate information. It appears that some of these visitors carry with them a certain reputation. I will go as far as to say that these visitors are not the fervent royalists they have led you to believe.'

'I am shocked, Inspector Bucke. Shocked that you could believe such a dreadful thing. And who is it has been spreading such vile lies? I shall be taking legal advice, Inspector, you can be sure. A vile calumny.'

Bucke shook his head sorrowfully. 'I regret to say that these are reliable sources, Jimmy, and it pains me to see you tricked in this way. You, an old friend. But I don't want you to worry. Not at all. Because there are some other people here in Swansea. People I know. People I can vouch for. They are eager to deal with any irritating little difficulties that might regrettably emerge.'

'Word has come my way, Inspector,' said Giblin warily. 'When just one person knows something, it is no longer a secret.'

'And I don't think either of us would be happy for things to get out of hand. In my opinion, anyway.' He threw out his hands expansively. 'Everyone's got different opinions about things and that is right and proper. But we don't want more bodies in carts on the Strand or propped up outside public houses. I am sure we agree on that.'

'Surely,' Giblin said, his eyes not wavering from Bucke's. 'I won't lie to you. I have given the matter some thought. It puzzles me that this sort of thing has happened recently. it hasn't happened before, not when we have been dealing with things ourselves.'

'Do you know, Jimmy? My thoughts exactly. Why now? When we have always been able to sort things out between the two of us, quietly.'

'You are not far wrong, Inspector.'

'You see, these new friends of mine, who are also in town, have come to see the splendours of the Prince and the Princess, of course.'

'A fine-looking woman by all accounts.'

'Indeed. But my friends are so easily distracted. And they might find other things that need their attention, other than waving joyfully from amongst the happy crowds.' Bucke paused. 'They are ruthless, Jimmy.'

Giblin nodded his head slowly. 'As are mine, Inspector. That does not make for the happiest of arrangements for either of us, as I think about it.'

'Not at all. And I wouldn't want anything to happen that might poison our relationship and the relationship the constables have with your people in Little Ireland. We have had a few good months, Jimmy. I don't want to lose that. It would take some time to rebuild any trust we might lose. And you can't rebuild lives, Jimmy. Not if they have been lost.'

Giblin scratched his chin. 'Always the trouble with outsiders, as I see it, Inspector.' He looked around the Tavern. 'I don't suppose they do a decent cuppa tea hereabouts?' He resigned himself to his disappointment. 'Tell you what I will do. You keep your constables away from the Hill. We'll make sure there is nothing that requires their presence. But leave me up there with my people and we will see what we can do. It is all about trust, in the end, isn't that right? You'll be too busy rehearsing the national anthem anyways to bother with us. You know, it is hard to believe, but some visitors get over-excited if they sees a policeman, as if they have never seen one before.'

'I can't promise to keep all the constables away, all the time. Be sensible. Anything might happen. Something that has got nothing to do with the visit. But I can make sure that there will be no regular patrols.'

Giblin shrugged. It had been worth a try and there was no shame in compromise. 'I mean, I can't persuade Greenhill to love the Prince and wish him good health and all that, now can I?

265

They'd rather see his liver fried with onions and, for me, they has a point. But this, Inspector Bucke, is where we live. Before this bloody visit and afterwards. And I might have made that point, if for argument's sake, I had had such an opportunity. I would, to be honest, be happy to share this with other parties again, if I had another chance and if they would bloody listen.' He picked up his coffee cup, looked at it and put it down again. 'Let's not be too black and white. That will get us nowhere. We can all muddle along together perfectly well, as I see it, with a bit of give and take, that sort of thing. And it is all very well certain people, who I will not name, telling me that there has to be big changes made, which I grant you is not a bad idea at the end of the day, but we have got to get on with each other afterwards. And I am not a man for feeling it is right to take away a child's daddy or, god forbid, his mammy. You don't want that on your conscience, now do you?' He looked expectantly at the Inspector.

Bucke thought he knew what Giblin was saying; he hoped he knew what Giblin was saying. 'So Jimmy, if I put our constables on different beats, because these are busy days as you can imagine, you might be able to stop something happening that could have serious consequences?'

'I don't want you to get the wrong end of the stick, Inspector Bucke. I would happily see the bastard Prince dead and an end to the British in Ireland, begging your pardon. But when that happens, and God help us it has to happen soon enough, I would be obliged if it could happen somewhere else and not in Swansea. So think on, Inspector. And see what you can do.'

'A step at a time, Jimmy. Let's start off by making sure that the Prince of Wales leaves Swansea alive, shall we?'

'It is hard for me to say that is my concern, Inspector. But if you could oil the wheels, as we say, that could help a lot, when it comes down to it.' Bucke waited. 'I don't know if you have noticed, but it occurs to me that some of them railway embankments between here and Bridgend are in a shocking condition. Once the noble prince, may he rot in hell, has got to Swansea, it would be a crying shame if one of them embankments

266

should collapse. You know, somewhere near Pyle, shall we say? Because the old royal bugger would then be trapped in Swansea, wouldn't he? Who would want that? And he has got places to go, him being so important. So they would have to send out a team of navigation engineers, wouldn't they?'

'Yes they would, Jimmy. Vital work. We couldn't have the Prince trapped, could we? Not when he must be in Monmouth on Wednesday.'

'And the lads who would have to do it would be disappointed something dreadful, on account of missing the royal party and their exciting procession. You can understand that, can't you Inspector? They would need a measure of compensation to take the edge off their disappointment.'

'Without a doubt.'

'And so do you think we should be considering double time, Inspector? It is only fair.'

'I always try to be fair, Jimmy. But if we receive news of such an embankment issue then we would have to respond straightaway, assuming of course that we could find a well-connected ganger who could put out a reliable team at a moment's notice. On double time. Of course.'

'You know, Inspector. It never rains but it pours,' said Jimmy Giblin, smiling, 'and that is when embankments collapse.'

Twenty Three

Just another day, just another day. Duggan had woken a couple of hours earlier and felt as if he had never been to sleep. How could he have expected to sleep? Today was the day when he might die. But then, so was every day, and it was beginning to wear him out. The constant vigilance. The constant violence. The never-ending, unwavering commitment. The belief in the cause. There were days when he wasn't sure what the cause was anymore. Surely there was more to it than just killing people who disagreed with you?

He looked at the dirty ceiling and sighed, the narrow, flimsy bed shaking in response.

These were dangerous moments. Once you became exhausted by the unrelenting conflict, you lost your edge, you became vulnerable. And Duggan knew he was vulnerable. What was the point? He had started to ask that question rather a lot, recently. What was he fighting for? Some days he could not have said. On the days when he remembered phrases like 'The Freedom of Ireland' and 'The Emancipation of its People,' he sometimes could not remember what they meant.

And was this the way to achieve that end? Cruelty? Murder? Dishonesty?

'I have no idea,' he said aloud and the sound startled him, for he thought this conversation was all taking place inside his head.

Everything had eroded. His belief, his energy, his faith. Everything was now a battle and he knew that eventually the greater force would triumph. And he would die. There was no sentiment. He would die because he had to be taken out of the game. He knew that this was a game from which you could not retire. And so was today the day? He didn't know. But one day it would be. Every day he was merely one mistake from death and he knew there was little he could do about it.

And, if that happened and he did die, his blood gathering in a gutter, would his death have made the world a better place? Would his death have served to enhance the cause of Irish independence? He didn't know. And would his death be a price worth paying? To give away the only life he would ever have, because it might make the lives of people he would never meet, better at some point in a future in which he would have ceased to play a part? These were things he would never truly know, but he spent long hours, sleepless before the dawn, worrying about such things.

Some days it was too much to bear. And he knew that those days were the most dangerous of days, because once he allowed those doubts to eat away at him, then there was no room in his mind for anything else. But he could not stop the questioning during these last few days. Grey was in town and he had a terrible fear that he was being outplayed.

Last night the Royals had arrived at the temporary station built for them at Singleton so that their transfer from platform to Abbey would be seamless and untroubled. He had gone down to see them, mixing with an excited crowd desperate to be part of a historic moment, barely supervised by a large number of irritable policemen. He had managed to catch a glimpse of them, these two people whose life and death rested in his hands, though they were not aware of this. They would relax, have a formal evening of toasts and handshaking, dressed in the finest clothes, in the most privileged of surroundings, and all the while the man who was arranging their deaths was only a short distance away.

This morning it didn't seem so easy. What was he doing? What was the point? After all the people he had killed, what had he actually achieved? And this is what his life had become. He was lying alone in a stranger's house a long way from home, in an uncomfortable bed, in a town where there were people he knew wanted to kill him, and if he asked himself whether he had been a force for good or for bad, the truthful answer was that he didn't know.

But he did know for sure that there could be no turning back. He had come so far, there was no point. He had to go on. But his conviction had been worn down. He wasn't an evangelist anymore. He knew that. It was not about a mission anymore. It was about survival. And this morning he didn't know how he was going to manage that. He sighed again and swung his feet on to the floor. Something cracked beneath him, ominously. Whatever happened, whether good or bad, he wouldn't be sleeping here tonight.

He often thought about what had happened, about how this life of his had all started twenty years ago. Or was it 21? He could never be sure. But now he had come to the realisation that the English soldier who shot Maureen on that day, probably did it accidentally. He'd gone over it in his own mind every day, and the anger had unexpectedly burnt itself out. For most of his adult life, the death of his betrothed had been a conspiracy, the deliberate act of a hostile, repressive state. But he didn't think that it was as clear as that any more. A frightened boy told to shoot into the sky and the gun had never been aimed at her. Perhaps it had gone off accidentally, but the love of his life had bled to death whilst he had been handcuffed in a police wagon.

It had become the rage that had fuelled him for so many years. But he now believed that the boy soldier had been given no target, no instructions to aim or to kill. He had fired his gun because he had been told to shoot, perhaps for the first time. He was just as much a victim as anyone in the crowd who had been protesting against rising food prices. He had been the same as them, a poor boy from a slum, except he was in a uniform. He never knew who the rifleman was. If he had known, perhaps it would have been easier. There would have been another death and his grief thus assuaged. Instead, he had entered this endless war and he did not think that he could do it anymore. He never left the battlefield; he took it with him wherever he went. But today he was facing an enemy as ruthless as the Fenians were themselves; Grey, an appropriate name for a man about whom no one seemed to know very much at all.

He stood up and stretched, then ran his fingers against his scalp, scratching to stimulate his brain. Then he stood before the washstand and splashed his face with the cold water.

Just another day, just another day. In which I kill someone.

270

Or in which they kill me.

And my blood will be pooling on someone else's floor.

He tried, but he could not shake than image from his mind. He needed to be positive. They had a plan. It was a good plan. But then the doubts once more. Would it work? Who could say? Would all of his team escape? Unlikely. They had clearly started to feel uneasy and he hoped desperately that he had managed to keep them committed to the cause, at least for the rest of the day. He hoped he had managed to persuade them – but he also felt guilty at doing so. Some would probably die.

They trusted him, trusted him to get things right. He knew that and it was flattering. But they didn't need to know the truth. Yes, some of them would die. He couldn't tell which ones, but they would. His responsibility was not to prevent death, merely to keep the deaths and horrendous woundings to a minimum. That responsibility had begun to weigh him down.

They were short of men, he knew that, which would be the worst failure of all. He had recruited young men from Greenhill who seemed willing enough but he was not convinced that he could rely upon them entirely, if, and when, bullets started to fly. They were foot soldiers and they were untrained and likely to die, because you needed more than enthusiasm. And Sellars would disappear to take Patagonia Jacques to Dublin. That was almost as important as the assassination itself. But Sellars was another man he could not deploy. And then there was the idiot policeman. He knew too much. He had to be dealt with. It wasn't as if there was nothing else to do. And where were his temporary policemen that he had imported? Deployed properly, he hoped. But who would check on that if he didn't? It was too much.

There were two sides in this conflict. But did those different arguments really matter? Was it worth it? Spin the coin and let that answer that question. Why not spin a coin to answer any question. Ireland free? Or Ireland enslaved, still? At least no one would die.

He splashed more water on his face. He was always apprehensive before a mission. Nervous. Consumed by self-doubt. But today it felt different. Deeper. Overwhelming. But then, he had never been asked to kill the heir to the English throne before.

He hid his face in the rag that passed for a towel. And then he wondered. What would be the consequences of what they planned to do? Would the assassination set in motion a terrible sequence of reprisals that would devastate his own country? On the other side of that coin, could it bring about independence? Or would it wipe villages from the map? This must have been considered, mustn't it? But if it had, then no one had taken any time to share those calculations with him. He had to play his own part in the plan, without ever knowing the rest of it. Same as it ever was.

Perhaps his name would go down in history, as his handlers said. But why? As the man who set Ireland free, so a hero? Or as the man who set fire to its people and thus a reviled villain? It was hardly likely he would ever find out. The same ideas were firing in an uncontrolled way around his mind and already he was exhausted. Too much thinking. He picked up the railway ticket that he had left on the flimsy chair. Tomorrow, Mr Cockaigne was taking the train to Llanelly to start a long and indirect route back to London. It wouldn't be what they were expecting. It had worked before so why not again? But he was worrying more these days. You could be trapped on a railway platform. Or in a room. Anywhere.

All he could do was to immerse himself in action. He had to clear his mind and lead his men. This was his duty; this was his role. He had to set their work in motion and to trust each one of them to carry out their part properly. He hoped that the British had no idea of the details of the plot but he knew that he could never be sure. He clutched at the thought that if Eli had ever known the details of the mission, he hadn't had time to share them with anyone, since they had worked out that he was an English spy quite early on. He'd been careless – being seen leaving a message in a hole in a wall on Croft Street was a basic and unforgivable error. That was something that he had to hang on to. It gave him hope that Grey didn't really know anything; that he was playing games. It was very sad. Duggan had quite liked Eli – or at least the part he was playing. But he had been removed because of what he might possibly know. It was just a game – with extremely high stakes. And there was the unanswerable question. Was his own time up? Was he about to be taken off the board?

*

It was cold and dark, for it was not yet day break, but already the streets were lined with those who had determined that a bleak night on an unyielding pavement was a price worth paying for an unblocked view of the royal procession. Bucke watched them, unable to understand the devotion they were offering to these people they had never met. He knew too well that those hopeful of the very best viewing points were soon to be bitterly disappointed, and he wondered whether their children, insufficiently wrapped in their best garments and thin blankets, would ever agree that this had all been worthwhile. Boredom had already inspired an endless stream of children to create makeshift toilets behind the walls that enclosed the small front gardens on Walters Road. What else were they to do? It was going to be an extremely long day for everyone.

*

Emily stood nervously in the hallway of Singleton Abbey, waiting for the royal couple, waiting for departure, and wondering why she had agreed to this. All around her stood elegant women, with carefully dressed hair and pearls, in expensive coats and the kind of hats rarely seen in Swansea. There were mature gentlemen in full naval uniform. It seemed to her that she was now inside a fairy story and in her bulky Welsh costume was merely a quaint and entertaining illustration. Everyone looked at her and examined the details, some smiled and admirals gently raised their bicorne hats, yet no one spoke to her, for she was nothing more than an embellishment. She felt conspicuous and completely out of place. An attendant to a woman with a gun? Why had she agreed to this? She was unable to anticipate what might happen and doubted very much that she could carry out the tasks expected of her, apart from providing the amusing spectacle of a cockle woman at court.

273

Therese appeared at her side and took her hand discreetly, squeezing it gently. 'Emily, you look perfect.'

'I feel so stupid, dressed like this.'

'Doesn't everyone?' Therese whispered. 'Don't be misled, Emily. All the people you see here, waiting in this hallway for the arrival of people with even finer clothes, are no different. They are all wearing their own uniform, just as you are. It is a disguise, nothing more. Look at my hair, Emily. You know it isn't real.' She put up her hand and touched the elaborately designed confection on her head. 'I could have a dead poodle on my head for all the difference it would make. You know that.'

'But I can't do what you have asked of me. It doesn't sound like a game anymore. I can't be brave. I thought I could, but I can't. All the things you have talked about, they are real, aren't they?'

'Emily. Please listen. You have already been brave in your life. Much braver than I have ever been. You have been scarred, but I know you are recovering, I can sense it. I am immensely proud that I have had the opportunity to have met you. No,' she said, when Emily tried to interrupt. 'Please listen. These are not empty words. Don't be taken in by this act of mine. It is all a sham. You see, Emily, I am damaged. Once I was an empty-headed young woman in expensive clothes, just like those over there, thinking they are important. I had not a care in the world. I was happy and in love. And then it all turned to dust in front of my eyes and I became what people think I am, because it suited me. I may appear reckless, but that is because it matters nothing to me, whether I live or I die. I am telling you the truth now, Emily. I don't care. Not one bit. Of course, I do not want to experience terrible pain, but if I could count to ten and then instantly cease to exist, then I would have done it years ago. You can only experience love as profound as the love I had, once in your life. I had it, but it was snatched away from me, and it will never come back. Everything else has been an afterthought.' She smiled at Emily. 'You are brave and you are a survivor, like me. The difference is that you want to survive and I am not sure.'

Emily did not know what she could say, as she stood on the threshold of a day that would be like no other she had ever experienced. She pulled at her shawl nervously.

'Don't be deceived, Emily. If you are acting, if all these people around you are acting, then so am I. And you are an essential part of this performance we must deliver. So chin up, Emily.' There was a distant sound of clapping and the resplendent figures around her, started to arrange themselves more formally. 'This will be the Prince and the Princess, late as usual. Come on, remember your part, we have work to do.'

Constance watched them together from across the hall and wished that she, too, could be having a serious conversation but with someone else. Rumsey had promised her that he would explain everything later and it had better be good. How had this happened? How was it that she, the town's whispered scarlet woman, was part of the Lady Mayoress' entourage? Surely Rumsey must have realised what a difficult position it put her in? The nudges, the comments, the disdainful nods. Unless he hadn't. Unless he thought that, in some strange way, she would be excited and thrilled at her proximity to royalty? Did he know nothing about her at all? Had he really been that pre-occupied?

All Constance could see was the disapproval of the people she knew, who were asking themselves how it was that she was there and they were not. She had neither asked for this nor welcomed it, but was now in the public gaze in a way that was entirely unhelpful. She felt ridiculous, fraudulent really. People who she did not wish to see, could see her. 'Who does she think she is? All airs and graces? No better than she should be. I could tell you a thing or two about her, don't you worry.' Whatever had Rumsey been thinking?

Flora was, of course, quite beside herself, with a fixed grin of bewildered ecstasy at her social elevation displayed indelibly across her face. Think of it! Princess Alexandra had been so close she could have reached out and touched her, though, naturally, she would never do such a thing. But my goodness she was so close. And Emily was even closer! If only David had been here to witness

275

it! He would have overcome his objections; she was sure of that. What a wonderful day, she thought, wishing only that she could slow down time. This triumph was disappearing far too quickly. A day that would live forever, was melting away before her eyes.

*

Bucke, was overwhelmed by the enormity of the task that confronted him. He laughed hollowly after he muttered to himself, 'I don't know which way to turn.' There was no one to tell him. But how could he possibly know? There were difficulties everywhere. How could he know what was going on across the town? How could he decide which was the best place for him to be?

Constance had said to him yesterday, in an attempt to soothe his anxieties, 'You can't be everywhere, Rumsey.' And that was entirely the problem. There was at least one potential crisis, sometimes more, for every yard of the procession.

And who actually was in town today? The whole population of south Wales it seemed. Anyone of them could be a maniac and, if any of them were, he could guarantee they were not wearing a badge that identified their status. The temporary constables, spread across the whole length of the route, were a gift from the Watch Committee that sent chills down his spine. They were to be deployed merely to control the crowds. In other words, to stop strangers falling beneath horses. And if one of these careless people, eager to be trodden on by a Hussar, was carrying a bomb? Was a beer-infused temporary constable going to stop it, he wondered?

There were no modern devices he could employ. His means of communicating with the constables, real or pretend, along the whole of the route, he had placed in the capable hands of the Hatstand Gang. Children, but at least they knew what they were doing, and he knew what he was getting.

Some children were still asleep wrapped in blankets on the pavement, oblivious to the noisy business around them. Bucke did wonder whether it was really a worth all this. But people wanted to be part of something that was unusual, that they could talk about, that they could look at proudly and say, 'I was there.' He hoped this wouldn't be for the wrong reasons. And amongst all these people, how did you identify those who were a threat? Where should he position himself? The real danger was that in trying to be everywhere, he would end up being nowhere.

He found himself standing on Walters Road, wishing that the procession would start. It was still only 10.00 o'clock and they had already made their first arrest of the day. Perhaps inevitably, that honour was awarded to Nick the Holly, who stole a pocket watch (without a chain) from a chemist from Neath who had foolishly left it on a bench in St James' Terrace whilst he refastened his shoelace. Holly was easily identified by his scarred forehead and arrested a few minutes later, bemused and irritated because, however cunning he tried to be, he always seemed to be caught so quickly.

At least when the procession started there would be a momentum to take his mind away from shapeless apprehensions of disaster. Each stage of the procession could then be ticked off successfully from his mental list, ensuring his concerns were reducing by every minute, and then - as he turned casually to see Dai Potato setting up his cart against a stone garden wall - he saw it; the barrel of a gun protruding from a half-opened upstairs window above his head. He ran, leaping over the low wall and attracting the puzzled attentions of this section of the crowd. He threw his shoulder against the door of the house which flew open with surprising ease and ran shouting up the stairs, desperately trying to assess the layout of the house as he reached the top of the stairs. Where was the window? Which room? Left? right.? A door opened and a man appeared. Was he armed?

'Police! Stop!' he shouted, whilst realising that he sounded especially feeble.

The man at the door looked confused. 'I have rented this room for the day, officer, Through my solicitor Mr Douglas of Temple Street. If there has been some misunderstanding… We are here to watch the procession,' he added rather ineffectually.

Bucke panting, pushed him against the door jamb and almost fell through the door, expecting to confront an anarchist with a gun who would fire at him at point-blank range. Instead he saw a family. An alarmed woman he assumed was a wife and mother, a puzzled teenage daughter waving a flag and a boy in a cap and short trousers pointing a toy gun out of the window and making shooting noises.

He felt so very stupid. He looked around the room, taking in the alarmed figures, the tired office furniture, the threadbare carpet and the expansive view of Walters Road. Bucke's silence instilled courage in the man and he began to manufacture outrage.

'I say, officer this is completely out of order. We have rented this room legitimately. I have papers. We are not intruders! I shall take up this issue with the chief constable at the earliest opportunity. He is a personal friend, you know.'

'I do apologise,' said Bucke, his mind racing. He didn't need an argument. 'I just wanted to check your arrangements. Make sure everything is satisfactory. Hope you have everything you need.' He smiled unconvincingly and slowly backed out of the room. 'Enjoy your day. Let's hope that the rain holds off, shall we?' He turned and scurried back down the stairs, suddenly feeling the weight of the revolver against his hip. He'd been stupid. He should have taken his gun out, even if it had been a false alarm. When he went up those stairs, he had believed the threat was real. The next time? Perhaps he wouldn't have time to regret his foolishness. He had been given a gun for a reason.

He walked down Walters Road, stepping over more children already bored by the waiting. Boys playing marbles, their parents gossiping, occasionally craning their necks to see if there was any real action starting up the road. Those marbles could become a bit of a hazard if they rolled off into the procession. Occasionally he had to step into the road to get past particularly intransigent groups of spectators, enjoying the holiday from work, however much it was costing them. Sand had been scattered as a precautionary measure in case the weather turned inclement and he skidded on it, almost losing his balance. The sand was unlikely

278

to be necessary. The weather forecast for the day was good. Some sunshine, a cold breeze, no rain until the evening. Bucke always regarded the weather forecast as nothing more than guesswork. He looked at the grey sky. There was a cold east wind blowing but it was dry. One storm had passed. Was there a different one to come, he wondered?

A temporary constable barked at him and Bucke was momentarily irritated. Didn't he know who he was? And then he realised that he probably didn't. At least he was doing his job. He saw one of the Hat Stand Gang and sent him off to find Sergeant Ball and ask him to remind the constables to stop spectators spilling on to the road. He knew that Royal Security required clear lines of fire; their feelings about the consequences of ricochets were less definitive.

Although it was still early in the day, Roe was already out amongst the crowds, selling last night's newspapers by describing them as The Prince's Itinerary. He had also introduced a potentially lucrative innovation– advertising. He shouted out very loudly the attractions of products that traders paid him to promote. He repeated his three advertisements so regularly and loudly that the crowd became seriously irritated.

'The Cambrian Hair Restorer,' he shouted, 'from John Williams of Nelson Street. Restoring hair becoming prematurely grey to its original colour.' Next it was, 'Nicholls and Sons of Waterloo Street for the best bread, delivered by their own van daily!' and then 'For a grand display of novelties, visit D T Edwards of Park Street!' He had hoped for more, but he was not sure that he would have been able to remember them all. He was repeatedly advised to move on and, as he worked his way down Wind Street, the remains of a Welsh batch were thrown at him. 'Will you stop?' he shouted with mock agitation. 'A man has to earn a crust.'

There were few embarrassing opportunities he was not prepared to embrace. Someone swore at him through the laughter. 'What do you mean? Idiot? Who is the idiot here, then? Me in the middle of the road or you crushed up on the pavement like that? Don't you forget. These arrangements around us have been made to suit a few favoured ones. Most of you lot will see bugger all. So wave and clap as much as you can, because you won't clap eyes on 'em.' Someone responded indistinctly, though obviously obscenely, and Roe turned towards them briefly. 'Your choice, my friend. You want to be a sheep, well that is fine by me. You enjoy being taken to market. Me? I'd rather be the dog that barks you into the abattoir.'

Twenty Four

Bucke didn't have to count them, because he had seen the list so many times. Two hundred and fifty of Swansea's finest, properly invited by letter, had formally replied and now found themselves gathered together in the Royal Pavilion at the top of Walters Road awaiting the arrival of royalty. And whilst it was true that life could not get any better, it was still very important for all of them to have their presence confirmed by others, to be noticed, to perhaps even be noticed and admired, if only briefly, by a Prince and a Princess. They had not, however, rushed to the Royal Pavilion to be gawped at by those outside as if they were other-worldly creatures, fallen in their finery from an orbit around a distant star into this tent. It was those outside who were intruders, who had not fallen from the sky but instead, had crawled upwards from the underworld. Something needed to be done, and quickly.

The contrast between those within the Pavilion, and those without, was stark and Bucke watched regretfully as the constables moved away those who would never have any clothes suitable for greeting a Prince, or anyone, really. He watched old men in mufflers and flat caps shuffling away in poverty, painfully aware that they were nothing more than a shameful stain upon the glittering aspirations of the town. He saw small boys in old, ill-fitting suits, scouring the ground for dropped coins as they, too, were removed. They were not wanted.

Bucke went to the entrance to the Pavilion as they were escorted away and looked inside. He realised that there were many people there who he had never, ever, seen before, at any time during his years in Swansea. But then why should he? Theirs were the sort of lives that never came into contact with his own, for they lived in a part of the town which he rarely had cause to visit. But today they were pleased to see him, his presence soothing the anxieties of these excited guests, relieved to see the expulsion of the undeserving poor to the wrong side of town. This was not an occasion for them. Today was the day for Swansea to put on its best face for the world to see. Not a day for that view to be obscured.

Later however, when all this was over and the finery was packed away, their deserved sleep would be disturbed in the darkest hours by that terrible, recurring, fear of their servants who, they were sure, would one day rise up in the night and slaughter them in vengeful violence. Others, though, would regard this as a delusion. Where would overworked staff find the energy?

There was an irony in all this, too. Bucke knew that those who were shuffling away, often had to deal with an inspector when they would always prefer to see a constable, because that would reassure them that their offence, whatever it was, was a minor one. Citizens like those inside the tent, never wanted to see a constable in any circumstances. They always wanted to see an inspector, for otherwise they never felt they were being afforded sufficient attention.

His musings were interrupted when he saw Evan Davies sitting, inexpertly, on a police horse. Who had authorised that? No one, he was sure. If that horse bolted it would cause mayhem, because Davies would never be able to control it. But it was even more alarming to see that Frankie Starr was standing next to him, stroking the neck of the horse. He was, of course, the most notorious horse thief in Swansea, who enjoyed regular respite from his busy trading in a cell Swansea gaol. And Evan Davies was introducing him to one of their horses? The procession had not yet begun and already he was horrified. Was there any chance at all, that things would get better? None at all that he could anticipate. At least it wasn't raining.

There was a series of loud explosions. It was an uncoordinated twenty-one-gun salute that announced the departure of the royal party from Singleton. They were late, but that mattered little; they were on their way and there were gasps of excitement. Necks were strained in the crowd on the pavement, although as yet there was nothing to see. Inside the Pavilion dresses were smoothed, hats were adjusted and watchchains draped just-so across prosperous waistcoats.

Bucke could hear in the distance the band of the Dragoon Guards, who were leading the procession. Waves of excitement were spreading along the stretched-out crowds and very soon he could see the white helmets of the Guards shining brilliantly in the encouraging sunshine. They were followed by fifty troopers on horseback and then finally, the gilded Royal Carriage, brought in at considerable expense from Marlborough House, with the other notables in alternative transport that was much less grand.

Suddenly they were here and a cloud of hysteria settled then surged through the spectators, who cheered and shouted and waved flags. The police horse remained unmoved and impassive but Evan Davies fell off and Bucke watched Starr help him to his feet, pat him down, rearrange his uniform and then assist him in remounting. It would be a considerable surprise if Davies still had his truncheon after all that.

The carriage stopped and Bucke could see the Prince and Princess. Around him people gasped; the cheers were louder. This was a magical moment, for the Prince and Princess were walking amongst them, like angels. People strained to catch the merest glimpse and suddenly there were complaints, for feet were trodden on, children were squashed. Bucke had met the prince some years ago, just before he resigned his commission. He had put on a little weight since then, but that was a consequence of good living, he thought. He was dark suited, with the obligatory top hat, his face trimmed by a neat beard. This was not, and never would be, an extraordinary man. He was a man like any other. Most men don't look much different, Bucke thought, whether they were miners or costermongers or dockers. It was the expensive clothes that made the difference; that and the bearing. Probably the same with the Princess too, he thought. She was dressed in peacock blue with a long dark jacket. Constance would explain it to him, if he was really interested. But they were expensive clothes, like a theatrical costume. Or even a disguise. The parts that made her a woman were exactly the same as those of Lizzie Thomas or of Mrs Lambrick.

He watched the couple doing what they did habitually – they

smiled and nodded, representing influence and power that did not change. Yet somewhere nearby there were activists who would attempt to do just that.

He was aware of movement behind him and Bucke turned to see members of the Royal Glamorgan Artillery Militia lining up along the Walters Road gutter to form an avenue of respectful loyalty, blocking the view of those who had shivered through an uncomfortable night on the pavements. There would be tension, he was sure of it. The insensitivity of the Militia was something you could rely upon; it was as regular and relentless as the Swansea rain. Bucke decided to move on to the next stage of this procession to check the arrangements there. He looked towards the Pavilion but failed to see Constance and so, disappointed, he walked briskly down the road. He would never be able to find his way through that crush on the pavement.

Therese followed the Royal party into the Pavilion and Emily walked behind her with some difficulty, for her clothes were thick and unwieldy. Therese had been right; her Welsh costume was a crowd-pleaser, a representation of national identity. Emily, though, was tense, consumed by nerves, suddenly unsettled by the attention she was receiving and realising, finally, that this was no game and that Therese was carrying a loaded gun, with permission to use it. She looked around the Pavilion and saw Constable Turner standing on the side and he smiled at her. This gave her some comfort before she dragged her attention back to her duties.

There was another, and unexpected, example of Welshness to greet her at the far end of the Pavilion, which Emily found most peculiar, for a man dressed as a Druid stood at a lectern and declaimed mightily, in English, to the assembled dignitaries

Thrice welcome, Prince, to this our loyal land

We hail thy presence, as the throbbing sea

Leaps up, in billowy gladness o'er the strand.

Suddenly there was a voice in her ear, whispering, which briefly alarmed her. 'Moving, eh? Dry your eyes, Lady Emily.' It was Grey, of course, but when she glanced behind her, he wasn't there.

Then the speeches began; it would be a day of speeches and before long she would be unable to distinguish between any of them. The first was delivered by Mr Thomas, the town clerk, although it had been written by the Lord Mayor. He described the visit as an *'opportunity which the town now seizes, of evincing their loyalty and affection.'* In fact, the mayor was so proud of his speech that he presented the Prince with a signed copy. For his part, the Prince of Wales managed his boredom well, Emily decided, certainly better than her, although she did notice Princess Alexandra discreetly pinch his arm at one point. Did they really have to listen to this sort of thing every day? Pointless speeches? Pointless presentations? Could you ever get used to this?

She looked around her briefly, as she was supposed to, for any potential dangers and saw her mother entranced and Constance embarrassed, though she had lost sight of Turner, which was disappointing. Then there was a movement, glimpsed briefly out of the corner of her eye, amongst the audience. She knew that Therese had seen it too and her hand hovered over her clasp, but they were both relieved when they saw it was an elderly man who had dropped his handkerchief.

All the way down Walters Road, Bucke admired the venetian masts that had been placed between each tree, which supported the wind-kissed bunting that had been stretched along the whole of this part of the route. Between the masts, bucket lamps hung from chains and Bucke watched them sway in the wind. He knew some had been hastily re-installed after the storm and they still appeared precarious.

At the top of Page Street, Bucke saw a most peculiar structure. This was The Tin Arch, through which the royal procession would pass. It had been designed by the mayor himself to express the industrial creativity of the town. The triumphal tin frame had been covered in crimson cloth and then decorated with designs cut from tinplate – men in armour, the inevitable Fleur de Lys, trains, ships, a set of miner's tools. It had blown down in the storm and then hastily re-erected. Bucke pushed at it gently, like an expert, to test its stability and was alarmed to feel it wobble.

He arrived on New Road, soon to be renamed Alexandra Road. He had examined the route as he walked and found nothing to alarm him – and everything to alarm him. He looked for Riverton, of course, but it was foolish to think he would be that careless. He saw so many people and almost any one of them could be an agitator, hiding deep within the crowd. How could you know? Grey must have his agents deployed, who should know who or what they were looking for. But they could not be everywhere.

Outside the Masonic tent he could see James Flynn looking smart in his resplendent dress uniform. They acknowledged each other from a distance. At least Bucke knew that this part of the route would be properly managed. Was James a mason, he wondered? He didn't know. It seemed unlikely, but you could never tell. The tent was festooned with banners, flags and artificial flowers and he hoped they had sorted out their seating arrangements without visible bruising. A greeting for the Prince, *'Hail Grand Master,'* was prominently displayed, as was *'Freemasonry, a code of the loftiest morals and of the truest philosophy.'* The Lodge were eager to be seen and have their status as benefactors paraded before the common horde. Their tent however, as far as Bucke could see anyway, had little to identify it as representing Swansea; it could have sprung up anywhere, in any town, to satisfy wealthy egos.

Opposite the tent there was the stand that had been erected for the Swansea Choral Society's two thousand voices. These voices stood there, expectantly, watching Mr T. Harlington Jones, tall, bald and haughty, with his baton poised, ready to direct them from a flimsy rostrum. The child choristers at the front, dressed in Welsh costume, were inevitably more restless, muttering the words of *'God Bless the Prince of Wales'* to fix them more securely in their memory.

Bucke turned away from the tent before the procession arrived and headed down into High Street, skirting another triumphal arch, this one made of wood and shaking in the breeze. It was a temporary glory; tomorrow it would be firewood. He could hear the beginnings of *'The Hallelujah Chorus'.* Obviously, the royal party were not far behind him. They were, however, slightly delayed, for when the Princess pulled on a rope to unfurl a flag at the naming of Alexandra Road, the tassel came off in her hand and stout shoulders had to pull directly on the rope to release it. Bucke was later told by Constance that the mayor watched all this with a fixed expression on his face, horrified by such unparalleled civic embarrassment.

Further down High Street there was yet another arch. This one was made entirely from wool and yarn, looking like something abandoned by a farmer and with the potential to smell when wet. The businessman who had erected it, Mr Rocke, was a prosperous trader, his generous frame crammed into his Sunday-best suit, which appeared to Bucke to be under considerable strain. He was standing proudly by the side of his arch, ready and eager for royal approval. 'Six tons, that lot is,' he said proudly. Bucke nodded, hoping fervently that it would not collapse until after the royal party and the press had departed. He hoped, too, that the structure did not contain any rats.

On Temple Street, the Theatre Royal had been decorated with banners carrying Shakespearean quotations, which at least made a change from the normal garish advertisements for unmissable juggling fire-eating acrobats. *The master is a just one and his worthiness does challenge much respect.* What nonsense, thought Bucke. They ascribe all these qualities to the Prince of Wales without ever having met him. *Welcome both at once, those that go or tarry* said another. Perhaps they couldn't find anything better. The Royal party probably wouldn't even see them. Some of the locals who doffed their caps to Bucke, in the hope that he might just remember their patriotism when he next tried to arrest them, had probably no idea what those banners said. What purpose did they serve? He watched Jack Dawes take a handful of change in exchange for a stained apple box on which a father stood his daughter in a vain attempt to allow her to see over the people in front of her. Bucke hoped for her sake that the militia did not relocate.

Wind Street was festooned. There was no other word for it. The offices of the Cambrian newspaper were draped with crimson curtains, already flapping insecurely. If the wind picked up later as promised, they would probably find those curtains in Neath. The windows of Fulton, Dunlop and Co were outlined in coloured lamps. Mr Williams, the hairdresser, had illuminations in his windows, too. He saw Morris standing impassively, like a statue, amongst those gathered outside the Plume of Feathers, the pub briefly 'owned' by Hamish Darr. He did not acknowledge Bucke at all, and he felt it best to leave him alone. He carried a huge amount in his own head, so many secrets, it seemed, from a life that appeared always to have played tricks on him. Once this visit was over, Bucke had to deal with Morris and what he had told him, as a matter of urgency. Although, apart from finding and arresting Riverton on suspicion of murder, he hadn't really decided where to begin. In normal circumstances Bucke could rely upon Morris to do his job properly. But could he still rely on him now? Bucke didn't know. But this was one of the tricker parts of the route to deal with.

The plan was that Wind Street would be cleared by 3.30 pm and only those with tickets would be allowed to remain. Effectively, the police were required to shut down the entire centre of the town to ensure enhanced security at the Music Hall for the Grand Ball. He wasn't sure why anyone would actually want to stay, in view of a predicted deterioration in the weather. He lived close by, he policed these streets and knew how difficult the area could be. It was a maze of alleys, dead ends and short cuts. It would be impossible to keep every street clear, with the notoriously unreliable street lamps that could plunge any street instantly into the darkness of an up-turned bucket. No, there was too much left to chance. All this, and Riverton on the loose. It wasn't a happy combination.

He looked at the crowds, ignoring the children and the obvious families, focusing instead upon the single men. Who were they? What had drawn them here? Curiosity? A desire to be part of a notable event? Or for something more sinister? He didn't like the look of some of the temporary constables either. Nervous, inexperienced? Vulnerable? Or sinister? Take your pick. Of course, if single men looked more suspicious than anyone else, then a political activist would not draw attention to himself in that way, would he? He would be in the crowd as part of a family group. Simply looking for single, suspicious men, was never going to be the answer. Anyone in the crowd could be a threat. Why did it have to be a man?

Nevertheless, he wished he knew where Riverton was. He had to be around somewhere. There was naturally the possibility that he was using the occasion as a cover for a series of lucrative and untroubled burglaries amongst the quiet residential streets of Swansea. He had done that before, of course. Some had servants on guard, whilst the home owners paraded their patriotic credentials, but not everyone. Perhaps that was where Riverton was today, helping himself in the suburbs they were unable to police. Or he might be settling old scores, distributing justice. They couldn't afford to put a police guard on Patagonia Jacques, even if they knew where he was. Not today, not tonight. Bucke had no choice other than to take a chance. Surely old events from Patagonia could wait one more day.

There was another unstable Triumphal Arch at the bottom of Wind Street. Across the top it read, *And more such days as these to us befall!* Bucke sincerely hoped not. He stopped and turned to look back along Wind Street at the excited crowd, at the decorations, the lights, the bunting, all too soon to be abandoned and discarded.

And then it happened. As the procession entered Wind Street the crowd behind them broke and ran in a shapeless, excited mass to pursue the Royal party to the East Dock for the naming ceremony. The crowd was too large to control. Some untrained horses were startled and the whole of the top of Wind Street was a seething, dangerous mass of congestion. The only explanation could be that some barriers had been removed and the crowd had surged through the gaps. It could have been that barriers had fallen over under pressure, or that constables had been pushed out of the way, but Bucke immediately suspected a plot; he was seeing them everywhere. Temporary constables had planned this, he was sure of it. Bucke found his hand resting on the handle of his revolver. Bucke thought he caught a glimpse of Colonel Grey in the crowd but if it was him, he was soon gone.

But his moment of alarm was unnecessary. The Royal Carriage was well protected by the Dragoons, who prevented any unpleasant intrusions, and soon the escaped crowd were carefully marshalled, although their numbers were swelling rapidly as others joined this disorganised melee, like battlefield plunderers.

The other members of the entourage, less of a priority for protection in the eyes of the dragoons than the royals themselves, were less fortunate and some of Swansea's finest faces were soon climbing on to running boards and leering through carriage windows to gawk at the finery within before they fell back to the ground, wheels somehow avoiding ankles.

The dock, very soon to be named The Prince of Wales Dock, was another nightmare, a complex environment that was impossible to police. Bucke had known this from the very beginning. There seemed to be thousands of people there and he felt he had made eye contact with every one of them – but had been unable to see any constables he recognised. Midwinter was supposed to be one of those supervising the stands, but perhaps he had been redeployed by Sergeant Ball. He hoped that was the case, though he could not understand why. He went to see if he could find him and then, failing to do so, patrolled the pavilion where waiters rushed around laying out cutlery on the white damask tablecloths.

One of the events at the harbour was a sea trip, which Therese knew had been keeping Grey awake at night. The elderly Lord Lieutenant was eager to show off his yacht, *The Lynx*. What the point was of a trip around the bay in October, in the middle of a whole series of formal presentations, no one could be sure but the Lord Lieutenant was a man who accepted no contradiction and certainly not today.

As the royal party assembled, ready to embark upon the choppy and uninviting grey water, a whiskered and braided man with the obligatory bicorne hat bowed respectfully in front of Therese

D'Auch. Emily heard him say, "Nothing better, ma'am, than the sensation of the lively sea. Allow me…'

Emily was shocked to hear Therese giggle childishly. 'Oh Admiral Leybourne! You naughty old salt! Not in front of the ladies, please! Best if we stay on dry land, for fear of over-excitement!' The Admiral bowed and backed away, wondering whether what he had actually said, had been what he intended or whether he had jumbled up his words again, whilst Therese whispered to Emily. 'Tiresome old man. One of many. We are better here. There is a crowd to watch and a quayside to observe. There is not much we can do if the Prince is shot by a rifleman from another boat. Need to think always about where you can see the greater risk.' With practised ease she persuaded the Lady Mayoress and her party, including Flora and Constance, to remain with them to make her refusal to sail seem less conspicuous, though they did not need much persuasion.

The brief trip around the bay was not a success. One of the accompanying vessels in this festive flotilla got stuck on a sandbank. Emily could see equerries pacing anxiously around the deck of *The Lynx* whilst they waited for the boat that blocked them to be freed. The subsequent delay in disembarking the Prince and the Princess did not improve the mood, since the carefully planned itinerary was crumbling before them. The inspection of the new facility was consequently cursory.

'A noble work,' the Prince muttered to the engineer, Mr Abernethy. 'Vast and well done, indeed.' He looked around for something else to say.' Excellent masonry,' he said and moved on. He was getting hungry.

There were more speeches, more presentations. Emily was amazed particularly by the fortitude of the princess and her capacity to contain her boredom. She was presented with a large and ornate pair of scissors with which to cut a ribbon to send a bottle of champagne to smash in the new dock, narrowly, but thankfully, missing two labourers ready to open the valve that would admit the water.

Emily's feet were getting tired and her costume was heavy and here was another huge choir to listen to politely, this time with a new anthem, '*With Loyal Hearts.*' A man suddenly appeared at her side and Emily was briefly alarmed and was unsure what to do. She leaned forward and pulled at Therese's jacket.

She did not turn around but merely spoke quietly over her shoulder. 'It's Colonel Grey.'

'Only here for the poetry,' he whispered. 'Listen. Quite remarkable.'

And thus, O Prince, thou hold'st the golden key
To hearts that beat both loyally and true-
To souls that throb with joy to welcome thee,
And round thy footsteps love's bright blossoms strew.

He shook his head. 'How wonderful. Enjoying yourselves?'

'Enjoying every precious minute, of course we are,' said Therese without turning round.

'It was so vigorously rendered, Lady D'Auch. Don't you think?'

'You make it sound like the perfect lover, Colonel.'

'Please, Therese. Remember your responsibilities to Lady Emily here. More decorum on such an august occasion would not go amiss.' He slipped away into the crowd.

There were yet more speeches by unidentifiable worthies, more presentations of trinkets and all the while the Prince of Wales was cruelly separated from the Royal Luncheon, to be served in a huge, ridiculously expensive and temporary, pavilion imported for the day. He was, quite rightly, better placed than some of the minor dignitaries who were still stranded on the *Lady Mary*, a boat which appeared be fulfilling the role of a distressed straggler from the Spanish Armada. They couldn't get off and so missed the first two hours of a protracted lunch, during which there were yet more speeches about the visit, '*a desire that has so long been cherished*' that had now been '*happily realised.*' By this stage Emily was, like the Prince of Wales himself, more interested in the range of hot soups and a cold menu prepared by Gunters of Berkeley Square. Her spirits were revived when she saw Turner once again, alert at the flap through which the waiters moved briskly. She raised her hand briefly to acknowledge him and was pleased when he smiled back at her,

Therese was not so easily distracted. She ate little, her eyes never still, and neither did Constance, who watched Rumsey patrolling the fringes of the pavilion, still consumed by horror at what he could see. Fifty cooks and 125 waiters, all from London. Who were they? Every one of them - every misplaced glance, every quiet word between them, every moment of eye contact, everything - was suspicious and ominous.

Bucke was wearing himself out, and he knew it He was becoming increasingly exhausted and concerned that he was therefore less alert, less effective.

But nothing happened. There was still the march past of the Volunteer troops to be observed from the steps of the Townhall. They were out of sequence, of course, as Bucke noted immediately, and then he looked around, but could find no one to whom he could express his considerable irritation. Who could be surprised about their incompetence? Their lines were as straight as a dog's broken hind leg.

But it didn't seem to matter. The day had been endured, everyone was exhausted, and now it was over. The Procession retraced its path through the town, back to Singleton Abbey, though at a greater pace. It was done. Not on time, but it was done. The town centre could not be cleared by 3,30 pm as planned, but 4.30 pm wasn't such a problem and the day was at an end and nothing had happened. Bucke was surprised but relieved. Prevention was always best, even though he could never be sure that they had actually prevented anything.

As the official party broke up, regretting that this wonderful day had passed so quickly, a hand appeared on Bucke's arm. It was Jack Dawes.

'Begging your pardon, Inspector Bucke, but the London gent is asking you to stay here in the Townhall for an important meeting. With Constable Turner too. I don't know what it has got to do with him, but it aint nothing to do with me, like. do as I am told. And that Missus Doosh and the stripey lady. Me? I'm off to High Street station – there will be crowds there. And everyone wanting something.' He winked and briefly flashed what looked like train tickets and then walked away.

Twenty Five

Colonel Grey had called a meeting of what he now called his security team, immediately he knew the Prince and Princess were on their way back to Singleton Abbey. But he had added Constance White to the group and that alarmed Bucke greatly. Why? What was his intention?

They were all worn out by the unrelieved tensions of a day that had not been perfect, in neither planning nor execution, but they were obviously aware that it could have gone so much worse and everyone slumped around, vacantly, in chairs scattered through the chamber. Bucke had hoped, as always, to speak to Constance, but Grey immediately led him away so that they could speak privately. As they went out into the mayor's robing room, he could see Therese sitting opposite Emily, leaning forward and holding her hands, speaking softly to her.

Grey closed the door firmly. 'You see, Rumsey, there are a great many issues here, some of which you might be aware of. Perhaps the most important of them is that poor old Bertie is losing a little bit of focus. It happens. The whole day has been a touch too long for him and who should be surprised? Too long for me, if I am honest. Of course, Bertie does like a ball, there is no question of that. He likes the dancing and the touching. But it is not safe. Can't take him to the Music Hall. How many temporary constables are there? Remind me. No, it is just too dangerous. So we are going to keep the Prince and Princess in Singleton Abbey this evening. There is so much to see you know, so many glories. How the Vivian family pulse will race when their treasures fall beneath the royal gaze once more. A chair from the Inquisition chamber of Venice would be my particular favourite, but there is a stuffed seal, Etruscan vases, a panel from Catherine of Aragon's wedding trousseau. And how could you forget a Caravaggio and a charming Rembrandt? Oh that I could have such an opportunity. But perhaps they are reserved for better people than ourselves, Rumsey.'

Bucke watched him closely, apprehensive about the final destination of this conversation.

'He is a remarkably important man, you know. He has the order of the Elephant of Denmark, the Black Eagle of Prussia, the Golden Fleece of Spain. He is a walking menagerie. Certainly not a man to be trifled with. He would probably eat it anyway. But he is not the greatest Brain of Bombay, Baghdad or even Bolton. No, a good fire and a good bottle and he will be as happy as Larry. The Dragoons will remain in Singleton and guard him and that is where he is going to stay. But we have the ball in the Music Hall and that is such an opportunity for us.'

'So it is not your intention to cancel it, since the Prince of Wales will not attend?'

'Absolutely not. You see, Rumsey, what is interesting me is that the Fenians had an opportunity today and they didn't take it. It was a perfect chance. When the crowd surged. Was that on Windy Street? Can't remember. Nevertheless, that would have been the moment – temporary chaos, probably arranged by these temporary constables of yours. They could have been alongside the royal carriage in a moment, and that is all they would need. Could have bombed it in seconds. But they didn't, so there is, as I see it, only one other chance for them. The Ball in the Music Hall. That must have been their plan all along. Want us to think they have all gone away, disappointed. They haven't. To be honest when you think about it, an attack on the Prince in the middle of a parade would have been what some would have expected. Maximum publicity, a story that would have carried Swansea's name round the world before breakfast time, even if it had failed. But if they are keen for success, then the Music Hall is another issue entirely.'

'So they are trying to deceive you, do you think, Colonel?'

'Oh yes. This is all essentially a guessing game. A deadly sport but a sport nonetheless. There has already been one assassination this year, as you will know, in July. President Garfield in Washington. You will remember the newspapers, I presume. Shot at a railway station.'

'Yes, I do remember. Finally died last month. There was an obituary.'

'That's right. Shot with a British revolver too, you know. I have worried about it for a while, as I am sure you will understand. I feared that it might plant a seed in someone's mind. A single assassin is all that is needed. I worried about your temporary railway station in Singleton a great deal. Flooded the place with my men. No sign of Fenians. So no attempt then or on the procession. So I now think we have the perfect chance.'

Bucke thought they were examining the Fenian's opportunities, not their own, but said nothing, his alarm growing.

'Duggan can't afford to wait until tomorrow in my estimation, because his constables in disguise have to go before they are identified, and his waiters will be expected to return to London. And all the waiters have been moved to the Music Hall for the grand buffet. Bertie always likes a buffet. But Duggan can get his men in there. Perfect cover.'

Grey folded his arms and leaned back in his chair. He raised his eyebrows as if he had asked a question and was waiting for a reply. Bucke still said nothing.

'To be perfectly frank, we have a chance. We have managed, I think, to get one step ahead of the Fenians and we really do need to flush out Duggan, once and for all. Not a chance that comes our way that often.' He paused again. 'We have to take it. And so we have a plan.'

'Well, if there is anything I can do,' Bucke said, and then instantly regretted it.

Grey gave a wry smile and scratched his chin. 'Well yes, there is. That's why I mention it. You see, from a distance you can pass for the Prince. Not close up, obviously, and certainly not for the people who know him. But the lighting in the Music Hall can be adjusted and I anticipate that the affair won't last too long anyway. But your good friend, Miss White? She can play the part of Princess Alexandra. It simplifies things for us, as you can probably see.'

That was why he had brought Constance here and he was appalled. 'I am not sure. I am certainly deeply unhappy about involving Constance. Obviously I will do my bit, but Constance is quite another issue entirely.'

There was a little more steel in Grey's voice now. 'Miss White will be expected to do her bit too, Rumsey.' He held up his hand. 'Let's be honest here, shall we? It is not altogether helpful to consider this as an invitation. Look upon it more as an obligation. You already have a revolver, of course and I know that you can use one. You will need to protect Miss White, whilst we deal with the Fenians. Oh yes, it is a risk, of course, above all since we don't know their plans. So, yes. It is dangerous. But you need to leave the dirty work to us.'

'And how is it possible to be so selective in the chaos of an armed attack? What do you mean, leave the Fenians to you?'

Grey ignored his objection. 'We can't afford to cancel the Ball, because we will miss our chance. Yes, there will be lots of civilians there to greet the Prince and Princess of Wales in the ballroom, but that might obscure the Fenians sight lines. It will also be full of elderly veterans dressed in uniform and golden braid. If anything happens, they will think that the hunting season has moved indoors and will fire at anything that moves. So my guess is that they will act quickly once the Prince has passed into the anteroom where the buffet will be laid out. They will know that Bertie would stride forward purposefully across sleeping babies to reach the easy meat of a buffet. And that is how they will see him. Easy meat, once he is in the anteroom. So that is my best guess.' He appraised Bucke carefully. 'I think Therese can lighten your beard slightly if necessary. But then, who down here has ever been that close to Bertie to know?'

'Inside the music hall? You are planning a gunfight?'

'Not ideal, I grant you. There will be all kinds of members of the royal household who will need to be told – which isn't something I welcome, but without them inside the room it will not look authentic. So we have the distinct possibility of Lord Wells of Tunbridge, or Lord Tunbridge of Wells, or Rear Admiral

Sinkhurst Green or The Right Honourable Balfour Hush-Heath or The Right Reverend Bassett of Foxchase doing something heroic and stupid. My problem will be trying to control them.' He shook his head. 'I hope there isn't one of those blessed ice-sculpture things. I have enough to deal with without a wet floor as well.'

Bucke was horrified. This casual acceptance of terrible risk for other people he found shocking. 'Will Constance be safe? Can you guarantee that she will be safe?' he asked desperately.

'What an unnecessary question. Of course not. I can't guarantee anyone's safety. And to be honest, Rumsey, neither can you. Have you seen the way they drive their carts in this town of yours?' He paused. 'I could tell you it's for the greater good, etc. You know; God, the country, the Empire. But it wouldn't impress you if I were to talk such nonsense. It is a considerable risk for us all. For Therese, Miss White, for young Emily, for me and for you. But it is what we have to do. My job is a success if the Prince and the Princess get home alive, perhaps I have told you before. Everything else is just a footnote. You know Miss White better than anyone, Rumsey, but I am quite sure I know how she will respond when I ask her to co-operate; you know what she will say.' He held up his hand. 'You cannot decide for her – or indeed for Emily, she is part of the royal household at the moment.' He emphasised his point. 'You know very well what they will say.' He raised his eyebrows. 'Your constable. The young one. We have already primed him as a photographer's assistant. We already have the two official photographers under house detention – Mr Chapman and Herr Goldman. Yes, I know. It is a liberty to have done it, but I don't have much time to ask anyone's permission. And to be honest this will not be an occasion when we want a photographic record. Rhodes and the constable will pose as photographers. It won't be a camera they will have.'

Bucke shook his head faintly. What a thing to ask. To make himself a target – no. THE target, with Constance by his side, as part of his cover? It didn't seem right. 'What is their purpose? The Fenians. What do they intend to do?' he asked, knowing and fearing the answer.

'I could tell you it is to take hostages and raise money through ransom. But it is not. It is assassination. You see, Rumsey. It is all part of this game that we are obliged to play. I have to guess what they are thinking and try to counter that. So they will calculate that if the Prince and Princess arrive at the Music Hall, then we know nothing of their intentions, because they murdered our man, Eli Feeney before he could speak. It is all about bluffing, an impossible game of chess. I calculate that they will believe we are ignorant of their presence. They will know the layout of the Music Hall, that is for certain, probably as a result of the Power Cobbe woman's visit.'

'How many of them do you think there could be?'

'Hard to say. Four? Twenty four? Look, I know duty has always been important to you. And this is what this is. We have the opportunity to prevent untold difficulties in the future if we act now. I understand your reservations. It is natural. I would be disappointed if you didn't have them, and I do mean that. I have mentioned duty too many times, Rumsey. So this time I will just say that we have a job to do.'

Bucke closed his eyes, sighed and nodded.

Grey paused briefly and studied him. 'Right then,' he said briskly. 'No time for a rehearsal, so let me draw you a rough plan.' He drew an outline of the room and then a rectangle in the middle. 'That is the long table down the middle that will be in front of you as you enter. It might actually be a number of tables but they will be put together to look like one continuous surface. Above you there is a gallery with stairs at either side. I would suspect that Fenians will try to take control of that because it simplifies their line of fire. Your task? You get Miss White under a table. Don't worry about Emily. Therese will look after her.'

Bucke nodded.' And how will I know who is on my side?'

'Generally speaking, if they are not dressed as a waiter. If they are and they start shooting at you, that should clarify things. If they look like policemen, they won't be, because we are putting no regular constables in the room. I have arranged that with the Chief Constable. Should make for an interesting night.'

Bucke's face hardened. Sometimes Grey's flippancy was completely inappropriate.

'But I do take your point. We could just cancel the whole thing and watch them drift away. But they would pop up again. This is the chance that we need. It is a risk, but we want Duggan. He's killed policemen, Inspector. And he will kill again, you can be sure of that. Tonight we have a chance to stop him. So we need to get you and the ladies back to Singleton in a closed carriage so that you can then return in all your finery for this splendid ball. Have a bite to eat too, if you are minded. There won't be much chance at the buffet.'

'Don't turn the lights down too much, colonel. It will be difficult in there, as it is. Being able to see has its advantages. And the Mayor?'

'Can't afford to say a word, Rumsey. You must realise that. If too many people know, one of them is bound to blab. Let him enjoy the surprise. Are we clear? Oh yes, and another thing. Very interesting. Must be that storm last week. An embankment has gone down near a place with that unfortunate name. Pyle, is it? Seems the line is blocked and Bertie and the fragrant Princess must away tomorrow to Monmouth and thence to the ruined castle of Raglan. Obviously he must see it tomorrow in case the ruins change by the weekend. But you're not to worry. A brave gang of men from Swansea have gone out to dig out the obstruction.' He paused. 'Such hard work. Someone should give them double time.' He looked steadily at Bucke.

'Who could argue with that, Colonel?' At least something had worked as planned. Would this?

*

Elsewhere, Duggan was beside himself with fury. What the hell had Giblin done? He'll answer for this, oh yes, he will. The additional men he needed for this evening had disappeared. His agent in the police had told him that they had been taken away to

301

dig out a collapsed railway embankment. Giblin had quickly put a gang together, which he did quite often. But not now. Not tonight. Of all the things to do. It was bad enough that he had lost one of his temporary constables to that bitch on the hill. Now he had lost his foot-soldiers. What was Giblin playing at?

Twenty Six

Bucke leaned back in his seat, occasionally extending a hand to wave at the cheering crowds he could not see. He was a silent, brooding, shadow of terror. He had witnessed executions and this evening he wondered whether this was how the condemned felt, that the awful distress they were feeling now would only ever be eased by the physical agony of death.

How had his life brought him to this moment, when his existence appeared to have been traded away in a transaction from which he had been excluded? Was his own life – and the life of Constance – available to be bought so cheaply, without their consent? And so tonight he was a man who must be a prince, to save the man who would be king. Because, it seemed, another life was more important than his own.

Constance was next to him in a long silk dress in mauve and was fluttering a gloved hand towards the road side, bright-eyed with surprise, excitement and considerable apprehension. Nothing in her life had ever prepared her for such a thing. To be chosen for something like this? It had never crossed her mind that anyone would consider her worthy, or indeed competent. But tonight she had been asked to impersonate the future queen. And she could do it, of course she could. It wasn't anything at all – as long as Rumsey was by her side. If he was, well she believed she could face anything.

'You look beautiful,' he said softly.

Constance smiled, though he could not see. 'You are talking to the dress, Rumsey. Stop it.'

'No, I am not. Not at all. If this is when we are to be parted, then I… I need you to know that…' His words faded away.

She looked closely at the silent figure that had retreated into the shadows, sensing his fear. He was wearing a formal evening suit decorated with the sash of the Order of the Garter, but with little conviction, as if, for him, they were the coarse garments of a convict, waiting to be hanged. That was an unfortunate idea and she didn't know where it came from. Constance knew he didn't want to talk; she knew he was frightened on her behalf. But there was no need; she was with him. How could she possibly come to any harm if he was with her?

And then she paused for a moment as she heard voices from the pavement. 'God bless your majesty!' and 'Int she bewtiful?' shouted a man who could not see her at all. A thought had suddenly been born in her mind, one that she could not now dismiss. Was Rumsey safe because she was there? And then she realised that perhaps because she was there, he was in greater danger. Perhaps he would look to her at that precise moment when he should be protecting himself. She too slumped back into the shadows. Oh my God. What have we done? She leaned across and felt for Bucke's hand. She squeezed it gently.

'Rumsey. Kiss me please. Tell me everything will be fine'.

He remained where he was, slumped in the corner of the carriage, and then, grasping her hand, leaned over and kissed her slowly and tenderly. It was a kiss like neither had experienced before and realised, as their lips finally parted, that there was a chance they would never experience it's like again.

'Words cannot express what I feel, Constance. And I cannot lie to you; I will not lie to you. I have never been so fearful in my life, about anything.' She looked deeply into the eyes she could not see. 'A choice has been made. For us? By us? I cannot be sure. But we go into this together and we will come out of it together. Dead? Alive? Who can say? But together.'

And all the while the wheels rumbled along the cobbles and the people, in their ignorance, cheered for those they thought were inside, and for the life that they could never have themselves, and for their own lives, from which this fairy tale day had offered a brief escape and which those inside could never properly understand.

The carriage drew to a halt outside the Music Hall and Bucke drew a deep breath. There was no turning back now. He had to make sure that Constance survived; nothing else mattered. He felt, rather than heard, the other two carriages stop behind them. He thought he should say something to Constance, but it would never be anything other than an empty platitude. It was too late now for anything. The time for thought and consideration had gone; now was the time for action. But he knew that he had no intention of doing anything, other than protecting Constance.

She leaned towards him. 'Come, Rumsey. Together. 'Amor Vincit Omnia.' Remember? You told me. I believed you then. I believe you now. So be a gentleman and help me from this fine carriage.'

There were people on the other side of the road, calling, cheering as they saw him take the Princess's hand to help her climb down. He waved abstractedly with the back of his hand, looking around for Grey, but not seeing him. Therese arrived by his side suddenly in the gloom of the suitably subdued lighting from too-few gas lamps. He could not remember ever appreciating the inefficiencies of Swansea's lighting before.

'Your Highness?' asked Therese with the merest of bows. 'Shall we proceed?' Then, just as suddenly, she wasn't there.

His mouth was dry and he did not trust himself to speak. Constance took his arm, waved at the cheering crowd and led Bucke forward. He looked towards the Music Hall and saw the familiar figure of the Lord Mayor, twisting his hands in anxiety in the gloomy twilight of the entrance.

'You are not the Prince!' hissed the mayoress, her eyes wide with anger and confusion. 'And you are not the Princess!'

It was a stupid thing to say, Bucke thought, telling him things he already knew. But he couldn't blame her. 'No, Mrs Jones-Jenkins. It is me. Inspector Bucke. Please remain calm,' he pleaded. 'For all our sakes.'

'For goodness sake, Inspector! What is going on? This is most irregular.'

'Something of the very greatest national importance, Lady Mayoress. Trust me and play along. Please, I beg you.'

She looked at Bucke quizzically and then, making a quick assessment, smiled. 'My poor husband is looking even more confused. I fear that Miss White's dancing skills may embarrass him.'

'Please reassure him,' said Constance. 'I can scarcely move in this dress. I am sure Princess Alexandra would have presented a much more intimidating challenge, but alas that is not to be. She is otherwise engaged.'

Suddenly the Mayor finally found his voice. 'What do you mean? Police Inspector you might be, but I shall have you arrested immediately!'

'Hush, John, please. This is obviously important,' said the mayoress. 'Keep your voice down.'

Bucke looked around for Grey but still could not see him anywhere. He could see elderly and prosperous military figures looking at him significantly. He felt their encouragement – and their apprehension. 'There has been a slight alteration to the protocols, Lord Mayor. There will be no dancing to begin with. We must repair immediately to the anteroom. The Prince is peckish and so, as the Prince, I shall lead the way and I suggest that that you fall into line towards the rear.'

'That is outrageous! I am the representative of the corporation of Swansea, the capital of Wales as so many people say. I should be escorting our Royal visitors, not skulking at the back like some kind of second-class hanger-on!'

'John! Keep your voice down!'

Bucke waved as cheerily as he could at the crowd once more. 'I do know that it sounds irregular, but it is only for a moment. Please Lord Mayor. Please trust me. There is a reason and I am acting in accordance with instructions I have received from the very highest level.' Bucke leaned towards him. 'National security. You will understand. Affairs of State. Your cooperation will be noted. And not forgotten, either.'

The Lord Mayor assessed a situation that he could not begin to understand and then came to a decision. He drew himself upright and set his face in an attitude of resolve. He adjusted his chain of office. 'When one is called, one must respond, not ask questions. Duty is everything, in my opinion.'

'Quite,' said Bucke. 'And if there is shooting,' and he watched the mayor 's face expand along with his eyes, 'look first to your wife and then to yourself. Let those for whom it is their job, do their work. Give them space and let them deal with it. But look always to your wife. She may see things you have no wish for her to see.'

'The Lady Mayoress is made of sterner stuff than you think, Bucke. She once witnessed a traffic accident and…' He paused suddenly realising that things might be far more complicated that he could ever have imagined. 'I say, Bucke,' he said, as his face lost whatever colour it ever had that wasn't grey, 'What is going on here?'

'Not for us to know,' said Bucke quietly.

Even in the thin light from the occasional gas lamp, Bucke could see the dark fear in his eyes. The mayor swallowed and then tapped the side of his nose. 'Quite, Bucke. Quite. Need anything, then let me know. I could look after myself, you know. As a lad.'

'I shall bear that in mind, sir. Thank you for your understanding. Please go to the end of the line but do not show any alarm.'

He shook Bucke's hand surreptitiously. 'You can rely on me. Like a coiled spring, Inspector. Say the word. I'm your man.'

Bucke nodded very slightly than blew out his cheeks as he looked at the steps of the Music Hall where liveried man were standing, doing their duty. How many of them know, he wondered? Are these the Colonel's men? Or are they the enemy? They could be anywhere in such a place as this. In the background, all he was aware of were eyes, and he knew that he was now at the very centre of everyone's attention.

He looked behind him and saw Emily in her designated place behind Therese, looking around her analytically, he thought. Alert; poised. Emily's heavy flannel Welsh costume looked cumbersome and too big for her small frame, but once again it prompted muffled cheers and some clapping.

Constance took his arm and squeezed it but he did not look at her.

He knew he had to do it. He had to move, his dread a heavy weight pressing down on him, squashing his chest. He had to move. There was no going back. Not now. His job was to lead them, but towards what? The Music Hall, a theatre of war?

Constance squeezed his arm again, more firmly this time and he walked carefully up the steps and through the entrance. There was applause, there were cheers. There may have been music coming from the orchestra pit but he could not be sure. There were those elderly men he'd been told about in their ornate uniforms, golden lanyards catching what little light there was, watching him carefully. Bucke was sure one of them winked at him. He could see old hands hovering over ceremonial swords. Heaven help us, he thought.

They entered the anteroom where the elaborate buffet was displayed, around the centre piece of ice, sculptured in the shape of a swan. Grey wouldn't be pleased, he thought.

And then their eyes met across that crowded doorway and locked on to each other. In that moment everything was revealed. It was Aoife in the black and white uniform of a waitress and she knew that this wasn't Bertie.

She desperately pushed her way roughly through the crowd. Therese had seen her too and was suddenly at Bucke's side, opening her clasp. He looked around, saw that Emily had turned to cover her back, her hat an encumbrance suddenly removed.

The elderly uniforms started to look suddenly confused. A woman with a gun? Oh! I say!

'I can't get a sight on her!' Therese cursed loudly. 'Where is the cow? She's better dead.'

'Quick, boys!' she shouted across the room, as she desperately pushed old men aside. 'We've been had!'

And then suddenly Grey was there. He approached her with a

happy grin. 'Good evening, Aoife! What a treat it is to see you once more,' he said cheerily, as he shot her in the heart at close range.

*

Everything became confused and confusing very quickly. There were screams and guests backed out of the anteroom, in a congested mass of fear. Someone tried to grab hold of Grey to detain him, but another man pulled him away and threw him into the auditorium, causing even more alarm. Elderly military men, triggered by the gunfire and driven by duty, tried to force their way into the buffet, ceremonial swords drawn. At the sight of Aoife's sightless eyes as she slumped against the door frame, waiters scattered in every direction. The two who drew pistols were shot by Rhodes and Turner, their camera tripod and hood set up at the rear of the room disguising a rifle. The waiters fell into the food displayed and the tables beneath the damask cloth separated and overturned, food and ice from the intricate sculpture, scattered across the floor. But as the smoke filled the air, it became impossible to identify targets. The room was big enough for a buffet, but too small for a firing range.

Bucke had been under fire before and he knew that the hardest thing to do was to remain calm amongst the explosions and amongst the terror. Your ears might be full of sounds but you had to keep your mind clear. Concentrate. Focus. Be decisive. Select an opponent. Eliminate him from the fight, in whatever way you could. This is what he knew. But here, it was hard to identify the enemy and he had never before had to do such a thing with the woman he loved by his side. There was a table lying on its side and he dragged it towards him as a shelter and then pulled Constance alongside him. The enemy, whoever they were, already knew they were not the real Prince and Princess, so there was no need to target them specifically, apart from revenge. But the assassination mission had changed with that single shot. For them it was now only about escape.

Something important was happening on the gallery above him, Bucke could see hand-to-hand fighting taking place on such a narrow landing. A loud crack signalled that the banister on the stairs had smashed. A man fell through it, thrown by his aristocratic assailant, and landing on his neck with a sharp crack that penetrated the echoing noise of gunfire.

One less to deal with. But how many Fenians were there? He didn't know. No one knew. Temporary policeman? None had been officially deployed in here, so any in police uniform were clearly a threat. Bucke saw Colonel Colquhoun clubbing a temporary constable with his ceremonial truncheon. That must have given him some satisfaction, he thought. But what about the waiters? How could they be sure they had them all? How would they ever know if one had escaped, had slipped back into the crowd in the auditorium, who would be pushing and fighting to escape from the confusion of stray bullets and death? What sort of horror could a waiter with a sharp knife create in a seething crowd like that?

Then his heart stopped. His breath became solid. The world slowed down, though his mind was instantly frantic, uncontrollable. He had turned to check on Constance and saw her covered in blood. In that instant the earth ceased to turn. His ears were roaring. Constance lost to save a Prince? All was suddenly meaningless. He realised that he had spent every moment of his life staring at his own grave; his life nothing but a short, brutal, meaningless interlude that had interrupted eternal oblivion... and then he looked beyond her, saw the old soldier on her other side, with blood gulping from a unclosable neck wound. Constance was vainly trying to pull the ragged edges together, the blood pulping onto her sleeve and soaking into her embroidered bodice. The man raised himself, his eyes fading rapidly. He tried to speak, but could not and fell back, his light extinguished. Dead, but a death that restored life in Bucke himself. He saw Constance look at the chaos around her in bewilderment, as if seeing it for the first time. 'Keep down, Constance! Take his sword. No good to him now.' And he raised himself and fired hastily at a temporary constable scurrying along the gallery. He didn't know whether he had hit him. He didn't care. Constance was still alive and she smiled at him faintly, as if his presence was enough to comfort her at this moment when the gates of hell stood open before her.

There was a brief lull in the shooting and Constance could hear the groans and the sobs of the wounded, cries for help, an Irish voice crying out for his mother. If there was such a place as hell, could it really be worse than this? The air was acrid and she tried to stifle a cough. Reloaded revolvers sprang into life again, bullets crashing into walls, dislodging plaster and then the gunfire was loud and incessant once more.

Bucke, confined behind the table, recognised that much of the shooting was not skilled and wasn't targeted. It was simply random, guns fired anywhere, just a noise. A comfort perhaps, he wondered? But then, how could there be comfort in unpredictability? Death from a stray bullet was still death. He pulled Constance roughly away from the table, for she was sitting with her back against it, dazed and terrified. A bullet could easily find its way into her back if it were so cruel. She was exhausted and lost in this world of violence and death that she had previously never know existed, holding a ridiculous ceremonial sword.

A thought occurred to Bucke, in all its simple clarity. The enemy - the Fenians, the assassins, whatever you wanted to call them - had made a terrible and inescapable error, and now found themselves deliberately trapped in this room. They could not escape through the doors that led back into the auditorium; that was impossible, there were too many people. They could only escape to the rear, and Bucke could see that Colonel Grey had anticipated that – which is why two of the conspirators were killed whilst they vainly tried to force open an exit that was firmly secured from the outside. Bucke knew that the shooting would continue until they were all dead, or until they surrendered. They would fail – that much was clear. The prince was far away, safe and oblivious, looking at vases or stuffed seals. They could never kill him. They had miscalculated and would pay a heavy price. But how many others would they take with them?

There were far too many of them, Bucke thought, providing too many targets. And then he realised something else, that explained the aimless gunfire. So many of the conspirators were merely simple recruits, an expendable distraction. Those temporary constables and the blood-soaked waiters so easily identifiable, they were never going to kill the Prince of Wales. Somewhere amongst the mayhem in the anteroom, the real assassins were waiting for their moment. And then he started to look at the room differently. Grey had done the same thing too. He had peppered the room with ageing heroes. His real agents were not so noticeable. He pulled Constance close to him. Nothing in this scene of smoke and carnage was certain. A deadly sport was being played out, in which lives were a commodity to be traded for a moment's advantage.

'Is it over, Rumsey. Is it done?' Constance wiped blood from her face with a stained gloved hand.

'I don't think so. This is when we must be at our most vigilant.'

'Then I shall try to be strong once again.' She did not think that was possible.

There was a scraping noise and the table shifted slightly. Constance gasped, but it was Emily crawling towards them, followed by Constable Turner. Bucke did not think this was wise. They didn't need anyone else next to them when their role in the deception could still make them an urgent target for revenge. 'Oh my God, Connie! There are bodies everywhere.' The streak in Emily's hair made her the perfect target, Bucke thought with alarm.

'Get down, Emily!' he ordered. 'Where is Therese?'

'I don't know. I lost her in the smoke.'

There was a burst of shouting and then more firing. He looked tentatively over the top of the table and watched a joint of roasted ham spilled from the overturned buffet thrown through the air to strike an elderly red-faced, military-looking man, on the side of the head. Gammon to gammon he thought, like a scene from a jolly Dickens Christmas tale. And then a group of men rushed the table behind which they were sheltering. A man chopped down viciously at him with a carving knife. Bucke managed to sway to the side and the knife crashed into the edge of the table. He was dressed as a waiter, his eyes empty, his mouth full of foul oaths and his clothes soaked in the blood of others. Turner jumped up to his feet and chopped at his neck with a rapid swipe with the side of his hand. Bucke had seen such fighting blows in India. How did Turner know these things? The man fell to the ground and Bucke was astonished – and horrified - to see Emily thrust into his gaping mouth a long sharp shard of ice from the toppled frozen swan. Her face had twisted itself into a mask of fierce determination and Bucke could see the revenge that was in her mind. This was the man who had bitten her; this was the man who beaten her; this was the man who had poisoned her. This was the man who had raped her.

But there was no time for reflection. Another rushed at Constance, with a chair raised, and Bucke instinctively fired his revolver into the man's chest, only to realise how close the bullet must have passed to her head. It was perhaps better not to think too much about what he was doing. Bucke turned, feeling surrounded, and fired at a figure coming towards them from behind, but his gun jammed. He wrestled frantically with it, all semblance of calm disappearing suddenly as he desperately tried to free the bullet. Someone else jumped on his back and they wrestled together desperately on the wet and slippery floor as the first attacker closed upon Constance.

She turned and waved her sword clumsily at her assailant and he laughed at her as he held up a gun, ready to shoot. Constance couldn't hold the heavy sword anymore and closed her eyes. She could not bear to look at the man who was about to take her life and wipe away all those hopes that had now suddenly been made irrelevant. But crucially, he was so excited that he wasn't paying attention. He had the woman who had tricked them in his sights and he would be a hero and so did not notice Therese appear at his side and fire her pistol straight into the side of his head.

Constance heard the shot but felt nothing. It was easier than she ever expected and was relieved, but then she realised that she was still aware of her surroundings and then she felt someone by her side. Was she alive? Was she dead? At that moment she wasn't sure. She opened her eyes to see Turner snapping handcuffs on a man groaning on the floor and Rumsey pulling himself up and rubbing his knuckles. She was alive. So was Rumsey.

'Pleased about that,' said Therese. 'It is so hard to get a clear shot in here, isn't it? Thank you for distracting him.' She reloaded her gun with bullets from her clasp. She had lost her wig somewhere in the confusion and her hair was prominent amid the gunpowder gloom. 'I would much rather that the buggers stayed still for a moment. Never trust a Fenian.' Then she stilled and focused on a figure across the room. 'Wait,' she said. 'That one there. He's mine.' She was calm, she was ruthless, and pointed her revolver steadily at Duggan in the far corner, retreating into the shadows by the exit door they had been unable to open. 'I have waited so …damn!' She exclaimed, as an old man with outlandish whiskers in an admiral's uniform stepped into the line of fire. 'Damn! Damn the man! What does he think he is doing? Never seen active service in his life!'

There was a volley of shots from the gallery and smoke ballooned across the room once more. When it cleared, the admiral was trying to drag himself off the floor, his hat elsewhere, and Therese couldn't see Duggan anywhere.

As always in battle, Bucke's memory became fragmented, his senses overloaded, and he was unable to pick out any sort of pattern or shape to the events. Some things never left him of course- and that inevitably included the clearest memory of all; the entirely unexpected and ridiculous moment that marked the end of the conflict. As the air cleared, and as he caught his breath after the fight on the ground, he saw Emily throw an hard-boiled egg inelegantly at the man he later learned to call Duggan, who was frantically trying to reload his gun. The egg hit him straight in the eye and for that moment he was distracted.

Turner watched Rhodes knock him to the ground and kick him in the ribs, then ran across the room to throw the photographer's camera hood over him and together they trussed him up. It was, Bucke thought, an ignominious end to a brutal career

The best estimate was that there had been fourteen of them. As the anteroom was cleared, they found ten bodies in the twisted shapes of death. Two were wounded, of whom the most seriously was not expected to survive and so they propped him in the corner on his own. A doctor had been called to tend to the wounds of the other. It was Dr Rowlands, so Bucke did not think that the prognosis was good but he kept that observation to himself.

Had someone escaped? They could not know. It had all been even more chaotic than anyone could have anticipated. But Duggan had been captured – and the cell that he had led effectively eliminated. There were bodies everywhere; some old, some not so old, but bodies nonetheless. A good evening's work, as far as Grey was concerned, as he toured the anteroom, looking for dangers, looking for those who might be dissembling, pretending to be dead before rising up for the last time. He shot a twitching waiter in the head, for reassurance, and that final gunshot echoed around the room that was fogged with gunpowder, littered with trampled food, dressed with fresh blood. And how long had it lasted? Three minutes? Five minutes? Bucke could not be sure. They were merely very short minutes in the Music Hall in Swansea, in which so many died.

Grey took Bucke by the elbow and whispered in his ear. 'Go out on to the steps of the Music Hall, take Constance with you, but please hide the blood stains, Dark enough so they probably won't see them, but you can never tell. Wave at the crowd in a cheery way, prove to them that the Prince is still alive. Let them go home happy and the press attention will be elsewhere – a small altercation, nothing more, probably caused by an undressed salad.' But Grey reloaded his revolver, just in case.

So they waved expansively at a crowd that cheered and cheered, their anxieties melting away beneath the inadequate gas lamps, whilst uncontrollable tears flowed down Rumsey Bucke's cheeks.

Twenty Seven

He had been inexpertly tied to the chair, and Grey was briefly irritated by the lack of precision used by some of the men he employed, but the untidy nature of the numerous knots was far less important than their effectiveness. When the time came for them to move him somewhere else, they would have to be cut.

Finally, after all these years, they had him; finally Michael Duggan was theirs. Grey looked at him, wondering how someone who looked so ordinary, so unexceptional, had led them such a dance. But then perhaps that was the point. He was able to pass unnoticed because he was unexceptional. Nevertheless, his achievements – if that is what they were – had echoed across the country and beyond.

'At last, Mr Duggan. You are mine. You cannot know how pleased this makes me.'

Duggan looked at him with contempt. 'As if I am going to speak to the likes of you. I promise you now, from this moment onwards, never shall I speak a word.'

'We shall see about that. I have heard this before, you see. The contempt, the bravado. As if we were not ready for it. In fact your offer of fearful compliance would be more disturbing and we wouldn't believe a word you might say. This is merely normal. And what you can also expect, in this little world of ours, is that very soon you will be begging me to listen to you. Do you understand? This is what happens.'

Duggan started at him unblinking, summoning up the courage he hoped had not disappeared forever.

Grey shook his head, in apparent sympathy 'You see, now you are mine. You belong to me, and my very skilled friends. You will do whatever they want. Be as brave as you like; it will make no difference. They will make you sing to me. You have no choices. You do not know what these people will do to you. They cannot wait to get started. Even now they are pacing round and round

316

their darkest cell in excitement. Oiling and testing all their ingenious equipment. How much pleasure you will give them. I do not believe it is possible for you to imagine quite how excited they will be.'

Duggan looked at him with hatred and contempt, though his mind was working at tremendous speed. He had always known it was likely to end this way. From now on he must be strong, stronger perhaps than he had ever anticipated. However futile resistance would be, he had to try. And that would be his legacy, his final contribution to a movement to which he had once devoted his life and for which he was now about to sacrifice it. Yes, they would break him at some point. That was inevitable, but he would make them wait as long as he could. There would come a point at which he would welcome the noose or indeed the unlikely firing squad, but every minute he delayed, every small lie he managed to construct, every piece of information he withheld – each one would be a small triumph. It was time for someone else to take over. Someone younger, stronger, less exhausted. If anyone could ever believe that they were fully prepared for the agony that awaited him, then he knew he was that man; this was his destiny and if he was not ready to embrace it, he was ready to accept it.

Grey turned to Therese. 'Thank you for your work. Once more, you have done a remarkable job. I cannot think of anyone else who could have achieved what you have done.' Therese nodded to accept his approval, though in truth she thought he was overstating her contribution, but then he usually did. She moved her clasp so that it hung by its elegant thread from her left shoulder. 'And you, Emily. Such an achievement in one so young. Thank you on behalf of the Prince of Wales and her Majesty the Queen. It will not go unnoticed.'

Emily was sitting on a blood-stained dining chair. She was still shaking and could not yet speak. Turner, who was standing behind her, laid a hand on her shoulder briefly then took it away. She turned to look up at him.

'Thank you, Charles. Kind as always. Such tiring days these, don't you find?' said Therese. 'All the noise and the smell. Quite overwhelming at times.' She walked up to Duggan, helpless in his chair, who suddenly sighed with relief when he realised what she was about to do. He watched her unfasten the clip of her bag and then withdraw her revolver, still warm. She pushed it into the centre of Duggan's chest.

'Therese, please, you are being silly,' said Grey ineffectually. 'That is quite enough.'

'I have waited for this moment. Through all those dark and lonely nights, my only comfort the memory of your face and the certainty that one day I would be here, with you. This is for my Alexander and perhaps now he can rest in peace.'

The muffled sound of the gunshot seemed to fill the room, bringing the walls ever closer until the reverberating sound receded and the room assumed its proper shape.

The chair had been blown on to the floor and Emily, bewildered – perhaps a little concussed – saw an expression on Duggan's face that was almost one of triumph. The empty eyes and the blood that was still collecting beneath the seat to which he had been tied, confirmed that he was dead.

'I am so sorry. My mistake, I did not know it was loaded, Charles. An amateurish error. The error of an untrained schoolgirl. I am very embarrassed. I shall ensure it will not happen again.'

'Oh, Therese! This sort of thing just will not do! That's grossly unfair! Most irregular. There were so many things he could have told us and you have gone and spoilt it all. There were so many questions I had for him, you cannot imagine. Acting in that way is most irresponsible!'

'Your time is terribly precious, Charles. And you would have been wasting it. He would have lied to you so much you would have lost track of what was true and what was not. It is better this way. You know that, really.'

'I really am quite cross, Therese.'

They exchanged a long look, like the friends who accepted their differences because they had never mattered, like the lovers they had never been, like the professionals whose greatest dread was to

318

hear of the other's murder. There was too much that held them together and there was too much unexpressed anxiety that one day they would be alone and that there would be nothing left. It was a profoundly deep relationship, one entirely unsullied and one that Therese knew no one else would ever understand.

'To be honest, Therese, this is most inconvenient, and don't you forget it. You can be most impulsive at times.'

'But it is not inconvenient for me, Charles, and I would be grateful if you would remember that. That vile creature shot my husband in the same way and it seems to me that this is right and proper. It won't bring Alexander back, but I have the satisfaction of knowing that he might be waiting for this bloodied leach on the other side. If I had realised my gun was loaded, then it wouldn't have happened and I might have had a chance to enjoy it. But I also ask that you remember that you shot the woman without giving anyone else a chance. You can't keep all the fun for yourself, now can you?'

She turned to Emily. 'I regret very much that you had to witness my ghastly mistake. But there is a lesson here for us all; always check the provenance of your firearms. In the heat of battle it is so easy to lose track of your ammunition.'

Emily was stunned by the events she had just witnessed. A man had died. A dangerous man, a fanatic, a killer and yet the feeling in this small room, still faintly echoing with gunshot, was nothing more than exasperation. She could only nod, as if she had been taught an important lesson that she would remember. Her eyes inadvertently found Aoife dead on the floor and Turner once more touched her, for longer this time, and she looked at him up at him once more. 'I will try to remember your advice,' she said faintly.

'Knew you would understand. Is it just me or do you find that carrying a gun soils your clothes? Gun oil is so difficult to remove.'

Bucke and Constance came into the chaos of the anteroom, looking battered and worn, stepping carefully over the aftermath of scattered food debris and broken furniture. The tears had disappeared into his beard, though Constance knew they were not far away, and he looked in confusion at the scene before them. He could not believe that those things he had witnessed had actually happened. But even as they watched, they could see an order slowly emerging from beneath a splintered table where it must have been sheltering. Elderly and confused dignitaries were being led past them towards their waiting coaches, whilst the rear doors of the anteroom had now been opened and bodies were being taken outside and placed in waiting carts. Agents were collecting discarded weapons and from somewhere two men with brushes and shovels had appeared and were sweeping the floor. He saw Emily bewildered and obviously shocked in her chair and felt Constance squeeze his arm as she went to her. He noticed that Constable Turner quite unconsciously, put his hand on Emily's shoulder. Constance noticed that too, and the fact that he did not take it away. Even when she knelt in front of her and stroked her cheek, willing those frightened eyes to diminish, Emily smiled at her and then looked, in relief, at Turner again.

Therese D'Auch took a lace handkerchief from her sleeve and dabbed ineffectually at the splatter of blood across her bodice. 'Do you think blood stains will feature in the latest collection of evening gowns from Paris? You know, I always think it is better to find someone else's blood on your clothing, rather than your own, don't you think, Emily? Ask Constance,' she said, nodding in her direction. 'I am sure she will agree. If that is her own blood on that shockingly expensive silk gown, she will have died twice. I have absolutely no idea at all about how we are going to explain the mess. What do you think would be best, Emily? Blame the Fenians?'

Emily could not think of anything to say and lifted up her hand and put it on top of Turner's where it still rested. Constance recognised a relationship budding, a seed recently planted and now germinating in the terrible stresses and terror of extreme circumstances. She knew all too well how these things happened.

Grey was leaning against the door and Bucke went to stand by him. He seemed deflated as he contemplated the remains of the horror that he had created. Two men carried Aoife's body past them, it seemed insubstantial, empty, without the fervour that had once sustained her. Rhodes was using a knife to remove the ropes that had once held Duggan, looking for support from Constable Turner and receiving none.

'A good day's work? God knows, Bucke. This is without doubt a filthy trade. Look at all this and tell me why it was necessary.' His sardonic air had disappeared. He was drained, worn out.

'I can't, Colonel Grey. Why do things have to turn out in this way?'

Grey did not appear to be listening. 'Tell me, Bucke, be honest. Am I better than the Fenians because my plan succeeded and theirs failed? Or are we nothing more than the opposite sides of the same coin that falls as it will? What do you think?' He looked at the opposite wall, where a huge blood stain surrounded scattered pieces of flesh, imperfectly attached to the plaster.

Bucke could not answer. His own life as a small-town police inspector seemed so much simpler. His task was to uncover plots; not to create them. He looked at he remains of the chaos that surrounded them. 'And you won, Colonel. Is that right?'

Therese had been watching Grey; Emily no longer needed her. There were others here now, more important than her, who would give Emily what she needed. She walked over to Grey and stood in front of him and held his hands, looking straight into his eyes. Then, very slowly, she rested her forehead against his and felt him shudder.

Twenty Eight

Midwinter scurried along the deserted streets like a rat, his weeping lips raw in the cold wind and his mind full of money. Clearing all the spectators away had been a real bonus; it made it so much easier for him to earn this essential little extra.

It was always money in the end, wasn't it? If any of the other constables asked him, he would tell them straight. Why should it trouble him if Patagonia Jacques got on a boat? Just escort him and his nephew through the streets and down to the South Dock. There was a boat there apparently, taking the old bugger away to live with this nephew, Irvine, who would look after him in his old age. Job and finish. It wasn't going to harm anyone else, now was it? In fact, it seemed wrong that someone should try to stop it. He'd get paid for it, but that is what enterprise is about, surely? Everyone happy with an arrangement that had been made, everyone getting a little something from it.

Some of the other things they had asked him to do he hadn't been too comfortable with. Like reporting what was going on in the police station. To be honest, he never heard anything grand. It was never his place to know. Some of the things they wanted to know were little more than gossip, who was up, who was down, who said what to whom. Did a man from London ever visit the police station? Was Rumsey Bucke right-handed or left-handed? For goodness sake.

He had heard rumours that Patagonia Jacques was the richest man in Swansea. How ridiculous. The stupid things some people believed. He dressed like a tramp, for a start. He was just an unpleasant old man, lucky that he had someone to look after him. Fat chance I will, thought Midwinter. It was not often that the streets were as quiet as this and it gave him time to think. It might have been better if he hadn't got involved with that circus troupe last summer. But that trapeze girl had been so supple. He missed her, Miss Eugenie on the Flying Trapeze. He hadn't expected to fall for her quite as he did. Silly thing to say about a trapeze artiste, falling for her. Always something you didn't want to happen. But she was nice. A breath of fresh air, as they say. A result of swinging around up there he thought, and smiled at his little joke. Fresh air. He hoped she would be back in February. She said the circus was coming back then. She wouldn't say where she was from, she wouldn't even tell him her proper name, but her accent made her sound a bit like Mrs O'Leary at the pie shop who came from Belfast, she said, wherever that was.

But a man has to have a bit of fun, doesn't he? It had certainly made the summer a lot more enjoyable. But happiness always comes at a price, they say.

And, to be perfectly honest, it didn't feel much like fun now, not with the regular, expensive pills and he wasn't sure that they worked anyway. There were these bloody ulcers around his mouth too. At the same time as the other thing. How unlucky can you get? And now Mrs Midwinter was complaining of being uncomfortable 'down under,' as if it was Australia. So he had to earn a spot of extra. What was wrong with that? All he had to do was get an old man through the streets and on a ship. What could be the problem? They would pay him, he was sure. They had been paying him for months now, regular, never a problem. He never told them anything important anyway, so it was money for nothing, really.

So everything had been fine. But then he had met Irvine Sellars. And he didn't think he liked Irvine Sellars too much. He had spoiled things. Much more impatient that the other one, more aggressive. More demanding. Never satisfied. Still, he would be gone soon and everything would return to normal.

More importantly though, he hadn't realised that Patagonia Jacques would be wrapped in blankets and squashed into a bath chair. It was really difficult to push, heavy and unwieldy, and it was really hard work. He wasn't talking much either, which also surprised Midwinter, because he would have expected him to complain about it. He complained about most things, after all.

So he was surprised at how quiet Patagonia Jacques was tonight, wrapped up and motionless in the bathchair that he wrestled with, through the littered streets down to the South Dock. The ship waiting for him was *The Drimnagh Castle*, ready and eager to take him back to Dublin. Midwinter had thought he might be chatty, cheerful even, though that was hard to imagine where Pat was concerned. But he was going off to his family who were going to look after him. Lucky bastard. Surely, he would be pleased. But instead, he seemed rather indifferent. He had always been a grumpy old bugger, with not much of a clue about anything. And they said Jacques was a millionaire? Don't be stupid, thought Midwinter.

Wind Street had been cleared of all visitors by 4.30 pm, as soon as was decent after the procession had finished; it had been later than had been planned but it hadn't made much of a difference. Only those with tickets to the viewing stands erected for the Grand Ball in the Music Hall were allowed in the town centre, so it was very quiet, the town now seemingly deserted after the stresses of the royal visit. Morris was supposed to be on duty on Wind Street but he hadn't seen him and was grateful for that. He had though met Constable Gill, who had told him of chaos at the railways station and so, under instructions, was hurrying there; he was rather confused why Midwinter wasn't going with him. Everyone was trying to leave town at the same time, Gill had told him. Too many tired and angry people, not enough trains, he said. Midwinter had smiled but said nothing, and pointed down towards the docks, as if he had duties to perform down there and so a disgruntled Gill walked briskly on his way.

But at least this ridiculous visit seemed to have passed off with any problems as far as Midwinter was concerned, and the imperious demand to empty the streets had been the perfect gift. He knew where everyone was at the moment, which suited him. There were still repeated loud noises however, but there were probably fireworks somewhere. He hadn't paid much attention to the arrangements, someone else's problem, they were. The planning seemed to have gone on for months now and it had never been needed. A fuss about nothing, as far as he was concerned. Why couldn't the nobs just turn up and wander down the streets for a while and then bugger off? Such a lot of work and nothing alarming had happened at all. What a waste of time.

Still, it was over now. All he had to do now was to take Sellars and Jacques to the quayside, help them get on *The Drimnagh Castle* and watch them sail away. And then his work was over and they would leave him alone. He picked at a scab on his lip which came easily away, but the satisfaction was merely temporary, for he could now taste the blood as it seeped into his mouth.

He pushed the bath chair over the debris of the day's celebration, through wet strands of ribbon and fallen banners, for a squally, wet wind had arrived, signifying the return of normality. There were scraps of food, some broken bottles, an occasional flag. It would have been difficult to deliver Jacques to the boat at the best of times, for the bath chair was intransigent and clumsy, hard to control and steer. But Sellars' constant complaints didn't help. 'If it's that easy,' grumbled Midwinter, 'you do it. I can go home then.' He couldn't hear Sellars' reply, which was perhaps just as well.

At least there was no one about and the rattling of the harsh wheels caused the scavenging dogs to scurry away, so progress along Wind Street was unhindered. Then, as he passed the end of Salubrious Passage, a man ran out and crashed into the chair and Midwinter struggled to keep it upright. The man fell on top of Jacques and there was a deal of fussing and struggling and loud apologies. Sellars swore and went to the front of the chair to push the man away. He, in turn, responded by pushing Sellars, and he stumbled backwards over an abandoned apple crate. The man continued to apologise, rearranging Jacques's disordered blankets, tucking them firmly under his chin.

'I am sorry, I'm sorry, I'm sorry, indeed. Yer poor Grandad,' he said in an Irish accent. 'I *never* meant him no harm, to be sure of it. My own fault, rushing I was.'

Sellars pulled himself upright but slipped on the remains of a wet pasty and fell to the ground once again. He was getting seriously annoyed at this unnecessary disruption to his plans. He started swearing and made incoherent threats, then fell down

325

again.

'Tell your man here that I don't require all his pushin' and swearin.' I done wrong and I am sorry but he's not doing nothing to make things right, now is he? Lying on the ground like that. Don't help nobody.'

'You should not be out on the streets,' said Midwinter, ineffectually, wondering whether he should reveal his identity as a policeman, but quickly decided that it might not be helpful. He watched the man finish tucking Jacques back into the bathchair, securing his muffler, making sure he was comfortable.

Sellars was not impressed. 'You just bugger off now, or I am warning you, I shall be coming back to look for you, right?'

The man looked affronted. 'I am mortified, sir. It is not right and that is the beginning and end of it. There is no need for you to be taking that attitude.' He stopped suddenly and pointed behind them to the top of Wind Street. 'Guards! Guards is coming!' and he turned, ran back down Salubrious Passage and then he was gone.

'Who was that bastard?' asked Sellars. 'Bastard!' he shouted into the darkness down the alley. 'Who was he?'

'How am I supposed to know, then? It is not as if I know every bugger in this town, is it? But he reckoned there were police back there, and I don't want to get caught, do I?'

'Ahh come on, let's get down to the ship. If I had the time I 'd feed his bloody spleen to the bloody dogs. I'll push the bloody thing now. You watch out for guards.'

Soon Sellars bounced the bath chair over the tramway on Victoria Road; the lines were hard and unyielding and bounced Jacques around in his chair, but still did not wake him. He certainly didn't complain. They proceeded briskly along Adelaide Street to the South Dock and then they were alongside a ship, that looked ghostly against the dark clouds. Midwinter could see men busy on deck in the yellow light of the oil lamps. There was a steady stream of smoke coming from the funnel. They seemed to be ready for departure, which suited Midwinter just fine. Get the old man on

326

the ship and this irritating episode would all be over. He watched two men, one tall, one short, who came down from the ship.

Midwinter looked across at Patagonia Jacques. He ought to say goodbye; it was only polite. He walked over to the chair behind which Sellars stood impassively. He leaned over and pulled the blanket down from Jacques's chin. He was still unconscious. He must have been dribbling, for his muffler was wet and there was a faint sheen on his chin, barely discernible in the flickering lights. He looked up at Sellars.

'Is he alright?' he asked.

'He is sleeping peacefully, Constable. An old man. Let him rest.'

'Doesn't seem to be sleeping to me. Can't wake him up.'

'Ah well you see, that'll be the potion, I 'll be bound. You're not to trouble yourself. Not now. You see, it's a little late.' His smile was like an open blade.

Midwinter looked at him and for that briefest of fleeting moments, knew that he had been tricked and used. And then one of the two sailors hit him across the back of his head with a mallet and what little he knew of what happened next, appeared to be happening to someone else.

The sailors moved with well-practiced precision. They picked up the sack full of rubble that had been long-hidden behind the crates and tied it securely to Midwinter's legs. They fastened his hands tightly behind his back as he groaned and tried to speak, but could not. A rope was thrown from the stern and was quickly threaded under his armpits and pulled tight. Then, with no ceremony at all, they threw him into the dock.

'Job well done boys. Let's get underway, shall we?'

They man-handled the bath chair, still filled with the insensible Patagonia Jacques, on to the deck and, shortly afterwards, *The Drimnagh Castle* steamed slowly out into the Bristol Channel, towing the invisible body of Constable Midwinter behind them. Sellars cut the rope that held him once they were properly out at sea, and his body sank without trace.

Their celebrations at the success of their well-planned escape from Swansea were, however, brief and premature. When they went to rouse Patagonia Jacques, to remove him from the uncomfortable bathchair in which he was slumped, they found that he was dead. His throat had been expertly slit and the blood had soaked into his muffler, oozed down into his waistcoat and then gathered on the seat beneath him.

Twenty Nine

When he had reached the end of Salubrious Passage, Riverton checked that no one was looking and then dropped the knife into a storm drain. Someone would find it, eventually, but not whilst he was still in the town, and there was little chance that they would be able to link it to the death of Patagonia Jacques. A job well done.

He climbed through the kitchen window of the deserted Plume of Feathers, the public house on Wind Street that Lardy Darr had turned into a failure. That was some achievement and it always made him smile. No matter what Lardy Darr ever did, it was always a failure. Like his whole life.

Riverton didn't need a light in the building. He had been working here for a while now and could find his way easily through the darkness and neglect. Tonight would be his last night in Swansea. His mission accomplished, just one job left, that was all, and it shouldn't take him long.

But something didn't seem quite right. The dead, cold air he walked into, as he went down the stairs, the air that he was familiar with, felt different. It wasn't even a smell. It was something else. What was it? As soon as he walked into the cellar he knew. He was not alone. He could sense a presence in the darkness, then a match was struck and an oil lamp was lit.

'I wondered where you were. Didn't think you were a fan of royal processions, Arthur.'

'Evening, Iago. Good to see you. I have been wondering when you were going to turn up, too. Had a busy day? Sorry I am late. I had business to attend to.' Riverton looked at Morris' uniform and shook his head. 'The things you have to do to earn a living, it doesn't make any sense to me. Out there? Amongst all of that? However much they pay you, it isn't enough. Still, you won't have to do it for much longer, will you? There is a way out of all this for you.' He paused and assessed Morris' face carefully. 'That why you

329

are here, is it? You have finally seen sense? Who could blame you?'

Morris ignored him. 'It has taken me a while. Not as quick on my feet as I used to be. But I have come to arrest you, Arthur.' He stared back at Riverton. 'I don't have any choice. Not that I want one. This is my duty and I am here to carry it out.'

'Is this some kind of joke, Iago? It is, isn't it? For goodness sake. Don't be ridiculous. Get over here and give me a hand. Look.' He gestured to the hole in the wall of the cellar that he had created. 'Taken me quite a while, Iago. Had to work quietly, see. But it is done now. And I am through. Into the Bristol and West of England Bank. That is where Patagonia Jacques's money is. I know.'

'I have told you before Arthur. I am on a different side now; I am not with you. The police gave me a life. Swansea gave me a life. I was rescued and I owe them. Not much of a life at times, but better that the one I'd had. Better than yours.'

Riverton sniggered. 'You are talking nonsense, Iago. Look at you. Not much more than a slave, that's what you are. Doing the bidding of aldermen and tobacconists, that's all. No freedom. Just protecting the money; someone else's money. Just looking after pompous old men and being grateful for it. Yes sir. No sir. Thank you very much, sir. For God's sake. Come with me and find your freedom, Iago. You deserve better than all this.'

'And where might that place be, exactly, Arthur? In prison? In solitary confinement, is it? Between beatings? Is that the life you are offering me?' Morris laughed hollowly. 'There is nothing you can say. There is nothing you can do. I shall have to arrest you.'

'Don't be stupid, Iago. You arrest me? Me? For god's sake, that isn't going to happen, is it? Come with me. We will be able to go anywhere, once we've got into the safe. Won't take long, you know that. It is not as if it is stealing, is it? That's our money in there. What we are entitled to it. Nothing more. Nothing less.'

'Doesn't matter what you think, Arthur. That was never our money in the first place. We stole it. We killed men to get it. We allowed a boy to be murdered, too. That was never right, was it?

We both knew that when it happened. We wouldn't get involved because we knew it was wrong.'

'That is far away, Iago. No one knows now. Except us. We did what was right and the others cut us out of it. Now, it is time we had our share. There is no one else left, is there? Not even Patagonia Jacques left now. And it is better we have it, rather than his bloody nephew. So you are not going to arrest me. That is not going to happen.'

'Oh yes, it is Arthur. I reckon I can arrest you for murder four times. It is the only thing that makes any sense. You see, you are released from Dartmoor and then Rhys and Molly, Fred and Lardy all die. And I been thinking and you are the only thing that joins them together, when you know what I know.'

'Is that a fact?'

'It is enough for me, Arthur.

'Best if you don't forget Patagonia Jacques then, isn't it? He would be very upset to learn that he has been left out. But you see, you don't know about that one, do you. Does anyone? So where are all the constables then?' He looked around himself scornfully. 'Or are you doing this arrest all on your own.'

Iago was forcing himself, concentrating. This meant everything to him and he screwed up his courage. He knew it had to be done. He could never rest if he did not act. So he went on regardless. 'They don't know. Inspector has suspicions I reckon, but no one else knows. This is between the two of us. We go back a long way. Arthur. You know we do. But I am not your mate anymore. I have got a new life now. And so I am taking you in. You can't enforce the law yourself. You don't have the right to decide what's right and what's wrong. You are not God.'

'Don't be stupid,' laughed Riverton. 'You will be telling me you go to chapel before long.'

'Yes I do, Arthur. Nothing much else comforts me.'

Riverton snorted in disdain. 'You have lost your grip, Iago.'

'Every Sunday, Arthur. Inside my own head I pray for forgiveness, for Aucaman. It's the only thing that brings me peace.'

'You are being ridiculous, Iago. What has God done about it, ever? Did he stop me wheeling Price's body to the railway in a wheelbarrow and dumping his body on the tracks? Did he stop me stabbing Craven to death on his filthy old bed? Did he stop me dropping Darr into the copper? No, he did not. So he doesn't actually care. Think about it, Iago. This is our money. They stole it from us. It wasn't a mistake. It was deliberate and it was a shocking injustice and one I can neither forgive nor forget. So it is ours, by right. And they killed the Indian boy. We didn't. We didn't eat him, either. And you know that is true.'

'But we didn't do anything to stop it? Did we?'

'So what are you going to do? Are you really going to try to take me in? Because four pieces of horseflesh have died? Who is going to miss them? No one. They were cursed by what they did. And they deserved it. We both know that. The Mapuche cursed them. They were doomed to die because of what they did to us and to Aucaman. That was their curse, not ours. Nothing could have stopped that curse. You can't blame me for that. But all I will say is that God didn't punish the bastards for what they did, now did he? It was me. Unless I am his instrument.' He laughed. 'That might be the answer you chapel boys like best. Arthur the Avenging Angel. I like that idea, too. And if I am, there is no need to take me in at all and anyway, I don't think you can do it; I am stronger than you. Always have been.' He paused. 'If you want a fight, you can have one. But you will lose.' He paused again. 'And I have got a gun.'

Morris smiled bitterly. 'You don't understand, do you? You leave this cellar with me now and we let the law take its course. Or you die here.'

'Well done, Iago, very cleverly thought out. I leave with you and I die on the gallows or I stay here and you, somehow, are going to kill me. What sort of choice is that? You never were the tightest rope in the rigging, were you? Let me make it simple for you. We leave as comrades. Or one of us can leave the cellar alone. And that is likely to be me, isn't it? With the contents of the safe.' He wiped his hands on his stained, tattered trousers, drying them, readying himself for combat.

Morris did not flinch. 'Best come quietly, Arthur. You don't talk sense anymore. I am not your mate anymore. I don't follow you anymore. I've got a new life now and it comes with certain obligations.'

'But not for much longer. And if you don't have a word with yourself, you'll have no life at all. The offer's there. We were friends once. We can be friends again. But you think it is right to throw it all away? It is here, in front of you. I have done the hard part. I have taken out the bricks. We are through. Just the safe now and you know I can crack a safe. The job's done.'

'I am arresting you, Arthur Riverton, for four murders. Molly and Rhys Price, Fred Craven and Hamish Darr. And –'

'Oh, you are counting Molly, are you? If you do that, then technically it is five.'

'What do you mean?'

'Patagonia Jacques. Cut his throat for him about ten minutes ago. I just told you. Weren't you listening? Are these important qualities for a policeman in Swansea, Iago? Not listening. Acting stupid.'

'Patagonia Jacques?

'Yes, Iago. Patagonia Jacques. Horace Jacques. I killed him.'

'But no one knows where he is.'

'For goodness sake, Iago. That is the problem with you coppers. You don't keep your ears open. Or your eyes. I have had lads watching and I have been expecting. So you see, it is all down to you and me now. We can take the money, which is rightfully ours anyway, and split it because that is the right thing to do. Or we leave it in the safe for the Fenians to have it? Don't be ridiculous. Let's away, Iago. You and me. Like the old days. Except this time with money. Our money.'

'I can't let you do that. I have worked too long dealing with right and wrong. I can't let it go now. It isn't about me or what happened in South America or anything. It is about the things that matter.'

'And that means what? That you don't matter? Is that it? Is that what being a policeman in Swansea has done to you? Or is it something else? Can't you stand the heat anymore?' he pointed at Morris's hand and grinned at the thought of his knuckles. 'We are wasting time, Iago. You are not making any sense. You can't stop me. Come with me and be a wealthy man or lie down here dead on the floor. Because I am going into that safe and then out of the door with our money.'

Morris stared back at Riverton. He didn't blink and put his hand into his pocket and produced a revolver. Then holding it carefully in both hands, he pointed it straight at Riverton's head.

'Well, well, Iago. That is a turn up for the books, now isn't it? You with a gun. Know what to do, Iago? Are you sure? Done it before? Because I have and I am ready to do it again. So that means, Iago, that you have just one chance. That is all. No room for hesitation or doubt.' Riverton smiled and raised his eyebrows. 'So what are you going to do? Shoot me?'

'I am arresting you, Arthur Riverton, on a charge – '

'With a gun, Iago? Are you allowed to do that? As a policeman? In Swansea? This isn't Buenos Aires.'

'On a charge of murder.'

'Where did you get the gun from, Iago? Not Fred's old gun, is it? Surely not. If it is, are you sure it works? Because if it doesn't and you carry on playing this ridiculous game, you are dead.'

'This is a very serious charge and I will remember everything you say – '

''For goodness sake. You can't even get the words right. Iago. You are embarrassing yourself. Put the gun down and let's just clear out the safe together, shall we? The town is quiet. We'll get away easy. No one will see us.'

'I am warning you, Arthur.' His voice was shaking, and so was his hand. His arms were aching. Riverton was sure he could see his resolve wavering.

Riverton spoke quietly. 'And I am warning you, too. Iago. Put the gun away before you hurt yourself. It is Fred's. It must be. And you can never trust anything connected with that liar. Look at you. You are not even holding it properly. Please think, Iago. Because there is only one way in which this will end.'

Morris glanced at his hand and pointed the gun at the ceiling to check his grip. It was involuntary and it was all the time that Riverton needed. When he looked back at him, he saw Riverton with his right arm outstretched, pointing his gun and smiling again. 'The thing is, Iago. I know for a fact that my gun works. And that's not your gun, so you can't be sure, can you? Where did you find it? Under Fred's pillow? On the street? In Sergeant Ball's desk? It is Fred's isn't it? So ask yourself why I didn't take it. Go on. Ask yourself. I will tell you if it is too difficult for you. I left it where it was because it doesn't work. Typical Fred Craven. It is useless. Like everything he has ever touched. No good to me. So why do you think it is any use to you? Tell me, Iago. Why didn't I take it?'

'I am warning you, Arthur!'

'No, no, no, Iago. You have got it all wrong again. I am warning you. Can't you see that? You are gambling. You can't be sure it will fire. But I know that one won't and that mine will.' His eyes did not waver. 'For goodness sake, Iago Morris. You haven't half created a problem for yourself, haven't you? How are you going to get out of this then?'

His jaw was clenched so tightly that it was a moment before Morris could speak. 'Perhaps it is your gun that doesn't work. Else you would have shot me by now.' He closed his mouth again. His teeth were aching.

'Don't be ridiculous, Iago. Of course I could have shot you. But I owe you, and that is important to me. So I am giving you a chance. You looked after me when I needed looking after. We worked together, we suffered together, we stayed together. I don't forget those things. But you have created this mess and you don't know how to get out of it, do you? So my advice is that we both lower our guns at the same time and then we can talk about it.' Riverton's eyes did not waver. 'On a count of three, Iago. Are you

335

with me?' Morris said nothing. 'On a count of three, we lower our guns. Are you ready?' Still Morris said nothing, but the shaking in his arm was more pronounced. 'One,' said Riverton, then he paused. 'Two,' and he paused again. 'Three.' And Riverton slowly lowered his arm so that the gun no longer pointed at Morris.

Morris did not move for a moment. His certainty and his confidence were fading. And then he, too, lowered his hands.

'Iago,' said Riverton, shaking his head. 'Iago.' He sighed.

Then he quickly lifted his hand and shot Morris in the chest.

*

The sound of the gunshot reverberated around the cellar, the noise bouncing off the stone walls like thunder. Through the haze of gun smoke that hung in the dark cold air, Riverton could see Morris's body crumpled face down on the floor. Riverton was surprised and wondered why he hadn't been thrown backwards by the bullet. Perhaps it had gone straight through him and the exit wound had thrown him forward. It was idle speculation, in the end; he had work to do. He was sure there would be no one around to have heard the shot and if they had, they would probably think it was something to do with the fireworks, but he didn't need to take any risks.

He picked up the bunch of forget me nots from the floor and scrambled through the hole into the cellar of the bank and went to the safe. It would not be a problem for him, he was sure. He needed to stay calm, to concentrate, to listen to the tumbling of the levers. But his ears were still ringing and he couldn't hear very much. He pushed his ear more firmly against the safe and gently turned his pick inside the lock but he wasn't making contact with anything.

He picked up the flowers from the floor, laid them on top of the safe, then shook his head again to clear his ears. He blew out his cheeks and then laid his ear against the safe once more.

*

He was lost in darkness deep within the earth. There was a rushing sound, as if he was beneath a waterfall in some inaccessible

336

cavern. Nothing seemed real and his head felt loose and wouldn't stay still. It was really very strange, as if he was in a different world. He didn't know where his hands were. Then his head hit something, the floor perhaps, and he remembered where he was and disconnected fragments of what had happened. Morris knew he had been shot and was surprised that he couldn't feel anything. He wasn't sure how his body was arranged and didn't feel he could organise it so that he could get up off the floor. He could hear a voice, muttering, though the sounds did not seem to be words that he could identify. Was there someone else here? Then he realised it was his own voice and he listened very carefully but it made no sense whatsoever. Who had shot him?

Arthur.

He remembered now. It was Arthur, his friend. He had shot him. And he was doing something and he had to be stopped. Where was he?

There was blood suddenly in his mouth and so Morris spat it out and found that he could lift his head. Then there was more blood, so he spat that out, too. He could see a hole in the wall because there was a light on the other side and so he crawled towards it. He was pleased that he had remembered how to do it, even if his toes suddenly felt much too big for his boots. But now he was short of breath and couldn't move properly. Why couldn't he remember what to do? Then he realised that he was holding a gun. That was why it was hard to move, he was sure that was the reason. Suddenly a wave swept over him that turned everything black, but he swallowed hard and that seemed to make the darkness go away.

And then he was at the hole. Morris didn't know how he had got there but that didn't matter because he could use the brickwork to pull himself up and he could see into the next room. Arthur was there, his head pressed against a large box. And then Arthur wasn't there anymore and in his place was a huge dark bird, with a shaved head, the cruellest of beaks and the coldest of eyes, staring silently back at him. He knew it was necessary to kill such an ugly creature and so he rested his hand on the edge of the bricks and pointed the gun towards it. And then suddenly he was shaking and he felt very cold and he was sure he heard someone shout 'Iago!' and his name seemed to echo and roar and then there was a noise like a thunderclap and his legs were twitching and then the bird spread out huge black wings like a cloak that wrapped itself around him and he couldn't escape its embrace but it seemed that didn't matter very much at all, and so he gratefully surrendered himself to a cloud of dark impenetrable feathers.

Thirty

She folded the newspaper carefully and put it next to her on the bench on the pier. Flora hoped it wouldn't blow away; she hated mess. This would be her last look at Swansea for how long? Who could say? She dare not say how much she missed it; how bitterly disappointing life in Aberystwyth had become. David would never come back to Swansea; he was too proud and there were many things he had said that he now regretted. But where did that leave his wife? In Aberystwyth, arranging flowers in a damp church for want of something better to do. All these thrills, excitements, old friends, all to be left behind once more. That hurt. as did the feeling, which had suddenly and unexpectedly intensified, that Emily would leave home just as soon as it was possible. And Flora wondered what would happen to her, if Emily was not there. Would her husband still avoid speaking to her? She had experienced such unexpected thrills in Swansea, things she could never have anticipated. But now it was back to reality.

She had thought until a few days ago that she would come back to Swansea as soon as she could. The shops, the people, the activity. Now she wasn't so sure. Emily appeared to have an unsettling secret of some sort. Something to do with the visit and the ball in the music hall, which for some reason she herself had been unable to attend. That had been very disappointing. She would have loved the dancing and the glorious gowns and the shining uniforms. Emily had attended, but seemed unwilling to talk about it. She said little more than, 'It was alright,' which was hardly sufficient. And why was it that Emily had gone to the ball dressed in traditional Welsh costume and then come home in an evening gown? The idea that she had spilled something on it was not very convincing. What was she hiding? But there was something else, much more worrying.

The new brightness in Emily's eyes was startling, particularly since it seemed to have been inspired by a police constable. What was wrong with the girl? It was good to see her escaping from the deep depression that had eaten away at her and the reappearance of hints of the old Emily was a joyous thing to behold. But a constable? Someone would have to have a word with her. She couldn't do it, obviously and she had hoped that Constance would offer some advice, but on reflection perhaps she wasn't the best person to do so. But then David couldn't talk to her either, not without it developing into an argument.

Constance was walking down the pier towards her with Inspector Bucke. Dancing with scandal, was Constance and she wouldn't listen to sense, even from an old friend. Flora shook her head. Constance was going to go with her to the station to bid her farewell and Emily had been rather too excited when she had learned that Bucke had given Constable Turner permission to escort her to the train. She was with him now, taking that dog of his for a walk before the train left. She had promised faithfully not to be late.

Didn't Bucke realise just how inappropriate such a friendship had the potential to become? That was the problem with Swansea. Too many modern ideas. She stood up and walked towards Constance and Rumsey, who raised his hat as she approached.

*

In an interview with the Cambrian newspaper, The Lord Mayor John Jones-Jenkins, said that it was a matter of great gratification to find that the splendid festivities of Tuesday last, in honour of the visit of the Prince and Princess of Wales, had passed off without the slightest disturbance to the peace and tranquillity of the town and that the great multitudes present had enjoyed themselves in a manner so temperate and orderly as to be creditable to themselves and all concerned.

He folded the newspaper neatly and returned it to the bench where he had found it. It wasn't the most important newspaper he had seen today and he returned to staring at the sea. The Royal visit was over and there were other things in his mind.

Bucke understood that he would never know the complete details of what had happened; but clearly no one else would. In fact, it never happened, depending of course on what 'it' was.

What he knew for certain, was that there had been far too many guns in Swansea for a few weeks now and not one of them had made the town a better place. You could write it as a play or as one of those dramatic stories published in weekly instalments and it may indeed be very exciting, but you would never truly know what really happened between those two men, those two old friends; you would never know what words passed between them; you would never know why those two men were found in pools of their own blood, one shot in the chest, the other shot in the forehead and blood splattered all over that bunch of forget me nots, next to Riverton - in memory of his grandmother perhaps? Or himself? Bucke would never know and so he wondered about the details he would never fully understand and the things he had confronted in recent days.

Jacques and Pugh. Riverton and Morris.

Old rivalries, old stories, old men. Relationships that for Bucke were always destined to end in death. He wished he had been there, to stop them happening, to bring justice and light to the dark hauntings that those men shared; to bring a proper conclusion to stories that had begun such a long time ago. As it was, so much would forever remain unknown.

He thought about what he regarded as the duel in the cellar. Who shot who first? Did it matter, in the end? The tableau he examined told its own story. A thick smear of blood stretched across the adjoining cellar to the hole in the wall where Morris was lying. Riverton had been shot precisely between the eyes and death had been instant; there were no other wounds, so there had been no moment when he might have been wounded but managed to reach for his gun. He was alive one moment and dead the next in the damp and the darkness of that cellar. A vault? Or a grave?

Bucke hadn't realised that Morris was such a sharpshooter. How it was that they had come to be there in the cellar of the bank was much more interesting. Were they partners in a robbery which went wrong? Was Morris carrying out his duty as a policeman. But on his own? With a gun? And the old question remained. Why? What exactly had brought them together at that time, in that place?

There was also the final irony of it all. All that effort wasted; lives thrown away in order to open an empty safe in a disused cellar. The safe no longer served a purpose; the world had changed and they didn't keep their money down there in the darkness anymore. There was a proper combination vault upstairs, shiny and modern. Riverton, like so many others in these sorry days, was locked away in the past.

Frankie Starr had alerted the police to the incident. He claimed to be passing and had heard gunshots. He had found the door to the Plume of Feathers open and so had gone inside…. No one believed him, of course. He had gone in with the hope of finding something – anything – that he could steal, but the sight of two bodies had made him reconsider his priorities very quickly, turning his shadowy slyness into an impressive expression of his public duty.

Now there was another constable dead in Swansea and Bucke was on the pier, at the place where a few days ago he had spoken to Iago Morris. He stood and leaned on the rail and looked down at the grey water beneath, just as Morris had done. The road to everywhere. And the road to nowhere, too. What a few weeks it had been. He had lost colleagues. The haunted Rhys Price, of course, and poor Iago Morris. And what had happened to Byron Midwinter? No one knew anything, but no one had seen him after he suggested to Gill on Wind Street that he was going to the docks. His helmet, found on the quay side, told Bucke all he needed to know. That somehow, whether accidentally or by his own hand, he was down in the water. His colleagues dragged the grey scummy water with a grappling iron in a desultory fashion but their hearts were not in it and they recovered nothing. So there was no body and Bucke wondered whether there ever would be. Was he the agent in the police station and had fled to Ireland? That seemed unlikely. What did he know that anyone else would want to hear? It was impossible to know for sure. Or was Midwinter just another faller, nothing more than that? There had been a few of those. The fact he was a policeman meant nothing. Policemen died doing their duties. Why shouldn't they? It was a dangerous job. And

Bucke knew that one day it could be him. Probably would be him, if he stayed here for much longer.

The piece of the puzzle that was missing was Patagonia Jacques. What had happened to him? Who could know? Almost certainly he had been spirited away. There was no sign anywhere of his alleged nephew Sellars. You could always get out of Swansea quickly if you put your mind to it; that had always been the case, and *The Drimnagh Castle* had sailed away. He had telegraphed Dublin and asked the police to keep a look out for Jacques, but he wasn't convinced they'd find him. Jacques was a strange and obsessive character, for whom wealth brought no pleasure, just hostility. He seemed to be at the heart of most things in recent days. Had he killed Iestyn Pugh? Or had Riverton killed him, somehow? Riverton appeared to have killed everyone else, so why not? He had said he was looking for Pughs.

There had been so much about revenge, so many scores to be settled and so much blood that had to be shed. And to what end, he wondered? What had changed, exactly? Some people were dead who would otherwise still be alive. Too many of them, too. And the Prince and Princess were still alive and everything they represented remained unshaken and Jack Dawes was already selling bullets from the Music Hall as souvenirs outside the market. Life went on.

All those people, all carrying with them, for better and for worse, their own shadows from the past. Morris, Riverton, Price, Therese – the list seemed to go on in his mind. Flora and Emily, too. All your own personal stories made you what you were. Sometimes they made you better; often they didn't, and the things you had done would never been forgotten. They came back to haunt you. And kill you.

He sometimes thought that the town was crying out for help. What it had become was never what had been intended. An identity as an elegant town on a beautiful bay had long since been abandoned. The soot and grime that clung to the walls, what was that? Dirty air? Or was it nothing more than a manifestation of misery, of the price a small number of people were ready for others to pay to facilitate their own advancement and wealth? He watched seagulls swooping low over the water. So much misery. He surprised himself by how radical he could sometimes be.

But amongst it all, the happiness shone like a rare polished diamond. Happiness that came when people found each other.

He turned and put his back against the rail and looked towards the town, Such a filthy place. So much sorrow, too. He had been part of that, once the perfect policeman for a troubled town, aimless, lonely, indifferent. But he and Constance had unexpectedly rescued each other and now nothing else mattered to them.

And now this. Constance had known for some days but had chosen not to tell him when he was so wrapped up in his work. But she had told him this morning. Mr Strick, her solicitor, had informed her of yet another delay. Her appearance in the High Court in London in pursuit of a divorce had been postponed again. The case was unlikely to be heard before the summer of 1882, she'd been told. 'Of course, things may change in an instant, Mrs Bristow blah blah blah... Fortitude, madam, fortitude blah blah blah...I shall instruct my clerk to draw up an interim bill for your attention blah blah blah...yes, we deal in guineas, Mrs Bristow blah blah blah...'

They had been so patient, but a further delay seemed so cruel. He was always troubled that one day he would go on duty and never come home - and every day that came always held that possibility within it. How much longer did he have before that came to pass? Could he afford simply to sit and wait for these legal proceedings to grind away so slowly, proceedings that had every chance of being postponed once more? How much time did he have left?

Grey had offered him a job in London, working with him. He hadn't mentioned it to Constance, but he would later, he knew it. Grey had been very persuasive. He was wasted, he told him. You deserve better, he said. You have much more to offer. We need you. But he knew it wasn't for him; the moral ambiguities Grey accepted, and worked with so easily, he would never be able to accept. It wasn't leaving Swansea that was the problem for Constance or himself. There was really no pressing reason for either of them to stay, other than habit. The problem was agreeing to accept a different set of values. He knew he could not do it.

He pushed himself away from the pier and walked back towards to St Helen's Road. He and Constance needed to talk. She had found an advertisement in a London newspaper left by a guest which she had picked up in the Mackworth Hotel, inviting professional people to move to South Africa. They still had some money saved for the divorce case. Why waste more of it on lawyers? They could do it – and Constance's daughter, Agnes, was there. She was sure they could settle in a new country and prosper together. After all, they were not chancing the insecurities of South America were they, those that had brought such trouble back to the town? And once the ship was at sea, who would ever know they were not married? Easy, and seductive. They had thought about this, they had talked about this, so many times. Perhaps now was the time.

Bucke paused for a moment and looked at the town before him, in all its grime and sorrow. So many stories. So much pain. A place for survivors. Was it really possible that he might leave? But for how long could he survive here before it ground him down completely, or killed him? No. Enough was enough.

'We have a right to think about ourselves, for once. Whilst we still have time. So, let us look at that advertisement,' he said aloud, for Constance was always with him, even when she wasn't there. 'Together.'

*

Alice grimaced with pain as her son helped her across the room to her bed. This was humiliating. Better to be dead than this endless torture, her mind trapped within a collapsing body; her mind angry that it had been so suddenly, so cruelly and so maliciously imprisoned. Please, she thought. Set me free from this useless frame that cannot even carry me around anymore. How had this happened? Moments ago, or so it seemed, everything had been well. Together, travelling the world. And now? Maynard was gone and everything was such hard work and the concept of dignity seemed to have been abandoned long ago. They even had to pay some stranger to help her go to the toilet. And yet try as she might, she was incapable of bringing death upon herself. These days, as the pain of a hot lance pushed its way up her leg and then along her spine, waking up every morning was such a bitter disappointment. She knew, more than anything else, that she owed it to her son to depart. It wasn't fair. His life seemed to be slipping away before her eyes. He deserved so much more than this, watching her apparently endless suffering. He deserved a life. He did not deserve the dried crumbs from her own.

Alice bit her lip until the pain had subsided and looked at her son, the only man she still loved and wondered what he had done to deserve the burden she had become. Poor Lemuel. She knew she needed to let him go, but she was still waiting for Maynard to come for her. Where was the old bugger? What was he doing? Bolting some metal together? Polishing it? Making it shine? It had always been the same when he was alive. Why should it be different now he was dead?

She looked at Lemuel, at his worried eyes. She did not want him to know how much it hurt, or how little any of this mattered anymore. Another day done, another day tomorrow. But in between? Her only purpose. Those dreams he made for her, where she and Maynard were immortal, where they were once again free, where the joy that had so quickly slipped through their fingers was now theirs once more, but this time forever. This was her joy; this was her heaven. She knew that she was an addict who would keep returning to this moment, to the twilight that lay between consciousness and sleep, for it was richer and more real than this grim, stained world of bodily betrayal; and, in those fleeting moments, her son's words would always set her free.

'And so, my son?' Where are you taking me tonight?' she asked as she settled back against the pillows he had arranged for her. She reached out to lay a gnarled, gentle hand on Vasco.

He looked quite serious tonight. 'We are not going far tonight, Momma. There is no need.' He looked at his mother with

346

undiminished love. What a terrible conclusion to a life, he thought. A once strong, independent, fearless woman, reduced to this; a beautiful picture trapped within a crumbling frame. She never complained, but he knew she must hate this. And all he could do, was to tell stories. He could not turn back the clock and restore her body. But he could lead her mind away from the pain and release her like a condor, to soar freely and easily above the endless scenery in her mind. And so he began to whisper to her his new invention, a story that came from his heart.

'A long time ago, when the world was a happier place, a Prince and Princess came to Swansea. It was a warm day, a beautiful day, and the streets were alive with happy, smiling people, for they loved the Prince and Princess. They walked through the town together, hand in hand, radiant in the sunshine and it was the happiest of times. The jewels of the Princess shone, as if the stars had fallen from the sky merely to be with her. The Prince was tall and brave, an ancient Greek god brought to life; he was Apollo, he was Zeus.'

'And with them they had brought their daughter, Princess Emily. She was the most beautiful princess in the world. She had a white band running through hair, where she had been blessed by a dove, a band of hope. Her eyes were things of wonder, dark and bruised perhaps, but full of love and hope and compassion, and everyone loved her, particularly a poor simple boy, who stood apart from everyone else, all alone except for his dog, and watched her.'

Perhaps sleep was coming upon mother earlier tonight, for there was a sense of serenity about her. But for some reason he thought it very important that he should finish his story.

'The boy knew she had endured such terrible times. She had been beaten by terrible storms; she had nearly died in darkness deep within the cold, pitiless earth The world had been very cruel to her. Perhaps she was being tested because she was so beautiful, and so she carried these terrible times with her in her mind. But the boy and his dog could see deep into her soul and they could see that she was the purest, most beautiful person in the world.'

Alice opened her eyes, her breath shortening, or so it seemed to Lemuel. 'And the boy with the dog? Did he love her?'

'Yes he did, mother.'

'Then he must love her forever. He must never betray her. He must never doubt her. He must know when to speak; he must know when to stay silent. He should always listen. And he should always love.' She raised herself up on her elbow and looked at her son. Lemuel thought there might have been a tear, but he wasn't sure, for he had never seen his mother cry. 'Do you think the boy with the dog can do these things? Because that is how she can be healed.'

'I know that he can, Mother.'

'And do you think the boy can be patient and wait, until the princess learns to love him too?'

'I think he can. He will write her long letters and he will wait, though the dog may be a little impatient.'

Alice settled back against the pillows again. To Lemuel she seemed suddenly relaxed. It was odd but she seemed lighter, free not imprisoned, a bird ready to fly away towards distant mountains, together with another.

She smiled at her son. 'It is the very best of your stories, Lemuel,' she said and then closed her eyes.

Afterword

This is the fourth novel in the Rumsey Buke series and, like the others, it is a work of fiction. It is not a history book. and was never intended to be so. However, as I have in all of these novels, I have used incidents that feature in contemporary newspapers to try and anchor the books, however imperfectly, in the reality of the late nineteenth century.

Chapter 1 takes place on Monday 3 October 1881 and the book ends on Friday 21 October 1881

The Prince of Wales did visit Swansea in October 1881 in order to open the sluice of what he named the Prince of Wales Dock. The Princess also named Alexandra Road. The arrangements for this exciting day, as outlined in the novel, can be found in the contemporary reports of 18 October 1881, though I have taken certain liberties and whilst events did not, in truth, turn out quite the way they do here, nonetheless the Music Hall was the location for a glittering ball, facilitated in no small part by the removal of all the seats in the auditorium.

The character of Patagonia Jacques is based, very loosely, upon James Brazil, also known as Jimmy the Brace. He made his fortune in property and mining in Australia and returned to live quietly and simply in Swansea. He was taken to Ireland by his cousin in 1908 and died a day after his arrival. His estate was valued in excess of £80,000 and Jimmy's will was disputed for years as a result of an ever-expanding group of claimants. I have no evidence that he had an obsessive interest in the lost treasure of Edward II.

Hamish 'Lardy' Darr is based on John Alexander Hoyes, a young man from a wealthy family who lost a fortune, lived in much reduced circumstances, worked in The Elba Steel works in Gowerton, and died in an industrial accident in 1914.

Josiah Padley murdered his wife on 1 April 1884 after telling the police on a number of occasions that he intended to do so. He then hanged himself alongside his kippers.

An argument over the ownership of the Plume of Feathers ended in a riot on Wind Street in 1848.

The Welsh settlement at Chubut continues to thrive and is an important outpost of the Welsh Language. Of course, the crash of Uruguayan Air Force Flight 571 in October 1972, and the survival of members of an Uruguayan rugby team in what became known as *Miracle of the Andes,* made its own contribution to a specific element of the plot.

The needle in the heart is a story from 1856 which warns of the dangers of hugging a seamstress, and if you take nothing else away from this book, please remember that piece of important advice.

Frances Power-Cobbe (1822-1904) is one of the most significant women of the nineteenth century and today is sometimes regrettably overlooked. She never came to Swansea for an anti-vivisection meeting but the references to her writing, her will and her political activism are accurate.

The Mutiny on *The Caswell* happened on the ship's return to Europe in 1876. A Greek seaman, Christos Bombos was executed in Ireland for his alleged part in it, though he adamantly denied any involvement. He died in a double execution on 25 August 1876 alongside Thomas Crowe, a political agitator. Riverton, Price and Morris were fortunate to discharge themselves as they did in 1875.

Rhys 'Dai' Price is based on Henry O'Neill who murdered his wife in 1898 and who had indeed been trapped in the ice on the *Para.* That is where the idea of the ghost and the buried clothes came from, too.

The murder of Eleanor Williams in Felindre in 1832, and the discovery of her body at the bottom of a well, is a notorious story. My version of the murder is entirely fictional but you can still see her poignant but fading gravestone in the grounds of the Nebo chapel there. I think you should go and pay your respects to the poor girl.

The arrest and execution of Catherine Harris is based on the story of Charlotte Long from Gloucestershire who died in 1832.

Arthur Riverton, a habitual criminal, escaped from Swansea Gaol in 1898 and was recaptured in Reynoldston. He was sentenced to ten years in Dartmoor following a burglary in Blackpill. He received twelve strokes with the 'cat' for assaulting a warder in 1902.

My grandmother was a market trader in Sheffield Rag Market and, as a young boy, I spent a lot of time with her. Every Saturday I used to watch a couple of men (plus a look-out) run a Find the Lady scam using a wooden crate as a table on the main walkway through the market and I have used those memories in the scene in Chapter 7. The bit I liked best was when the police turned up and they grabbed their cards and fled. Wooden crates were very easy to come by. I always fancied the job of look-out. My great grandfather, who I never met, used to sit in a crate in the same place every week in the market and sold bananas from a box, but that is another story.

As you can see, I still strive to restore Rumsey Bucke's reputation. I believe it is time that his dismissal from the Swansea Police Force in 1872 for the theft of a yew tree was overlooked and that he and Constance, abandoned by her headteacher husband, also in 1872, are allowed to find enduring happiness together, wherever that may be.